ROMEO SPIKES

JOANNE REAY

Beautiful
Books

First published 2011.

Beautiful Books Limited
36-38 Glasshouse Street
London W1B 5DL

www.beautiful-books.co.uk

ISBN 9781907616297

9 8 7 6 5 4 3 2 1

SF
Pbk

Copyright © Joanne Reay 2011.

The right of Joanne Reay to be identified as the author of
this work has been asserted by her in accordance with the
Copyright, Designs and Patents Act 1988.

All rights reserved. No part of this publication may be reproduced,
stored in or introduced into a retrieval system, or transmitted,
in any form, or by any means (electronic, mechanical,
photocopying, recording or otherwise) without
the prior written permission of the publisher.
Any person who does any unauthorised act in relation
to this publication may be liable to criminal prosecution
and civil claims for damages.

A catalogue reference for this book is available
from the British Library.

Cover design by Head Design.
Typesetting by Misa Watanabe.
Printed in and bound in the UK by Clays Ltd, St Ives plc

To Emma and Katie
...and in time, Georgie.

BOOK I

1

'. . . but I say, life's too short.'

She ignores him. Her lacquered fingernails agitate the cashew bowl.

He forges on. 'Fifty-five. But firmer than I was at forty. Lotta fruit and fibre. And fish oil.'

A blast of breath. He has moved closer. 'What's your secret?'

'I eat six pounds of grapes a day.'

'That's a lot of grapes.'

'Not when you squeeze them down to wine.'

She turns to him. 'The night is young. Fish elsewhere.' She feels the ripple of his departure. Turns back to the bar and taps the bowl of her wine glass.

The young barman responds to her semaphore, gathers a bottle and approaches with a boyish grin. His hair is surfed into a halo of gold. 'It's the Rioja, right?'

He twists the cork, dialling up the volume of his appeal. The woman tilts her chin. Not in answer to his question, but to pull taut a hammock of neck flesh.

She watches as he pours the glass brim full. Pirouettes her fingers about the stem. 'Won't you join me?'

'I'm working.'

'Join me later?'

'Aren't you waiting for someone?' Her fur coat swamps the adjacent stool but she wafts a finger in a dismissal.

'Just company business.'

'Well, if you're wanting company, ma'am' – the barman motions a finger between his chest and hers – 'that's business too.'

Her purse snaps open. She pulls out three twenty-dollar bills. 'What does that get me?'

'Fresh nuts.'

She withdraws, jaw tight.

'Lady, this is Manhattan.' He taps the cash. 'And that don't get you a man.'

She rolls back her shoulders, hoisting her breasts. 'Ten years ago, I would have been your fantasy. I looked very different.'

'Did you look like Spiderman?'

She grimaces. Froths her hair with furious fingers. *How young* is *he?*

He moves to take the bottle, but she snatches it by the neck.

'I'm not finished. Not yet.'

The barman gathers up one of the twenties. 'That should cover it.' Glances at the bottle. 'It's just the dregs.'

She watches as he turns and walks away. *His whole life ahead of him.*

And mine? She inhales deeply. All her best years lay behind, spilled like the trail of a dancing drunk. *Squandered. Scattered.*

The young Annie Torgus had graduated top of her class with a doctorate in psychiatry. Her speciality was the early diagnosis of suicidal tendencies. The perception may be that suicide is a practice of the poor, but evidence shows that a life of dull luxury is a sharper spur.

Renting costly offices on the Upper West Side, she imagines a wealthy clientele clamouring for her services. Anxious parents, perhaps, of a teenage girl who festers in her bedroom. To draw her out, Mommy and Daddy have applied a poultice of promises: a new Porsche, a trip to Paris, a pony in the upper field – but nothing has worked. So they urgently call upon Dr Annie Torgus. And she comes at once, and at quite a price.

Easy money.

But the young doctor is kept awake by the sound of her phone not ringing. Her debts rise and so, to raise her profile, she rushes to publish, submitting a lengthy article to the *New Scientist*. With a racy title, 'How the Kids Hang in the Hamptons', the article exposes a culture of self-harm and suicide within the wealthy teens of New England. Snatched up by the *New York Times*, her shocking data flies across the Sunday pages. Radio stations ring for interviews and television soon chases after, faster still once it discovers that Dr Annie Torgus is young and big-breasted. But as the media spotlight intensifies, it becomes an invasive, burning heat, igniting her research and turning it to ashes. Dr Annie Torgus, it transpires, fabricated the statistics and falsified the teenage testimony. The glitter she saw surrounding her career turns out to be knives and blow by blow, amid howls of derision from her peers, her professional reputation is destroyed.

Sliced. Shredded.

Sued by everyone, she struggles on, living off store cards. Until she's thrown out of her Broadway and 4th apartment, landing back in the swamps of Louisiana where she was born. And where the only local employer is Morphic Fields Penitentiary. The black brick structure looms like a mausoleum and appropriately so, as more prisoners await their execution here than any other facility.

There is a position available and, with little local competition, she secures the job of chief psychiatric officer. Her duty is to monitor suicidal tendencies amongst the inmates. The urge to kill oneself is a prime indicator of insanity and a suicide attempt is all too often used by appeal lawyers to certify an inmate's unsound mind. A stay of execution frequently follows. The governor of Morphic Fields, who resents any interruption to the natural flow of death within the prison walls, decides to create the post of Prison Psychiatric Officer to stifle this trend. On her first day, walking into the concrete bunker of her office, Annie

Torgus assesses her job as this: to stop death-row prisoners from taking their own lives. The irony is not lost upon her.

Her sense of purpose is lost for ever.

She works alone, day after day, year after year, examining the inmates, declaring them sane and signing away their last chance of appeal. Clutching her clipboard and ticking the boxes, she idly imagines that Governor Duggin may eventually decide to extend her responsibilities one degree further, one gesture more – to swish her signature and then plunge her pen deep into the inmate's carotid artery, ripping wide a hole, a gushing slash . . .

She splashes the last of the wine into her glass. Knocks it back. Thirty-five years she has been at Morphic Fields. Her whole life . . . a life sentence.

The glass stem lowers, unleashing her reflection on to the mirror behind the bar. She grimaces at the old woman who stares back at her.

Hair too black, too brittle. Eyes wrapped in wrinkles. And those hands, those ancient hands. Spotted, scaly, fatless claws —

The bitter self-attack continues until she slams down her fist and loudly orders another bottle; drags an angry cuff across her eyes. *God, no wonder when people off themselves, they shoot their head.*

She inhales slowly. Eases back a sleeve to expose her watch. It is later than she thought. She pulls her coat from the adjacent stool. He could arrive at any moment. She needs to compose herself. Remember why she is here. Remember at least his name.

She urgently fumbles in her pocket, retrieving a business card. Holds it at arm's length, straining to read the small cursive print: '*Christopher Hatchling, Senior Buyer, Phobos Books*'.

On the journey out from Louisiana, idling hours at the airport, she bought a Phobos title: *Pharos from a Far-flung Star*. A brick of a book, it promised to 'stun the reader'.

If it falls on your skull, then perhaps.

Torgus peeled back the gold-embossed cover and her heart sank as she scanned the trashy text within. But she ploughed on, congratulating herself that she was, at least, doing some research. Then a thought Chinese-burned her brain: *If I'd done my research thirty-five years ago, I wouldn't now be reduced to this.* Offering a tawdry publishing house what she knows to be an earth-shattering manuscript.

How could they ever appreciate the thrall it holds? So very, very rare . . .

But this raw material had fallen into her hands and it will be her salvation.

She pulls her spine straight. Lifts her chin. Reminds herself that Annie is short for Anstice: a Greek name, reflecting her roots. It means 'resurrection'. She will rise again.

I'm not finished. Not yet.

She pulls a small mirror from her purse. Checks her teeth for lipstick and her lips for teeth marks. Her habit is to bite down hard when nerves attack. The mirror twists in her palm, searching the bar behind. She'd like to see Christopher Hatchling before he sees her. She needs that fractional head start, to drop her face into a casual cradle of welcome.

The mirror picks up a man. His hair tumbles in thick curls. Dr Torgus thins her lips. She had hoped for someone older, as suggested by the epithet *senior* buyer. But *Hatchling* it is. Fresh from the egg of his ambition. He strides across the carpet, nose up and neck extended. She recognises the gander-gait of a man arriving for lunch with a mystery woman. She waves her hand and as his eyes connect, his swagger slows.

'Dr Torgus, I'm sorry I'm late.'

I'm sorry I'm old. She delivers a shallow smile, so as not to ripple more wrinkles. 'You're quite on time.'

She takes a deep swig, fluffs her hair. 'I can recommend

the Rioja, if you would like a glass.'

'Too early for me.'

Too young, too young . . .

She tosses her hair and inside her head, the alcohol swills the rim of her skull.

I can do this!

Her voice drops, husky now. Or haggard. She can no longer tell. 'So, Christopher, are you ready?'

She lifts her bag between her legs, reaches deep into the old, brown folds. 'I have something very special to show you.'

And from within, she lifts a tightly bound file.

2

An EAGLE ARCS ACROSS THE SKY. Its head swivels down, drawn by something below. The glint of a rifle, sliding from the corner of a watchtower.

Down the length of the barrel gazes a prison guard. His head dips, drawn to the exercise yard below.

A flash of metal.

The guard primes his rifle. Then removes his finger from the trigger and waggles it in his ear to pop a wave of atmospheric pressure.

One helluva storm coming.

The finger returns to the trigger and his eye presses down against the eye-piece.

Dammit, he saw *something*.

He swivels the rifle-sight towards the most likely location of a shank. *Always bet on the Petra Loa.* The shaven-headed Haitian gang arcs across the centre of the yard, owning it.

In their midst stands a flat-faced giant of a man, who once went by the name of Little Bit. A rising rap star, the heat of the Cajun Hip Hop scene kept his ears and wrists nicely iced. Until the Louisiana State police gave him bracelets on a charge of Murder One.

The trial was big news. Little Bit towered in the dock, so warped with muscle that they had to find a fatter chair to take his weight.

But his defence was slim. His prints were on the gun. His legal team argued for accidental shooting: the victim, little LouAnne Titley, was caught in the cross-fire of a long-standing feud. 'But she isn't standing no more,' said the young District Attorney as he brandished a blow-up of LouAnne's blasted body. The fine ladies of the jury, with their shoes and totes carefully colour-matched, wept into white handkerchiefs and, with matching southern values, swiftly condemned the black man to death.

Little Bit was led from the courtroom, headed for the big chair.

At Morphic Fields, news of his arrival caused a stir amongst the guards. They all wanted the bragging rights to his admission. *Yeah, it was me who stripped that big ass rapper to his nappy.*

Right up to the moment when the bus shuddered to a halt outside the prison gate, elbows were flying amid the guards, each man pushing himself to the fore. Until Little Bit thuds down from the bus, one giant boot and then another landing in the dust. The guards ghost back towards the gates. Not spooked by his size. But something more. A dark force that surrounds him, like an invisible fur, hackled high.

Elbows jostle again, this time forcing one of the guards to the front, allowing the others to shelter behind. The elected officer waggles a hand over his holster and barks an order. *Strip down!*

Garments gather in the dust.

An hour later, steel chains now his sole accessory, Little Bit lumbers to his cell, dripping from the hose-down and greased up from the hand-search. But the guards know that he still carries something. Something hidden deep, where no frisk can ever reach.

Bad voodoo.

The watchtower guard shifts his shoulder against the rifle. Blinks against the eye-piece.

Real bad voodoo.

His thumb flips on a two-way radio. 'Molloy, you got your ears on?'

The speaker crackles a confirmation from far below.

'I saw something. Shined like a shank. I wanna see the Petra Loa lay out hands.'

Guard Molloy peels his spine from the base of the watchtower ladder. Pokes up his hat. Surveys the gang, who stand with their backs to him. They seem to be chanting.

Molloy cocks his thumb against the two-way. 'I don't see nothing.'

The chant has the raw rhythm of an incantation.

'What's your problem, Molloy? Too chicken cause they're toastin'?'

Toasts are dark poems, once composed by prisoners, cursing and celebrating the street life that took them to jail. They are acknowledged as the origin of rap, but have long since been forgotten. Little Bit decided to use his time on death row to revive this vibe. So he killed off Little Bit and became Kon'Verse. And whilst Kon'Verse is imprisoned, his albums get released twice a year. *Doin' Time and Makin' Rhyme* just went platinum.

The gang are riffing lyrics. With slow, deliberate strokes of a pen, Kon'Verse commits to paper the verses of *Kentucky Fried Suicide*. Eyes down, deep in the flow.

Molloy thrusts the two-way into his belt, readying himself. Just picking the moment.

Takes a step forward, moving against the tide of the other prisoners, who spread out from the centre of the yard, as if the boom-box beat of the Petra Loa causes sonic waves.

Only one prisoner dares to wander close to their perimeter. A thin, white man who barely fills his prison blues. Agnus Day staggers in chaotic circles and clasps in his hand a sheet of paper.

He scrawls furiously with a blunt pencil across the paper, gibbering as he writes one word – the same word – again and again, his fingers too twisted to move fast enough.

Molloy halts, observing the old man's perilous path. *Sweet Jesus, no . . .*

The Petra Loa are dead ahead, but Agnus lurches on,

eyes down and unaware. The paper falls to shreds between his fingers, the pencil carving deep. With a howl, he bursts through the muscled gang and stumbles towards Kon'Verse, snatching fresh paper from the black fist. With frenzied strokes, Agnus crosses out the existing lyrics and writes on the reverse his one chosen word, again and again, filling the sheet.

Kon'Verse slowly rises. To a boom of thunder.

He unfurls his giant arms and launches forward. Lightning explodes about the yard and in a rush of rainfall, Kon'Verse engulfs the tiny man – with tender care, gathering him up against his giant body.

The wind roars, straining to pull the storm closer. Sirens wail. The prisoners respond to the command and abandon the yard. Molloy is already by the gate, gun drawn, herding them through the lashing rain, two by two.

And through the deluge comes the last of them. The silhouette of Kon'Verse. And in his arms he cradles the twitching figure of Agnus Day, who still madly scrawls.

Molloy tugs down his hat, emptying a brimful of water on to his shoes. He is determined not to look up.

The boots of Kon'Verse heave up to the gate. They halt and Molloy jerks back as a thin, white hand thrusts out, forcing a scrap of paper beneath his chin.

Molloy's hand stays low, refusing to take the paper. Instead his palm waves an order for Kon'Verse to pass.

But the boots do not move. And so Molloy surrenders an upwards glance, to read the silent command in the eyes of Kon'Verse.

And with a trembling hand, Molloy obediently takes the paper.

3

Ice clatters in a cocktail shaker. Christopher Hatchling has ordered an extra-dry martini with Carpano Antica vermouth. His face is turned towards Dr Torgus but she senses that he awaits the pouring of his drink with more interest than anything that may emerge from her mouth.

She forces a smile. When she rang the New York offices of Phobos – a cold call, in effect, as she had no introduction there – the flirtation that crackled between them had nudged his agreement to meet her. She watches now as Hatchling sips his freshly decanted drink. His disappointment with her is palpable.

His smile is for the barman. 'Perfect.'

The boy gathers a generous tip from the counter. Turns to Dr Torgus. 'Another Rioja for the lovely lady?'

The compliment is crushed beneath his emphasis on *another*.

'Thank you, but no.'

She inhales deeply, mustering calm. Then relaxes back, uncrossing her legs and spreading wide her leather file. Scraps of paper flutter across the bar. Each fragment is covered with what looks like the dense spikes of a seismograph read-out. But a closer inspection shows that it is in fact a manic text, written tight and tall to make use of every inch of paper. Hatchling picks up a fragment, flipping it round like a candy wrapper, trying to determine where the text begins.

'Let me first explain.' Dr Torgus nips the the paper between her nails with a surgical precision and returns it to the file. 'The story I bring to you concerns a patient of mine.'

13

'A patient?'

She concedes a correcting smile. 'A *prisoner*.'

Hatchling sucks down his olive. 'I'm aware that you don't have a practice, doctor, just a penitentiary. According to the notes I read.'

He has notes on me? Dr Torgus hides her unease in the folds of her skirt, which she busily rearranges.

'Prison work is a vocation . . . a calling.'

'The kind you answer when the phone stops ringing.' Hatchling bats away his own quip with a raised hand that catches the barman's eye. 'Another martini. And make it dirty.'

He knows about my past. My dirty past! Dr Torgus shakes her head, admonishing herself for hearing innuendo in Hatchling's every comment.

She closes her eyes, finding focus. Opens them to see that now a striking redhead has taken the stool next to Hatchling. Torgus exhales through gritted teeth.

'The prisoner's name is Agnus Day. And his case, without doubt, is the most extraordinary that I have ever seen.'

Hatchling flashes a boyish smile at the redhead.

'It begins twenty years ago.' *When you were still waiting for your balls to drop.*

Dr Torgus thrusts out a photo of a man in a white laboratory coat. It serves to momentarily snap Hatchling back. He glances at the image. 'The prisoner was . . . a scientist?'

'One of the most eminent of his generation. A highly respected neurophysicist. His area of expertise was telomeres.'

Hatchling's blank expression confirms a need for further explanation.

'Telomeres are the molecular threads, coiled in the centre of every living cell. Each time the cell divides, the telomeres shorten in length. When these threads have dwindled to nothing, the cell stops dividing and dies. In short, telomeres control how long we live.'

He snatches a glance at his watch. 'Will this take long?'

'I'll speed things up.' A smile, significant only to her. 'Life's too short, right?' She plucks at the cashews, quickly recalculating a new route through her pitch. 'Agnus was researching ways by which these threads could be controlled, extended even. In short, Agnus was looking to create an ever-extending lifespan.'

The adjacent redhead shimmies out of her coat, revealing legs that define for ever. Torgus runs a hand through her dry hair, crackling static, then slides closer to Hatchling, determined to keep his attention.

'One factor, however, continually confounded the work of Agnus Day. Each time he found a means to extend the telomeres, the cell would turn cancerous. A likely complication, when one considers that cancer is essentially a human cell refusing to cease its reproduction.'

Hatchling and his thirty billion sperm are focused on the redhead. His stool swivels away from the doctor, as if her story is concluded.

Torgus slugs the last of her wine, tasting defeat. Then brings down the glass.

I'm not finished. Not yet!

She raises her voice and presses on. 'Agnus' mind became locked on resolving this conundrum, an obsession doubtless driven by the death of his daughter. She'd been a troubled teen —'

Hatchling suddenly swivels towards to Dr Torgus.

'A *suicidal* teen?'

Torgus is taken aback by his sudden re-engagement.

'Well, actually, no.'

'You sure about that, doctor?' Hatchling smiles like a paper cut. And now she divines his true intent. He's been waiting for this opportunity. 'You were something of an expert in the field of teenage suicide, from what I read.'

Torgus twitches her lips. '. . . in your notes.'

'I did my research. Quite thoroughly.' The deliberate dig strikes her hard between the ribs.

She straightens her spine. 'It wasn't suicide. At fifteen, his daughter had succumbed to a brain tumour. After her death, the papers Agnus submitted for publication rapidly went from ground-breaking to perverse. Telomeres became more than his research. They became his mania. His sanity collapsed. The final paper he submitted, handwritten, sprawled across the page, contained no reference to his study. It was instead an incoherent diatribe against the Three Fates – the women of Greek legend who control human lifespan by the pulling, spinning and cutting of thread.'

'Yeah, the Three Fates. I've heard of them.'

Dr Torgus nods, feigning delight in his familiarity with the fifth-grade element of this story.

'When those close to Agnus tried to intervene, to get him psychiatric help, he disappeared. In his laboratory, there were signs of an attempted suicide and – inexplicably – a burned void in the floor as if a human body had combusted.'

Hatchling's face now betrays a burgeoning interest. Torgus smiles. If this were a bedtime story – *and, dammit, I am old enough to be his mother* – this would be the moment to turn the page and show the child a vivid picture.

She pulls a photo from the file, but keeps it face down, not ready to reveal it. Leans in deep. 'He was not seen again until the night of the murder.'

'What murder?'

Gotcha!

'They called it "The Slashing at Sulphur".' Torgus peels the picture over. Hatchling bolts back on his stool, unprepared for what he sees: the naked corpse of a young girl, torn into long strips that uncoil from her chin to her pelvis.

'Jezebeth Hooger was just fifteen years old, the same age as Agnus' daughter when she died. They found her like this

– raped, ripped – in a motel bed in Sulphur City.'

Torgus produces a second photo. This one shows a man, covered in blood, lying beside Jezebeth's corpse. His eyes are wide and his jaw is clenched in spasm. Hatchling looks closer at the agonised face. It is Agnus Day.

'Wh-what happened to him?'

'They found him in some sort of catatonic coma. The blade was still in his hand.'

Hatchling pushes the pictures away, disturbed. But his lingering fingers suggest a desire to know more.

'And he did this?'

'So said a jury of his peers.' Now Torgus seizes the moment, drilling her gaze deep into Hatchling's eyes. 'Though I would say that Agnus Day has no peers. Not any more.' From the file comes a clutch of crime-scene photos. 'What he is now is . . . beyond compare.'

From the stack of photographs she pulls a blow-up of Jezebeth's torso. On the narrow stretches of flesh that cling between the knife wounds are words, handwritten words, tall and thin and densely scrawled.

Hatchling's fingers trace the text, severed between syllables. 'What does it say?' He picks up photo after photo, eyes wide. 'And why did he . . . ?'

Each chunk of corpse is overrun by writing, the ink as copious as the blood.

'It is called hypergraphia: a manic imperative to write. And it is a symptom of Geschwind syndrome.' She rolls her shoulders, relaxing back. Now she's in charge.

Hatchling waves the barman away when he threatens to approach. And beckons Torgus to continue.

'Those afflicted by the syndrome feel their cognitive powers overwhelmed by visions. Powerful, violent, inhuman visions. The hypergraphia arises from a compulsion to record these visions before they dissipate. Any surface will be indiscriminately utilised: walls, floors . . . human skin.'

Now it is Torgus who signals to the barman, transmitting

17

with taps to her wine glass the decision to have another.

'Geschwind syndrome is rare, but not so rare that I would pin my hopes of publication upon it. There must be another reason why I travelled all this way.' Now she even dares to stroke the back of Hatchling's hand. 'So let me tell you what that reason is.'

She reaches once more into her bag. 'I have copies of all the murder investigation files. Standard practice, because I am Agnus Day's mental-health worker.' She taps the folder. 'And, by any standard, they make good reading. A fifteen-year-old girl, entered and then eviscerated by a crazy scientist, who then writes all over her precious body. There's your novel, or at least the start of it. But that is where the police let it finish.' She pulls a final file. Not police-issue, but pink, precisely bound . . . personal. 'What was written on Jezebeth Hooger's body – the actual text – to the investigating officers, well that was . . . irrelevant.' Torgus lays her hand across the file and spreads her fingers wide. 'But not to me.'

Hatchling smiles and moves his hand over to the file, but Torgus is quicker and shunts it tight towards her body.

His fingers tap against the bar. 'Let's not play games.'

Torgus shakes her head. 'I need to know you're interested. That there's a deal to be done here.'

Now Hatchling drops his smile. 'Dr Torgus, I have to say that, of everything you've told me tonight, the only thing that interests me is what you now *won't* say.' He points to the file. 'If what you have uncovered is suitably . . . sensational, then perhaps we have a deal. Without it, you have just another murder that I could catch on cable. So let's not waste any more time.'

Dr Torgus swills her wine about the glass. 'It is sensational, Christopher. It is end-of-the-world, death-of-humanity sensational. And I believe that I have told you quite enough for you to make an offer.' She fluffs her hair, laughter bubbling in her throat. 'I mean, it's not as though your readership cares what particular flavour the apocalypse comes in.'

Her laughter twists to silence as she catches sight of Hatchling's reaction. 'Christopher, I'm so sorry. I didn't mean to imply for one moment that your readership is . . . that Phobos caters only to the —'

His face is set hard, killing her tumbling apology on impact. 'Listen, *doctor*, the psychiatric community sniffed you out once before. If you think that by descending from those lofty heights you'll find a second chance, think again. If there's one thing that the pig-ignorant know, it's the smell of shit.'

His hand rises to both silence her and to demand the check from the barman. 'I'm sure Phobos wasn't your first choice. This meeting was, no doubt, a fishing trip.'

Torgus grabs at his sleeve. 'That's not true, Christopher! Believe me, I —'

Hatchling pulls his cuff free and slams a fifty on the bar. 'I suggest you try elsewhere.'

4

OFFICER WALLACE MOLLOY STARES INTO THE MIRROR that hangs inside his locker door. He takes a comb and, with slow, careful strokes, shifts a ginger quiff half an inch to the right. His hair is so sparse, its entire arrangement takes only a few strokes. But this evening, Molloy seems impossible to satisfy. He combs it again and again. And now his eyes leave the mirror, rolling left and right, searching out those who still remain in the locker room. A handful of guards linger, shrugging on civilian shirts, ready to sink some beers. Their voices echo off the tiled walls, a barrage of bar suggestion: 'I say the Kicking Mule, bound to have the game on . . .' amid bids to 'have a good night' and warnings to watch out for the rain, 'cos she's a slippery bitch'. The last reverberation is directed at the locker in the far corner: 'You comin' Molloy? You can't get no prettier.'

'I'll catch you up.' Molloy still claws at his scalp with the comb. 'You go ahead.' And now his purpose is clear. He is waiting for the room to empty. To be the last man standing. Pondering. Panicking.

The click of the old door latch declares that he is finally alone. He slides his fingers into his breast pocket and pulls out the sodden fragment of paper forced upon him by Agnus Day. The confusion of the storm meant that none of the other guards saw him receive it. Molloy wants to keep it that way.

Not that the guards would comment, even if they knew. They never talk about Agnus Day. Not even to each other. It's a rule they all adhere to. An unspoken rule.

An unbroken rule.

Since Agnus arrived at Morphic Fields, almost every one of them has received a similar piece of paper. At first, the scribbled messages were met with derision. This soon shifted to fear.

The notes revealed secrets, personal to each man. Exposing a truth about their lives. Something that had happened . . . something that was about to happen.

Some guards persisted in their bluff, mocking those who feared the sudden thrust of Agnus' hand.

Some guards became withdrawn, anxious.

But all of them agreed on one thing, since Agnus' arrival, the inmates were altered.

Molloy's wife, kept awake one particular night by his nocturnal churning, had demanded that he tell her what he meant. '*Changed exactly how, darlin'?*'

Molloy had risen to his elbow, struck a match and lit a cigarette, slowly sucking it into life. 'It's like this, Trudy. The prisoners have a law all of their own. A jungle justice. And a child-killer . . . well, the law demands that demon must receive a particular punishing. Take Ring-Pull, for example.'

Molloy pauses and taps his ash into the neck of a beer bottle. *What in God's name did that kiddie-molester do to get such a nickname?* He exhales a ring of smoke and continues.

'They beat Ring-Pull up so goddamn bad, Doctor couldn't put his face back together. But Agnus Day. . .' The cigarette lolls between Molloy's lips. 'He ripped a fifteen-year-old girl apart like a fish. But the cons, they don't lay a hand upon him. Not a single finger. It's kinda like they . . .' He wafts the glowing tip, searching the dark for the right word.

'. . . *protect* him?' offers Trudy.

Molloy shakes his head. 'No . . . no. They *revere* him.'

'And you have no idea why?'

21

Molloy hesitates. He could tell Trudy about the secrets . . . the revelations. But instead he pulls her close to him and tenderly kisses the crown of her hair. There's nothing she can do. Best keep this from her.

Along with all the other secrets he keeps from her.

In the locker room, Molloy slams the metal door hard, shutting out all thoughts of his wife.

Screwed to the metal plate is a clip, holding his work roster.

The date of Agnus Day's execution is looming.

The guards have never once said it out loud, but they all sense the same, like the coming of a Louisiana storm: the day the life of Agnus Day is taken, the inmates will respond.

There will be trouble.

Governor Duggin has refused to make the execution date public. It will be announced just hours before, to minimise the inmates' opportunity to prepare any protest.

Molloy can only ripple his lips with the same prayer every night: *not on my shift.*

He folds up the paper fragment in his hand and shoves it through the locker grill. Then closes his eyes and inhales deeply, smoothing his face into a mask that his wife might recognise as her easy-going husband.

A crash of rain draws his eyes up to the window. The glass shivers. *What's with this weather?* Molloy can't remember a cloud-burst going on this long.

He pauses, then snatches his locker open, reaching quickly inside to pull out a thin macintosh. He prepares to slam the metal shut for one last time. But then the paper fragment falls to the floor, refusing to be ignored.

Molloy grits his jaw. Finally stoops to snare the paper and opens it, eyes locked on the single word within.

What the fuck does it mean?

His fist rolls shut and he thrusts the fragment deep into his pocket. *Grotteschi needs to see this.*

5

IN THE METAL WORKSHOP of Morphic Fields, machines lurk in lines like a hostile robot army, waiting for some spark to revive them. Even in this dead-metal state, they have fought against the prisoners. Fingers, feet, scalps and (on one memorable occasion) an entire face has been ripped and chewed by these unmuzzled machines. It is not so much that they are dangerous, more that there is an absence of interest in the prisoners' well-being. Morphic Fields gets paid by the volume of metal goods it produces and so, for the sake of speed, all safety gates have been removed. Many an inmate has gone to the chair with limbs already removed, as if his execution were part of a lay-away program.

One machine churns away in the far corner, throwing sparks. An inmate is hunched over it. When he shifts position, it becomes clear the hunch is not a stance of concentration, but a deformity of the spine. The prisoner's hands, however, are nimble and elegantly manicured. This is Charles Grotteschi.

The metal tube he welds together is part of a plumbing device but it reminds him of the sculptural pieces in which he used to deal, before his arrest.

Never seen without his trademark onyx monocle, he was known in every coffee house on Manhattan's East Side as the curator of the Hunkypunk Gallery. He dealt in what was known as 'wet art': work from up-coming artists, some of it so radical, like a smear of human sputum on canvas, that critics would often fail to agree on whether it was art or idiocy. All of which made for an excellent environment if, like Grotteschi, you are a confidence trickster, selling worthless 'masterpieces' to gullible clients.

It was never Grotteschi's intention to become a criminal. The real crime was how he had been ruthlessly rebuffed by the legitimate New York art crowd. The cause was his hump, the result of childhood spina bifida. If he was to be excluded from the classics and the modernists, he would deal with those stupid enough to spend ten thousand bucks on a lacquered twist of dog shit. They deserved to be duped.

In Morphic Fields, Grotteschi's academic learning was well known. It was the trick upon which he traded to keep himself removed from the usual prison routine of rape and rough-housing. And since Agnus Day arrived within these awful walls, Grotteschi's services had been much in demand. Every prisoner who had received one of the obscure revelations had come to Grotteschi, in the hope that his vast knowledge would shine some light upon its meaning. And just as many guards had sought the same service, sweeping Grotteschi aside, somewhere unseen, swearing him to silence as they unfolded some paper scrap.

Grotteschi is always happy to offer up his cryptology skills, in return for cigarettes, soap or soft towels.

He lifts his head from the welding machine, sniffing the air. Turns to find that Officer Molloy has appeared behind him. A boon of some sort is slid into Grotteschi's pocket. Whatever it is, it smells of lily of the valley, a particular favourite of his.

Molloy must want some very immediate attention. Grotteschi turns, his hump sweeping just inches from Molloy's chin.

'Good evening, officer.'

Without a word, Molloy presents him with the paper. Grotteschi neither needs nor expects any accompanying conversation. All he requires is his onyx monocle, which his privileged position has allowed him to preserve. He withdraws it from the top of his sock, huffs a cleansing breath and then screws it deep into the wrinkled knot of his eye.

It almost falls free as Grotteschi's eyes pop, locked on to the single word riven across the paper: 'Scox'.

Molloy lunges forward. 'What does it mean?'

Grotteschi pauses and brings a delicate hand to his temple as if awarding Molloy's revelation the greatest care. In truth, Grotteschi is indulging in a little drama. If his interpretation comes too easily, too lacking in lustre, then its apparent value will diminish. He wants Molloy to feel that there is weight enough in his revelation to merit eight ounces of soap.

Finally, Grotteschi speaks. 'This is what I can tell you of Scox. The name refers to an ancient god. He appears in many cultures – Egyptian, Mayan, Nazca – but most prominently in Voodoo, where he takes the form of a stork.' Grotteschi inhales, ready to embroider this further, but Molloy is already pacing backwards, his mouth pumping air, inflating an agonised wail.

'LaTisha's pregnant. That little bit o' trash is goddamn pregnant and she's going to tell my wife. That's what she always threatened to do, but I didn't believe her. But this . . . this . . .' His finger wildly agitates towards the paper. 'This is a warning! A stork means a baby. And you said Scox is a stork. Oh, this is bad. This is very bad . . .'

Grotteschi shrinks back as Molloy rails and then storms away across the workshop floor, loudly lamenting the unbidden secret that his mistress now seems destined to expose.

If Grotteshi's shoulders were not fused to his neck, he would shrug. *Such is human nature.* Give people the thinnest thread of an idea and they will weave their own meaning from it. What he told Molloy about Scox was true, but as to whether that paltry, adulterous incident was the revelation intended by Agnus – who knows? *Who cares?* Grotteschi withdraws his hand from his pocket and sniffs his pristine bar of soap.

A PLEASANT HOUR LATER, freshly showered and smelling like his mother, Grotteschi lays on his lower bunk bed. He has the cell to himself, a luxury arranged by the accommodation officer. A few weeks previously the officer had received a prophecy from Agnus and Grotteschi had maintained that to crack the obscure reference, he would need an extraordinary degree of silent concentration. That same day, a transfer was ordered to a private corner cell, *with a window no less!* Defying his deformity, Grotteschi danced a little jig that day and cracked the lunatic scrawl of Agnus within the hour. Not that he delivered the deciphered text to the accommodation officer until three days later, declaring loudly that it had drained him dreadfully.

The privacy he now enjoys is precious, but more wonderful still is the window. By day, the hues of sunlight and by night, sometimes, the sound of rain. A gentle patter to transport him back to autumn in New England. But tonight . . . tonight is quite different. The rain clatters like nails against the glass and the howling gale reminds Grotteschi that the derivation of this portal's name is 'wind's eye'.

Grotteschi wriggles deeper beneath his blanket, uneasy.

There is a while to go before lights out. He pulls from under his mattress a selection of books. Dusty and devoid of pornographic content, these academic tomes are rarely borrowed from the library trolley. The only reason the inmates ever request them is because the ancient, thick paper makes great roaches.

With a puff of dust, Grotteschi opens up the appendix to Rabey's *Compendium of Myth and Lore*. He finds the precise reference to Scox and, with a moistened finger, he peels open the book at the appropriate page. As his one good eye scans the chapter, he slowly nods, commending his own memory. Scox was indeed a stork-god. But Rabey elucidates further. Whilst some cultures attach him to the idea of new life, hence the myth of delivering babies, Scox is far more prevalent in cultures as an omen of evil. Grotteschi wriggles up on to his elbow, curiosity mounting as he reads that in the Voodoo culture, the stork appears as a 'loa' or harbinger of the most feared evil of all, an apocalyptically destructive spirit force that goes by the name of —

Grotteschi eagerly looks at the next page to find the name. Only to find the page gone. Torn out. Just a neatly severed strip remains, the rest no doubt smoked. Grotteschi grunts with frustration. His interest had been genuinely piqued and now he will never know what great evil Scox heralds.

He thuds the book shut, the resultant gust blowing up from his blanket the fragment of Molloy's revelation. Grotteschi had quite forgotten to file it with the rest.

He reaches below his bed once more, this time withdrawing a shoe-box. Beneath the lid lies an avalanche of paper shreds, each one covered in Agnus' manic scrawl. This is Grotteschi's stash, collected from worried recipients, eager for interpretation.

Few of his clients ever asked for their revelation to be returned. Grotteschi could understand that. *Here's your awful truth. Would you like a receipt with that?*

But Grotteschi was a natural hoarder, a lover of *things*. His tiny apartment in Manhattan had an entire wall stacked with leather-bound boxes, filled with knic-knacks and gee-gaws, pictures and letters. His deliberately perverse filing system labelled each box with the name of a Greek god. The irony that the one box he could muster behind bars was labelled 'Nike' still delighted him.

He presses Molloy's revelation deep amid the rest. But as he moves to close the box, something is exposed: an envelope crudely taped to the underside of the lid. Just as a dealer may separate the darkest herb for his own smoking,

Grotteschi keeps within this envelope the more obscure revelations. The ones that he has yet to decipher to his own satisfaction.

He rummages around the envelope with a careful finger. Amongst the scraps are some of the earliest revelations given to him. Way back then, Grotteschi found each one fascinating. The whole mad distraction of Agnus Day was, after all, still a novelty. And Grotteschi had his own opinion. He readily assumed that this highly intelligent inmate was creating a confidence trick. Behaving in a mad and mystical fashion, in the hope that Dr Torgus would rule on his sanity, commuting his death sentence to life.

So if it is a hoax, thought Grotteschi, who better to uncover it than a kindred gifted trickster?

But as time passed, and further revelations spewed from Agnus, Grotteschi was forced to admit that something other than deceit was at play.

The more he studied these fragments of text, the more he had come to believe that something fascinating lurked within.

The first bell of lights-out sounds. Ten more minutes of contemplation. Grotteschi pulls out a few of his favourites, running his eyes over the text, committing every detail to memory so that, as darkness is thrust upon him, he can roll his mind like a marble between the mysterious words until sleep finds him.

The first is a fragment where the handwriting of Agnus is so agitated that only a single repeated word is partially legible. To Grotteschi's eye, it says 'Chiaroscuro'. This, Grotteschi knows, is a school of art where light and shadow interplay in the extreme. A style much favoured in the seventeenth century by the Italian and Dutch masters. *But what does it mean?* On its own, perhaps nothing. But Grotteschi has another fragment. It bears the name 'Emanuel de Witte', once again written repeatedly and with such fervour, Agnus' pen has ripped through the paper, carving great holes. De Witte was a seventeenth-century Dutch artist, famed for his perfect perspective. His works are largely church interiors, all pillars and vast arches. He did not paint in the chiairoscuro style. So what, other than the particular fury with which Agnus wrote both these gobbets, is the connection?

The other fragment that equals these, in terms of manic execution, is Grotteschi's favourite. Its content causes his mind to divert and distract so violently that during these moments of contemplation, he forgets where he is. His mind, at least, escapes the jail.

This fragment bears the name 'Archilochus'. Grotteschi's passion for the classics means his knowledge here is deep. Archilochus was a Greek poet. His greatest work was called 'The Moera'. This is the Greek term for the Three Fates. The word Moera means '*part*' or '*portion*' and it refers to the way the Fates pull the thread until the extent of each portion is reached for each individual human. The thread is then cut and the human's mortality set – their span defined.

What intrigued Grotteschi, when this fragment first came to him, is that the Greek word *moera* is the root of the word *telomoera*, which became '*telomere*' – the thread that determines the life of a human cell. This had been Agnus' field of research.

The final bell of lights-out sounds. Grotteschi's cell is plunged into darkness. The endless storm rolls on outside and Grotteschi's mind churns: *what is the connection between Archilochus, the Moera and Agnus' previous research into human lifespan?*

6

DR TORGUS FLOSSES HER TEETH, lips snarled back like a dog. She rinses the clotted thread in a basin. The bathroom is attached to the private quarters of Governor Duggin, who smokes on a pull-out bed in the adjoining room. She runs the faucet to drown out the sound of him.

Dr Torgus arrived an hour ago, as she did each Friday afternoon, to hand-deliver her weekly report. This particular Friday, she had allowed Duggin's hand beneath her blouse. More routinely, she would rebuff any attempt at intimacy. But if the occasion arose that Dr Torgus should need something – a few days' vacation, an increase in her gas allowance – she would let his fingers twist open her buttons while she wrestled with his fly.

Today had been such a day. Torgus now finds herself in the bathroom, brandishing a flannel, completing the usual kitty-lick that still leaves her feeling dirty.

She pulls on the light-cord above the mirror. The bare bulb blasts like an X-ray, revealing the skull beneath her face. Torgus averts her eyes.

Sex and death. She shakes her head, a thought coming to her mind that the French call an orgasm *une petite mort* – a little death. She understands why. She tongues her teeth. They feel loose in her gums. She pulls another length of floss. And as she does, her mind flies in another direction, to the Three Fates, pulling their thread. She severs the floss and wonders *how much longer do I have?* Her life is passing too quickly. There is so much more she wants to achieve.

She's not finished. Not yet.

Torgus bends low, forcing her lips about the faucet, filling her cheeks with water, spitting hard. This does nothing to rid her mouth of the taste of Duggin. The whole building tastes of him, smells of him.

But no matter how distasteful the prospect may be, she must re-enter the room and continue her seduction. She still has to gain the permission she seeks . . . a very special permission.

She has failed to get any publisher interested in her book on Agnus Day. Her past academic misfires have worked against her. So she has devised another plan. A means by which she can get a worldwide platform for Agnus' work. But she needs Duggin to bless this latest and most brilliant enterprise.

If he will just give me a chance to explain my idea. She tousles her hair and tugs off the light, gaining ten years of youth in the gloom.

Her hand snakes around the door jamb, finds the light switch to the main room and flicks it off. A beam of yellow light persists. Duggin has turned on the television and the corner of the room is bathed in its flickering glow.

Torgus shimmies out of the bathroom and moves towards the window, pulling the curtains shut. Duggin's voice grunts from the sheets.

'You lookin' to go another round, doctor?'

An apt description as you barely last two minutes. 'Suppose I am, Governor. Are you going to refuse me?'

Duggin pats the bed. 'Since when did I refuse you anything, cher?'

She slides to the next window. Stares out at the lashing storm. Presses her forehead against the cold glass, as if willing an idea to distil.

She must act carefully. One wrong word and he will sniff out her intent too soon.

She listens to the snatches of sound as Duggin flicks past the quiz shows in search of the Friday night games.

'One final chance to get this right, Bobby or it's a sudden death round . . . '

'. . . All eyes are on him as he takes aim . . . and with the seconds on the clock, this has to be the last shot . . .'

Duggin flinches as the remote is pulled from his fist. He finds Torgus stroking his arm, demanding his full attention.

'And what have I done to arouse such a healthy interest, doctor?'

Torgus peels back a smile. *One final chance to get this right.*

'I have a proposition to put to you.' She aims her words carefully. 'Something that could be so very good for the reputation of Morphic Fields —'

Before she can shoot, Duggin rolls up from the bed, a rictus grin spread wide. *Sudden death personified.*

'And here it comes.' A chuckle catches in his catarrh.

'What do you mean?'

He swoops down, naked flesh swilling. 'Let's hear it! C'mon now, let it out!' His mouth is just a spit-bubble away from hers. 'It's Agnus Day, isn't it? You want Agnus Day.'

'I don't want *him* I simply want the opportunity to —'

'— bring down these walls like fucking Jericho! You think you blow my trumpet and get what you want?'

He drags a bathrobe from the back of the door, wraps himself within and tugs on the towelling cord, as if this binds his resolve tighter still. 'You think I don't know what you've been planning? Those trips to New York, cocktails with this editor and that . . . You think I only open the inmates' mail, doctor?' He bares his teeth more broadly still. 'I like to slide my knife where that tongue of yours has licked. Peel open that soft manilla.'

He wags a finger before tapping it against his eye-socket. 'I've seen inside. I know what you've been sending out. What I didn't know is how long you'd burn your knees on my carpet before finally finding the courage to beg for what you really want. My permission to publish.'

Torgus rises now, pulls sharply away. Utterly silent as she contorts her face from a caustic fury into something quite coy.

'Really, baby. You're acting as if I was deliberately keeping this from you. If I was discreet, it was because I thought you'd be pleased. A wonderful surprise – that I had created something that would attract such worthy public interest in Morphic Fields . . . in you.'

She wants to underscore her words with a tender gesture, but her fingers refuse to unclench from a fist. So she sweetens her voice another spoonful. 'Just imagine the magazine headlines: "The visions of a prisoner, brought to the world by a visionary governor . . ."'

He cuts across her like a truck. 'I want Agnus Day dead. I want my prison back to how it used to be. A place of simple evil. Can't you understand that?'

His breath comes in rasps, slowing slightly as his bare feet pace the cold tiled floor. He says nothing further. *A good sign perhaps?* His temper may be cooling.

Torgus moves once more to the window. A single pane has bent open a crack and is being sucked against its hinges by the wind. The metal creaks under the mounting strain.

She appears to busy herself with pulling the glass shut. She can hear the repeated snap of Duggin's lighter behind as he attempts to ignite a cigarette.

Her back is still to him. She slowly inhales.

And with seconds on the clock. This has to be the last shot of the match . . .

'Baby, I just want you to consider the —'

'Answer's no.' His cigarette jabs towards the back of her head. 'Do I make myself clear Annie? Whatever you're planning . . . it's finished.'

Duggin cannot see her expression. He cannot see the quiver in her fingers as they twist the window latch, tighter and tighter.

She turns to him with a straining smile. Barely moving
as behind her —
— the glass shatters under the force of the rain.

7

A WHITE SHEET UNFURLS. Twisting through the air. Caught at the corner by a tattooed hand. One of many hands that claw upwards, catching at cotton.

The prison laundry is alive with activity.

A long line of inmates heave sheets from shelves as water floods across the concrete floor. The freakish storm has overwhelmed the prison's sanitation system and water is bubbling up through the drainage grills.

The inmates work with a strange urgency, billowing the sheets like sails of a flotilla. The guards on duty are focused on the rising water and seem unconcerned by the prisoners' silent synchronicity.

At the back of the laundry is the event that the inmates are concealing. Agnus is on all fours, a lump of charcoal in his hand. Crawling back and forth across the plashy sheets, writing madly as if the cotton were canvas. His entire body quivers. Saliva froths at the corner of his mouth.

And from the shadow of the doorway, Kon'Verse looks on, delivering a signal with a flick of his eyes. A Petra Loa foot-soldier nods and disappears, his mission understood.

THE FIRST THAT GROTTESCHI knows of his summoning is the grip of a hand about his throat, followed by a sharp yank. His socked feet skitter to stay upright as he is hauled across the flooding floor, arriving like so much wet laundry at the feet of Kon'Verse.

Grotteschi rises, wiping a wet cuff across his eyes. Then bolts back at what he sees. Agnus, convulsing and retching as he scrawls across the vast expanse of sheets.

35

Never before has Grotteschi seen him work on such a scale. And this time, he writes not a word but a symbol. The same symbol. Again and again. His hand clawing at his own creation.

Grotteschi rubs his eyes, mumbling in excitement. 'How long has he . . . ?' 'How have the guards not . . . ?'

Kon'Verse towers above him, dark eyes imparting the only question that matters. *What does it mean?*

Grotteschi reaches down, fumbling at the top of his sock. Pulls out his monocle and smudges the lens against his cuff. Sinks it into his eye-socket and stares again at the symbol.

Jagged lines surround a dark centre, in which Agnus writhes, blackening the sphere deeper and deeper with heavy strokes.

The Black Sun, could it be? Grotteschi has read of this symbol in many of his books. He knows its origins in Germanic mysticism and that it always portends evil, but what could it mean here?

He looks on as Agnus scrawls the jagged lines further across the sheet, turning the rays into something else, something jointed. Like legs. The black sun now appears . . . alive. Like an insect.

What manner of creature? And what does it mean? Grotteschi pokes a thinking finger in his ear, winkling an interpretation forth. He opens his mouth, unsure of what will emerge. And then —

A bestial roar erupts.

Not from him, but from Agnus, as his arms and legs violently spasm. He falls to the ground, eyes rolling into the back of his skull.

The cry draws the guards who now splash the length of the laundry room. Before the first of them breaks through the ring of prisoners, the sheets have all been pulled away and bundled into a giant wicker basket. Leaving just the body of Agnus to be discovered, convulsing in the water.

A bellow from the senior guard commands the prisoners to disperse, but they are already marching out in a silent exodus lead by Kon'Verse. He lumbers past Grotteschi. A look is cast. The command is clear.

Figure this out.

The jab of a baton in the small of Grotteschi's back moves him out towards his cell.

Even before he shuffles into the corridor, he is running an imaginary finger along the spine of books massed beneath his bed.

This symbol, this black and mutant sun, does not appear in any of Rabey's illustrations. And in *Le Grand Grimoire*, an ancient tome he knows so well, never has Grotteschi come across a cryptogram like this.

His eyes dart up as a phalanx of guards pass by. The inert body of Agnus swings between them.

As they round the corner, the limp head lolls and Agnus' face is revealed.

Grotteschi flinches back against the wall, riven with fear. Until the baton jabs once more into his hump.

He resumes his shuffling stride. Back to his cell . . . to his books. Which he now suspects will be of scant use.

Grotteschi closes his eyes, seeing again the flash of that face . . . that mask of inexpressible terror.

Shakes his head, certain now.

The meaning of this last symbol does not lie within his library. Nor within his vast learning.

Indeed, it does not lie within this human realm.

8

SHE BREATHES SLOWLY. A black canvas hood, heavy and smelling of someone else's saliva, has been buckled about her head for the last two hours.

She has been instructed not to remove the hood until ordered to do so.

Her hands, though not cuffed, lie obediently in her lap. She knows that she's been disarmed. Her holster feels lighter. Her .44 Magnum is gone.

She likes her gun. More than the average detective. But that's Alexis Bianco – always more than the average detective. Her police file is testament to that fact: a collage of commendations for bravery and reprimands for breach of protocol. A senior officer once said that if a police dog had a record like hers, they'd put it down. She was unsafe off the leash.

They'd even made her do a psych test before her sergeant's exam. The doctor had noted at the start of the session that there was little on file for her before the age of seventeen. He had requested, in gentle, sing-song tones, that she recount her childhood.

Even as Bianco drew breath, she knew that telling him the truth could flip those sergeant's pips way out of reach. But here's the thing with Bianco – she has her creed.

Tell the truth and face the consequences.

So she kicks off her shoes and stretches out along the couch, a long story coming. Beginning thirty-five years ago, at the very hour of her birth.

Wrapped in a blood-splattered grocery bag, printed with the words 'We Deliver', she was abandoned outside

St Hilda's, a children's home in Bayou Cane. There was no note left by her mother as far as she can remember. And, in truth, she can't remember much.

Her memories, etched deeply by events, begin the day that she turned five. The same day that St Hilda's burned to the ground. She knows it was her birthday because a small, dry cake had been presented to her that morning. She wished it had been a proper birthday cake with icing and candles, but this dull muffin was all St Hilda's felt obliged to provide. The fire must have started soon after breakfast as she has no memory of ever eating the cake. But she does recall that amid the hysterical aftermath of the fire, with police and social workers running and remonstrating, she had heard a girl's name talked of in the same breath as the blaze. At first, she thought that they had given the fire a name, as they do to hurricanes. It was too late by the time she realised that the girl's name was her own and its association with the fire was brought about by a deep suspicion that she, by means of a stolen candle, had wantonly started it.

A week later she was dumped in a foster home. Her new parents, Sterbon and Monica, didn't much like God or his little children but they worshipped whiskey, a devotion observed from Sunday to pay day. They stretched the liquor with a combination of lemonade and federal aid; a weekly sum of ninety dollars came through their door as long as the kid was under their roof. They never got round to giving her a name. Their dog had always just been Dog and so Kid would work well enough for her. She could have accepted this lack of a label more easily if Sterbon and Monica hadn't taken the trouble give the broken-down shack that they called home a name. The plaque on the porch read 'Bonica', a union of their names' last syllables. They should have selected the first two, making 'Monster', as this is how they appeared to the Kid. A two-headed beast, locked together, fists flying as they drunkenly raged about

39

the room, hurling accusations, threats and glassware.

And then, just as fast as any fight would start, it would finish and Sterbon would stagger to the Kid, half-hidden by the door jamb and slur her hair with the palm of his hand. 'Y'see, Kid, always best to tell the truth, take the consequences and move on.'

Monica would woozily nod, making the wads crammed into her bleeding nostrils quiver like tissue tusks. 'He's right, honey. Truth's always gonna come out, so you just make sure that it comes outta your mouth first.' Monica would finish these good parenting homilies with a smile, lacking many a tooth lost to the truth.

As soon as she grew big enough to lift her bedroom window, the Kid was out of there, sliding down the tiles, feeling the first bone-jarring thud of freedom. A life on the streets began, but at least the life was hers.

With her loose mouth and even looser fists, the girl with no name got a reputation fast. She'd tell it as it is, call you out, spit the truth and take the consequences. Her appetite for a fight meant that the first two letters of the alphabet she ever learned were E and R. The nurses were kind enough and knew the score, but there's only so many times they can stomach a girl with gunshots to the belly before they call the cops.

So she had to go elsewhere. Word on the streets talked about an old swamp Mambo who would patch you up with spit and spells and take payment in liquor.

She took the raft out to her cabin one night, when a wound between her ribs refused to close. The old Mambo asked for her name, but she said nothing. The Mambo clucked, 'Well, I believe I know who yo' are. I hear talk of the filly who weighs no more than a feather, but is forever crowing for a fight. And seeing as you won't give me a name, I'll give you one. I'm gonna call you Bien'Cou. It's voodoo for Crow and it means 'a lot of neck'. Cos that's what crows are – kinda pushy.'

And the name stuck. When she came to New York she changed it to Bianco; Italian-American was an easier blend than Bayou-Voodoo. But what didn't alter was her pushy nature. She soon attracted the attention of a recruitment cop who worked the ghetto beat. He saw something in her. Took a risk and gave her a book on law enforcement. She ate it up, demanded more. Quick fists soon became quick wits.

The day after her twenty-first birthday, she aced the entrance exam and signed up as a cadet.

At twenty-seven, she made uniform sergeant. At thirty-one, she was moved to plain clothes and joined the toughest ranks of vice. At thirty-three, she made detective with special firearm privileges.

And from the day she strapped on her restricted-issue Magnum, one thing was clear: Bianco would always be more than the average detective.

And if she were anything less, she wouldn't be here now. In darkness and alone. Summoned to the most secret of debriefings.

Bianco twists her cheek against the bag. The air inside now tastes of her last meal. Houmous was the starter. Had she known what was to start just moments later – a thump to the skull, a clamp of canvas – she would've had the salad.

Someone will come. The hood will be removed. The debrief will begin.

Or maybe it won't.

The summons, after all, had come from SCURO.

This shadow agency investigates all reports submitted by law-enforcement officers which reference 'unorthodox events'. The word 'supernatural' is expressly forbidden by the SCURO Bureau.

Some cops call it the 'Screw Loose Bureau'. Such locker-room ridicule serves to mask a deep unease in the rank and file about the agency and its obscure operation. No one knows to whom SCURO reports and rumours occasionally rise of cops who get summoned and never come back. But Bianco didn't get to where she is today by listening to rumours.

She explores the rough floor with the heel of her shoe. *Not that I know where I am today . . .*

But there's one thing she is sure of. She knows why SCURO pulled her in. It was a report she filed on a missing girl called Maddy Pool.

It was a strange case from the start. Maddy was an overweight teen with bad skin and braces. The club where she worked as a coat-check girl was an elite joint, frequented by thin, tattooed creatures with black-painted lips. Any flesh not pierced was scored with self-harm scars. It was an underground club in every sense. Set up in the old city sewers, its long track record of member 'self-deaths' found an ironic echo in the joint's name: 'The Sewercide Club'.

Bianco had been called here to bag up wrist-cut sluts too many times before. But this body collect was different.

There was no body. Just a strange carbon burn mark on the floor of the coat-check kiosk, in the shape of a fat corpse.

Filling out her report, Bianco had used the words 'spontaneous human combustion' even though she knew this phenomenon belonged in the realms of science fiction.

The file must have gone straight to SCURO.

That was more than a year ago . . . maybe more. No, it can't be that long. Her thoughts are blurring. And with a rush of fingers, she claws at the hood. She is losing consciousness, her brain operating now on adrenalin alone. With a wrenching tug, the hood comes free. Long, dark hair tumbles out, crackling with static. Heaving back as she gasps for air.

What in God's name . . . ? Were they just gonna let her suffocate in there?

Or were they testing her? How long before she defied

orders not to touch the hood?

Breathing deeply, she rakes back her hair, revealing a pale face, sharp with cheekbones. The eyes are dark and deep, close-set like a predator.

She looks left and right about the room. She's in some kind of derelict loft. The vast space houses vats and pumps, rusted remnants of a soap-making factory. There is still the faint smell of lily of the valley, strangely at odds with the sinister chill that creeps down Bianco's spine.

The only available light seeps through the barricaded windows. The rays are thick with dust and strain to bounce a few feet from the floor. And so a darkness fills the void above her.

Silent. Still. Rushing as —

— something hurtles down, skimming past her skull and crashing into the floor.

Bianco jolts, looks down. At the foot of her chair is a clipboard. A crude artefact of plywood with paper clamped beneath a rusty clip.

Bianco glances from the floor up to the darkness, unsure if she should expect anything more.

Silence. Nothing comes. Then —

— a deafening howl, which blasts to white noise and resolves with a loud sonic pop.

And a cough, as a deep voice crackles from an unseen speaker suspended somewhere in the gloom.

'We ask that you record the events that you witnessed. Be accurate. Be truthful. Good afternoon.'

A second *pop* signs off the command.

Bianco pauses, then she gathers the clipboard. A pen dangles from knotted string.

You gotta be kidding?

The most feared of all federal agencies and SCURO turns out to be a clipboard and a biro?

Bianco flips the paper. Clicks the pen. Is this another test? If she cracks some combination will she activate a secret entrance to the real headquarters hidden below?

Her fingers explore the pen shaft and soon she finds a button which, when pressed, releases the barrel. A spring flies from within and a moment later she makes a discovery.

That she can't put the fucking thing back together.

It's just a pen. In fact, without the spring it's less than a pen as no amount of clicking now can force the nib out.

Bianco frisks her own pockets, finds a pencil. She stares at the rounded point, almost worn away, and wonders if enough graphite remains to commit her account.

And then she stops, smiling at her own stupidity. Shouldn't she be asking herself a different question?

Am I going to tell them the truth?

The top brass already fear that she is halfway cut to crazy. What she writes here could confirm it and kill her career.

Bianco licks the pencil's soft tip.

She hasn't lived her life by many rules, but one: truth . . . and consequence.

She grits her jaw, not about to change. And with bold strokes she begins. Three words, writ large: 'TORMENTA: THE FACTS'. She moves to underline the title and then halts, remembering she's short on graphite. She needs to keep this brief. Just tell it as it is.

'Walking amongst us – looking, sounding and acting just like us – are a type of demon called Tormenta. And as demons go, they are totally . . .'

She pauses. Searches for the right word, settling for: '. . . fiendish.'

Then her pencil halts again. So much to say.

Maybe she should tell it just as Lola told it to her. Because, dammit, that girl sure had a way of making it sound simple.

Bianco thinks back to that moment when the two of them, still strangers, stood in the dark. Lola's hand gripped hard to Bianco's shoulder, the muzzle of her own Magnum less than an inch from her chin.

'Do I have your attention, detective?'

Bianco mustered a nod.

'Then listen good.'

Lola's voice was no more than a whisper but it seemed twisted tight, sinking like a needle into Bianco's ear.

'Humans are born with a pre-determined lifespan, an allotted number of years to live. Some consume their span to its limit and pass away. Some have their span prematurely snatched from them by murder or mishap. But some surrender their life by choice. Humans call it suicide. Tormenta call it opportunity.'

Bianco felt the grip on her shoulder loosen a fraction. When she didn't move, it loosened further. But the gun was going nowhere. Bianco could still smell its metal breath.

'At the moment of the suicide's death, Tormenta can siphon the surrendered lifespan. Every unspent year refuels them. Rejuvenated, they will live out these stolen years. And when those years come close to expiration, the cunning Tormenta will begin the search for the next fuel-stop. The next fragile human. Because the lifespan must be surrendered, not taken. This is the only way it retains its purity and potency.'

Slowly, the Magnum lowered.

'From their method, comes their name. They torment their human prey into giving up their lives.'

Bianco swallowed, attempting to speak, but no words came. She licked her lips, easing a path and tried again.

'You – you say these Tormenta walk amongst us . . . in plain sight.'

'They are everywhere.'

'I've never seen one.'

'Weren't you listening?' The Magnum twitched, not committed to retreat. 'They look like humans. In fact, they are mankind's closest demon relative.' Lola swept the finger of her free hand. 'Take mankind one evolutionary step back in the natural world and you find the Great Ape. One step forward in the supernatural world and you find the Tormenta. They share much with us.'

'So you're saying that I have seen one, but I just didn't know.'

Lola leant in closer now, almost chummy. 'Ever heard one of those stories about the old guy with a trophy wife who drives him to drink and then to divorce. Stripping the house of everything he's ever worked for. But maybe she deigns to leave him just one thing. His study desk. The one he keeps his gun in. She's probably gone no more than a day before, broken and bawling, the guy blows his brains out . . . Or how about the story of the little girl in the church choir, so pretty, so tempting beyond her tender years, she seduces the young pastor. He hangs himself from the church rafters, no doubt compelled by her threats to expose him. Or maybe it's the tyrant boss, who promotes some kid so fast and then, just when he's bought the car and the penthouse and run up a ton of debt, he fires him, with the whole floor watching. They pull the poor kid's body out from under the train the very next day . . .'

Bianco felt her head nod. The department's suicide file was full of scenarios just like this.

'Tormenta come in every human form, each with their own particular grift to get you to surrender your span.'

'So Maddy Pool . . . someone in the club tormented her and then she . . .'

A silence hung.

Lola holstered her gun. 'It's a lot to take in.'

'No, I get it.'

'Take a minute. Have a smoke. You'll have questions.'

'You're right. I do.' Bianco pulled her soft-pack, tapped a stick. 'Who the blue fuck are you?'

A bell suddenly shrills from the soap factory wall. Bianco jolts back to the present. Looks at the paper on her lap.

She has written nothing.

And she knows why.

The truth matters. It is her creed. But sometimes, there's a truth that matters more.

Being a cop is about right and wrong. Working with Lola is about this world and the next. And maybe the one after that.

With a loud shunt, a narrow hatch slides open in the floor below her chair. She waits for a command, but none comes. And so, with careful fingers, she eases the empty clipboard into the slot, feeling something snare it below, snatch it away.

She's given SCURO nothing.

That may be bad.

The slot snaps shut.

Too late now.

9

THE LONG BLADE OF A WINDSCREEN WIPER slashes
back and forth. It clears the path of a bus as it hurtles
through rain. The side panels of the vehicle are splattered
with high-velocity mud, as if the wheels have burst the
road's carotid artery.

Beneath the mud, a design on the bodywork can be
discerned. Painted in black, it stretches the length of the
vehicle. It is the skull of a long-beaked bird.

In giant letters below the skull is one word: 'STORK'.

With a shriek of hydraulics, the tyres twist around a
tight bend.

Inside the bus, the driver lurches at the wheel and
howls with laughter. Or perhaps fear. His full expression is
obscured by long, black hair that dangles to his chin.

His hand unclamps from the wheel and fumbles across
the dash, searching for a CD. The album cover bears the
stork-skull logo. With one skilled hand, he slides the disc
into the slit of the player. Stabs at the volume.

A death-metal track blasts from the speakers. The
driver leans back, resparks his joint and mumbles along
to the music. The only discernible phrase from the chorus
seems to be '. . . death is the breath that I wanna inhale . . .'

He glances up to his rear-view mirror. A collection of
heads, hung with unwashed hair, mosh to the droning beat.

A girl removes her leather jacket, studded with the word
'STORK', revealing beneath a black T-shirt printed with a
list of stadium dates; the path of their pilgrimage.

She folds the leather with shroud-like care and then
examines her forearm. Old scar tissue hatches the flesh.

Between her fingers she twirls a razor blade. The edge comes to rest on a fresh patch of skin. She intends to score her name – her new name. The label given to you by your parents has no meaning, that's your slave name. Once you are awakened, as Stork awakened her, you choose a name that has true meaning . . . true destiny.

The band's lead singer, Fell Watson, had set an example. When Stork's original front man blew his brains out, he was quickly replaced by a Japanese guy called Hash-Tu. The fans were appalled, until they realised that Hash-Tu was not his birth name. He signed it thus – #2 – a name that respectfully signified his position behind Fell Watson as the band's second front man. Immediately, the fans were won over.

She doesn't imagine that she will come up with anything quite so brilliant. But still, she carefully considers all her options. The logical thing would be to select a name made from straight lines. Carving an 'o' or an 'e' could be messy. She smiles to herself. Even now, so far evolved from the nerdy girl she used to be, she still likes things to be . . . neat.

She bites down hard on her lower lip and cuts three verticals and two careful obliques – Livi – and then smiles, as the neat incisions barely weep.

There is a rationale behind her choice. The psychiatrist, hired by her parents at the first sign of their daughter's sudden obsession with Stork, had once let her file slip from his briefcase. She glimpsed her allocated patient number: '57'.

Just another can of worms for you to label, eh, doctor? Fifty-seven varieties of crazy.

And so she chose Livi, a version of the number 57 in numerals. She's kinda rearranged the Roman rules a little bit, but what the hell? No one will ever figure out the meaning of her name. That's the point. Your name is your own private destiny. And her destiny is to follow the band. From coast to coast. Continent to continent, hemisphere to hemisphere. From this world to the next.

Her iPhone blips and flashes up a road map. Livi checks the mileage and then wrinkles a frown. They are gonna need to stop for gas soon. She flicks her tongue against her teeth, clicking a silver stud like an abacus as she does a quick mental calculation. *We can make another fifty miles.*

Her residual love of order has put Livi in charge of this phalanx of die-hard fans, and she performs these duties with appropriate style. When the fan club was forced to comply with certain federal regulations, Livi had grabbed the papers from the City Hall clerk and, whilst he watched, she cut her palm and signed the Health and Safety form in blood.

Livi looks about the bus. Blades and needles roll about the seats. Bodies flop against the cool windows. Of all the kids travelling, only half are conscious at any one time. It was no sure bet that the driver would be one of them. More than once the bus had been known to swerve wildly off the highway, the wheel-spin worsened by his attempt to stamp out his burning joint, thudding his foot indiscriminately between the gas and the brake.

As the person in charge of their safety, Livi knows she is doing a pretty poor job. But she mentally blots that drop of guilt. That's the kinda thing that would have bothered her old self. Livi now knows better. *Death is the breath I wanna inhale.*

A pale face lurches up in front of her. The eyes are deep green and the lips are painted black.

'Hey . . . hi . . .'

Livi stares at the eyes. They are so dilated, the pupils look as though they are about to roll down the girl's cheeks like tears. Livi's voice is stern. 'How many Vicodin you taken, Ghost?'

Ghost shrugs, the effort dropping her back behind the seat. A sprout of blond hair slowly reappears as she claws her way upwards once more.

'So . . . yeah . . .' She inhales, determined this time to get a little further into her question. 'Doncha think the skinny kid with the real big . . .' Her fingers loosely circle her eyes, suggesting spectacles. 'Doncha think he's kinda . . . weird?'

Livi looks to the bespectacled boy sitting a few seats in front. Accusing any one kid on the Stork bus of being weird is pretty meaningless. They all exist way beyond the bounds of normal. But Livi has to agree with Ghost. This kid doesn't fit.

She has her own suspicions as to who he might be.

Ever since the media labelled Stork a 'suicide-cult' band, various do-gooders had attempted to infiltrate the fan-base. Teen counsellors had dressed up in leather jackets and turned up at gigs, the most dedicated amongst them committing to a little self-harm, to blend their scars like tiger stripes amid the true followers.

Livi had watched the skinny kid. The way his eyes swept back and forth behind those big glasses, observing . . . absorbing.

And yet Livi had not moved to expose him. One thing prevented her from being sure. She had been around enough psychiatrists and counsellors to recognise the suffocating air that surrounds them. They might come towards you with open arms, but what Livi saw, held between their outstretched hands, was an invisible feather pillow, ready to smother her. This vision was so strong, so real, that the last time her psychiatrist tried to embrace her, Livi swore she could smell feathers.

But this skinny kid . . . he didn't trigger that nerve. Livi knew this from the time she had come close to him. Just a few days ago, when Ghost had taken too many downers and couldn't be woken.

Livi had found the boy bent deep over her body, his lips almost touching hers. Livi had thrust her hand forward and wrenched him away. And that was when she saw it . . . in his eyes. A flash of *something*, there and gone too quick for her brain to give the expression a label.

His face clicked to a picture of simple concern. 'I was just listening . . . to see if she's breathing.' As Livi protectively gathered Ghost's head into her lap, the pale mouth had twitched and groaned, confirming life. The skinny kid exhaled with apparent relief. 'Looks like she's gonna be all right.'

As he walked away, sliding back into his seat, Livi's brain had churned over and over, searching for options: is he a church-worker? A newspaper reporter? She shook her head, knowing none of these was right. He didn't smell like feathers. *He smelled like . . .*

Her brain finally nailed it . . . *a fucking vulture.*

Livi remembers bolting at this strange conclusion. Unsure of what her own instincts were telling her. She decided, there and then, to keep it to herself . . . until she could make sense of it.

That was two days ago. Livi hasn't spoken to the skinny kid again. But he has never been far from her thoughts. And now Ghost shares her ill-ease.

Livi pats her hand. 'Don't worry. I'll take care of it.' She looks at the green eyes, which flicker shut. 'You look like shit, Ghost. Get your head down.'

And with a violent jerk, Ghost's head is thrown down on to the seat. Because the whole bus is lurching.

Livi braces herself against the window, adrenalin forcing her to her feet as she yells at the driver. 'What the fuck, Tez!'

He sweeps around his mop of hair. He's probably facing her but no features are visible, just the roar of his voice: 'Suck and chuck, people, we got company.'

And now Livi sees it. A pulsing blue light, closing in behind them.

Followed by the whoop of a siren.

And in one smooth action, every window in the bus is

pulled open and barbs, baggies and burning joints burst out of the vehicle as if it were a well-struck piñata.

The driver yells again: 'We clear back there?' In his rear-view mirror, he sees Livi give him a thumbs-up.

With a squeal of rubber, the bus swerves off the road and pulls to a halt. The patrol car slides in smoothly behind.

The driver bundles his long hair back into a ponytail and from under his seat comes a bus company cap. It has a banner wrapped around: 'Your driver is TERRY'. With a grunt, he pulls it on.

Fuckin' cops.

His eyes go now to the side-view mirror.

A woman exits the patrol car.

His mouth drops open and his eyes crimp with confusion. He leans closer still to the mirror.

She sure don't look like a cop . . .

10

A **WOODEN SIGN** once bore the name of this place, but no living soul can remember what it said. All that remains is the sign's uppermost post; the rest has been sucked down, year after year, in gentle sips. And the same thirsty mud gave this plot the name by which it is known today: Swamp Gravy.

An ugly name, but it is rarely spoken. So the need for something better is unlikely to arise.

The rain is a frequent visitor, dimpling the thick mud, making ripples that radiate out to a low, lone hut that perches in the middle of the swamp on bowed wooden legs. These stilts were once intricately carved, covered in a scaly design that fanned out into feathers. The impression is that the cabin stands on chicken legs. Flecks of paint suggest that, long ago, a careful hand took time to paint the stilts a rooster red. But the paint has peeled and the cabin is now plucked of any comfort. Roof tiles have been shed, exposing rafters, and the wooden steps droop into the water like a broken wing.

The porch boasts just a single shingle. Beneath this shelter squats an old woman, her body arranged in thick, comfortable folds. Dyed yellow hair is piled high on her head like pond weed. Old Fan Fan Bohica twitches a fishing rod and sinks it over the edge of the stoop.

She chews on tobacco and a song throbs in the stretching chamber of her neck. The melody, if such it can be called, revolves around and around, deeper and deeper. And each time she inhales to begin a phrase anew, she seems to suck the world towards her, drawing the wind around from the east, bending the reeds away from the tide. But throughout her song, Fan Fan's eyes never divert from the tip of her rod.

And so it is with fury that she turns to call behind her, 'Ain't I told you once too many times about your shadow?'

A massive black crow lowers itself on to the back of her chair, wings still beating.

Fan Fan jabs a finger at the water. 'Stickleback's got eyes on the top of his damn head.' She jabs the rod at the bird. 'Maybe I'll just put you in the pot. Problem solved. Problem eaten.'

The crow ignores her, shaking the rain from its feathers as if used to weathering the storm of Fan Fan's irritable welcome.

She slowly sets down the rod and shuffles the folds of her body until her massive form confronts the crow. She looks the bird straight in the eye.

'So – she's back, is she?'

The crow emits a rasping caw. And Fan Fan nods, clapping her huge hands down upon her thighs.

'Guess I shoulda been expectin' her.' She heaves to her feet, now talking with the absent care of someone who addresses empty air. 'But there's gonna be trouble if she's brought more than one . . .'

Her tongue is already tutting as she collects a long wooden pole and shuffles to the side of the cabin.

'Last time she came, I told her. Told her straight . . .' She pokes and prods the tip of the pole into the swamp. 'I'm kinda full t'bustin' . . .'

In the black water below floats a slew of bloated corpses.

THE POLE SINKS AGAIN. Each shunt now propels a crude raft. Fan Fan is paddling across the water, through the thick bayou vapours that roll and part to reveal another cabin. Painted black, the windows are barred and the doors are studded with metal plates. This hut was built to keep

55

something in . . . or something out.

Candles burn within. It is late, but Lola won't be asleep.

She never sleeps, not in the way the living do. She might shut her eyes and her breathing may slow. But her mind remains hitched to the switch of her adrenalin. Ready to respond to the slightest sound, the merest movement.

Which is why it comes as no surprise that the ripple of Fan Fan's raft arouses a shotgun snout. It slides through the bars.

'Jus' me, child. Jus' me.'

The rifle retracts. And, one thigh at a time, Fan Fan heaves herself on to the tiny porch.

Inside the hut, the walls are hung with weaponry: short knives, long-nosed pistols. A six-foot rocket launcher is braced above the door.

And the tiny tip of a needle glints. It pulls a length of surgical suture through pale skin.

Lola sits cross-legged on the floor, closing a slit in her shoulder with a final stitch.

Fan Fan grimaces at the depth of the wound, and then inhales, knowing better than to pass any comment. Instead she lifts a green flask of Old Artemis liquor from her apron. 'I brought fresh supplies.' Her eyes dart to the stack of empty bottles in the corner.

Lola grabs the flask and jerks it like hot sauce across the sutured slit. Then she jolts a shot across the back of her head. Her pale blond hair is shaved short and four fresh rips, raked by fingernails, run down her neck.

The last slug is saved for a split across her eye. The flesh swells blue. But the eye beneath is bluer still. The liquor hits and her lashes thrash against its antiseptic bite.

Then her fist swings and the flask swoops and smashes into the top of the pile.

Fan Fan pulls another bottle, uncorks it with her teeth. 'You know, one day you might try drinking it.' She takes a deep chug, smacking her lips and wiping her chin with the back of her hand.

Lola picks up her shotgun, snapping it open, checking the chambers. Picks up a cloth and begins to clean the weapon.

'Now, cher, what's troublin' you?'

'She said she'd be here.'

Lola's tone is almost petulant. Times like this, Fan Fan is reminded that the ruthless hunter sat before her is just a girl. She couldn't have been more than nineteen when destiny dealt her this cold hand.

'Bianco's doing what she has to do. And you should pity her.' Fan Fan reaches out, touches the back of Lola's neck. 'She doesn't have the freedom you enjoy.'

Lola pulls sharply away and Fan Fan inwardly curses her poor choice of words. *Enjoy?* As if one moment of Lola's dark existence is something she can enjoy.

'Child, I simply meant she's a cop. She got her duties.'

'She's off duty. Today and tomorrow. She said she'd be here.'

'Give her time.'

'One hour.'

'I meant, give her time,' – Fan Fan eases herself into a chair – 'to understand your world.' Her big feet spread wide. 'You got her into this, remember. Your decision.' She kicks off her shoes, stretching her toes. 'You needed someone to get you information. Trace number plates, tap telephones. Without a cop on your side, it would take you twice as long to find your quarry. And you knew she would roll with it. You saw that crow-crazy look in her eye and that lust o' hers for danger – and you worked on that.' A fat finger rises and wags at Lola's head. 'But remember this, my lil' muffeletta, the day you chose Bianco, you gave her no choice at all. You just turned up and hit her with the truth. And I don't doubt that everything you revealed is ripping her in two, even now.'

Fan Fan exhales; her finger drops to her belly. 'An old

57

Mambo like me, familiar with the dark side, I can accept you . . . and all that comes with you. But Bianco's different. Her life is in the real world, at least what she thought was real until you came along. She needs a little time to adjust . . . to believe all that you are asking her to believe. But no matter how hard it is for her, I can tell you this, Lola.' Fan Fan's voice drops to a whisper. 'She believes in you.'

Her old hand reaches out, strokes the back of Lola's head. 'She brought you to me, didn't she? To Swamp Gravy, a place where she once felt safe. A place to heal, to hide what you are . . . and what you do.'

Lola slides the polished bullet-chamber back into the belly of her Winchester. She rises, pulls on a long black leather coat. Then pauses and looks at Fan Fan. 'The job we do, that's the real fight. The only fight. So how long before she gets that?'

'Soon, child, real soon.' Fan Fan taps a finger to her temple 'You already got her here. She understands.' Her finger then drifts down towards her chest. 'But she's gotta believe. You need to get her here.' Her finger taps her heart.

Lola points to the empty space beside her. 'I need to get her here.'

She pulls a gun-holster from the wall, buckles it about her hips. Tugs a belt of bullets without looking up.

Fan Fan exhales. 'Then I guess you're going.'

Lola's lean frame moves towards the door.

'But, missy, one more thing.' Lola turns to see Fan Fan's finger jab towards one corner. 'When you gonna clean your room?'

A sticky trail of blood arcs across the floor, leading to a bundle of tarpaulin. From one end pokes a pair of bloodied Pumas. From the other, a pulped skull.

Lola exhales. 'When I get back.'

'No, no, uh-uh. We do this now.'

Fan Fan withdraws a large, leather-bound book from deep beneath her apron and spreads it wide across her lap, pawing through pages of handwritten notes until her fingers find a fresh page.

'So let's begin.' She nips her tongue between her lips and licks the tip of a pencil. 'What was his grift?'

Lola crosses her arms, resigned. 'He was passing himself off as a member of a fan club.' Lola nudges round the dead head with the tip of her boot. It is the skinny kid from the bus.

'He was following a death-metal band that's famous for its fan-base. Bunch of self-harming, soon-to-be-suicides. Pretty rich pickings for a Tormenta.'

Fan Fan writes in slow, careful strokes. 'What was the name of the band?'

'The band? seriously?'

'Every detail, cher. Every detail.'

Lola exhales, taps her fingers against the holster. 'Stork. And the bus was an Isuzu Gala Twin-Drive Diesel. Light blue. Maybe duck egg.'

Fan Fan puckers her lips. 'My love, you may laugh. But I have ambitions.' She pats the book. 'Come the day the world is ready to know the truth, this little opus is my sure-ass passport to Oprah.' She nibs her pencil to the page once more. 'How long would you say this boy's been around?'

'Long enough.' Lola tenses her shoulders, as if reliving their encounter. 'He had a fistful of fight styles.'

Her mind flashes back. She's inside the bus, her fist smashing into the skinny kid's skull. He dives down, deflecting the blow, his legs spinning round, cracking her behind the knees, forcing her into the aisle.

'Korean kick-house, for one.'

Fan Fan moves her pencil fast across the page, keeping up. 'What else?'

'Hapkido. Wrist-lock style.' Lola's fingers ripple, remembering.

She is tumbling out of the bus, pulling the kid with her. Two bodies thrashing through the mud, the rain falling hard. The kid leaps and twists, contorting his hand into an impossible punch that reverses back, connecting with Lola's jaw, jousting her high. She smashes hard into the back of the bus, falls on all fours, gasping for breath. The kid responds with a roar, ripping himself free from the last of his T-shirt. The torso revealed is racked with muscle. He lunges forward. Lola is still on the ground. Defeated. . . or perhaps deceptive. She suddenly launches upwards, a length of metal in her hand – the bus fender, ripped away. Too close to halt his attack, the kid swoops down. And, with a sucking thud, the metal plunges through his belly. He falls – dead.

Lola rises from the impaled body to see the other kids lined up against the bus, spread-eagled, eyes averted as Lola had commanded. Only one pair of eyes dare to look around: a girl with the name Livi scored on her forearm. She stares through the rain in a shivering silence as Lola extracts the fender from the kid's flank. Then Lola halts, sensing eyes upon her and slowly tips her head to meet the girl's gaze. And with a dark smile, she hoists the bloody fender. 'Death metal. My style.'

Fan Fan turns the page, her old hand racing to record Lola's account. 'Ah, cher, your wits were quicker than his fists. But he was good. Hapkido and kick-house – to learn that many disciplines takes time . . . and travel.'

'Including Peru.' Lola pulls a knife and slices the twine that binds the tarpaulin. 'There was some Capoeira, Wari style.' She nods towards the unrolling tarpaulin. 'Not from the kid. The other guy.'

A second head slumps forward, striking the floor.

Fan Fan looks up, eyes wide. 'What was this bus – a Tormenta nest?'

Lola shrugs and cranks her jaw, a jab of pain taking her back to the fight.

She's bent over the kid's corpse, momentarily distracted. A fist launches from the shadows, smashing her to the mud.

She leaps back to her feet, to see a figure hurtling forward. A cap catches in the light, a name upon it declaring that her attacker is Terry. But now the driver's eyes are ablaze and his movements fast and powerful, revealing his true nature. He drops his body low, swings his legs high. Boots smash, catching the side of Lola's face as she swiftly deflects. Blood blasts between her teeth as she crashes down, twisting her torso, her hands thrusting upwards. Fingers tensed, hard as a blade. Scything into the driver's neck that cracks hard to the left. Gasping for breath, but too late as Lola grabs his long ponytail and wraps it round his neck, forcing her knee into the base of his skull. As he writhes, his cap rolls into the mud. Lola mumbles through split lips, 'Your driver is sorry.' Then yanks back hard on his hair and, in one jerk, garrottes him.

Fan Fan's pencil pauses. She looks up. 'And then?'

'He died. In no particular style.'

With a thud, Fan Fan shuts the book and waddles over to the bundled bodies. 'Well, if you're done, let's see what they reveal to my old mambo eyes.'

She tugs at the tarpaulin and the corpses collapse on to the floor, face down.

Fan Fan begins her examination with the kid, peeling off the last of his clothing. The cotton cracks with hardening blood, revealing beneath a fresh tattoo spread across his shoulder blades. It is the bird-skull logo of Stork. Fan Fan pulls a bottle from her pocket and shoots a stream of liquid across the dead skin. At first, the impact serves to wash away the blood. But as the liquid settles, it begins to sizzle, its acid nature reacting with the air to produce a scalding brew that burns away the surface skin.

With her hand balled into a fist, Fan Fan wipes away the bubbling blisters, revealing beneath an older tattoo that stretches across his shoulder: a spider with eight eyes. 'I seen this one before.' Fan Fan flicks through her book, her finger finding a sketch of the same tattoo. 'It's the mark

61

of the Ocho Ojos, from Tecate. But that gang hasn't been active since the late 1960s.'

She jolts another slug of acid across the forearm. A number bubbles from the flesh.

'A prison tag, inked deep. I'd say he did time at the turn of the century.'

She rolls the corpse and slugs the last of the acid across his chest. As the flesh boils and Fan Fan scrubs and rubs, another image appears, buried deep in the flesh.

A bird, long-beaked, wings spread.

'What's that, another stork?' Lola leans in close, reaching forward. Until Fan Fan smacks her hand away. 'No, no, cher. This tattoo is deep. Real old.'

She prods at the flesh. 'Back when he got this, he wasn't following no stork. Because that right there . . .' She tentatively circles her finger above the bird. '. . . is Guacariga.' She pauses. Then with a sudden resolve, she shunts the second body over. An identical tattoo is spread across the driver's chest.

'Well, well . . . fresh ink, I'd say. Which makes this skink a new disciple.' Fan Fan slumps back on to her haunches, tapping her chin in contemplation. 'It would seem the followers of Guacariga are gathering once more.'

Then her hand reaches down. She pulls a lump of tobacco from her pouch, agitating it between her palms. 'What does this portend . . . that he comes again?'

Lola knows that phrasing. The way Fan Fan will half-finish a thought, dangle a question. She is playing the wise but haughty Mambo who must be cajoled into her tale.

'So, great Bohica. You gonna tell me who this Guacariga is?'

Tracing her teeth with the tip of her tongue, Fan Fan selects the right place to begin her story. 'The Nazca desert, in Peru. You ever seen the creatures drawn in the dust?'

Lola nods. 'Yeah, I've seen pictures. A spider, a monkey . . .' She frowns and then raises a finger. 'And a hummingbird.' She points to the tattoo. 'It looks just like this.'

'And the hummingbird represents a god called Guacariga. And to the Taino people, he is the god of death.'

Fan Fan settles into her tale with another bolt of tobacco.

'Taino legend tells of two great spirit clans who were at war. The House of the Fly and the House of the Lily. Each house had a son and a daughter who fell in love – ancient precursors of Romeo and Juliet. Their love was forbidden because the Fly was a filthy creature who fed off death and the Lily was a thing of vivid beauty and life. So the Fly did a terrible thing: he stole rays from the sun and turned himself into a glittering creature whose wings were every colour of the spectrum. And so was born the Hummingbird. But the Sun God discovered what the Fly had done and he cursed him. So when the Hummingbird at last sank his beak into the sweetness of his beloved Lily, he found himself driven to suck . . . to suck the very life from her. In that moment, racked with grief and fury, the Hummingbird became Guacariga, the destroyer. His coming signals death, just as it did when he was the Fly. Those who bear the symbol of Guacariga believe he will return. And when he does return, death will come to all mankind.'

'How d'you know so much about Taino culture?'

Fan Fan flaps her hand as if it should be obvious. 'The Taino people came from the Nazca deserts. They spread to Trinidad and Haiti and then to Louisiana. And that's where Taino culture grew into Voodoo.' She taps her chest. 'Even my own name, Bohica, is evidence of this ancestry. In the ancient Taino language it means 'priestess'. So I take that as a sign that I was always destined to become a Mambo . . . even though some may doubt my powers.'

A silence falls. Lola looks up. 'I know how powerful you are.'

A dark smile passes between them. Lola looks away, unwilling to let Fan Fan see what rises in her eyes.

'What is it, child? Are you having regrets?'

Lola says nothing.

'I sense that something's stirring in you.' She pauses, draws a subtle breath. 'Do you want to remember?'

The blond head remains averted in the shadows. 'I don't know . . . maybe.'

Fan Fan reaches out, pats Lola's hand. The gesture is gentle but the old woman's fingers are stiff with tension. 'No, honey, believe me . . . you don't.'

11

GROTTESCHI WHEELS THE LIBRARY TROLLEY along a narrow corridor. It leads to the Isolation Wing.

He has secured this duty by calling in a favour from the young guard who accompanies him. Not that Grotteschi ever itches to dirty his hands with the labours of a prison trustee. But today he has a particular mission in mind.

There is one prisoner he wants to talk to and this is the only way that he can secure an audience.

Because this is no ordinary prisoner. This is the one they call Ring-Pull.

The wheels of the trolley squeak, a rhythmic pulse that echoes off the walls like an alarm.

They approach the last security gate that quarantines the corridor. The young guard slows his pace. His eyes flick to the unlit length ahead. 'So . . . you goin' right inside his cell?'

Grotteschi exhales. 'No, my plan is to remain outside and slide his book choice, page by page, beneath the door.'

The young guard pauses but Grotteschi waits, knowing that sarcasm moves in slow motion round here.

Finally the guard grunts and nods. 'Yeah well, let's see how funny you are when you come out.'

His key churns in the lock as he ushers the trolley through the gate.

'I'll open his cell when you get there.' The guard dangles a hand above a panel of buttons. 'You got three seconds and then the door shuts, real quick. Could slice that hump o' yours like ham.'

Grotteschi shunts the trolley forward. Shuffling towards

the farthest door. Then, quite unexpectedly, a shiver struggles up his spine. Grotteschi halts and tugs at his ear, confused.

How strange!

When he walked down the first length of corridor, the young guard's evident unease had served as a distraction. Now with him gone, Grotteschi feels exposed to the pounding of his own heart.

Can it be that the prospect of this prisoner unnerves me?

Grotteschi had felt nothing, not a flicker of fear as he read the transcripts of Ring-Pull's trial. Even as he scrolled through the tabloids, crammed with gory detail, his hand had never flinched. He appreciated, of course, the ghastly magnitude of Ring-Pull's crimes. To fail to do so . . . well, that would be inhuman; seven little boys, blond beauties every one, abducted and killed. All in the same way: starved to death in a shed in Bayou Cane.

But none of this aroused outrage in Grotteschi. What consumed him was curiosity. The opening argument from Ring-Pull's defence was beyond extraordinary.

It contended that Ring-Pull was not in his right mind. More than that . . . not in his right *body*.

His real name – that is to say, the name upon his birth certificate – was Todd Lily. A roadie who lugged gear for every heavy-metal band that rocked the east coast. When his sacrum finally cracked, Lily turned his massive hands to a new trade and opened up 'Rinky Dink Ink', a tattoo parlour on New York's Lower East Side.

Aged fifty-two, he gets blood poisoning from a dirty needle. Falls into a coma and is pronounced dead.

Laid out in the morgue, the pathologist makes his first cut and finds running blood. Lily is still alive . . . or back from the dead. Same thing. *Kinda . . .*

When Lily comes round, he announces that he is Tenzin Nara, a Buddhist monk. He has no memory of his life as Todd Lily.

Once physically recovered – and with no coverage on his HMO for psychiatric help – he is discharged. And disappears.

Ten months later, he turns up in Louisiana with seven little boys, all dead. When arrested, he said nothing, only that he meant the children no harm. He was simply performing his duty, in search of the Rinpoche.

The county court of New Orleans was not much bothered to investigate what lay behind this one repeated word, settling to respond with just one of their own: execution.

The inmates of Morphic Fields talked eagerly and endlessly of his arrival and soon bastardised this Rinpoche guy to Ring-Pull.

Grotteschi's interest was piqued. Tales of reincarnation had always fascinated him. Lily's belief that he is now a Tibetan monk sounded like a classic case of delusion. He was keen to speak with him.

But Grotteschi was denied any opportunity for such a conversation.

On his first night in Morphic Fields, Ring-Pull's head was so savagely pulped against the lip of a urinal, his jaw could not be reconstructed and now the lower half of his face is held together by a crude wire brace.

Grotteschi is not even sure whether the man can speak. But he has to find out. Because Ring-Pull is the one who can give Grotteschi the answers he seeks.

He arrives outside the cell. Wipes his palms down his thighs, conscious of their heavy sweat.

The young guard, standing far away on the other side of the gate, presses the button and the door shunts open. The space beyond is windowless and dark.

Grotteschi sees nothing, but his other senses quiver to the rasp of wet breath and the sharp tang of urine.

As his pupils dilate, a shadow gains form. A face turns, meshed in metal.

Grotteschi grips his trolley as if he might at any moment wield it as a weapon. Then, with a jagged intake of breath, he finds his voice.

'Namaste . . .' He places his hands together and bows, using the downward motion to conceal the removal of a particular book from the bottom of the trolley. 'I am in need of your wisdom.'

The silence is filled with the shadow's breath, sieved through saliva.

Forcing himself onwards, Grotteschi slides the book across the floor. 'There is a symbol that defies me. It is not one of our world. I believe it belongs to the realm of the dead. And so its meaning may lie within this book. I ask for your learning to help me understand.'

An arm uncoils from the darkness, draws the book closer. A torch snaps on. Finds the book's title.

Bardo Thodol: The Tibetan Book of the Dead

Grotteschi's taps the cover. 'It is a 1950s' imprint, but wonderfully complete.'

The torch beam swings up, catching the edge of Ring-Pull's metal face. Grotteschi spasms, his knees buckling behind the shield of the trolley.

He gathers himself, quivering a finger. 'The relevant page, I have marked it.'

Ring-Pull rises from the corner and slides through the darkness towards his bed. The movement releases a fresh stench of human decay and Grotteschi feels a cannonball of bile bowl up his gullet. He swallows it down as Ring-Pull spreads the book across his lap, fingers tracing the selected symbol.

Grotteschi musters a whisper. 'You know its meaning?'

A noise shudders from Ring-Pull. A deep, bestial grunt. That comes again, faster now. Harder. Louder.

Grotteschi's hands clench on the trolley.

And as the sound explodes about the cell, he realises that Ring-Pull is laughing.

12

BIANCO CAN NO LONGER SMELL THE LILIES. The old aroma stuck to the walls of the soap factory has not diminished. But she's been there so long, her nose has dulled. She looks at her wrists where her watch should be, remembering now that she was stripped of it.

Then her fingers descend to the floor and ripple through ripped shreds. It's the paper upon which her testimony should have been written, torn to pieces. Real small pieces. Stripping and ripping has been the only way to pass the intervening hours since she made her decision.

The right decision. To say nothing.

She owes Lola her life.

Because a new life began for her the moment Lola revealed all that exists beyond the human realm.

And the fact that Bianco's alive today, that's down to Lola too.

Because one night, everything changed.

LOLA WAS BLEEDING SO BAD, the floor of Fan Fan's cabin was slippery as a slaughterhouse ice-rink. It took a yard of cat-gut and all of the old Mambo's sewing skills to patch her up. And as Lola lay in the corner, forced into slumber by a flask of Old Artemis, Fan Fan turns to Bianco, her voice low.

'Yo' gone tell me what passed tonight?'

Bianco tightens her mouth, twitching her cigarette.

'Ever since I've known you, Crow, you got a sickness. I call it lock-jaw.' The old woman thrusts a bottle of the green liquor beneath Bianco's chin. 'Here's the cure. Take as required and talking comes easy.'

Bianco grabs the neck, swills the bottle. And memories lick the back of her mind. 'Do you remember how this all began, Fan Fan? Way back, when you and I knew nothing of Tormenta?'

'Child, I always had my demons.' She raises her bottle and, with a smile, takes a deep swig. Then her smile slackens and she reaches out to pat Bianco's hand. 'You got regrets?'

'No, it's just that . . .' Bianco grinds her cigarette, slow and hard. 'I was a cop. Plain and simple. Or as simple as homicide gets. Then I meet Lola. Her DNA says she's one-time dead because her suicide file is on my desk. But here she is, alive and kicking the shit outta anyone who gets in her way. And then she and her Magnum give me a fast education in Tormenta. Because she needs my help.'

Bianco flips a smile. 'Of course, she doesn't call it help. Lola can take care of herself. She knows how to hunt. She knows every Tormenta game, every grift. She says that all she needs from me is information. The paperwork and passes that will get her closer to her mark. But the kill – that's down to her. She goes in solo, every time. And I obey. I stay away, every time.'

Bianco pulls a fresh smoke. 'Except this time.'

Her eyes go to blood on her hands, cracked across her knuckles. She taps the soft pack. Presses on.

'We went to Vegas. Lola said it's a prime hunting ground. A lot of Tormenta operate there. She made it sound like we were going into duck country at the height of the season. But there was one guy she wanted. A casino owner called Jimmy Finny. She knew his grift. He gets a punter deep in debt and then sends his boys round to collect. It doesn't take many visits before the punter opts to blow out his own brains before the boys achieve the same result with a baseball bat.'

Bianco sparks her smoke. 'That's top grade tormenting.' The match flicks to the floor, joining a pile of many. 'Finny had built up quite an empire. A ritzy joint on the Strip. A ton of security. Getting close wasn't gonna be easy. Lola needed inside information. So I swing by the Las Vegas Police Department with some cold-case cover story. Ask them about Finny. His movements, his routine. Detective Dirk takes me for a coffee, gives me one of his fancy French cigarettes and lays out some even sweeter information. He tells me that Finny will always take a face-to-face meeting with the Gaming Commission. Those guys, he keeps close. So if I'm going undercover, Dirk recommended I get myself a Commissioner's ID. That way I can walk right in. I pass this on to Lola. She gets herself suited and booted and dammit, ya know, she looks badass even with a briefcase.'

Fan Fan chuckles, encouraging her on.

'I get her a Commissioner's ID. And in she goes. Tells me she'll call when she's done. Like she always does. I'll drive by, pick her up and then we're smoke.'

Bianco grinds out her cigarette, barely touched. 'I figure I've got fifteen minutes. I walk over to a tobacco booth in the lobby of the Bellagio. I'm looking for that fancy French brand that Detective Dirk gave me. The guy in the booth has a real attitude.' Bianco tightens her face, doing an impersonation of the clerk as she replays their exchange.

'"Is Madame looking for anything in particular?"

'"Thinking about changing my brand. I'll take a packet of the Vichy Grand."

'"That'll be forty dollars."

'"Forty dollars?"

'"It's a lovely cigarette."

'"If I owned the casino, maybe. Wrong brand for a cop."

'"Maybe you're the wrong brand of cop."'

Fan Fan pops her eyes at this comment. And Bianco nods.

'Yeah, it hit me too. No way could Dirk afford those smokes. Unless Dirk is dirty. In which case, I just walked my partner into a set-up.'

Her fingers flex into a fist. 'I got there in under five. And there she was, under fire.

'First time I'd seen her fight. The way she moved, taking all those goons out, one by one. Until Finny stands alone Then it begins. The main event.'

Fan Fan pulls her notebook from her pocket. 'Slowly now, I want to get this down.' Her long tongue slicks the tip of a pencil, but Bianco accelerates, lost in her own tale.

'It was spectacular. Fists flying like whirly-birds. And Lola's pulling blades and pumping bullets, any hand, every direction. And Finny – he's just as fast. Faster even. That's what it looked like. Because suddenly, Lola's down. And I'm not thinking. I'm on instinct override. My gun is out and I'm going in. Then I realise – too late – she's not hurt, she's faking. And I've fucked it up.

'Finny turns to me and gets a shot away. And I hear it hit, metal mashing flesh. I know that sound. But I'm still standing. And then I see Lola, right in front of me, twisting through the air, falling and firing her Winchester. She hits Finny. Nukes his neck. And then she's rolling at my feet. A hole this big, right through her chest. She took that bullet.'

'I pull her arms around my shoulders and drag her out of there. We're in the car. I'm driving like a maniac. I'm saying, "I'm sorry, I'm sorry."'

Bianco closes her eyes, head down.

Fan Fan nudges the bottle in her hand. 'She's gonna be all right.' Ruffles Bianco's long hair. 'You're still her partner.'

'We're not partners.'

'She's your friend.'

Bianco dunks a smile. 'We're not friends.'

'She'd die for you.'

'I'm not sure what that makes us.'

A BELL SUDDENLY shrills on the factory wall, rousing Bianco.

The last shreds of paper drift through her fingers, falling to nothing.

She stands up straight, smooths her suit. She doesn't have a single regret. But she's disobeyed SCURO, so she has one question.

What fate awaits? She doesn't know. Perhaps no one knows. That's how it goes with SCURO.

It's an easy task for them to make a cop disappear. Just deliver some soft-soap story about recruitment to a special operation. All your chief knows back at the precinct is that you'll be on other duties for a while. He won't know where or why or how long until you come back . . . if you come back.

A light blasts on above her head. Bianco blinks, looks about her, seeing for the first time the room that holds her. And instantly she learns a fresh fact about SCURO.

They gotta sense of humour.

The faded sign on the wall reads: 'The Soft Soap Factory'.

The slot in the floor shunts open for a second time. Something bulges up, soft and rubbery. Flopping out and uncurling on to the floor. Bianco gathers it.

It is a rubber party mask. Of Einstein.

The loudspeaker on the wall shivers and crackles. A voice booms.

'Place the mask on your face. Exit the room. Do not speak. Do not remove the mask.' A loud pop punctuates the end of the order as the speaker clunks off.

Bianco slides on the mask. The skin smells of latex and clings to her nostrils and mouth. She exhales as the door to her room clangs open.

Chin up, she walks out.

13

GROTTESCHI PUSHES HIS TROLLEY DOWN THE CORRIDOR, fast away from Ring-Pull's cell.

The wheels have lost their squeak, as if the knowledge now borne by Grotteschi is so astounding that it has the power to silence not only him, but all he touches.

The body of Todd Lily holds the mind of another.

At first, Grotteschi could not untangle his own thoughts because the fear that shrieked within his skull was so distracting.

Only as he acclimatised to the stench of the cell and the vastness of the shadowed form before him did another feeling start to clamber across his heart: a heavy calm.

The breathing of Ring-Pull, at first so wet with threat, now seemed to impart a soothing rhythm.

And the voice, when it finally came, was deep and round. Grotteschi found himself sitting like a patient child as the mind of Tenzin Nara spoke to him through the mouth of Todd Lily.

'The life that we call ours, we borrow only. Once we die, the lifespan returns to the eternal cycle and awaits to be reborn. This cycle was my care . . . my duty to protect.'

Ring-Pull pauses, noisily hawking up the drool that escapes from his split lips. Grotteschi shifts, waiting patiently.

'I belong to an elite brotherhood of Buddhist monks. Our sworn duty is to seek out the human vessels into which the spans of our beloved masters – our Rinpoche – are reborn. For centuries, this tradition has been upheld. Monks such as I travel from village to village, examining every boy, searching for the reborn span of our masters to appear in what we call the Unmistaken Son. But we must move quickly, as once the boy is five years old, it is too late. Human emotions, unwittingly instilled by his parents, will have destroyed his gifts. In short, his mind will now be locked into the human realm – and the spirit of the Rinpoche trapped for ever.'

Ring-Pull suddenly lunges forward, roaring. Behind his metal mask, his face contorts as if another body is trying to burst out.

Grotteschi shrinks back. *The fight between Tenzin Nara and Todd Lily is not done with!*

Ring-Pull bellows again and then ferociously inhales, swallowing back down the restless fury into the belly of his being. A silence hangs and, slowly, he continues with his story.

'When I first died as Tenzin Nara I found myself reborn into the body of Todd Lily. I accepted this as just another stage in my search. The duty to find my Rinpoche remained. I sought the boy in whom he may be concealed. I was not killing these children. I was merely opening their mortal shell.'

Grotteschi listens in wide-mouthed fascination. 'Venerable Nara, you indeed have knowledge beyond this world.'

He has almost forgotten his original purpose in coming to this stinking cell. Then – he jabs a finger at the symbol on the opening page of *The Book of the Dead*.

'A man . . . not of his own mind . . . drew this symbol.'

Ring-Pull nods and rolls up his sleeve to reveal the identical symbol tattooed on his own arm. It is spherical like the sun but the rays are jointed, like insect legs.

'The man Todd Lily was familiar with this symbol, though he had no knowledge of its meaning. The *Bardo Thodol* has long since been an inspiration for skin-ink artists. He was simply drawn to this particular totem.'

His fingers trace a gnarl of scars that surround the tattoo.

'It was this that he was applying when the infection set in. I sometimes wonder if that is what called me to his body . . .'

Ring-Pull's eye crinkle with a contemplative smile. Grotteschi urges him on.

'So you know the meaning?'

And with those words, the calm is ripped from Ring-Pull's eyes like a morgue-sheet, revealing beneath a face racked with fear. 'Yes, I know its meaning.'

His voice strains. 'Amid the flow, there are certain spans that come with great power. The power to inflict upon the human realm . . . infinite alteration.'

Ring-Pull grimaces. 'I never thought to witness it . . .'

The cell door shudders open. The guard is calling time.

'Witness what, venerable sir?' Grotteschi's body is knotted with anticipation.

Ring-Pull taps a filthy finger on the symbol. 'This means he comes once more . . . the accursed fly . . . the Mosca.'

BOOK II

14

A FIGURE SITS IN THE DEEPEST REACH OF THE
ARCHIVUM. A set of shelves, stacked with books, obscures
the body and a table lamp blasts a beam below but not
above. And so the figure's face cannot be seen. But still,
there are some clues that prove his identity.

For one, the cuffs.

They tumble from his sleeve, light and lacy. Some might
dismiss these trims as dandiness but he delights in them. As
he does in his hair, cured into coils.

Another clue: the cards. A handsome golden deck, laid
out in the careful ranks of Solitaire. They pass the time, and
much time is passed here.

And that's the final clue, the one that categorically
confirms who sits within the shadows: the sheer lateness
of the hour. Who else would endure the night chill of the
Archivum, other than Dali?

He looks about him. He need not move his head. His
eyes are large and roil in the sockets, back and forth, soft
and silent.

He is alone. His favoured state. He gathers up his game
of Solitaire and slides the deck within a velvet pocket.

And then he waits a moment more. Patience too is to
be prized. He breathes in deeply, smelling the leather and
the vellum.

And then he slowly extracts a long silver pen, setting
it down like a surgeon's scalpel. For, in a way, he is about
to operate . . . to make better. The Archivum holds many
documents in need of his tender care. Works that contain
inaccuracies, half-truths. They need correcting, like a

crooked spine.

This addiction of Dali's to add and append, he knows whence it comes. It is an urge instilled in him from his youthful days, when he worked as a scribe to a scholarly priest. Père Corbeau studied the ancient works of the philosopher Trismegistus. Ten thousand years before the birth of Christ, when the world worshipped a host of deities, Trismegistus wrote of one God who would some day come to Earth in the form of man. Père Corbeau pored over every word and every time he discerned some deeper meaning, he would charge his young scribe with the task of annotating his copy of the text with a tiny asterisk. Then he would dictate his interpretation and the boy would write, in a fine, light hand, a footnote at the bottom of the page.

This apprenticeship lasted barely two years but even in that short time, the young scribe became aware that the old priest's mind was growing ever more troubled. With each interpretation, the old man found his faith twisted ever tighter towards the teachings of the Rose-Cross monks, who had long since held the works of Trismegistus as the cornerstone of their faith. But the Rose-Cross brothers, or Rosicrucians as they came to be known, were deemed a radical sect and were vilified by Rome. So if Père Corbeau's notes were ever discovered, he would be castigated as a heretic. So the old man hatched a plan.

The rules of typography are such that a second set of notes must be signified by a fresh mark – not an asterisk, but a cross-shaped symbol called an obelus. And so it was that the young scribe returned to the works of Trismegistus and, at the old man's command, added obelus after obelus to the original annotations. Père Corbeau then gave him a new, blank book. These footnotes, in all their rose-coloured, heretical glory, must exist in this tome alone. A slim, hide-bound book that the young scribe came to refer to as *The Obelus*. And at the end of each night's annotation, this book would be snatched up by the old priest to be hidden away.

A hide-bound book indeed . . .

And so this continued – until the night that Père Corbeau was discovered on the floor of the church scriptorium with his throat slit, still wearing his habit, dried hard with blood.

Dali never worked as a scribe again. But old habits die hard. And his passion for books continued unabated. He loves not what a book reveals, but what it does not. The insidious intent. The masquerade of meaning. The subtle subtext, sliding another message like a razor blade beneath your eyelid.

Dali leans back in his chair and looks about the Archivum one last time. He is now quite certain of his solitude and so he reaches up and eases a book from the shelf, gently as if it were a sleeping baby. Then he sets it down upon the table. This publication will be the first to undergo tonight's process of correction.

The cover is black leather, worn to a shine. Embossed across the front is the title: *The Sinestra Manifestum.*

Dali had first been instructed to read this manual years ago as part of his induction. Standard practice when someone is enlisted from the outside. And Dali was – in every sense – an outsider.

The information contained within *The Manifestum* is rudimentary, no more than a collection of cold, disjointed phrases. In Dali's opinion, it raises the reader's awareness of the Sinestra much as a tent might be raised, in slow, slotting stages. His instinct was to add a little colour and verve and, as a result, the manual now sparkles with asterisks.

Indeed, even the very first sentence was one that Dali felt obliged to embellish. The original line read: 'The Sinestra is a division of Lo'World security dedicated to safeguard the dispersal of span. Its sworn purpose is to ensure that mankind is protected from those other entities who endeavour to despoil the span allotted to humanity.*'

At the foot of the page is Dali's inky tinkering.

*Let us start at the true beginning. For in the beginning, there was the Source. And the Source created man and bestowed upon him a measure of life. A span of existence. But those dark forces who exist beyond the reach of grace, those foul and fallen miscreants, soon found a way to steal that span. And so the Source sent an army of Angels and they were called the Sinestra. And they were charged with the duty of protecting man's span from all those demons that sought to suckle it.

The ink in which this footnote is inscribed is soft and grey, an indication that Dali made this note more than a century ago. In those early days, he was still finding his feet within the Sinestra. All he wished to do, by means of this addition, was to record the division's angelic origins.

Then the years passed and his knowledge grew. At first, just facts. But all the same, he felt the need to note his learning and expand again *The Manifestum*'s shallow account. The second chapter is entitled 'Span' and an asterisk beside leads to a footnote, writ small and at length.

*To understand span, one should think of it as an echo, reverberating round and around. Span passes from one human to another, as birth follows death. Span has no memory of itself as it cycles. It is just a dose of existence, apportioned measure by measure. But it comes from one shared resource, a whole that connects all mankind. And this universal mass is called the Spanorama. By opening their minds – a process some might call prayer – the Sinestra can tune into the echoes of the Spanorama and detect any untoward fluctuations. If an attempt to siphon span is detected, a Hunter will be despatched. That Hunter will leave the Hypogeum and walk amongst human society, to seek out and destroy the demon responsible.

As Dali reads this now, he knows that he should refine his own addendum and add a further footnote to explain the term Hypogeum. But this can wait. It is a simple matter and can be dealt with quickly. The Hypogeum is the subterranean structure in which the Sinestra dwell. The name itself means no more than 'under-earth' and the location of the Hypogeum has changed many times since the Sinestra's inception. *The Manifestum* records the first as lying beneath a field called King's Reach in Staffordshire, England. In 1686, three hundred years after the Sinestra had abandoned this Hypogeum and moved to another, the giant stone slab that marked its entrance was discovered by the delightfully named Dr Plot. With the aid of a hefty labourer, he opened the slab and descended the stone staircase that lay beyond, entering the maze of tunnels beneath. Upon his return, he refused to disclose what relics he found therein, but Dr Plot later became a professor at University College, Oxford, where – by chance or by design? – he dedicated his life to the study of echoes.

The move from King's Reach had been necessitated by the growing workload of the Sinestra. Mankind was expanding across the globe. The task of monitoring the Spanorama threatened to overwhelm the Sinestra's resources.

A new Hypogeum was established beneath Nottingham Castle. A deep set of tunnels, including a cave known as King David's Dungeon, lay beneath the foundations and their vast expanse gave the Sinestra the space they required as their ranks grew. The dungeons were chosen because at their heart was a deep void called Romylowe's Cave. It provided the perfect conical chamber in which the Angeli Superiores could pray. They was a new hierarchy within the Sinestra, created in response to their growing task. They were commissioned to do nothing but sit within the void, deep in prayer. And with their minds laid open, they would monitor day and night the flux of the Spanorama.

The division of labour within the Sinestra spread far beyond the creation of the Angeli Superiores. Interpreting the fluctuations in the Spanorama and then mapping these disturbances across the globe became a task of its own and a sub-division arose for this purpose. And as the number of Hunters grew, they required management and so it was that another tier of administration came into being.

It was at this time that Dali joined the Sinestra and he was allocated the role of Handler. Into his care was placed a clutch of Hunters. His task was to train them, allocate their targets and oversee their missions. Within a few years of his arrival the number of Handlers and Hunters had grown ten-fold.

But this expansion was not the only change that Dali witnessed. There was another. A monumental alteration to the Sinestra.

And it caused the abandonment of King David's Dungeon.

In *The Manifestum*, this move receives scant mention. A single sentence records the date of resettlement as May 1956, and the location: Kingsway, beneath the streets of Holborn in London.

The entrance to Kingsway is a small door at 32 High Holborn. Behind it lies a lift-shaft that descends one hundred feet below the streets of London, arriving in an underground city: mile after mile of iron-clad corridors and low-ceilinged chambers, all painted in a dull beige. This subterranean maze was built as a wartime refuge, capable of sheltering thousands. But from the time of its construction, there was always a sprawling portion kept secret from the public. These covert corridors housed a monumental telephone exchange capable of connecting the entire western world in the event of an atomic attack. After the war, as the threat subsided, the tunnels of Kingsway were given over to the Public Records Office and 400,000 of the Allies most sensitive documents were hidden here, safe from public scrutiny. When the Public Records Office moved out in 1956, the Sinestra moved in.

The actual means by which they came to take possession

is referenced in *The Manifestum* in just one short line: 'The Sinestra cooperated with terrestrial authorities to effect the occupation of Kingsway.'

This line is marked by an obelus. A sign that Dali has made an addendum here. But no footnote exists at the bottom of this page.

Dali's hand reaches into his coat and he pulls out a small, hide-bound book. Its cover is marked with a cross that might, to the untrained eye, suggest that it is a bible. But any scribe would recognise it as an obelus. Just like his old mentor, Dali has created his own book to contain those additions that are too radical to sit safely within the manual's original pages.

He turns to the page that contains this particular footnote.

This entry is absent of Dali's florid prose. Instead the tone is stark, suggesting anger. It begins thus:

By the following means, the Sinestra is forever altered.

(i) It has made certain human agencies aware of its existence and its operations.

(ii) The Angeli Superiores, now termed the High Command, no longer monitor the echo of the Spanorama.

(iii) That duty – the precious duty that lies at the very heart of the Sinestra's existence – now rests with a machine, the Helix Vivat. And it was solely in order to install the Helix Vivat into the telecommunication chamber that the Sinestra moved to Kingsway.

The entry concludes with a final scrawled note, unnumbered and disconnected from the rest.

Trismegistus once wrote, 'As it is above, so it is below.' The great man was referring to the Heavenly Kingdom and Earth, but my point is this: the human world occupies the streets above, where mankind runs around, blind and bewildered, governed by ego and self-obsessed order ... and so it is below, in our underground world. The Sinestra has become an obsessive bureaucracy with a machine at its heart.

Dali bends the neck of the table-lamp, rolling its beam across this old entry. He smiles at the lettering, raw and ragged, reflecting the fury with which it was inflicted on the page. Back then, Dali did indeed deplore the Helix Vivat: a machine swarming with officious operatives who jump at every twitch of the gauge, gripping their clipboards, jotting notes and filing reports.

But Dali has an eye for beauty and he cannot deny that the Helix Vivat, towering tall with its valves and pipes and glittering lights, is a spectacular creation. Throbbing and thudding, it plays to Dali's ear like music, urging him to bow and bend those long elastic legs of his. A fey weakness perhaps. But as Dali likes to say, everybody dances to their own boom-boom.

His obvious delight in the Helix Vivat resulted in the High Command awarding him the honorary title of Master of the Machine. There is little actual duty that comes with the title, but Dali bears the keys to the engine room and he revels in that.

He has held the post for decades now and on those evenings when he is not in the Archivum, he can often be found wandering amid the throbbing coils, polishing dials and tapping valves.

The machine does a fine job of monitoring the Spanorama and, in truth, these days there is just one miscreant species remaining that subverts the smooth flow – and that is the Tormenta.

Of all the demon breeds that walk the Earth, Tormenta are the most closely related to humankind. So similar is their physiology that Tormenta can harvest span directly from a human host, as long as the span is surrendered, and not stolen.

The Manifestum's entry on these vermin is extensive. But that holds no interest for Dali tonight. He thumbs past those pages, reaching a directory at the back. Drags a finger, finding his own name, listed with his honorary title, Magisters Machinae.

He smiles, wondering still whether it was his famous passion for the Helix Vivat that won him the title. Or was there a darker irony to be found?

Did it perhaps amuse the High Command to make him this award, knowing how Tormenta bedevil his beloved machine?

Knowing that he was once a Tormenta himself. Before his defection . . .

Beside his name in the directory is the date on which he joined the Sinestra: 6 June 1857. And next to the date, a faint cross, confirming that somewhere Dali has expounded upon his own history.

He peels open the pages of his *Obelus*, finds the appropriate place.

The entry is extensive. It is a confession of sorts.

† This account should begin with a date of birth, but there is none. The boy who was to become Dali was born an orphan. He lived amongst the Taino tribe in Trinidad with nothing but a fierce desire to survive – which he did by virtue of a silver tongue, his only gift. He was fed by fishermen, whom he persuaded to share their catch, and he was clad by women, beguiled to give him garments.

When the French arrived and trade began, he saw fresh opportunities. Strong and lithe, he'd stow away unnoticed, pocketing small portions of cargo and then selling it beneath the noses of the French in the Louisiana markets where they docked. He was caught, of course, that was inevitable. But once again, his powers of persuasion saved his skin. He fiddled with their fury until they saw the funny side. They took him in like a member of the crew and gave him a seafaring name, Tret. It is a term that means the fraction of cargo that is always lost in transportation. The boy was rather taken with his name.

He decided to remain in Louisiana. The prospects would be brighter for a boy such as he, young and hungry for success. The only impediment to his plan was the lack of a patron, someone to provide basic victuals whilst he made his mark. His prayers were answered by Père Corbeau, a local priest. He took the boy under his wing and trained him in the skills of a scribe. The priest showed the boy nothing but unbridled kindness, in stark contrast to the beatings he bestowed upon himself. The boy knew that the priest was suffering from a trial of faith, but there was something else eating away at the old man's conscience. Night after night, the boy would hear him thrashing at his flesh with many instruments of penance. Why he should punish himself so was a mystery, until the night that the old man crept into the corner of the scriptorium where the scribe slept and tried to lay his old hands upon the boy's naked body. Then he finally understood the urges that had plagued the old priest. He should have killed him there and then. But something stopped him. An urge of his own that he could not grasp, or put a name to. But its draw was strong. An instinct . . . not to snap the old man's neck, but to break his heart.

One dark night, he hears Père Corbeau ripping at his flesh with leather straps. So he enters his room and puts that silver tongue of his to work. Taunting him, teasing him. Whipping him into a frenzy of lust . . . and self-disgust. Of such loathing for his own sick desires that death can be the only salve. And passing him a knife, the boy rouses the old man, there and then, to take the final stroke. And he does. To great effect.

The blood, the boy was prepared for. The horror came from what consumed him next: an overwhelming compulsion to press his lips to the old man's mouth as he lay dying. He fought the urge and, in a frenzy, he washed the room, burned the habit and bundled Corbeau's body into a bayou.

As he suspected, the old priest was not missed. And

without opposition, the scribe claimed his lodgings in the church. And that was where he saw her first. His beloved flower ... Rosa Cruz.

She was barely thirteen, but this was a girl for whom spring had slipped soon into summer. Those rounded hips of hers took rest in the pews of the rich, one black bonnet among many. And yet the merest tilt of her brim inflamed him like a rising skirt; a glimpse of thigh could not have roused him more than the flash of her eye. He was bewitched. His heart's sole counterpoise was found. But she was rich and he was poor. These circumstances might have deterred a lesser suitor, but young Tret was persistent. And persuasive.

Every Sunday, he would follow her home. Outside her bedroom window was a balcony. Tret would climb the adjacent lamp-post and leap across, calling to her, wooing her with well-chosen words and wild antics. He may have had no coin, but the boy had charm. And he had dreams. He promised Rosa that he would make something of himself and return to marry her. If she would promise to wait.

The night she makes that promise is the night that Tret first tastes her upon his lips. But his mouth can barely suck her flavour before his ears are drawn to the click of a lock. Her bedroom door is opening. Her father is entering and the sound in Tret's head becomes the pulsing thud of his blood as he runs to the window and leaps for the lamp-post. His hand misses; his body falls. His chest impales upon a set of iron spikes that crown the post. In New Orleans, these deterrents are called Romeo spikes. And the longest spike pierces Tret's heart.

The next thing he remembers is awakening. That was most unexpected, compounded further by the fact that the slab on which he lies is in a morgue. The tag upon his toe reads 'DEAD'. Before he can begin to fathom what has happened, a hand is clamped upon his mouth and, from above, a man's voice comes, urging him to silence. He tells the boy that all will be explained. The man is lean and wrapped within a dark cape. Just a wisp of white hair escapes from beneath his three-cornered hat. He inhales a long, rattling breath. Then, peeling his fingers one by one from the boy's wet mouth, he begins.

'You, my dear boy, are not human. You may look human, you may feel human, but you are not. You are something so much more.'

The caped figure pauses, allowing each word to settle like a pebble in the boy's mind before continuing.

'If you look back, you'll realise that perhaps you always felt a little different from your peers. That you had an insatiable appetite to taunt and tease ... to reduce those close to you to self-disgust. Many children feel this, because many children are not human. Imagine, then, their relief when a kindly, avuncular figure appears one day – perhaps in the park, or as they walk home from church – and gently explains that they are special . . . very special indeed. Just as I am explaining to you ... that you are not a man-child. You are in fact, a Tormenta.'

Now the boy's eye slowly dilate, like blotting paper soaking up the information. And then, cautiously, he speaks. 'Père Corbeau ... I could have killed him. But I knew ... what I wanted more, was for him to take his own life ... the sin of suicide ...'

The man claps his hands together, as if witnessing baby's first steps. 'Of course, of course! And then you felt an urge to place your mouth on his.'

Eagerly now, the boy leans forward. 'Yes! Yes! The thought of it revolted me, but still –'

'– you longed to do it. Because that is how we feed. We suck up the span the human has surrendered. Unspent by them, we can take their allotted years. And this is how we live.'

He rests a hand upon the boy's shoulders. 'This is how we live ... for ever.'

The fingers slide down, arriving at the gaping wound in the boy's chest. 'Now this ... should not have happened quite as it did and the fault is mine. I failed in my duties. And so I failed the Legion of Gehenna . . .'

He tugs the boy's shirt up to cover the ragged chest wound and rolls on with his explanation. 'The Legion of Gehenna are an elite group of Tormenta, chosen for their skills, to seek out and awaken those of our kind. It is a great honour to be called as a G-Man and each is designated an area to monitor – a beat, if you like. We fit ourselves into society as best we can, doctors, teachers . . .' He taps his own chest. '. . . the local undertaker. And when we see a child that harbours a Tormenta spirit, we watch and we wait, choosing our moment to awaken the child to its true self. And this we accomplish by use of our clave.'

He now lifts a long, iron shank that hangs from his belt. At one end are jagged teeth, like a key. 'We thrust our clave into the child's heart. This act, of course, kills him as a human. But his Tormenta self will then take over and consume him fully.'

He lets the clave fall back to his side. 'My intention was to induct you in the usual way. I was simply waiting for the right moment. But too late. Before I could make my move, you fell and there I found you, impaled upon the Romeo spikes. I pulled you down and told myself that there was nothing I could do. If you die before your Tormenta self is awakened, then it is over. You expire as any human would. I thought the very least that I could do would be to bury you. And so I brought you back here, cleaned you up and then – to my astonishment – you revived. Of your own accord. I can only guess that the spike through your heart served the same purpose as my clave. So I suggest we do not dwell on how it came to pass.'

The G-Man grabs the tag that hangs from the boy's toe. Taking a pen, he amends the word 'DEAD' to 'ALIVE'. 'Because there is much for you to learn about Tormenta ways. For example, it is customary to take a new name at the beginning of one's Tormenta life. And you must choose carefully. Names have enormous potency! Humans vaguely know this – they sense that a given name can sometimes shape their future. But most dismiss this as the stuff of superstition.' He shakes his head at this further evidence of human ignorance. 'If they but knew the true power of a name . . .'

'I have a name. It's Tret.'

The G-Man's hands fly upwards. 'No, no! We must change it and I will tell you why.' He jabs a finger high, to indicate his first reason. 'You are of Taino descent. Not good.' He leans in close. 'Many centuries ago, the Legion of Gehenna was betrayed and it was by a Tormenta of Taino descent. This Tormenta was allowed into the inner sanctum of the Legion and then deserted, taking the Legion's secrets with him. He returned to his tribe and much of what he disclosed became woven into the Taino mythology. For this reason, Tormenta have viewed the Taino with particular suspicion, as humans who know too much. Thankfully, the passing years have fogged the meaning of these stories, and with each retelling, they have blurred and drifted away from the dangerous Legion secrets that they once contained. But all the same, we need a name that erases anything of your Taino past. Second' – he jabs another finger towards the boy – 'the name you got from the French sailors, it has a different meaning in Creole. Tret means "traitor", so if you're set on staying in Louisiana, you may want to rethink that.'

The man smiles. 'A name will come to you. Trust me.'

Tret's eyes go to the wound in his chest, then his fingers follow, exploring this body that he thought he knew. That is no longer human. No longer dead, nor alive.

What name befits a creature such as he?

His eyes finally arrive at the tag on his toe. The G-Man's hasty alteration has crossed out all but the last 'D' of 'DEAD', before adding 'ALIVE'.

The boy's eyes widen. He sees it now. 'D-ALI'. Just as he is between two worlds, so his name will be between two words.

And from that day onwards, he lived as Dali . . . and lived as a Tormenta. He thrived in this new role, exhibiting a talent for tormenting. Humans fell like apples and he rose quickly up the ladder of Tormenta society, inevitably catching the attention of the Legion of Gehenna. They recruited him to their ranks, presenting him with his own clave. Each clave is cut uniquely like a key, so that by its bite, it can be seen who effected any awakening. And over the years, many Tormenta bore the scar of Dali's clave. Because Dali served in spectacular fashion, until the day arrived when he

Dali closes the *Obelus*. The entry continues but he has spent too long on this distraction. His original intent was to find another name within the directory. His finger flicks at speed. And then he finds it, listed numerically amid the index of Hunters: 101A.

She was one of his operatives, a protégée in whom Dali had taken a particular interest. But now she has gone rogue. Exiting the Hypogeum on a mission, never to return. Deceiving him. Deceiving them all.

He should perhaps have seen it coming.

In her eyes, there had always been a spark . . . the girl had *something*. She was without doubt the best Hunter he had ever trained. Fast, strong and without mercy. He had never seen her like before. But more than that, he liked her. For all her brutish prowess, she had an enquiring mind. Forever asking questions.

He remembers the last question she posed as he was strapping her into her weapons, readying her for the hunt. Her eye had gone to the implement that hung about his own belt.

'Why do you still wear your clave?'

Dali had smiled, choosing his words carefully. 'Ah cher, to reflect upon the horrors of one's past is the surest means to keep one's future pure. I cleave to this tool, lest I forget.'

Dali leans back in his chair, creaking the wood like bones. Looks across the table to the seat opposite.

Hunter 101A had accompanied him to the Archivum many times, discovering, to her own surprise, a love of reading. He introduced her to the works of Trismegistus and she was much intrigued by the fact that the philosopher's name translates as 'the greatness of three'. Her natural curiosity led her towards the other works of faith, inspired by him.

Dali had cherished her companionship and such was his ease, that one cold night he read aloud to her the contents of his *Obelus*. He expected many questions as he closed its covers, but just one came from 101A.

'What happened to Rosa?'

Dali had flinched, as if this question were a bullet. Then he slowly inhaled, straightening his tie.

'Do you know the story of Romeo and Juliet, cher? Their hopes of reunion were held in the hands of a priest.' His eyes had suddenly locked on to hers. 'Never to trust a priest who keeps his hand hidden.'

Dali stares at the now empty chair and then slowly closes his eyes. Picturing 101A. Gun in hand.

She is out in the world, killing Tormenta. That much the High Command knows from sporadic reports received. She has been sighted in Las Vegas, New York, London. But she is not killing to order. She is killing as she wishes. On her terms. By her choice.

But why?

Why turn her back on the Sinestra? Under their care, she is kept safe in the Hypogeum and regularly supplied with span, allowing her to live forever if she wishes. But out there, in the human world, she will live only as long as her last dose endures. And that could be months, years . . . or days. That's the thing with span, you just don't know.

But she is gone. And Dali has his suspicions. He believes that what ignited her rebellion was something that she read. Something she discovered hidden in one of these books. A revelation that turned her mind . . . twisted her heart.

His large eyes roll from left to right, looking at the vast array of shelving that once held 400,000 secret documents and now contains as many books of the Sinestra with perhaps as many secrets.

He slides his *Obelus* into his pocket and rises to leave. The High Command will not care as to the cause of 101A's desertion, only that he allowed it to happen. Or even encouraged it. There is every chance that they may suspect him of provocation. Because Dali, the infamous defector, cannot escape his past.

He strides from the Archivum, entering the low, iron corridor that leads back towards his quarters. He needs to feel the cool touch of a flannel and refresh his collars and cuffs. Because soon he will be summoned to account for her desertion.

And when that moment comes, he must convince the High Command of one thing. That he is determined to retrieve her . . . dead or alive.

15

A FLAG RIPS AND ROLLS AGAINST ITS POLE, caught in a raging wind. It bears the insignia of Cherry Point Military Training Base.

Far below, mud flies. A platoon of marine cadets double-time it through the dark.

Their bodies are humped with munitions. Their boots barely clear the ground. They have been at this since daybreak and now night has fallen and the air has dropped below freezing. Exhaustion gusts from their mouth like exorcized ghouls.

Alongside them runs their drill sergeant, seemingly untouched by the gruelling exercise. He chews on his cigar and bellows another chorus of call-and-response: 'You can't fail, that's what I said.'

The marines respond: 'Sergeant's gonna shoot us dead.'

He pounds up front. 'Only way to save your pride . . .'

'Do it first with suicide.'

With a roar, the drill sergeant finishes the cadence with the cry of 'BOHICA!' The marines all know what this means – Bend Over Here It Comes Again – as the drill sergeant blows his whistle and breaks out into triple-time. The shattered marines dig deep, strive to keep up.

The drill sergeant waves them past, looking for the stragglers. Allows the cadets to disappear into the night as he watches and waits for the one he knows is missing. He bites down hard on his cigar and smiles. 'Looks like we're outta Tampax.'

His head swivels at the sound of distant boots. A silhouette appears, stumbling with exhaustion.

The name sewn to the pocket reads: 'Paxos'. Blood falls on to the khaki, dripping from the young cadet's mouth. At first in thin dribbles, then a gusting spume as – *whack* – a fist thuds into his jaw.

'You goddam piece of green Greek shit!' The drill sergeant launches another blow, cracking the cadet across the back of the skull, hurling him down into the mud.

'You know why I call you Tampax?' He yanks the cadet's bloody face up from the mud. 'Because every month I see you back in basic, and every goddam month you bleed.'

The boy attempts to speak, but his mouth is pulped by another blow.

'When you gonna learn, Tampax? You'll never make it. And each month you try, you achieve just one thing. You bring down every other cadet. Because one fails, we all fail. That's the marine way. And thanks to you, everyone is gonna have to run the course again tomorrow. Now won't that make you popular? Bet you can't wait to tell the boys. But my advice is this: don't sleep tonight, Tampax. Cos in their wild excitement, in their unbridled happiness, your fellow cadets may get rowdy. They may express their joy . . . physically. You git me, Tampax?'

The drill sergeant bends to whisper. 'I'd say you're a dead man, Tampax. An' worse than that . . . a dead man without dignity. So here's my deal. I'll leave you now to contemplate your fate. And I'll leave you this . . .' His gloved hand produces a single bullet. 'Now, rules forbid me to distribute live ammunition. But this is how I see it: I'm not giving you a bullet. I'm giving you a way out.'

Private Paxos tries to take the bullet, but his hand jerks so violently with sobs that the sergeant is forced to take the boy's fingers and wrap them tight about the shaft.

'That's one inch of honour you're holding there, son.'

The silhouette of the sergeant disappears into the darkness. Private Paxos falls into a ball, howling. As he gasps for breath, he drags a muddy sleeve across his eyes, breathing deep and rolling to his knees. With one hand, he reaches up, pulling his gun from its strapped position across his backpack. His other palm uncurls, revealing the bullet.

He sniffs hard, gathering concentration as he slides the bullet into the chamber.

It takes both hands to place the gun against his temple. One bears the weight of the weapon. The other tries to quell the violent tremor of his fingers. The snout connects to his head and —

— *Ka-boom!* A boot kicks the gun from his fist, thudding him into the mud. He looks up, stunned, to see the long silhouette of a woman beside him. Walking away towards the approaching figure of the drill sergeant.

Over the crashing rain, the cadet can barely hear their exchange.

The woman seems to say, 'Close, but . . .'

The drill sergeant furiously chews down on his cigar.

His fingers twitch over the gun holster at his waist. The two shadows stand in silence then both hands fly, guns draw, shots explode.

The cadet watches as the blasted body of the sergeant sprawls into the mud.

The woman slides her gun back into its holster. Strides past.

'Get up, kid. And make yourself worth saving.'

And she's gone.

SLAMMING DOWN INTO THE SEAT OF A MILITARY JEEP, Lola yanks the casing from the steering shaft, twists the starter-motor and guns the vehicle, splattering mud across the massive corpse of the drill sergeant.

Size counts for nothing. Lola learned that long ago. It's about how long a Tormenta has been around. If they keep stealing span, they stay alive. And if they're smart, they use their time to hone their fighting skills. Because Tormenta can be killed: a weakness born from their close evolutionary relationship to humankind.

And all Tormenta know that there are Hunters out there, despatched to bring them down.

But that guy, he shoulda been sharper. Sure, he had a good grift going. A hard-core cadet is fast to fall on a bullet if dishonour looms. But Lola sees it often; if the grift is too easy, the Tormenta gets lazy.

She mashes the gas and glances in the rear-view. The cadet is staggering to his feet. Lola shrugs to herself. She got the job done. That's what matters.

And then she sees it. The cadet pulls on his fallen helmet.

And something bolts into her mind. Sharp as a bomb-frag.

A memory.

Too quick for her to grasp it . . . more a feeling. *She was once in training.*

Even though she had told Fan Fan to take her memories, wipe them clean, right back to that moment when all the hurt began, she can remember some of what happened before.

She wasn't born with this ability to fight and kill. Someone taught her.

She knows who, she knows where and she knows why. But what she no longer remembers is . . . why did she turn against them?

Lola shakes her head, erasing the moment. It doesn't matter. Every morning, she gets up and she knows what she has to do: *kill Tormenta.*

She needs no more than this to function.

But in recent weeks, something has been stirring within her, like a waking beast.

Her hands grip the wheel. She did the right thing. She is safer, stronger . . . not knowing.

She has a duty. She has a purpose.

But maybe she needs more than this to live?

16

DALI SITS ALONE in the gloom of the High Court. The narrow tunnels of Kingsway do not allow for any grandiose chambers. Instead, to gift this grey-walled place some pomp, the walls are hung with paintings of classical interiors, all marble pillars and lofty cupolas. The largest canvas, by Emanuel de Witte, shows the interior of a Dutch church, a masterpiece of precision and perspective. But Dali suspects that it hangs in pride of place because at its centre, painted small, is a group of magistrates seated around a table. And stretched before Dali is a table. In due course, his accusers will sit around it.

Dali knows the drill. They will make him wait. Force him to settle on the chair with the small, spherical seat that buries into his buttocks, as if this pelvic prod is a foretaste of the probing questions yet to come.

But Dali does not feel it. For him, the agonies of the turncoat reach much deeper. Into the realm of self-respect.

When he was a member of the Legion, he ranked highly. Seen by many as the brightest star, destined for greatness. And none revered him more than Vassago, a long-serving member of the Legion who had failed, for lack of flair, to further himself. He could only stand by and watch in awe as Dali would detect, distract and divest Tormenta children of their human selves, releasing them swiftly, painlessly into their new existence. Oftentimes, Vassago would break out into applause, gushing praise, scurrying to Dali's side as if sharing his shadow might siphon some of this skill. But Dali would side-step, slip away. He found Vassago's fawning adoration sickening, like a stinking lily, too sweet beneath his nose.

It was Dali's one gnawing regret that when he defected to the Sinestra, Vassago slavishly followed.

But what's done, is done.

Those days are over. Dali enjoys no glory here. The maverick genius he exercised as a Tormenta finds no favour in the rule-bound regime of the Sinestra.

He casually crosses his legs, neatening the seam of his pants as the iron door to the High Court groans open. The tribunal panel are entering.

The silhouettes settle one by one into their seats, their faces masked by shadows. A figure to the right of the table speaks.

'Since the Sinestra accepted your defection, we have done much to accommodate one of your . . . type . . . within our ranks. We supply you with span so that you can endure without needing to feed your habit by other less acceptable methods. And more than this, we have shown you enormous trust.'

'Which I have nevah' abused,' Dali forcibly reminds them all, his deep Creole twang resounding.

Another figure leans across the table. Even before the face hits the light, Dali knows who it will be. And the glinting eyes confirm it.

Vassago. Of course.

He smooths a long, black wig, evidence of his senior rank within the Sinestra. And with the tresses slicked against his scalp, he serves up a smile. The expression seems one of support but the cold pleasure it radiates suggests that Vassago is enjoying Dali's discomfort.

'I am sure Dali does not question for one moment the sincere regard that the Sinestra has for one such as he. After all, both he and I defected at the same time, under the same circumstances, and witness how high I have risen. There is no prejudice at play here.'

Just a preference for dull obedience. Dali returns the

smile like a twisting blade.

Leaning back in his chair, Vassago tips his palms upwards as if his next comment is of no consequence. 'My only question is why you devote so much time to the care of the Helix Vivat. Your honorary title does not require that you spend hour after hour – for want of a better word – tinkering.'

He leans forward, eyes tight. 'Don't you think you should explain yourself, Dali?'

'For want of a better word, no.'

A silence hangs, ruffled only by lace as Dali tweaks his cuffs.

Vassago grits his teeth, retreats. 'Very well then. To the business in hand.' He thuds a thick file on to the table. 'The unfortunate matter of Hunter 101A.'

Dali has his face under absolute control. No twitch. No tremor.

Vassago takes his time, peeling open the file, smoothing his palm across each page.

'She has been rogue for quite some time, it seems. But she continues to target Tormenta. So . . .' Large eyes roll up to meet Dali. '. . . should this fact make the High Command think her desertion acceptable?'

'I say it would be uppity to presume what the High Command thinks, or even that it thinks at all.'

Wigs turn and glances are exchanged as if searching for a handle on this insult.

Vassago presses on. 'We do not find it acceptable. Not at all. Rogue is rogue, regardless. And still you have done nothing to retrieve her.'

'I had hoped to resolve the situation before it required intervention.'

'What you hoped, Dali, is of no consequence. What you did, was subvert protocol. You do not have the authority to make such a decision. Need I remind you of your rank?'

'The frequency with which you do suggests a great need

on your part.'

Vassago shivers, his entrails thrashing to find a riposte. But a silencing hand rises from the figure at the head of the table. A face partially peels into the light. No element of the wig can be seen, but the eyes are enough to determine that this man will have the final word.

'With regret, Dali, I order you to retrieve Hunter 101A and oversee her termination.'

Dali bows his head, respect to this man readily given. 'Ver' well, Commander General. There is a Hunter available whom I believe . . .'

'I will determine the choice of Hunter.' The Commander General snaps his fingers towards Vassago. 'Lord Chancellor, your recommendation.'

A flash of enamel confirms that Vassago is smiling as he passes a single sheet into the Commander's waiting grasp.

Dali stiffens, knowing what comes.

'You will send Hunter 666A.'

17

IN THE INDEX of *The Manifestum*, 666A is not listed among the other Hunters. His entry is included in a final appendix, entitled simply '*Postscriptum*'.

And there is no asterisk beside his name. Just an obelus, suggesting that whatever annotation Dali chose to add, it was for his eyes only.

Dali sits now in the gloom of his quarters, *The Obelus* open on the table before him. His fingers find that particular addendum. It says only this: '† Remorse, you are made flesh in him! More ruthless than the act that first begat you.'

It is dated October 1858. But the encounter that forced Dali's hand to this cryptic quip is still fresh in his mind.

He closes his eyes, summoning the memory. And sees himself as he was, dressed in the crimson hues he favoured in those days. He is walking to the farthest reach beyond King David's Dungeon, bound for a low, domed structure hewn from the rock. It is known as the Megiddo and it welcomes few.

Nothing of its obscure entrance and narrow walls invites investigation.

As he enters, what strikes him first is the stinking air. And the guttering light from a rack of candles. They are suspended high above a naked body, prostrate on the floor.

The skin is alive with wounds, bubbling upwards as wax falls from above, striking hard, sizzling hot.

The naked figure lies unflinching, arms spread wide, devouring the agony.

Rising smoke summons up the stench of burning skin and Dali plugs a kerchief to his mouth, the white lace flashing as he sinks further still against the wall. Hunter 666A is drawing breath, rousing himself, rising slowly. His body uncoils muscle by muscle.

Eyes open, black as exit wounds. Narrowing as they detect a figure in the shadows.

Dali dabs his lips and devotes undue attention to his kerchief as he plants it in his pocket.

'Please forgive if I transgress yo' time of contemplation . . .' Stepping into the candlelight, Dali sees strange artefacts hung upon the walls of the Megiddo. 'Your time of worship, perhaps. My ignorance is shameful, I apologise.'

A final flourish to his kerchief. 'Yo' see, I myself follow no faith. Live and let live and let die and let live, that's what I say.'

Nothing issues from the mouth of Hunter 666A, but the eyes make a clear demand.

'Of course, to the cuttin' of the crap.' Dali draws a file from within his coat. 'A mission, most urgent.'

Dali extends the bundle of papers, awaiting the Hunter's gathering hand. But nothing disturbs the air. The only movement from Hunter 666A is to pull a black cloth tight about his loins.

Ah, silence. The half-brother of insolence.

If Dali is going to assert his authority, this is the moment. He may not have trained Hunter 666A, that duty fell to a member of the Sinestra over a thousand years ago, but he still outranks him. He need not endure this . . . this . . .

. . . this what, exactly?

Dali runs his tongue across his teeth, sharpening his smile sufficiently to skin this rabbit. 'I hear nothing but praise for your dedication. Your impeccable preparation. And I sense now that you'd appreciate some detail.'

He flicks open the papers. 'If you don't mind, I'll read straight from the file.'

Dali emits a dry cough. 'The mission is to retrieve Brother

Spino of the Chiro Scuro.' His eye drifts down. 'I spy a tiny footnote here, to which I shall refer.' Another cough, drier still. 'The Chiro Scuro is a human vigilante force, founded four centuries ago by a Rosicrucian monk called Brother Magen. Its sworn duty is to combat demon infiltration on Earth. Brother Magen, an exceptional scholar by all accounts, was translating the works of Trismegistus when he fell foul of violent visions. Endless, raging brainstorms that revealed to him the many realms of the Lo'Worlds and all the demon creatures that dwelled therein.'

Dali taps the page. 'For a footnote, I find this rather fetchingly described, don't you?'

Hunter 666A responds in the same way that granite doesn't. Dali goes on.

'Brother Magen committed his visions to a great series of books and around these revelations, the Brotherhood grew. It took the name of Chiro Scuro: the Hidden Hand. The name reflected the need for the Brotherhood to maintain its secrecy. The Holy Roman Church was fast to denounce them as dangerous fanatics.'

A fingertip is licked, a page turned.

'And so the Brotherhood sought the protection of Ignatius Loyola, the Black Pope. Such is the name given to the leader of the Jesuit Church. Ignatius shielded the Chiro Scuro and allowed them to pursue their hunt for demons. He created a library called the Collegio Romano and within the endless bookshelves, the revelations of the Chiro Scuro were successfully concealed. Every book was written in a coded language devised by Brother Magen. And without doubt, the most precious, the most momentous of these books is . . .'

The final page is turned. '. . . the *Kata Strepho*.'

A short pause, as Dali leans forward. 'The title is Greek for "I Overturn" and I do believe the word "catastrophe" derives from it.' The briefest of smiles. 'I knew a priest, long ago, and I acquired a little talent for translation.' In the ensuing silence, Dali's eyes sink back to the page.

'The *Kata* tells of Brother Magen's most fearful vision – a mighty conflict. But more than that we don't know. It is written in his most baffling code. That is quite the pity of it all.'

Dali closes the file, smoothing the cover with the flat of his hand. 'That a human, a lowly monk, should have been gifted these visions . . . let us just say, it is most frustrating. It is hard enough for the Sinestra to police mankind and safeguard their existence without humans themselves getting involved. We constantly feel like a peace-keeping force plagued by local, amateur guerrilla activity. But the Chiro Scuro cannot be ignored and so we have learned to tolerate them. However, relations have suffered a severe setback because the Sinestra has accepted into their ranks a certain defector.' Dali arches a gentle hand upon his own chest. 'It seems the Chiro Scuro will never trust a Tormenta, no matter what badge he wears.'

With a smile, bitter as a lemon slice, Dali turns on his heel, pacing the floor. 'Relations have recently worsened further still. King Victor Emmanuel of Italy has embarked upon an onslaught against the Holy Roman Church. The Vatican is to be plundered. The books of the Collegio Romano are undoubtedly in danger. So I myself, as an avowed lover of books, have made an offer to the Black Pope. I've suggested that the tomes of the Chiro Scuro be sent to the Sinestra, where I will oversee their care and personally ensure that they are cherished. The Black Pope has reluctantly agreed and all the books have been delivered into my care . . . all, that is, but the *Kata*.

'This book has been born away by one rebellious monk, Brother Spino. He seems determined that it shall not be surrendered to me. But now we have got word he is in Prague. One assumes the book is still with him. So, he must now be found. And when he's found, he will tell us where the book is hidden.'

Dali pauses, suddenly aware that his hand has clamped into a fist. He casually concerns himself with each uncurling finger. 'I hope that I have made it quite clear that if the the *Kata* were evah to get into human hands, if they were to decipher its contents . . . well, let me jus' say this. Once you find Brother Spino, yo' must question him without mercy.'

Dali rolls the file into a baton and presents it again. His voice follows, tightened to a whisper. 'I understand that it violates protocol to retrieve a human. Indeed, some in the Sinestra have voiced doubts that any Hunter will accept this mission. But my retort is this: 666A is not *any* Hunter.'

Dali thrusts the baton closer. 'So, what say you?'

To the best of Dali's recollection, he said nothing. Not one word. But Hunter 666A took the mission and returned three days later from Prague, bearing in a sack the severed head of Brother Spino. The face, crushed beyond recognition, confirmed that no amount of questioning had elicited where the *Kata* had been hidden.

And it is with the memory of this pulped skull clear in his mind that Dali rises from his chair and exits his quarters in long, furious strides. Down an echoing hallway that narrows to a stairwell, twisting to a spiral, sharpening his fast descent until the last raked incline delivers him to the door that yawns open, drawing breath. It reveals a bunker, lined with lead so thick it can withstand an atomic blast. It may not be the Megiddo, but its purpose is the same. It is where Hunter 666A comes to suffer his remorse.

Dali enters the blackness and traverses the cold floor. The chill is the same as the old Megiddo. And it is filled with the same aroma of burning flesh. Hunter 666A rises from the floor before him. Just as before. But this time from Dali, there come fewer words.

Just two –

'Go fetch'

– as he passes over the file on Hunter 101A.

18

THE WALLS OF THIS BUNKER MAY BE LEAD, but one is secretly hinged, opening inwards.

The space behind would feel like a tomb were it not for the ceiling. It is hung with knives, strung from chains.

A hand, scarred and hardened, reaches up. The blades twist and dance like wives in a harem, flirting for selection.

One by one, the knives are picked and plunged point down into a table. A figure, clad in black leather, battered to a shine, steps from the shadows. His gaze falls upon the weapons.

'Have I not chosen you twelve and one of you is a devil?'

Hunter 666A reaches forward, collecting a knife that quivers in the centre of the table. It is made from a single seamless shaft of silver.

He slides this blade into the sheath against his heart. Then, one by one, he conceals the remaining weapons about his body. The last item gathered is the mission dossier, passed to him by Dali. Hunter 666A smooths his hand across the file-cover and then bows his head, the movement coming with the beat of a ritual.

'What will ye give me, and I will deliver her to you?'

With a slow tenderness, he kisses the target's number: 101A

Eyes open, his head rises, the ritual of departure complete – almost.

His torso heaves against the leather as he bends to attend to his final task. Picking up a delicate china jug, he pours water into a flower pot. It holds a bloom.

By candlelight, it has the silhouette of a rose but the colour is hard to determine. Darker than red, deeper than blue. The flame finally reveals it to be that rarest of things: a black rose.

On the pot is pasted a label, hand-inscribed: 'The Judas Rose'. The paper is cracked and yellowed; it was pasted to the terracotta almost two centuries ago by the hand of Brother Spino.

THE YOUNG MONK could never have imagined that a day begun by labelling roses would end with a Hunter's knife pressed to his throat. But his life since joining the Chiro Scuro had been wonderfully eventful.

Brother Spino was recruited to their ranks in 1855, selected for his great skills as a cryptographer. The hidden language of Brother Magen was fast slipping from the Brotherhood's grip and with each passing generation his original learning was becoming ever more obscure. To forestall this encroaching ignorance, the young Spino had been assigned the most urgent of tasks: to complete the translation of the *Kata Strepho* before the onslaught of Victor Emmanuel reached the doors of the Collegio Romano.

But with the sound of hooves pounding, Brother Spino found himself running from Victor Emmanuel's mounted soldiers, clasping the *Kata* to his chest like a breastplate.

He knew his orders. In the event of an attack, he must deliver the *Kata* into the charge of the Black Pope. A deal had been struck and in these desperate times, the protection of the Sinestra was presented to the Brotherhood as the only way to keep their sacred scripts secure.

But Brother Spino ran and ran, as he had never run before.

Dear Lord, if they but knew the prophecy that I have here deciphered, they would never surrender the Kata*! Not into the hands of a Tormenta defector!*

For six days Brother Spino ran, neither eating nor sleeping, determined to make it over the Alps. His final destination was decided by his feet. Worn down to the bone, they called a halt in Prague.

The same feet also found him a friend. The eyes of an elderly apothecary were drawn to the monk's sandals, which seeped blood. He introduced himself as Jorgi Baresch, extending a hand so knotted with ague, it seemed a poor advertisement for his craft. But his insistence that he would help the monk, with no desire for payment, proved irresistible.

Clutching the *Kata* below his robes, Brother Spino's feet were soaked in pungent unctions and wrapped in cotton. The tender treatment took hours, but Brother Spino said nothing. Exhaustion played its part but more, the fear of discovery kept him silent.

None can know who he is, nor his purpose.

The silence is filled by old Baresch, who juggles a jolly conversation as he works upon the wounds, boasting of his ability to diagnose an illness through observation alone. He tells of a liver rot he diagnosed by the way his patient allowed his tongue to loll from his lips. And of a lover's complaint identified by the way the lady used her fan.

'And you, Brother, I know that these are not pilgrim wounds. You are in flight, for your very life.'

The comment is tossed, but the upward roll of Baresch's eye reveals his intent to surprise. And he finds the young monk's mouth ajar.

'Do not fear, Brother. I will say nothing.' He seals the last of the healing cotton strips across Spino's feet. 'You cannot know how glad I am of your coming. Dear Brother, I am much in need of a holy man.' His old head drops and his hands fall into his lap, balled into crude prayer. 'This is why I ask for no payment. So that you may serve me in return and hear my confession.'

Brother Spino reaches out, fingers clasping the old man's

shoulders. He feels the old muscles twitch with tension as Baresch tells his tale.

'The priest of our church, I cannot go to him. He condemns my trade in potions and calls me sinful. But believe me, I practise no magic. The ways of darkness, I abhor. And that is why I know, in my heart, that what I sense, what I see – these terrible visions – they come from God.'

'What do you see, old man?'

'I beg you, do not think me insane!' Already on his knees, Baresch slumps further still, grasping the hem of the monk's cassock. 'I must confess that when I look into the eyes of a certain woman, I see a demon staring back at me.'

His words tumble out, old hands wringing back and forth as the story of his suspicions gain form. Emily Duvall arrived in Prague a year before. Unknown to any in the city, she soon gained a foothold, taking over the old flower shop that stands just two doors down from Baresch's apothecary's shop. Her golden hair and clear blue eyes attracted customers but most were quick to comment that it was her delightful conversation that drew them more.

Baresch himself was struck by Emily's clever quips and one insightful comment in particular stuck in his mind. One day she tossed up the observation that those who come to a flower shop are always at the extremes of ecstasy or agony: buying a bouquet for a new lover, or a wreath for a loved one lost. She told Baresch that she liked this best about her profession, that she met mankind in such exquisite throes.

As he bid her farewell, Baresch felt his shoulders shaking at her wit. With laughter, so he thought. But when the shaking refused to abate, he realised to his horror that what shook him was a creeping chill, an abstract of unease. As the lovely Emily talked of her clientele, he had seen something in her eyes . . . something hungry, something waiting . . .

'. . . like a vulture, Brother Spino. Like a vulture, certain that a corpse is bound to drop. Now, you may say, what would this pretty creature want with death, but here's the thing . . .' He beckons the young monk closer, as if lowering his voice diminishes the madness of his words. 'That flower shop has stood for forty years, but only since Emily Duvall took charge have so many grieving widows and broken-hearted Romeos ended their woes in death.'

Baresch brings his hands together in prayer. 'Forgive me, Brother Spino, but I believe there is an evil in her. She takes hearts already broken and, with cunning words, she crushes them.'

His hands now spread across his face, as if he fears his eyes should meet those of the young monk. But then he feels the gentle touch of Spino's fingers.

'You are not mad, old man. Far from it. You see more clearly than most.' Brother Spino smiles. 'You have done right to confess your fears. I know what manner of demon she is. And she will be despatched.'

That night, Brother Spino sent word by way of messenger to the Black Pope, telling him that the Sinestra must be alerted to the presence of a Tormenta. He gave the location, but asked that no one be told the information came from him, for fear of his own whereabouts being discovered.

Whilst he waited for a Hunter to be sent, Brother Spino determined to use the intervening days to do as he had been taught by the Chiro Scuro: to interfere in Tormenta activity.

The first step is to get close, and this proves no problem. His monk's robes are quick to attract the eyes of Emily Duvall, as he samples, sniff by sniff, the flowers in her shop. The touch of her fingers, lingering too long as she helped him wrap lilies, reveals her ruse. She will see if this celibate monk can be seduced into despair.

He plays along, requesting to spend more time at the shop as he does so love to be amongst the blooms. He tells her of his skills in calligraphy and offers his services. He could label the pots, if that would please her. She agrees with eyes wide.

And now, praise God, Spino would play his part in a grand perversion of Emily's intent. He will eavesdrop on her conversations with each fragile customer, until such time as the Hunter comes.

Which turned out to be a Friday. And it began for Emily Duvall much as any other. She watered the blooms and brushed bugs from the leaves, careful not to disturb any spiders. Arachnids she admired for their webs, works of such patience and precision.

She places the prepared pots in the window and opens the shop door with a smile. And with a slash too fast to flee, a second smile is opened up across her neck. Blood gushes upwards. Through its heavy descent, a figure looms, knife in hand. Raised to strike a second time.

Emily clamps a fist to her own throat, stifling the flow, and pulls a blade. Thrusting at the black mass that descends upon her as might a meteor.

The advantage of that first strike is too much and overwhelmed, out-bled, Emily falls.

She knows this Hunter that slays her. He walks tall in Tormenta legend. And so she knows his signature of death. With her own hand, she sweeps her hair clear of her neck. When the blow comes, her tresses hang uncut, in all their glory, from her severed head.

The silence that ensues is broken only by the lightest of footsteps. In the doorway has appeared Brother Spino. He looks about the debris of combat, flowers fallen, pots cracked.

'I will see to this, Hunter. Your work here is done.'

The monk averts his eyes as the head of Emily Duvall is thrust into a coarse sack. But the Hunter's voice draws his attention back.

'My work here has not yet begun.'

Brother Spino has barely the time to crease a frown

of confusion before a knife creases a sliver of blood from his neck.

'You are Brother Spino?'

The monk twitches a nod. He cannot see the Hunter's face above him, hidden in the shadows. But he feels the voice, hot and wet with sweat.

'Upon your pride, I relied. You unmasked her. She was yours. So you came to see her die. And now you are mine.'

Brother Spino tries to speak, each word forcing the blade deeper into his flesh. 'You seek me? But why? I am no one!'

'You are Brother Spino.'

The Hunter's face sweeps down, bursting into the light. The monk's eyes bulge; his voice gulps. 'I know who you are . . . who you were.'

His pale finger rises, no longer shaking, stiff now with excitement as it jabs towards the Hunter. 'I see you . . . *Judas Iscariot.*'

At the sound of his name – unspoken for centuries – the Hunter recoils. The blade twists in his hand. Brother Spino feels the edge sink deeper, then – a slight release.

'How do you know me?'

The monk inches along the tightrope of his explanation. 'Some within the Sinestra are sympathetic to our Brotherhood. We hear word of what occurs within the Lo'Worlds. And we heard of you. Your arrival was indeed of extraordinary interest to a Christian brotherhood such as ours.'

'Call me traitor, I care not!' The knife resumes its original bite. Pushing on against the pain, the monk inhales.

'We do not call you traitor. Because we know of Boaz.'

Slowly, the knife peels from his throat. But the tip still tilts towards the monk's heart, a sign that Hunter 666A is curious, but a fast thrust away from killing him. The merest twitch of the tip commands Brother Spino to continue.

'Before Jesus called you, you were a fighter. A rebel against Roman enslavement. Young and headstrong, you believed that when Jesus said he would free his people, it would come by a great uprising. Imagine your confusion, then, when Jesus said that there would be no war. That the battle must be fought in the hearts of men . . .'

The Hunter grimaces, grinding down whatever emotion threatens.

'Boaz had been a rebel with you. Fought at your side against the Romans. He whispered in your ear. "Judas," he said, "we are men of action! We need to raise an army. And every man who follows this prophet is one less for our ranks. He is not come to free us, but to make us happy in our slavery."'

The Hunter's head sinks, the first impulse of a nod.

'The truth is, Boaz roused you to betray Christ. But the moment your lips touched your master's cheek . . . you knew what you had done.'

His chin upon his chest, the Hunter's voice is crushed to a whisper.

'He turned to me and said, "What thou doest, do quickly," and I knew I had betrayed the Son of God. But too late . . .'

His voice plummets to a grunt, dull with hurt. Then just breath, drawn hard.

'Go on, my son.'

'In fury, in despair, I drew my sword in search of Boaz, bent on his death. But he was not to be found. And as I stood alone, I knew his slaughter would mean nothing. The only death that would bring relief was my own. I looked up to find myself beneath a tree, boughed like a gallows – a sign from God. I pulled a belt about my neck. I remember the bite of the leather, the swell of my tongue, rupturing against the roof of my mouth. And then – nothing. Darkness. Until I awoke, chained by the hand and foot. A face above me telling me, with deep assurance, that all would be explained.'

Judas shrugs, gathering himself, hardening his tone. 'The

rest you can guess. You know well enough the methods of the Sinestra.'

Brother Spino shakes his head. 'In fact, no. I'm aware only of the tales passed down from generation to generation within the Brotherhood. Many aspects of the Sinestra's operation are unknown to me. So please, reveal.'

The knife is suddenly back, thrust up hard into a nostril, slitting blood. 'Is this your game? To trick me into betraying my new masters, some fresh treachery for Judas?'

Brother Spino tries to shake his head but the action screws the knife deeper. 'No, no, my son. I have no such intent!'

'How can I trust you!'

'For this reason alone. No matter how we finish this exchange . . . as allies or as enemies . . . my death will ensue, at my request. And so nothing you tell me will ever be heard by another.'

The knife slowly exits. 'You are a curious man.'

The monk delicately dabs at his nostril, sniffing up the blood that threatens. 'Curious indeed. To know more.'

Judas lowers himself to the floor, sliding the knife into the sheath beside his heart. 'The Sinestra always appoints a Handler to induct each new arrival. I received mine. His first task was to explain what had come to pass, what I had become, the domain that I was now in and – most importantly – the choice that lay before me.'

'So what had come to pass?'

'Boaz was a Tormenta. He had identified me as a furious young man, volatile and therefore vulnerable. He played upon my passions and drove me to an act that was certain to destroy my mind. When I came to surrender my life, he was waiting. But he must have been much in need of my span because he struck too soon. Death was not fully upon me when he pressed his mouth against mine. To attempt to siphon span before it is released . . . this is the greatest sin a Tormenta can commit. Because in this way, there is a mixing of essence and a human gains Tormenta traits.'

Brother Spino leans forward. 'And that same human, now neither dead nor alive, human nor Tormenta, arrives in the Lo'World, dark realm of the Sinestra.'

Judas nods. 'Tormenta make this mistake rarely, and so the delivery of such a human is a precious gift.' He exhales, half a smile roused by the memory. 'The Sinestra are good at what they do. Most persuasive. They soon convinced me that I had a purpose. The Tormenta trait I now harboured would act as a disguise, allowing me to move within Tormenta society, get close enough to kill them.'

'And the Sinestra would train you to fight, until your skills matched theirs.'

'My own death had been denied me. I saw no other road to repentance.'

Brother Spino flinches at this. Then he finds his voice, eyes wide. 'You still seek forgiveness?'

'Yes.'

'From whom?'

'From God.'

The young monk tries to sound indifferent, but he delivers the next words with the tension of tossed china. 'You still believe?'

'I still believe.'

Now Brother Spino cannot contain himself. 'Then you are truly of our calling. It was not by chance that you were sent. The Sinestra selected you because they thought you heartless enough to kill a holy man. But they could not know what higher force was at work. The one force beyond all others. The One True God.'

Now he meets the eyes of Judas with cool assurance. 'This simple world of man, the obscure realms of the Lo'World . . . and the many, many domains beyond . . . they are all just folds in God's robe. This is what we believe.'

He leans in close. 'This is what you believe.' Now daring to place a hand on the shoulder of Judas, his last words come with a smile. 'And this is why you will heed

118

my calling to serve.'

Brother Spino's hand slides within his cassock, withdrawing a thick tome. The gold script on the leather reads *Kata Strepho*.

Judas's eyes fall heavily upon it.

'So you know of this book.' Brother Spino allows himself a wry smile. 'But you will not know of the prophecy it holds.'

As he opens the book, the ancient pages crackle. 'I myself have deciphered only the first few chapters.' His fingers explore the waxy text with a lover's tenderness.

'The Bible tells us that the End of Days will come, when the Enemy will rise and Christ will return to defeat him. But though that may be the last battle, it will not be the first. Before that final onslaught, the Enemy will send forth his creatures of destruction. To wreck mankind, to bring him to his knees. And the worst of his envoys is the Mosca. The Mosca is a Tormenta of extraordinary power. He will draw all other Tormenta to him, to lead them from the covert existence and demand that Tormenta take their rightful dominion over mankind. His coming is talked of in Tormenta legend. And did they but know this, the beast has come before . . . He was risen into a human form, but upon each occasion the Sinestra has succeeded in his death before the Legion of Gehenna could find and awaken him. The Legion have little to go on, just what legend tells them. That to find the Mosca they must look for Scox, his harbinger, who will blaze like a star and reveal the Mosca.'

Brother Spino inhales, suppressing a fresh quiver in his voice. 'Each time the Mosca has come into a mortal shell, the Legion have got closer. We fear – I fear – that the next time, they will succeed. The G-Man they despatch will awaken him. And if he does, only one thing can save mankind. It says within the *Kata* that if the Mosca rises, God will bring forth its counter-poise, the Moera.'

Brother Spino raises a hand. 'I know what question

comes.' He slowly closes the *Kata* with a soft exhalation. 'What is the Moera.' He slides the book back inside his cassock. 'To that I have no answer.' He rises now, tightening the rope of his belt. 'I did not have time to decipher that far. So I cannot say from where or when the Moera will arise. But I can tell you this: someone within the Sinestra is intent on its discovery and its destruction. And that is Dali.'

Judas rises slowly. 'I have been loyal to the Sinestra for two thousand years. You ask that I act against one of their number, upon this – the word of a stranger.'

'We are brothers in God. Strange only is the bond that binds us.'

As if in prayer, Brother Spino places his hands together, gathering patience. 'I am sure of it. Dali plans some treachery.'

This word sweeps past Judas's ear like a spear. 'What manner of treachery?'

'He watches for the Mosca, to usher his arrival into the human realm.' Brother Spino shakes his head, mouth tight. 'The Chiro Scuro has never given credence to his defection. And with the Brotherhood disbanded, some other force must keep the *Kata* from Dali. I believe it should be placed in the hands of Man. God will find a way to bring the book before the eyes of those who can decipher it.'

'So what do you ask of me?'

'The Moera has been sent to save us and this time, Judas, you must become this saviour's best defender.'

'You would entrust me with this task? Knowing who I am – what I have done?'

'God knows what you have done, Judas. And he chose to bring you here, to me . . . today.' He bends down, collecting a potted flower that stands alone on a shelf. It is a black rose. He thumbs the label that he himself inscribed. 'To keep remembrance of what we once were is the surest way to keep our future pure.' He lifts the rose and presents it to Judas. 'You were once Judas the traitor. Now you will be the thorn that protects the precious rose.'

Judas accepts the plant in cupped hands.

Brother Spino exhales. 'And now you must kill me.'

Judas grits his jaw, stifling confusion. But Brother Spino just smiles. 'If you don't, they will suspect you. Hunter 666A never returns empty-handed. You must defile my corpse, a sign of your frustration that I would tell you nothing. Then return to them unchanged, the same brute they despatched. In this way, you will keep Dali's trust. Until such time as you can unmask him as a traitor.'

Judas draws himself up, inhaling slowly, sliding the silver knife from the sheath at his heart.

Brother Spino kneels and tilts his head forward. 'What thou doest, do quickly.'

The hand of Judas flies.

TWO CENTURIES LATER, the Judas Rose quivers in his tender touch as he pours the last of the water from the jug. Then Hunter 666A rises, pulls a long coat about him and strides towards the doorway.

This fresh command to retrieve a rogue Hunter – he welcomes it. It provides him with the chance to walk abroad.

Because the time has come. He is sure of it. He has gathered information and intelligence from every quarter. He has studied every sign and portent.

He knows it. He *feels* it.

The Moera is about to rise.

As the doorway slides shut behind him, the chamber trembles and above the rose, the whole wall shimmers. It is alive with black petals. The bush grows huge across the wall. And Judas's commitment to his secret cause is now as vast across his heart.

19

A LIBRARY SOARS, bold with a grace born of the fact that it belongs to Yale University. The silence within is thick and only one sound chips at the air: a rhythmic tick of wood. A walking stick perhaps, though the impact seems more weighty.

The sound increases as a figure nears. Swaddled in chaplain's robes, the old man bears no stick. But the inch between his cassock and the floor reveals the source of the sound. A wooden leg, heaving onwards as the old man makes his way between the library tables. A gentle nod and smile to each student blurs the purpose of his journey. There is only one table that genuinely holds his interest. It stands at the farthest end of the library and, despite its giant length, it seats just one student.

He is shrouded by a tangle of long, unruly dreads. It is only when he jerks back his head, to jolt the dregs from a Fanta can, that his face can be seen. Dark skin. Green eyes. His ear-buds throb to a hip-hop sub-base.

A South Central baby born to a junkie mother, some kind of freak-gene made him a genius and so he was riding a scholarship outta the ghetto. That's what he told everyone and it made for a good story.

The truth was somewhat different.

He was born to Mr and Mrs Massenberg, a wealthy professional couple who lived in the trimmed garden borders of Hancock Park, Los Angeles. His mother, victim years ago of a traffic accident, did have an addiction to painkillers. In her late forties, she was reconciled to a childless future and so was shocked to find that pregnancy, not menopause, was the cause of her recent malaise. Her first horrified thoughts were on the effects the painkillers she had been taking might have on the foetus. She was indeed warned that the baby's development may be affected.

But Mary Masseberg is a woman of faith and, praise God, the boy child is born healthy. The first year of life for Norris Massenberg Jr passes without incident, but come his second birthday it is clear that something is amiss with the boy's mental development.

It is happening too fast.

In kindergarten, rumours of his prowess are leaked to the press. In a review by a local black magazine of a piano recital given by young Norris, the journalist coins the mo' better name of Mo'Zart.

His talent for music was just one facet; mathematics came just as easily. A memory for numbers meant that at just seven years old, he could reproduce equations more than a thousand characters long.

At eighteen, he was snatched up by Yale.

No big deal to Mo'Zart. He thinks this brain-funk thing is overrated. He knows the Mayan alphabet by heart, but so what? He's one month off nineteen and he's never seen a woman naked. You wanna try milking your man-ham to a headful of hieroglyphs.

He'd taken his arrival at Yale as a chance to reinvent himself. The smart church suits, so beloved by his mother, have been replaced with baggy jeans and New Religion underpants.

But the threads and dreads change nothing of his brain. It is a beast inside his head that demands feeding. And night after night, Mo'Zart finds himself back here. Drawn to the library.

Compelled by one book.

The same book that is spread before him now. A thick, ancient tome. Mo'Zart's fingers slowly trace across each page. The dark, waxy text within is a mass of symbols, arranged in complex patterns across the parchment.

Beside the book is a pad, crammed with notes. Mo'Zart's pencil dashes again as he sees a symbol reoccurring, recording its position.

He jolts as a hand falls on his shoulder. Then exhales as he sees the familiar old face above him.

'How ya doin', Father Wexler?'

'Good, good, my son. And you?'

'Kinda slow today. The code has changed again. Every chapter. I feel like I'm always going back to first base.'

The hand pats a gentle reassurance. 'You have made great strides, Mo'Zart. But tell me this, what you've found today, in this chapter, does it alter anything of . . . anything of your last translation?'

Mo'Zart flips back a page in his notebook. 'Nope, I'm still pretty solid on that.' His finger finds the line as he reads it aloud. '. . . the three will become one and then it shall rise.' He shrugs and taps his pencil like a drumstick on the table's edge. 'Question is, *what* will rise?'

He flips his pad to another page. Revealing a sheet filled with one word – *Moera* – densely doodled.

'I mean, what d'you think, Father? What *is* the Moera?'

Mo'Zart feels the old hand rise from his shoulder, but he does not see the uncontrollable tremble that now possesses it.

Father Wexler turns away, his voice strangely hoarse as he tosses encouragement. 'Keep at it, my son. With persistence, I'm sure . . . all will become clear.'

And he is gone.

Mo'Zart returns to the manuscript, then —

— bolts back in his chair.

A man in a sharp black suit now sits opposite him. Mo'Zart blinks.

Where the hell . . . ?

He looks at the departing figure of Father Wexler. Did the old chaplain bring him here?

The man in the suit flashes a smile at Mo'Zart and then looks down at the reading matter in his own hands. His brow furrows, suggesting that whatever he studies, it is something as testing as the manuscript before Mo'Zart.

Mo'Zart jabs his pencil between his dreads and scratches his head, resisting the temptation to ogle what lies in the man's hand.

His eyes fix once more on the maze of glyphs before him and, with a crack, he turns the ancient parchment to a fresh page.

The man responds with a deep inhalation. Then, loudly: 'I don't understand this.'

Mo'Zart glances up. The man's hand taps his reading matter, roused to irritation.

'Most baffling.' He thrusts up the paper.

It is a take-out menu.

'The way it's written . . . very confusing.' He jabs a finger at the laminated words. 'The pizzeria's called Treble Belly. Very clear. That's written right here. You get three slices of pizza for the price of one. Then down here on the right, it says, "Thursday night is three-for-one". But no explanation. What does that mean? Three people can get triple portions for the price of one treble meal? Or that one person gets three trebles, which would make nine portions of pizza? Really very unclear. The way it's worded.'

Mo'Zart says nothing. Looks left and right. *Someone punkin' me?*

Looks back to the guy. Flashes a smile. 'You know, dude, if you venture to the diner, you will find there many wise women who will reveal all to you. Called waitresses.'

The man says nothing. Then with a sudden thrust, he thuds his hand down on Mo'Zart's giant manuscript. 'That's some big book all right.'

Mo'Zart flinches, then snaps his shoulders forward, mouth tight. 'You don't touch that.'

The man relaxes back into his chair, long legs extending,

ignoring Mo'Zart's tension. 'I read it. Some of it. Years back.'

Mo'Zart chills his tone, keeping it cool with the weird dude. 'You didn't read this book. This is the Voynich Manuscript.'

'No it isn't.'

Mo'Zart taps two fingertips on to the parchment. 'Yeah it is. This *is* the book.'

'It's the *book* of course it's the *book*. But Voynich —?' The man shakes his head. 'It only got that name by chance.'

'Right. And you, the dude with the mind-fuck menu, you know all about it?'

'When it was discovered by old Jorgi Baresch, the cover had been removed. So no name. No title. That's where the mystery began.'

Mo'Zart lays down the pencil and pushes back his chair. He stares at the man, taking in the cropped red hair and long copper sideburns that frame his face like a centurion's helmet.

'You want to talk to me. You seem pretty set on that.'

The suit says nothing.

'I don't know you, man. You're too old to be a student and dressed like that, you ain't on a professor's pay-check. I mean damn . . .' He takes in the cut of the black suit in long, admiring sweeps. '. . . those are some sick threads.'

With one hand, the man smooths the jacket. 'Hand-reeled Thai silk.' His fingers flip the lapels, revealing the merest flash of a gun.

Mo'Zart tenses, hands flat on the table. Exhales slowly.

'What do you want?'

'Pizza.'

THE BACK BOOTH IN THE TREBLE BELLY PIZZERIA is in almost total darkness. A yellow bulb splutters above.

The face of the man, once again seated opposite, flickers as if lit by flames. This hellish effect is unnecessary as

126

Mo'Zart's wack-o-meter is already jacked to the max.

He jerks back against the booth as a fist lunges forward. Then uncurls and hangs mid-way across the table. 'My name is Agent Petrus Bex.'

The hand is tentatively taken. 'Mo'Zart.'

'Except you got that name by chance. Your birth name is Norris Massenberg Jr.'

'You the law?'

'Yes.'

'What kind? I mean state, federal . . . how high we talking?'

'The highest.'

Petrus Bex rolls his hands upwards to reveal a tattoo in the centre of the palm. It is three crosses, combined to make one crucifix.

'I . . . I don't understand . . . '

'Good, that means we're getting somewhere.'

He signals for a waitress. A steaming coffee pot appears and two mugs are filled to the brim.

'You guys ready to choose?'

'Give us a coupla minutes.' Agent Bex flashes a smile that makes him appear, for less than a second, like quite a nice guy.

The waitress slides over a bowl of sugar and sashays away. Bex pulls three sachets of sweetener and opens them one by one as he talks.

'Jorgi Baresch was an apothecary with a small practice in Prague. In 1858, he finds a book abandoned in his shop. The cover is ripped away and the pages within are filled with an ancient coded text. Baresch was already thought by many to be a practitioner of the black arts. His local church had excluded him because the priest claimed Jorgi was possessed with demonic visions. So when he was found with this book, rumours raged that it was the work of the devil. These accusations worsened when Baresch stubbornly refused to say how the book had come into his hands. One story said that he was given it by a murderous monk, who slaughtered a local florist called Emily Duvall and then disappeared into the night.

'Baresch laboured hard to clear his name, insisting that the book held a message from God. The rest of his life was devoted to deciphering the code. But time was short. He died a broken man just two years later, with not a single page of the mysterious book deciphered.

'He had no close family and those relatives who descended to pick at his carcass were quick to sell off the manuscript, which had, by this time, gained some notoriety amongst cryptologists and collectors. It was bought at auction by the wealthy philanthropist Wilfred Voynich.

'Voynich treated it as a fanciful oddity and delighted in showing it to his high-society friends. It becomes known as the Voynich Manuscript and is celebrated as a marvellous conundrum. On the death of Voynich, his widow bequeathed it to Yale University. Where it has remained ever since.'

He takes a jolt of coffee, wincing at the bitterness. 'I was a student at Yale. Years ago. Mathematics was my forte. But something drew me to the manuscript, as if it were an equation that, with one revelation . . . that value of x . . . I might resolve.'

He stirs in another storm of sweetener. 'It took time before I realised that the purpose of the manuscript is more than just a code to be cracked. It is a lure, a magnet – to draw out those minds destined to join us. Minds like yours.'

He samples another sip. Sufficiently sweet, he drinks deeper, taking his time. Mo'Zart taps the table, urging him to say more.

'To join what?'

'SCURO.'

'What-who now?'

Bex smiles through the steam of his coffee. 'You cannot imagine what you have achieved. More than I ever did. That manuscript is the *Kata*. It tells us of the Mosca and the

128

Moera. You translated the one line that proves everything. That to rise . . . the three must become one.' The eyes of Agent Bex, for a moment, seem lost in some strange ecstasy. 'That is our creed.'

'Whose creed?'

'SCURO.'

'Yeah, you keep makin' that noise.'

Agent Bex sets down his coffee, eyes sharp. A perfunctory smile. 'Once you join us, all will become clear.'

'But not before? Like some crazy game-show shit, huh?' Mo'Zart mocks a quiz-master's voice. 'So, kid, you wanna take the car or open the mystery box?'

'You want the car – it's yours.' A set of keys tumble across the table towards him.

Mo'Zart gathers them up, eyes wide on the fob. It dangles with an Aston Martin icon.

'It's parked outside. Every agent gets one. And a suit. And as for the mystery box? Well, you've already opened that, kiddo. You cracked a crucial clause of the *Kata*. So that tells us you got the right stuff.'

Mo'Zart's eyes are still fixated on the glittering fob, but he hears the voice of Agent Bex rolling on.

'We're looking for the Moera . . . the three becoming one. You wanna jump on that train? Or d'you want to go back to your old life and forget this ever happened?'

Mo'Zart jerks as another voice cuts in. The waitress has returned.

'What's ya choice, kid?'

Agent Bex answers for him, jabbing a finger at the Thursday night special. 'He's gonna take the three for one.'

20

AN OLD HAND SMOOTHS THE PARCHMENT of the Voynich Manuscript. The pages have lain silent since Mo'Zart's recruitment. But the old chaplain knows it is for the best. It had been he, after all, who informed the Primus Pater of the Chiro Scuro, Umberto IV, that another mind had been called to the *Kata*. And it had been such an unexpected pleasure to see Agent Bex again. Wexler had made the call that resulted in his recruitment almost thirty years before.

But Mo'Zart he missed more than he expected.

Even the pages of the manuscript seemed to mourn his loss. Father Wexler strokes the parchment as if giving the ancient tome some comfort. But as he moves to turn the page, the edge catches his finger, slicing it thinly, drawing blood. Before he can lick the tip, the slit has opened further still, ripping like a fault-line down his finger, along his arm. Splitting faster, reaching his chest and racing up his neck to deliver a deep and gaping wound, as if drawn by a knife, severing his neck to the spine.

And then —

— his old eyes flash open. He is standing upright, untouched. His finger barely snagged.

His mind playing tricks . . . no more.

He exhales. He has not been plagued by such a vivid event since the days of his youth, when he first joined the Brotherhood. And even then he was ordered by the abbots to suppress these 'attacks of the mind'.

He remembers protesting, loud and long. Was it not through violent visions that their founding father, Brother

Magen, had first seen the truth?

But he was silenced. The Brotherhood, he was told, is not the same as it had been in those early days. It had been altered for ever by the attacks of Victor Emmanuel. Driven to disperse, hounded into hiding, much had been lost from their learning during these dark years of suppression. It was to be more than four decades before the Brotherhood would gather again, at the turn of the twentieth century.

They amassed in Spinkhill, England, under the protection of Joseph Pole, patriarch of a powerful Jesuit family. To reflect the changing times and to aid in the concealment of their true agenda, the Brotherhood assumed the name of the Society of Curators for the Understanding of Religious Orders.

Amid a fashionable Edwardian interest in spiritualism, the Society attracts little attention and continues its work as the century rolls on.

Then comes war. And the world changes again. Responding to information that Hitler is collecting relics and recruiting occultists, a secret contra-unit is established by the Allies under a covert title: the Ministry of the Unnoticed. Its task is to halt the Nazis' mastery of magic. And it is under this initiative that the Brotherhood finds an opportunity to truly reunite and return to being an active force.

Brother Wexler was one of the many young monks transferred from the Chiro Scuro's quiet cloisters to join the Brotherhood's field operation. Still technically operating under the guise of the Society of Curators for the Understanding of Religious Orders, this new pro-active division took the acronym SCURO.

Agent Wexler relished his duties in SCURO. He proved to be effective in the identification of Tormenta, who were enjoying a juicy existence within the ranks of the Nazi High Command. But his active career was brought to an abrupt halt. Word reached them that a Tormenta had infiltrated a branch of the Maquis, the French Resistance, and was persuading many young underground fighters that the only honour left to them, in the face of Nazi rule, was suicide. Trekking across a field in Northern France in search of the Tormenta, Agent Wexler found a land mine first, which blew his leg away at the knee. For him, the war was over.

He was relegated back into the cloisters of the Chiro Scuro, where the monks quietly supported the field operatives of SCURO with a combination of prayer and paper-pushing. Brother Wexler soon learned, to his dismay, that the fight against evil demanded an absurd amount of administration.

It therefore came as something of a relief when he was offered the post of chaplain at Yale. The Chiro Scuro had used their contacts within the university to subtly control this position for many years; ever since they had reason to believe that the Voynich Manuscript was in fact, the *Kata*. Whilst the extraordinary powers of the Chiro Scuro could have easily had the book removed into its care, Primus Pater Umberto IV had seen an alternate opportunity. Some of the greatest young minds in the western world would pass through the doors of Yale. If the mysterious tome was ever to be decoded, where better to seek the right minds to help accomplish this feat?

Father Wexler, as he would now be known, accepted the chaplain's role willingly. And over the coming decades, from the elevated halls of Yale, he observed the ever-more extraordinary evolution of SCURO.

By the end of the twentieth century, SCURO operated as a shadow agency aligned to the many other obscure offices of US Intelligence and Homeland Security. Funding from the deep coffers of the Jesuit Church ensures that SCURO is well resourced. The church's connections reach high into the realms of politics, military and law enforcement. Their powers are as wide as they are dark.

Which is why the extraction of a student from Yale is such an easy task. All the papers required to explain the temporary research post offered to the student are furnished to the university administration, friends and family.

But still, Father Wexler had been sad to see Mo'Zart go. Perhaps because he knew how special the boy was. He succeeded, after all, in deciphering that most precious gobbet of the code. But in his heart, Wexler knew it was more than that. He had a real affection for the boy.

Is that why he haunts my visions now?

Because the horror the old man has just experienced was not a warning to him, but a clear knell of danger to the boy. The manuscript was charged with his energy. It was to him that the pages spoke. And they were speaking to Wexler now, urging him to pass their warning on.

They pursue the boy. The Legion Of Gehenna will find him.

The manuscript thuds shut.

And the robes of Father Wexler fly as he slips through a doorway at the back of the library and hurries down a darkened hallway that runs beneath the library. His destination is a chamber, deep within the underground archives. A telephone was installed there, a secure line where Father Wexler could call directly to the Chiro Scuro. He used it rarely. Sometimes to deliver good news that a fresh student had shown interest in the manuscript.

Sometimes to declare danger.

He increases his pace, the clatter of his leg echoing from the walls as they narrow towards the doorway.

Then he halts – and the echo falls silent a moment later. But a moment too long. He heard the fragment of another footfall. Wexler turns, peers into the gloom. Sees nothing. And pulling his robe tighter about him, he presses on, opening the door to the chamber. Reaching out, raising the phone, his hand extending towards the old dial.

A HAND GRASPS A SHOULDER and gently shakes. 'Primus Pater, I am sorry to wake you. But there is a call.

Father Wexler.'

Silk sheets roil in the half-light. A voice rumbles. 'Wanting what?'

'He won't say. Just that this is a matter for the Primus Pater and no other.'

A fist uncurls from the sheets. A golden ring, carved with the symbol of the three crosses, is wrapped about a finger which snaps against a thumb, demanding the phone.

A large black receiver is delivered. Dry lips approach, slicked by a tongue. 'Father Wexler. You have my attention. Use it well.'

Nothing comes from receiver. Just a muffled gasp that rises into a desperate shriek that twists into . . .

. . . a dull buzzing tone.

The telephone line is dead.

21

BIANCO BREATHES SLOWLY, this time inhaling the sweet latex stench of the mask she wears. Einstein's nose inflates and flops with every exhalation.

She looks through the eye-holes, surveying this new space. It is a vast, dark warehouse, stacked with crates. The only light comes from the open door to the chamber that held her.

And from two other doors, to two other chambers.

And now she realises that two other figures stand alongside her in the darkness.

One wears a Tweetie-Pie mask. A small man in a crumpled suit and slip-on shoes. Bianco knows he's a detective even before she sees the badge on his belt.

His fingers fidget. Bianco recognises his type; this place will be freaking him out. He's just a simple cop who does things by the book. No arguments. No questions. He'll have written everything down, just to get outta here.

Bianco smiles beneath her mask. *Bet you sang like a canary.*

Then she hears it, a muffled voice. The detective is mumbling something . . . one word.

'Sulphur. Damned sulphur . . .'

Bianco leans in. 'I'm pretty sure, that smell – it's lilies.'

The figure to her left snaps its finger, reminding them to stay silent. She turns to see a tall frame, big chested. His neck is topped by a mask of Marilyn Monroe. Bianco sweeps her eyes past the detective's badge, down a long pair of legs to his feet. Size thirteen at least.

And something sparks in Bianco. *Dammit, I know*

those feet!

A sound smashes the memory before she can grasp it. A rhythmic beat. Loud and echoing.

All three masks turn towards the footsteps. A silhouette strides through the darkness, haloed by a blinding beam of light suddenly released by an unseen door.

Before the figure comes to a halt, a voice fires off an introduction. 'My name is Agent Petrus Bex. Detectives, welcome.'

His lean form thrusts from the light and falls into an easy pace, circling his guests. Bianco's eyes go to two deep, ragged scars that slit the agent's skull where his ears should be. The wounds look fresh. From behind her mask, she tries to take a closer look, but he circles away, striding on.

'Thank you for your attendance here today. Your reports will be reviewed and researched and in the event we find cause for further investigation, we will do so with a wonderful rigour. So rest assured, you have done your duty and whatever you saw . . . whatever you *think* you saw . . . it is now in the hands of SCURO.'

His lips stretch wide into a smile, as if wedged around a stick of dynamite. The threat is clear. 'From two of you, we require nothing further . . .'

His fingers snap and a second figure appears from the shadows. It is Mo'Zart, sporting a sleek, black suit. His unruly dreads have been bound behind his head. A second impatient snap prompts him to produce all three clipboards and pass them to his boss.

Bianco exhales behind her mask, low and slow.

She can see that two of the boards contain a mass of handwritten notes. Hers is the only one empty.

'There is, however, one of you . . .' Bex glances up, his face clenched like a fist. '. . . with whom I must speak at greater length.' His eyes swivel. 'Detective, this way please.'

Bianco jolts as a heavy hand drops on to Tweetie-Pie's shoulder, leading the little man away towards the door. The young agent follows behind.

Agent Bex's voice bounces from the darkness. 'Do not remove your masks until instructed. Do not attempt to leave before the timed lock disengages. Do not hesitate to ask if you have any questions.' A pause – less than an atomic second. 'No questions. Very well. And so we thank you both. Good afternoon.'

The door slams shut.

A bolt shunts.

Then silence.

Marilyn Monroe shifts from one huge foot to another. 'So, what d'you figure?'

Sweat runs down the side of Einstein's face. 'Fifty-fifty that we're fucked.'

The rubber muffles her voice and she's glad of it. She wants to maintain her anonymity until she is sure who Marilyn is. She has a pretty good idea. Even though the probability of this being correct is so whacked out, it would blow even Einstein's mind. But life's like that. One big curved universe, throwing balls.

She looks again at those feet. *It has to be Bambi Siggurson.*

It's been ten years at least, but her mind replays the sound of those size thirteens, pounding the gravel of the training circuit at Cadet School.

This was where they met – sort of. It was more like they met, then pulled away, then met again on the bend, then pulled away on the last five hundred yards of track that leads back to base.

Bambi Siggurson was her biggest competition for the Silver Wings, the badge awarded to the cadet who graduates with the highest marks.

And back in those days, Bianco had been all about the competition. Maybe because she knew where she'd come from, a one-time perp trying to step over that thin blue line. But something in her told her she would need to be twice as fast as the next kid to stand a chance of outrunning her past. She'd sized up the other cadets on her first day and saw no physique to touch hers. But the Siggurson guy, she had to admit, looked good. Long-legged, lean . . . and a loner. That's what made him dangerous. She knew his type. *He ain't here to make friends.*

She'd need to keep an eye on him.

And right there was her first problem. Siggurson was so goddam fast, she'd lose sight of him before he hit the first bend. He would easily outpace Bianco over the first two miles. But she would smile as Siggurson, along with most of the other male cadets, pounded past her.

Yeah, bye-bye guys. I'll be seein' ya.

After all those teen years spent fleeing from the cops, when she just kept running – mile after mile until she made it all the way back to Swamp Gravy – her legs are now limbs that don't know how to quit. Bianco may be slow on the sprint, but over distance, she's a goddamn machine. By the third mile, she's thudding past red faces. By the fourth mile, her knees are pounding high, weaving through boots that can barely clear the dirt. And by the sixth mile, there is only Siggurson left ahead of her. The last five hundred yards to the finish would see them shoulder to shoulder. Sometimes she'd take it. Sometimes Siggurson. Always in silence.

They never spoke. That's how they both liked it. And how it stayed, until that one particular day.

It had stormed since morning. Only Bianco and Siggurson were dumb enough to still attempt the circuit.

Bianco feels the rain thrash hard against her face. And behind, gaining ever closer, is the thump of Siggurson's Reeboks. Her muscles burn with lactic acid, starved of oxygen in the soaking air. But she can't stop. Won't stop.

Must stop! as a lightning bolt shears a branch. A ton of wood drops hard into the mud, missing her skull by inches.

Bianco swerves, grasped by a hand that pulls her below

the shelter of a massive oak.

The hand then relaxes, releases. Sinks down to hers, palm extended.

'Bambi Siggurson.'

Bianco takes the hand, shakes it, aware of the weirdness. They've seen each other every day for five weeks and with just eight days to go, they're getting round to this.

'Alexis Bianco.'

The hands drop apart. There is no more to say. But the silence held between them grows too heavy and it slips first from her grip.

'Bambi? That's kinda . . . unusual.'

'Yeah, well . . . my mother was killed in an accident. A hunter in the wood shot her dead. The local kids saw the funny side. Called me Bambi. So I took the name on myself. Then it stopped being funny.'

Bianco grimaces and shifts uncomfortably. 'That's some story but, hell, you could tell it better.'

She glances up. And sees the expression on Siggurson's face. Their long resistance to conversation means that Bianco can read him from his eyes alone. And now she knows, with absolute certainty, that he has never shared this story with anyone before.

Siggurson's hands agitate the hood of his tracksuit, pulling it over his head. 'Rain's easing. We can make it back.'

Bianco watches as he tugs the cords tight, concealing his face. Then she jerks a thumb at the track. It's awash with mud.

'OK, but we walk. Game over. No points to anyone, agreed?' She extends her hand to shake on the deal and Siggurson takes it.

At an easy pace, they start back towards base. Random topics of conversation drop into Bianco's head like bowling balls, all of them dull, detached, designed to pass the time. So she jolts with surprise when her own brain makes a weird selection and rolls out of her mouth: 'Ya know

Bianco isn't my real name.'

Siggurson says nothing but he turns to look at her from inside his hood. Bianco shrugs and continues.

'I chose it. Or more like it chose me. Bien'Cou. It means crow. And I guess I got the label because I'm always crowing. Like I just can't keep quiet about how many times I've beaten you at weapons assembly. And how I always ace you on the shooting range. And how many times I beat you on the Seven Mile.'

She grins at Siggurson and through the rain she sees his eyes narrow, suppressing a smile.

'Yeah. Suits you. Got those scrawny crow legs too.'

'All the better for beating you, Siggurson.'

He yanks down his hood and jabs a finger towards a dirt track that cuts through the woods. 'The Ten Mile. Right now.'

She holds her palms up to the torrential downpour. 'In this?'

'You chicken, crow?'

She grins and, with a surge of mud, she's gone. Accelerating down the track. Siggurson pounds after, heels flying.

He beat her. That time.

And every time after. If Bianco thought that anything had passed between them that day in the rain, she was wrong.

Siggurson never spoke to her again and for the remainder of the training, Bianco savoured second place so many times, it tasted like vanilla.

She licks her lips, releasing the mask that clings to the inside of her mouth each time she inhales. She looks at the familiar line of Siggurson's body. The years have been good to him. Doesn't look as if he's gained a pound.

Bianco rolls her shoulders, feeling the weight of everything she knows bear heavily upon her. She may look the same, but she has changed beyond recognition.

She exhales. Reaches up, ready now to remove her mask.

22

A DRUNK SLUMPS across a bar, tink-tinking his empty shot glass, looking for the barman. 'Hey, man! Where you hiding?'

He lifts his glass and peers through it, as if the thick base might bring his world into some sort of focus.

He cranks his head left and right and something catches in the prism. A wisp of gold. He lowers the glass to see that on the bar is a deck of cards, spread in columns. The back of the cards glitter with an intricate gold design.

A figure sits by the cards, close to the window.

The drunk lugs his head round. 'Pretty dandy cards, man.' His eyes pucker, searching for the figure's face. But nothing can be seen. The gloom of the bar conceals his hair and neck, and what escapes of his face is hidden behind an enormous pair of binoculars, pressed to the eyes.

The lenses are turned towards the window. They survey the only building opposite: a derelict soap factory.

The barrels of the binoculars twist, fixed on the factory door. The figure slowly exhales.

Patience. With patience this plan might just work.

The cards at his elbow suddenly flutter upwards.

'Solitaire, eh?' The drunk clumsily pokes at the half-completed columns. 'How 'bout you ditch that game and deal a duet.'

The barman appears, wiping the bar and nudging the drunk's sprawling arms back into a manageable mound. 'Eyes front and centre, Donny. The dude don't want to play.'

The shoulders of the figure tense and then roll; a shrug perhaps.

'No inconvenience, my friend.' His pale hand descends, collects the cards. Slowly shuffles. 'I have time to kill.'

'There ya go, man!' The drunk snorts, slaps his hand down on the bar. 'Name the game.'

'I propose a battle of my own design.' A smile flashes, like the silver plate on a coffin lid.

'Sweet, man. What's the rules?'

'The aim is to find the Mosca.' The hands cease to shuffle. 'The rules are constant, unchanging. The rules of eternal balance. And they state that if the Mosca rises, so will the Moera.'

The cards are placed one by one face down on the bar. 'But where to look?'

The hand hovers over a card. 'The Legion have played this game many, many times . . . and lost.' He turns over the Ace of Hearts. 'This being so, my plan is to change the game-play. And if we cannot find the Mosca, then we will seek out the Moera.' The Ace of Hearts is set down on top of another. 'And it will lead us to what we truly seek.'

He turns over the card underneath. It is the Ace of Spades. 'The Mosca and the Moera. Their fates are locked together for eternity. Like star-crossed lovers . . .'

The drunk rumples his face, trying to keep up. 'So how d'you win?'

The figure sweeps up the aces, and then adds a King and Jack to his hand. 'You get your enemy to play into your hand.' A long finger taps the King. 'To the death.'

The drunk grunts. 'I don't get it, man.'

'But you will, *man*.' The hand gestures to the mash of humanity in the bar. 'You all will.'

The figure is already turning away, binoculars rising, racking focus. Fixed upon three silhouettes that exit the factory opposite. It is Agent Bex, Mo'Zart and the small detective, shuffling in tow.

The Chiro Scuro seek the Moera. So follow the agents and when they find theirs, we shall find ours.

Fingers snaps as the figure orders another pomegranate martini, dry with a twist kicked to the side. Knowing that elsewhere, his precise orders are already in action. His plan has begun.

The martini glass is jerked forward, purple juice spilling on to the card caught beneath. The hand slides the card out, glancing down.

It is the Joker. *Of course? How perfect!*

A bitter smile, as the card is crumpled deep into his palm. Too long has he been regarded by the Legion as a trickster. Worse, a traitor.

But when he succeeds in finally awakening the Mosca, the Legion will embrace him again and forgive his past betrayal.

He would have succeeded long ago, were it not for Agent Bex. Bex has indeed proved to be an admirable adversary. He covers his tracks to perfection, contains the information he garners with a fist of steel. No word on the Moera has ever slipped his grip.

There have been times when the entire enterprise seemed doomed to failure. But a new recruit has been taken on. A kid who has not yet acquired Bex's invulnerable exterior.

A chink in SCURO's armour.

The challenge then is to find the right gee-gaw to distract the recruit. Something that can get close to him. Something . . . or someone.

The hand slowly slides a Queen between the King and Jack.

23

THE TREBLE BELLY DINER is alive on a Saturday night. In a back booth, a pair of hands toy with a menu. Opposite, another pair of hands fold and unfold a piece of paper, glancing at the text within.

'Says here you like music.' A boy swallows hard, bulging the collar of his shirt. 'I like the classics.'

The girl opposite has her hair pulled tight into a ponytail. It tugs her face taut. 'What, like Springstein and shit?'

'Debussy . . . and shit.' He exhales hard. Unfolds the paper again. 'So, what else do you like?'

He halts as a voice comes from above.

'I like this booth.'

Someone stands by the table, clad in a long, hooded coat. The boy attempts a smile, tips up his palms. 'Hey, guy, we're on a date.'

The hood swivels from the girl to the boy. 'I don't like your chances.'

The figure thuds into the booth, the ripple of the impact launching the couple on to their feet. They hurry into the aisle.

Booted legs uncurl below the table. Long and muscular. Hands rise to the hood. They are pale and delicate.

From beneath the fabric, a tumble of blond dreadlocks fall, concealing a face that is etched by a strong jawline. Only when the face turns, pierced and tattooed, does it appear to be woman. An amazonian creature.

Her features are African but her skin is white. Eyes ice-blue. The woman is a black albino.

Everything about her – colour, race, gender – seems to

be a contradictory mix.

She snaps her long fingers, demanding coffee.

A waitress stomps up. 'Black or white?' Maybe she intends the jibe . . . maybe not. One cold glance from the woman and the waitress quickly proffers the cream, resolving any doubt.

These fucking humans . . .

As the waitress scurries away, long black fingernails tap the table. Then idly gather the sheet of paper abandoned by the boy. It's a dating agency profile sheet. The top box is filled with a name and the box below is labelled: 'TELL US A LITTLE ABOUT YOURSELF'.

The woman grins. *Yeah, just imagine that . . .*

The name box she could fill in: Bee-Bee. But only a human could fit their life into a single text box.

Bee-Bee's life stretches more than four centuries.

She was born in 1544 in Trinidad. At the age of fourteen she was captured as a slave and shipped to New Orleans where her strange albino looks attracted much attention. As a thing of interest, she was sent across the Atlantic to the French court. Painted in her tribal colours, with a black stripe across her eyes, she was presented to the young Dauphine and given the name Melissa, from the Greek for bumblebee, prompted by her black and yellow colouring.

Melissa soon became a favourite and her quick wits brought her to the attention of the court's High Chancellor. He controlled the espionage that ceaselessly flowed between the French and Spanish courts as the New World brought them closer and closer to war. Melissa's strange appearance meant that she could pass as any nationality, because no one had ever seen her like before. More important still, it had become clear, in the midst of the lascivious antics of the French court, that Melissa's sexual preferences were wonderfully fluid. Men and women found her irresistible and she happily obliged both.

A marvellous quality in a spy.

And so it was that Melissa moved between the two courts, playing both sides, politically and sexually. Her prime loyalty, always to herself.

Until the day she met Perfidia.

She was a handmaiden, newly recruited for the Spanish queen. There was something about her that was both cruel and magnetic. A perfect contradiction. No wonder that Melissa fell in love, fast.

Perfidia encouraged these passions, telling Melissa that their destiny was to be together. When Melissa was ordered to return to the French court, she refused. The savage punishment she received at the hand of the Chancellor all but left her for dead.

Yet to Melissa, death would be preferable to separation from Perfidia.

As Perfidia washed the deep lashes across Melissa's back, she whispered a proposal. They would commit joint suicide and be united forever in death.

Melissa willingly agreed and swallowed down a spoonful of poison.

As the last gasp left her body, her consciousness flickered. She saw Perfidia not lying beside her, but bearing down, thrusting her mouth upon hers, violently sucking . . .

And then . . . nothing. All that was found by the chambermaid the next morning was a smoking carbon ring upon the floor.

And Melissa awakens in the Lo'World, delivered into the Sinestra's care. When her new masters explain that Perfidia was a Tormenta and that she duped her, Melissa's fury knows no bounds. Her first instinct is to break free of this place, return to Earth and seek Perfidia's death. Then her Handler in the Sinestra explains that Perfidia is already dead; her failed attempt to take Melissa's span will have condemned her. Melissa rages that she must have vengeance and so what sweet relief she feels when she is told that there is a means by which she can get even. She can be trained

146

to become a Hunter and whilst Perfidia may be gone, she can vent her fury against every other Tormenta that crosses her path. Without hesitation, Melissa agrees and becomes Hunter 696B.

She soon gains a reputation as one of the most ruthless ever to serve the Sinestra, taking mission after mission, slaughtering Tormenta. Until one day, when she learns a certain truth about Perfidia. About her motives all those years ago . . .

And as a consequence, Melissa's loyalty to the Sinestra is instantly and forever destroyed.

Her old duplicitous ways return. She drops her Hunter number, releases her yellow dreads, reinstates the black stripe across her eyes from her tribal days and takes the name Bee-Bee.

A killer for hire.

Part human. Part Tormenta. Entirely mercenary.

Another snap of her fingers brings the waitress back to her table.

'What's hot?'

The waitress jerks a pencil towards a picture on the menu. 'Hottest we got. Three types o' chilli.'

Bee-Bee smiles. 'The Treble Rebel. I like that.'

She peels a ten-dollar bill from a roll. 'You make it quick, and you make this.' The bill goes down on the table.

The waitress bobs and scoots away, all smiles now.

Must be my Tormenta side that makes me expensive, cos humans are so damned cheap.

The money roll slides back into her pocket. The generous girth suggests it must be ten thousand thick.

She has just accepted a new mission. She has a new target.

And she expects him at any moment.

A GIANT KEY SWINGS and Mo'Zart slides it into the lock of the factory door. One grinding clunk and the mortise slides shut. Mo'Zart attempts to slip the key into his suit pocket, but its long shaft resists, as if the key is determined to poke from his pocket and observe the journey the boy makes to the back of the building.

Agent Bex awaits in the darkness, a cigarette in one hand, the other resting in a relaxed, and yet restraining, fashion upon the shoulder of the short detective.

His voice carries cleanly on the night air.

'Detective Gobis was just telling me he hails from Sulphur City. Born and bred.'

'And soon to be dead?' Detective Gobis titters at his own grim jest. 'Hey, just joking, guys. I know that SCURO aren't . . . that you would never . . .'

He looks from one agent to the other, searching for some chink of camaraderie.

Agent Bex opens a smile, like the priming of a bear-trap. 'I suggest you forget any preconceptions you may have about SCURO. We are not what you think we are.'

Gobis shifts from one foot to another. 'You don't know what I think you are.'

'Believe me, detective, you do not have that calibre of imagination.' Agent Bex waggles a hand, instructing Mo'Zart to approach closer. 'The cellar door, please.'

Mo'Zart fumbles inside his jacket, taking out another giant key and slotting it into a padlock that seals a set of storm doors in the ground. The thought strikes him that the last time he manipulated keys so large in proportion to his hands, he was a baby and the keys were strung across his pram.

And working with Agent Bex, he sure feels like the baby. He has yet to see any real action. And tonight looks set to be no different, as his boss ushers Detective Gobis down the cellar steps and then raises a flat hand that halts Mo'Zart in his tracks.

'You may not attend this interview.'

Mo'Zart grimaces, head down. 'So this is how I learn?

The three-monkey method. See nothing. Hear nothing —'

'Say no more. And avoid insolence.'

Bex pulls a cigarette, sparks a match, draws deep and slow. Taking his time. Either the cigarette is sweet enough to savour or Bex is considering, with unusual care, what he utters next.

'This detective worked on a homicide.' Smoke ekes from the side of his mouth. 'A fifteen-year-old girl was found in a motel room, ripped from neck to hip one hundred and forty-four times.'

Mo'Zart jigs in the cold. 'Did they get the guilty guy?'

'*She* was the guilty one.'

Mo'Zart baulks, eyebrows up. 'What did she do?'

Bex taps his ash like a ticking bomb. 'Maybe nothing.' He takes a long last drag. 'Maybe everything.'

The same jerking gesture that casts down the cigarette instructs Mo'Zart to leave.

'Go get some fresh air.'

Ten minutes later, Mo'Zart finds himself stomping through the dark streets. He's been through the agency training programme – when will he start to get a taste of the good stuff? When's 007 gonna get the girl?

. . . *speaking of which* . . .

Mo'Zart glances at his watch. Maybe he can make good use of his time. A few nights back, he met this cool chick, or more like, she met him. The girl had some stones, just sliding into his booth, smooth as . . .

Mo'Zart smiles. She was kinda tall and the thought did cross his mind that she might be more man than him. But all suspicions were allayed when she allowed Mo'Zart's drunken hands to roam free. Suddenly, the boy got game. And he got her number.

Mo'Zart pulls out the napkin with her digits and flips his cell phone. She picks up on the second ring.

What d'ya know . . . she's in the Treble Belly, just down the street. Says she's gonna order for him, so be sure to get there quick.

'How do ya like your coffee?'

'Like my women.' Mo'Zart cringes at his own bad line.

In the diner, Bee-Bee leans back and snaps her cell shut with a smile. She's not sure that they serve tri-sexual coffee.

24

THE BASEMENT OF THE SOAP FACTORY smells quite different. It has a sweet, searing tang that forces Detective Gobis to jam his sleeve to his nose. He knows the stench well.

'You got a body down here?'

Agent Bex strides ahead between a maze of vats that fill the basement. 'What you smell is the old rendered fat.'

Gobis relaxes his sleeve half an inch. 'Smells human.'

'I believe they used pigs. Now please, if you will . . .' Bex gestures to a metal chair that stands alone amid the vats. 'Make yourself comfortable.'

Detective Gobis fails in this first task as his buttocks overspill the small, cold seat.

'Do you smoke?'

'Why, you gonna set fire to me?'

'You are quite the joker, Detective Gobis.'

'Guess it's a defence mechanism.'

'Not much protection against a bullet.'

Gobis shrinks back as Bex's face sweeps down. The scars of his severed ears ripple as he hikes a smile.

'I jest, detective.'

Something cold and hard suddenly presses into Gobis's chin. His eyes roll slowly down, pooling with relief as he sees it's just the metal edge of a clipboard.

'Your testimony.' Agent Bex urges the metal edge a little deeper into the folds of the detective's chin. 'It contained certain facts relating to the case of Jezebeth Hooger. Facts for which you could find no adequate explanation.'

'Sir, I just saw what I saw and reported it. I'm only a

cop. I don't need to know everything.'

His words twist to a gasp as the corner of the clipboard kinks his windpipe.

'But I need to know everything.' Bex withdraws the board. 'In your own time.'

Which feels to be fast running out, so Gobis draws breath and begins. 'It started the day that Jezebeth Hooger was murdered —'

A thin finger rises, wags disagreement. 'It started a long time before that, detective. The true beginning, please.'

'All right, we can do it that-a-way round.' Gobis shifts on his seat as if his ass is searching for the start of the story. 'So this is going back some but, yeah, I was the detective on duty the night of Agnus Day's suicide. Or supposed suicide, because there was no body. Just a goodbye note and a big ol' carbon burn ring on the floor. And no corpse. Now, if it had been anybody else, the file would have been shelved as a missing person. But this guy had a fancy academic reputation and the Chief wanted us to show some huff'n'puff, a little effort. So we dusted for prints, took a bunch of pictures. Then I filed it as a missing person. And forgot it.'

He halts, jerking a finger up towards his mouth. 'I do smoke, if you got one.'

Agent Bex produces a soft-pack, taps a cigarette. Gobis takes it, glancing at the logo.

Never heard of this brand. But I guess that figures.

Agent Bex clicks his lighter, like the snap of fingers, commanding him on.

'So the Agnus Day case goes cold. And seventeen years later, I get called to a homicide scene. A motel in Sulphur City. Sounds routine, until I get there.' He glances up at Agent Bex. 'You musta seen the pictures? They were everywhere. Every newspaper. Every news channel. Little Jezebeth Hooger, fifteen years old and all raped, ripped up and written on. And lying on the bed right alongside, catatonic and covered in her blood, is her killer, Agnus Day. Not that I knew it was him. No way. The pictures I'd seen when he went missing, he was this skinny, bearded scientist. This guy was all muscled up, a machine. But the DNA pegged him. And that was surprising. But then the lab boys take Jezebeth's prints and what d'you know . . .' The half-inch of cigarette sizzles. 'Coincidence is a funny thing.'

'God's favourite joke, I hear. Continue, please.'

'They match her prints to a set of unknowns taken from the scene of Agnus Day's disappearance. But Jezebeth Hooger is only fifteen years old. She wasn't even born then.'

Gobis takes a last, long drag. 'So I filed a report. And this one I ain't forgetting any time soon. Until the Chief takes me aside and says that I'm to wipe my memory clean of those prints. The prosecution has an airtight case. The killer was found with the victim. What nobody needs is a piece of the puzzle that doesn't fit. It has to be an error. And he promises me personally that he will send the prints away for review. And meanwhile, I should keep my mouth shut until Agnus Day is safely put down.

'I thought I could live with it. It's not like I'm so clean. I got dirt under my fingernails, what cop hasn't? But when Agnus went on death row, that dirt on my hands . . . felt sticky like blood. So I told the Chief, I want to know what happened to the evidence review. I wanted proof that the fingerprints were some kinda freak mistake. Guess you could say I made some noise. So when I get brought in by SCURO, I'm thinking two things: either I'm gonna get some facts. Or the facts are gonna get me.'

He looks up to see that Agent Bex is writing something on a piece of paper. The shred is ripped from the clipboard and passed to Gobis.

'Please look at that number. Have you ever seen a man with this number tattooed on his arm?'

Gobis takes the paper, glances at the number. Shakes his head.

'He may have gone by this name.' Bex gestures with his finger that Gobis should look at the reverse of the paper. 'Is it familiar?'

Gobis' flips the paper fragment and now his eyes bulge wide. 'Well . . . well, of course I know this name, but how could I ever . . . how could he be . . .'

With a waft of his hand, Bex draws him to silence. 'Thank you, I just had to be sure.' His lips tighten. 'So, we are grateful, Detective Gobis, for what you have provided. Thanks to your concern for the truth, we know where we should direct our search.'

'For what?'

'That is not your concern.'

'So what now?'

Agent Bex slides back his jacket, pulls out his gun.

25

'So, d'you make sergeant?'

'I scraped some stripes.'

'Thought you'd be way up there. You were always so hungry.'

'Maybe I lost my appetite.'

'You – never!'

Siggurson's words follow Bianco as she drops her mask and walks away across the warehouse, her attention caught by something. A glint of metal. She arrives at a crate and reaches in between the slats. Smiles as her fingers feel the familiar outline of her gun. Retrieves it and slides it into her holster. Siggurson is immediately by her side, fishing his own weapon from the box.

'All right, so I say we blast the lock and get outta here.' He buckles the gun tight beneath his arm, looking about the warehouse for the door. 'I don't know who or what SCURO is, but soap never smelled so much like bullshit.'

He glances up at Bianco. She is slowly buttoning her jacket over her gun-belt, taking her time. 'Hey, what's with you? Don't you want to get out of here?'

'The door's at twelve o'clock.' She jerks a finger towards the back of the warehouse and then sets off, following her own command. Siggurson moves up alongside.

'You've changed, Bianco.'

She strides half a pace in front of him, voice low. 'I've seen some things. Now the world don't look the same.'

'C'mon, we both work homicide. I've seen every way a man can die. You deal with it. Move on.'

'Yeah, you're right. That's all there is to it.'

Siggurson shakes his head, unrolling a smile. 'Don't tell me there's a little bit of real woman buried deep down in there? That whole job-is-not-enough thing. There-must-be more-to-life shit . . .'

'There's more to death, Siggurson.'

A gunshot explodes. From somewhere deep below.

Before the echo dies, Bianco and Siggurson are pounding towards the door. Siggurson pulls his gun and shoots the lock. In a shower of sparks, the metal bursts open. The stairs beyond shudder under their descending feet.

Gunfire erupts again, directing their pursuit down towards the factory cellar. They survey the floor looking for an entrance. Race outside. Find the stormdoors wide apart.

Siggurson is first down the steps, gun high. Bianco sweeps behind, ready to cover. Back to back, in tight formation, they enter the basement.

And then they see him: Agent Bex, aiming his weapon at the figure of Detective Gobis, who stands quivering with his back to one of the vats.

Siggurson shouts an order to Bex to drop the gun.

As Bex turns, Siggurson sees only the approaching mouth of the agent's Luger.

But Bianco sees something else – a strange expression on Bex's face. Which twists to agony as Siggurson's bullet sheers through his hand.

And as he falls, his skull explodes upwards. Struck by another bullet. Another shooter.

And then Bianco understands.

The barrel of a sawn-off shotgun emerges from behind the vat. Followed by a shadow with its arm tight around the detective's neck. The attacker had been holding Gobis as a human shield, until Bex was fatally distracted, allowing the attacker to let off a kill shot.

Realisation passes like lightning from Bianco to Siggurson, a moment before a bullet slices past their heads. Siggurson's neck is hooked down by Bianco as she reacts first, releasing a shot as the attacker pounds up the steps of the cellar, the limp body of Gobis slung under one arm. Bianco's bullet rips through a storm of blond dreadlocks that swirl as the attacker turns, firing with one hand. Effortlessly. Accurately.

Bianco's shoulder explodes, the force of the impact cracking her backwards and hurling her to the floor.

Siggurson reaches out, grabs her jaw and twists her face to look into her eyes. She's alive. Then he sweeps his gun through the darkness, finding only silence.

Leaping to his feet, he strides to the body of Agent Bex and rolls him over. His halved skull rocks like bowl of bad fruit.

He strides back towards Bianco. Hauls her to her feet and, bearing her weight, makes for the stairs to the storm doors.

In thudding steps, he rises and hits the air, stumbling as something tangles in his feet. Spread on the concrete is the motionless body of the other young agent. Blood seeps from the back of his skull.

Siggurson moves to walk on, Bianco now his priority. But he halts. He cannot escape his training. He sets Bianco down and goes back to the kid. Listens for breath. Nothing.

Feels for a pulse. Nothing . . . then, something. Faint but real.

He is alive.

Siggurson's eyes shoot up. Sees an old Ford Tahoe in the abandoned yard of the factory.

The hood pops. Wires fizz. The engine revs.

Mo'Zart rolls unconscious across the back seat and Bianco slumps forward on the passenger side as a size-thirteen boot crushes the gas and Siggurson roars into the night.

26

LOLA'S CHEEK LOLLS against a leather headrest. She is slumped in the bucket seat of her '71 Dodge Challenger.

Her eyes flicker open, looking across to the passenger side. The seat is empty.

Bianco should be here.

Then Lola shakes her head, mouth tight. *My weakness. That I want her with me.*

She tenses her spine, stretches her neck. She doesn't need her for anything.

Apart from maybe keeping her awake. On these long stakeouts, Bianco's conversation was as relentless as the radio.

When was their last hunt together . . . a month ago? They'd been in the car for three hours and Bianco hadn't stopped talking.

'Hey Lola, you ever shot with a .44 Magnum? Massive kick-back. It pulped my palm black and blue the first few months. But I've never seen you carry one. And ya know, I got an interest in what weapon you use. I'm your partner. You should try it. You'd like it. You like Clint. And Clint likes Magnums.'

'Clint hates having a partner.'

Bianco laughed. Lola liked the sound of it. Hard and loud, like a dog's bark.

She can't remember the sound of her own laughter.

A lot of things I don't remember.

Lola's eyes close. She breathes deeply, feeling fatigue fold about her. Opens them again, fixed on the empty seat. The only thing that rolls on the leather now is a carton of half 'n' half.

Without Bianco, Lola needs coffee.

A hot cup sweats on the dash, capped tight with plastic. Lola picks up the half 'n' half, places it between her teeth and pierces the foil lid with her incisor, a standard cop manoeuvre for avoiding spill.

She'd learned that from Bianco.

She'd learned a lot from Bianco. About how to tap phones, bug buildings, trace registrations. She can even log on to the police database for fingerprints and bullet matches.

And Bianco had gained some skills in return. She was getting pretty quick at spotting Tormenta grifts.

Lola plugs in an earpiece and looks up at the building where she's parked. The Hoyle School of the Dramatic Arts.

This stakeout had been Bianco's idea.

She was buzzed to tell me. Her first find.

Bianco had taken her to a sports bar on the outskirts of town.

She'd leant across her frothy beer. 'I was watching this show about acting classes, how they break the students down, really mess with their minds, telling them that they have to destroy their own persona to get into the mind of another character.'

Bianco talked at speed, excited by her own discovery. 'So I'm thinking, drama students are pretty tender meat. So what happens if you add some devastating criticism, tell them they will never be good enough . . .'

'Is this going anywhere specific?' Lola hated this bar. She wanted out.

'It's going right there.'

Bianco pointed out of the bar window to the Hoyle Academy opposite. 'Hilda Hoyle, prime English bitch and the toughest acting coach outside of New York.' A photo slid over. A small woman in winged spectacles. 'Students pay a fortune to get enrolled. They say that Hilda will either make you or break you. So I pulled up the student

159

records. Seven suicides in nine years.'

Lola lifted her chin, eyes front. Bianco has her attention.

'Even to an amateur like me, that school looks like an Oscar-winning grift.'

The listening device crackles in Lola's ear. A class is getting under way. A woman's voice shrills.

'You were deadly dull last week. All of you. I hope today that someone might light the darkness with a glimmer of talent.'

Lola slugs down the last of the coffee. Its bitterness jerks her tongue. But still her eyelids fall.

The leather seats are hot. Almost midday.

The half 'n' half carton drops from her fingers. Lola's breathing slows.

Then —

Her body spasms, like a falling dreamer. Words crackle in her ear-piece: 'I want you to take a good long look at your face. You see the problem? No-one else wants to look at it.'

Lola's eyes roll beneath the lids. The words trigger something. A memory . . .

A fat, pallid face stares into a mirror. Removes thick glasses. Tries to apply red lipstick, but the downturned mouth is sobbing, lips quivering, sending the lipstick in chaotic scrawls down the chubby chin. The image shifts . . . the lipstick becomes a trickle of blood, running down a slashed wrist.

'You will never succeed. Your life, my dear, is worthless.'

Lola's bolts forward in the car seat, breathing hard.

How long was she asleep?

Slams from the vehicle.

Boots pound up the stairwell. Burst into the studio to find the room in darkness.

But Lola's eyes soon adjust to see a familiar congress taking place in the far corner: a young girl's body is sprawled across the floor, pale and lifeless. A tell-tale froth bubbles at the corner of her mouth. In her hand is a bottle of pills, spilling outwards.

Lowering down, jaws agape, is Hilda Hoyle. She presses her lips hard on to the girl's mouth and begins to suck.

A glistening, twisted coil of span rises, snaking down Hilda's throat. She gulps hard, drawing it further. The last coil rises. Hilda inhales, ready to ingest, when —

— she hears the thud of approaching boots.

She rises. Her outward appearance is a bundle of knitwear and pearl-rimmed glasses. But as she opens her mouth and roars, her Tormenta nature rises to the fore.

And Hilda strikes the first blow, showing that she has put her all her years to good use. She hustles left and right, back and forth, with dancing speed, her fists, clad in heavy rings, lashing and smashing into Lola's defence. The back of Lola's hands pour blood but she matches the old woman, blow for blow. Until Hilda bobs low, landing a punch deep into Lola's belly. The breath blown from her body, Lola staggers backwards. A dangerous dip in her guard, forced apart by Hilda's lunging fist that cracks across Lola's temple.

Lola swirls back, aware that her opponent is drawing up her fist for a final blow to her skull. And as the old woman's small feet dance in for the kill —

— her shoes skitter, rolling chaotically, the soles sliding across the pool of pills spilled from the bottle of barbiturates.

As Hilda flails and falls, Lola grits her fist and launches hard, cracking back Hilda's head until the neck snaps.

The old woman falls dead.

In the corner of the room, the girl does not move. A pulsing coil of span, half-extracted, trails from her mouth. As she suddenly gasps for breath, the span sinks back down. Its last few inches, pulled from Hilda's mouth, is tainted black.

The girl bolts upright. Looks around her. 'What happened

. . . She said I should . . . and I wanted to die . . . but . . . ?'

Her eyes go to the body of Hilda and then to her own hands, that wiggle with life. With a smile, she looks up at the tall, blonde stranger who stands before her.

'You saved me?'

'Kinda.'

'I'm alive!'

'Half 'n' half.'

The girls frowns, confused.

Lola pulls out her Aviator shades – 'Everything will be explained' – and slides them over her eyes.

She knows what's coming next.

In a blinding blast of light, the body combusts. Leaving just a charred void in the floor.

Lola turns and exits.

27

A **BLISTER SIZZLES,** brown and sticky. The glowing tip of a cigarette rises from flesh. The filter slides between the lips of Bee-Bee who sucks hard, refreshing the heat before she lowers the tip back on to her forearm, searing another circle.

Then twists her wrist, admiring her handiwork.

The length of Bee-Bee's arm is covered in a delicate trellis of scars and blooming blisters. Her neck is ringed with kiss-cuts and carved on to her chest, above her heart, is an inverted K.

She sucks on the last inch of her cigarette, creating just enough heat to score another swirl. The hot tobacco bites and a cry explodes.

Not from Bee-Bee. From a man, in agony.

Why won't this dumb fuck just give up what he knows?

Bee-Bee is bored and wants this over with. She pulls a small mirror. Checks her reflection. Sweeps back her dreads. The edge of the mirror, prettied with pearls, captures a gruesome sight behind her. Gobis is stripped naked and bound to a chair, a mass of needles implanted into his flesh.

His interrogator sits in silhouette beside a table. On the table is a box, coiled with wires. Beside the box, gold cards turn. His captor is playing Solitaire. Passing time, as he waits for Gobis to recover from the last pulse of pain. And as his bloody head lolls up, another blast is discharged.

His body spasms.

Bee-Bee exhales, fluffing her hair.

Talk or die. Or better still, both.

She snaps her mirror shut. Inquisition is definitely not a

spectator sport. 'Why don't you let me try?'

The interrogator declines her offer with another voltage blast.

Fuck you, I could make this sweat-ball talk.

Bee-Bee has recently discovered a talent for interrogation. She always knew she was a skilled assassin. Her training in the Sinestra taught her how to kill with repetitive efficiency. Same moves, like a dance routine.

But since she became freelance, she's added her own little half-step.

Before she finishes her target, she takes a moment to ask a few questions. More precisely, one question.

Do they know where she can find Perfidia?

Because Perfidia is not dead. She lives!

The Sinestra lied to her. Just as they lie to all the half-dead humans whom they wish to turn into Hunters.

Bee-Bee knows this because she asked the right question, of the right Tormenta.

The finest Tormenta she ever had the pleasure to make bleed.

Her fingers trace the K carved on to her heart. It stands for Kave. And Kave stands for no one.

This was all she knew of him the night the Sinestra sent her on a mission to kill Kave. She was still an obedient operative back then. Her hard-core commitment was the reason she was selected for this particular task. Because to bring down Kave meant almost certain death. No Hunter had ever succeeded. But now, she was told, it must be done. There had been 'an incident'. Most unexpected. But it elevated the destruction of Kave from something that the Sinestra might simply relish, into an event upon which they now relied.

She found Kave easily – too easily. That was the first thing that made her suspicious. He was alone in an old salsa dance club. The grey-green walls were soon splattered with blood as she and Kave fought furiously. Hand to hand, blow for blow, she felt the casual sweep of his attack as if he were merely deflecting her fists until something more fun suggested itself.

And then, as she gasps for air, mustering a last assault – he smiles.

'Such spirit. I see now why Perfidia fell for you.'

At these words, confusion combusts with rage and she launches forward, crashing him to the ground. He falls with effortless grace, and does not resist as she strips his torso bare and chains him to a chair, a knife drawn and pressed against his throat.

'What do you know of Perfidia?'

Kave rolls his head, dark hair falling across his face. 'It hurts to even say her name, does it not?'

The blade whips, delivering a careful, shallow nick at the base of his neck. Bee-Bee's voice is hoarse with fury. 'I ask you again. What do you know of Perfidia?'

Blood slicks down Kave's sternum. He lifts his chin, eyes unblinking. 'Cut me as you wish, Hunter, I will not be persuaded. But cut yourself and I will talk.'

She jolts, confused.

But Kave smiles. Something in his eyes, his voice . . . something she cannot explain. Only feel. And she feels her knife rise.

'Above your heart, make a cut. Downwards and oblique.'

Her hand shaking with a strange tension, she finds herself obeying and as the knife opens her skin, her lips part releasing a soft gasp.

'Exquisite agony, that lessens the pain of a broken heart.'

The tip of the knife shivers from her flesh, attempting to return to his throat. 'Tell me of Perfidia!'

'I will not be persuaded by my own pain. Yours, however, I find irresistible.'

The knife slowly curves back towards her own body, as

if born on the wave of his words.

'I can tell you three things, Hunter. But I want a cut for each. A triangle, of sorts, is what we shall carve. Because what we have with you and Perfidia, is a love triangle. You have made the first cut.' He looks at the delicate oblique incision. 'And so, the first thing you should know is this: the Sinestra lied to you.'

He relaxes back into the chair, as if the chains that hold him could be shrugged from his shoulders at any time. 'Perfidia is not dead.'

She feels her muscles twitch. Kave has instilled the mere sound of Perfidia's name with an agonising power.

'So now to your second question, which I guess to be this: why do they perpetuate this lie?' His eyes move like magnets to the knife. 'A second cut, please. One end touching the other, to form a point.'

Bee-Bee stares at her own fist as it raises the blade, cutting deep. The blood comes fast.

Kave nods, satisfied.

'They know that when they tell a half-dead human what has befallen them – and, more importantly, who did it – the victim's first instinct will be to wreak bloody vengeance against that particular Tormenta, the one who drove them to take their own life. But the Sinestra cannot let that happen. They need a Hunter to kill according to command. They must serve just one cause. So they tell the Hunter their assailant is dead and in so doing, hope to divert all that hatred towards the world of Tormenta in general. Not that you should hate Perfidia. She did nothing but love you.'

The knife wavers in Bee-Bee's fingers, like a metal tongue.

'Which of course begs the question: why did she persuade you to your death?' Kave smiles. 'The third cut, when you're ready.'

The blade arrives on her skin as if to finish the triangle along the base. It halts at the sound of Kave's voice. 'No.

Not there. Place it across the top, balanced on the point.'
He flashes a smile. 'You must not complete the triangle
until you find her.'

With a steady hand, Bee-Bee obediently makes the
last cut.

'This mark will remind you always that the one you
search for will complete you.' He tips his head to one side.
'And, by chance, it looks like a K, so you will not forget
who taught you this lesson.'

She mutely looks down at the raw edges of the scars.

'Now this I tell you as a kindness. So be grateful and
come to your knees.'

Bee-Bee mutely drops down before him. He parts his
legs, the action commanding her to bring her torso between
his thighs. Her head hangs in submission.

'Closer. Chin up.'

Her ear arrives at his lips. His tongue brushes the soft,
pink ridges as he whispers.

'Perfidia loved you, but you were a human and she
a Tormenta. She could never change. But you . . . some
part of you could become Tormenta. She could bring that
transformation upon you. By committing the greatest sin
known to our kind: take a human span, your span, whilst
you still lived and so ensure your arrival in the Lo'World.
She knew then that you would be returned to Earth and
although the Sinestra would have caged and controlled your
Tormenta traits, by making you hate that part of yourself,
Perfidia had to believe that fate would cause your paths
to cross again. And when you meet . . . when your hands
are once again upon each other's body, the love you once
shared would return and prove stronger than the hatred
instilled in you.'

Bee-Bee's head dumbly rolls back, mouth open.

'What she did, she did only so that you and she could
one day reunite and be together for ever. Perfidia loved you.
She still loves you.'

Kave sinks his mouth. 'Release me.'

And as the chains fall to the ground, so does Bee-Bee, hard on to her back – with him fast upon her. Pushing her down. His breath thundering into the curve of her neck as he forces the last of her humanity from her, filling her with the hot rush of Tormenta ferocity.

And so it is that Hunter 696B walks away as Bee-Bee.

And each time she looks upon the K cut into her chest, she sees a triangle that awaits completion. Its final side, to be moved into place. So that each of the three lines conjoin.

Three becoming one.

BEE-BEE JOLTS AS GOBIS SCREAMS – this time a cry that gargles to a deathly silence.

The interrogator rises up in the darkness. Lays down his cards.

'Well, there we have it.'

Gobis's limbs slump, lifeless.

'Or, more accurately, there we don't.'

Bee-Bee saunters towards the corpse. 'You want me to clear this up?'

The interrogator hisses furiously, like escaping steam. 'What I want is information!' He inhales, calming himself. A gloved hand taps the curve of his chin. 'What was it that he told Agent Bex?'

His head turns at the slightest of sounds. Something falling from the uncurling hand of Gobis. A shred of paper. The yellow colour reveals it to be the scrap given to him by Agent Bex, when he asked him if he recognised a particular name.

The gloved hand sweeps the fragment up. It is so soaked with sweat, the ink has seeped from the paper. It is illegible. The fingers crush it, thwarted.

Bee-Bee kneels down, prising open Gobis's fist. The ink has left a reversed imprint on the palm.

She pulls her mirror, holds it against the mark. The

reflected words read: 'Judas Iscariot 666A'.

The gloved hands slowly come together, fingertips tapping in contemplation. 'Judas. Well, well! We must find out what he knows.'

Bee-Bee pulls on her long coat, preparing to leave.

'If you want me to bring him in, the price is double.' Knives slide, one by one, into her belt.

Her employer emits a pellet of laughter. 'I would never use you for such a task. This one requires sharp wits.'

Bee-Bee spins the last knife in her hand, tempted to show him just how quick her thinking can be.

28

A HAND THRUSTS a knife upwards. 'Could we get another? This one's dirty.'

The old waitress at Fat Tuesday's whips the steel away and lashes out another with a grin that makes you wonder what she's thinking.

'And more coffee, please.'

A steaming pot appears, carried by a bus boy. And as he tops off the two cups, what he's thinking is clear: *Why the hell is she with him?*

The woman has creamy skin and auburn hair that curls like maple syrup. The older guy beside her, balding and hunched in a waffle-knit cardigan, looks like a dessert delivered to the wrong table.

But their intertwining hands declare them lovers, to the untrained eye.

A figure sits behind their booth. And listens in with a highly trained ear.

It is Lola, slowly stirring her coffee.

The couple are discussing their hurried wedding plans. Lola smiles as she hears the man excitedly anticipate the reaction of his friends and family.

'They're gonna adore you, Love Muffin. Just adore you.' He nervously kneads her hands like dough. 'They'd never think I'd catch a peach like you.'

'Ah, Bubsy, you silly man.' She giggles, eyes down.

He sweeps a fat hand across his head, drawing up a skein of hair from the top of his neck, arranging the frayed ends like a quiff. The woman tweaks his cheek.

'Bubsy, don't fret. You look just fine.'

'And I feel even finer.' He sniffs and smiles. 'I was only half-alive until I met you.'

Lola sweetens her coffee, shakes her head. How many times has she seen this particular grift – the old Heartbreaker.

Most Tormentas have plied it at least once in their careers. They may invest it with a little variation, but in essence it remains the same. The target's hopes will be raised beyond reason, then dashed at a time designed to deliver maximum shame and pain.

And for this guy, tonight is the big night.

THERE IS NO MOON, which serves her well. Lola takes up position in the shadows of the parking lot. She watches as Bubsy's battered Saturn pulls up.

She knows the plan.

Bubsy will go into the café first, to gather his family and deliver the wondrous words of introduction to his bride-to-be. Their devotion may seem sudden and, to some eyes, unlikely. But they are in love. And with every reassurance to his incredulous family that this woman is sincere, he sows the seeds of his own imminent humiliation.

Love Muffin will be alone in the parking lot, waiting for her cue to enter.

Lola checks her weapons belt, pulls it tight, ready to take out her target before those cute kitten heels hit the tarmac.

The engine is killed and the headlights dim. Bubsy squeezes from the driver's door. As he waddles round the car, he sweeps his hair forward, tugs down his shirt. Then turns back into the open passenger door.

'You sure you want to do it like this, honey? We could just walk in together. They're gonna love you, I promise.'

Love Muffin smiles coyly from beneath her curls. 'You've never brought a girl to meet your family before. I want this to be special. I want you to tell them how much in love we are.'

He strokes her cheek and his voice catches and cracks. 'Didn't think a day worth living till I met you.'

She tenderly collects his hand and returns it to his side. 'Go along now.'

'I hate to leave you.'

'Honey, we got the rest of our lives to be together.'

Bubsy wipes a cuff across his nose, sniffs happily. 'Yeah, you're right. Till death do us part, eh?' Then his face twitches as a thought stings. 'Speaking of which, you got the gun in the glove-box, right?' His eyes scoot about the desolate parking lot. 'I don't like to think of you out here alone.'

'I'll be fine. Nothing's gonna happen to me in five minutes. But yes.' She flips open the compartment. 'It's right here. Loaded and ready. You happy now?'

He looks about the darkness one more time. 'Never can tell what's out there. Always plan ahead.'

In the shadows, Lola exhales hard.

Plan ahead. Right.

It's only because Lola kinda likes this fat-boy fool that she's put so much thought into this hit.

If Lola makes the kill here, the cops may find evidence of murder. And Bubsy may just top himself from grief.

So instead, she's gonna render Love Muffin inactive, take her and the car away to another secure location and finish it there. That way, for at least the first few days, Bubsy can think that his love bird has just done a flit. Nerves. Cold feet. But she'll be back.

Sure he'll hurt, but he'll have friends and family around. With luck, he'll get over it.

And if he doesn't?

That's life.

Lola pulls on her gloves, flexes her fingers, creaking the leather.

She slides her eyes from the shadows, watching him waddle towards the café. He turns back for one last wave.

And Lola finds her eyes drawn to his face.

Not his face . . . his eyes. The look in his eyes.

That heaving emotion.

. . . and something ignites, exploding across Lola's brain.

A spasm grips her. Forcing her to the ground. Her arms lash about her head as blinding pain erupts. But in her mind, a memory blazes.

A man. Long dark hair. Eyes, so blue. Gazing at her, with that same yearning. That desire.

That love.

His mouth, so close. Whispering words amid kisses.

'I am not who I was, Lola.'

His hands on her breasts, his arms tight about her. Her body surrendering. Rising up, as —

— a voice shouts loud.

'Miss? You all right, miss?'

Her eyes bolt wide.

She doesn't know how long she's been out. It is a sheriff's boot that rouses her from the tarmac. The parking lot is strobing with blue lights.

'A nasty sight, fo' sure. Guess you just fainted plain away. How's them legs now? Can you get up for me?'

Lola slowly rises, breathes deep. Looks around. Yellow crime-scene tape flutters about Bubsy's car. His body lolls from the passenger side, his bald-spot problem permanently cured, as the back of his skull lies somewhere across the tarmac.

The Sheriff raises his palm, shielding her view. 'Best not to look. All very sad. Some kinda Romeo and Juliet heartbreak, far as we can figure. But he did it himself, we know that. His gun, his hand. So don't you worry now.' The deputy glances about the parking lot. 'There ain't no gun-crazy on the loose. You're safe to go on your way. Quite safe.'

But Lola is already gone, striding into the darkness.

Thudding her fist against her treacherous brain.

The memories are coming back, like a cancer.

And now they are affecting her ability to do her duty.

She has never before lost a human. But in the space of a few days, she barely saved the drama student and now this – the mark is dead and the Tormenta is fed.

Lola flips up the collar of her coat. She's gonna get this head of hers taken care of. Fan Fan Bohica can do whatever it takes, pull her frontal lobe outta her nose with a coat-hook if she has to.

She is better, stronger . . . not knowing.

Lola thrusts her hands in her pockets, turns a corner at speed. And flies hard against the wall as a metal pipe smashes into the back of her skull.

29

A HAND MOVES up Lola's thigh, forcing her hips to the ground. She feels her spine sharply arch, but not in resistance . . . in compliance. Her head rolls, extending her neck as a heavy breath rushes against her skin. Her mouth releases a groan that rises from her belly pit. Her face twists again. Finding the chill of a stone floor, she —

— snaps hard into consciousness. Bolting upright. She is alone. It was a memory.

Her eyes rapidly adjust to the gloom. She appears to be in the crypt of a church. She attempts to look about her but her head throbs at the first twist. She lifts her hand to explore the back of her skull, to find her wrist jerked to a halt just a foot from the floor. It is bound by a rope that's attached to —

— something. She can't see what. The light source illuminating the wall suddenly moves. Swinging from side to side. It comes from a lantern and the movement suggests that whoever holds it is approaching.

A figure arrives above her, thrown into silhouette by the low-held lamp. Lola shields her eyes with her free hand. 'Who are you?'

The voice is cracked and low. 'Are you prepared to listen?'

'That wasn't my question.'

The lantern lowers further still, the glass now hot against her face. 'Are you prepared to listen?'

Lola sinks back against the wall, her body relaxing. Then with a roar, she lurches forward, loading her full weight behind a raging punch that wrenches at whatever bolts the rope. Feels metal give with a groan. Punches outwards again, the rope cutting deep into her skin. But this time, the tension holds. She shrieks and thrashes a third time. Blood flies. She remains tethered.

Sinks back down, jaw tight.

'I'm listening.'

The lantern retracts, shrouding Lola once more in darkness. But she feels the figure come closer.

'The Sinestra released me on a mission, but I walk the world on a cause of my own.'

Lola's eyes narrow. 'OK, now I'm really listening.'

The lantern rises, illuminating a face scored heavily with scars. 'My name is Judas Iscariot. But you knew me . . . knew *of* me . . . as Hunter 666A.'

Lola nods, smiles darkly. 'Yeah, that's right. You refused to quarter with the rest of the Hunters. I kinda respected that.' She grins now. 'The Weirdo in the Megiddo.'

Her smile drops at the rush of a blade. Judas lunges, metal flashing, slicing deep —

— across the rope that bind her wrists. The coil falls to the floor and Lola slumps back against the wall, exhaling hard. Then she rolls her wrists, feeling the blood seep back into her fingers.

'Thank you.'

Her hands jolt as a book is dropped into them. The purpose of her release is now clear. She gathers up the small red volume, twisting it back and forth, looking for a title. And as the lantern is swung close to give her light, the spine glitters. Embossed in gold leaf are three words: '*Fuga di Spino*'.

She moves to open the cover, but a growl from Judas halts her.

'You do not know how to read.'

Lola cocks her head. 'Yeah, I kinda do.'

'With your eyes perhaps. But not with your heart. And your heart must be open, or a book will deliver just words

176

and no meaning.'

'Meaning what?'

'That first, you must listen.' The light bathes the book in her lap. 'A *Fuga* is a diary kept by those who are in flight from persecution. It often represents a last chance to record the creed that condemned them. When all is lost and capture is nigh, the *Fuga* will be left in trusted hands. This is the *Fuga* of Brother Spino. He left it in my care. Because it holds his lasts words on the Moera and the Mosca.'

'The what . . . and the *what*?'

The lantern rises and slides on to a nail in the wall. As Judas lowers himself on to a stool beside her, Lola sees him entirely. She recognises the bite of many blades and the puckered kiss of bullets. But across his torso, like the surface of the moon, are strange, cratered wounds. Some ancient, some fresh. But all of them, she is certain, self-inflicted.

Judas drags the stool closer. 'I will tell it to you, just as it was told to me. In simple terms. But then you must read.' His finger thuds against the book. 'So you can fully understand.'

He closes his eyes, as if taking himself back to the moment when he first heard these words. 'The Mosca is the dark Messiah of legend, whose coming will unite all Tormenta. The Moera is the defender of humanity. If the Mosca rises, so must the Moera. But the Moera can only rise when three become one.'

Lola sits in a moment of silence. 'And that's your idea of keeping it simple?'

'You have questions?'

'Always.'

Judas rolls a hand, encouraging the first.

'Tormenta screw the system all the time. And they don't have any kinda messiah making them do it. So I don't see what difference it will make if this Mosca rises. What's one more dick at an orgy?'

'Such disrespect!'

'Just my kinda simple.'

Judas clenches one hand into a fist. Wraps it in the other and grinds it slowly, milling particles of patience. Then, with immense control, he speaks.

'Tormenta are lone creatures, highly competitive. Fighting for each other's hunting ground. This internal competition keeps them fragmented as a force. If a leader were to rise, with a promise of domination, Tormenta may unite. And with this army at his command, the Mosca can deliver on that promise.'

'Because mankind wouldn't stand a chance.'

'Not without the protection of the Moera.' He raises the *Fuga*. 'Brother Spino recorded the portents of its coming. And how we can protect it, become its guardian and hold it safe until . . .' He leans in close, his voice low. '. . . the three become one.'

'Meaning what?'

Now Judas leans back, a dark smile spreading. 'Ah, the *meaning*.' His eyes gaze into the darkness. 'If words are flesh and bone, then meaning is *spirit*.'

Lola snaps her fingers. 'Hey Jude-dude, feels like we're at the city limits of simple again. Turn around and run it past me one more time.'

Judas grunts, stiffening his spine. Then he nods. 'You are right. It is important you understand this. Though Brother Spino barely grasped it himself. He had just begun deciphering this phrase when he was forced to flee. But in his *Fuga*, I read his attempt at interpretation.'

Judas gathers up a length of rope from the floor. 'When we are born into our human selves, we have one life. When our span is taken, we enter a second state, part-human, part-Tormenta.' He folds the rope in two and twists the lengths together. 'What, then, if we were to find the Tormenta who holds our original span and – somehow – claim it back, would we not then enter a third state?' Judas bends the rope a third time, twisting the three lengths into a single thick pillar '. . . stronger and stronger. Three, becoming one.'

Lola's eyes lock upon the rope and she feels her mouth form words. 'The greatness of three . . .'

Judas looks up, eyes narrowing. 'What did you say?'

Lola shakes her head as if freeing her mind from its own grip. 'It's . . . I think it's something that I read. Something I remember.'

'It is the meaning of Trismegistus.' A voice comes from the darkness. 'You have read his works. Well, well! I am impressed.'

A hooded shadow shuffles forward, arriving before Lola and uncurling a hand from within a long sleeve. The flesh is withered from the bone. It hangs unshaken.

The old monk acknowledges Lola's refusal with a nod. 'Of course, my bad manners. You wish to know who offers you welcome.' He lowers his hood. 'My name is Brother Jolusa. I belong to the Chiro Scuro.'

The shaven head beneath is pulpy with black and purple rot. He smooths a last shred of hair across his scalp and settles into a throne-like chair that Judas sweeps beneath him.

'I apologise for my appearance.' He wipes a hand across his muddy habit as if that were the thing that offended. 'As a Brotherhood, we rarely venture forth. But these are serious times.'

His eyes then rise like embers and land upon Lola's face. Burning deep. 'We appreciate that we are asking you to absorb a vast amount of information. But time is short. And our enemy is strong.' A grey fluid, like ashes in milk, bubbles at the corner of his mouth. 'I should perhaps say "enemies" as the Legion of Gehenna number many. And their sworn duty is to awaken Tormenta, not only in the hope that they will find the Mosca, but to ensure than when he rises, his army is vast.'

He lifts his left hand. This one is sheathed in a glove. The fingers wrap about a rose-coloured cross that hangs at his neck. 'The calling of the Chiro Scuro is to counteract the Legion. We must therefore guard the Moera. But before we can guard it, we must find in which body it will rise. No easy task, but one in which Judas has miraculously succeeded.'

Brother Jolusa reaches out like a proud father, stroking the bowed head before him. 'He followed the instructions in the *Fuga*, looking for the signs and portents, gathering information from all quarters, heavenly and human. And by these means, after many long years of searching, he discovered Agnus Day.'

Judas suddenly jerks up his head, eyes alive. 'It is he! I am certain of it!'

Brother Jolusa twitches his gloved hand, silencing this interruption. The glove then continues upwards, dabbing the drool that drips from his chin.

'And thanks to his relentless searching, not only do we know *what* Agnus is, we know *where* he is. Locked inside a penitentiary called Morphic Fields, where he awaits execution. Now this should present no real obstacle to our accessing him because the Brotherhood has under its command a powerful agency – SCURO.'

His mouth twitches. Not a smile, something other. 'Ah, SCURO! Our public face. Our eyes and ears and, inevitably, our fists when action is required. But over the centuries, SCURO has forgotten its sacred origins. Increasingly it behaves as a secular agency. One that still professes to serve our holy order, but, all too often, questions its orders.'

He sinks back into his throne. 'Judas went to the head of SCURO. The illustrious Agent Bex. And he told Agent Bex that he had found the body in which the Moera was about to rise. He asked for SCURO's intervention to get Agnus Day released. One call from Agent Bex could have effected that. SCURO is empowered by the Brotherhood's lofty connections within the ranks of human governance. But Agent Bex failed to hear his higher calling . . . and did not make that call. He agreed only to conduct his own investigation into Agnus Day. If he should find sufficient proof, he would act.'

Brother Jolusa jerks forward, his mouth tight as an anus. 'I ask you, where was this agent's faith? Was he so far fallen that he should demand proof! Faith is belief in the absence of proof!'

He sinks back. 'But Bex was not prepared to listen.' A smile rises. 'So what use were those ears of his?' The smile lets laughter escape, like smoke beneath a door. 'So you know what Judas did? He pulled his knife and in two strokes he sliced those ears clean off Agent Bex's head.'

The laughter erupts into a roar. 'One two, one two and through and through . . . !' The old monk claps a hand upon his thigh, throwing back his rotten head and bellowing with delight. Until his eyes catch Judas, whose head is bowed and quivering.

Brother Jolusa swallows his last guffaw. '. . . a vile act, of course, for which Judas immediately repented.'

Judas grunts, his voice low. 'I found a church and I fell to my knees.'

'And there I found him. In the White Lily of the Trinity, that little church beside the old soap factory.' The monk turns to Lola. 'Perhaps you know it?' She shakes her head and Brother Jolusa smiles. 'Of course you don't. One such as you, so young, so lithe and healthy.' His baggy eyes linger on her body. 'The Lily of the Trinity is famed as a place of holy cure. I went there seeking a miracle – and found Judas. A miracle indeed.'

His gloved hand dabs his chin, careful not to dislodge the rotten flesh that still clings. 'Judas told me of his discovery and of what had come to pass with Agent Bex. I assured him that I would help. I would insist that SCURO offered more than just a promise to investigate Agnus Day. I would make Agent Bex take action.'

Jolusa taps his gloved fingers against the arm of his throne. 'But that course of action is no longer open to us. Because Agent Bex is dead.'

Lola snaps her head up, eyes locked on the monk now as he struggles to his feet.

'And as a consequence, action falls to us.' Yellow eyes sink down to Lola. 'And to you.'

'Me?'

'Judas and I must go to Morphic Fields and effect the release of Agnus Day. You must halt the Legion of Gehenna.'

'At the risk of repeating myself . . . *me*?'

Brother Jolusa signals to Judas. 'Restore her weapons to her.' Then he turns with a flash of black teeth. 'You will not face the Legion in its entirety – although from what I hear, a Hunter such as you would relish those odds. By tradition, the Legion selects one from their number to seek and awaken the Mosca. It is deemed quite the honour. So you find that glorious G-Man and finish him, before he completes his task.'

'You know who the G-Man is?'

'We are certain of it.' Jolusa shuffles close. Lola shrinks from the warm, wet stench. 'It is the deceiver, the duplicitous defector . . . it is Dali.'

Lola feels her fists instinctively clench. 'You're wrong.'

'We expected some resistance. You and Dali were close. Like father and daughter.'

'Like Hunter and Handler.'

'He favoured you. And yet you weren't the best.'

'He must have thought I was good enough.'

'I don't think it was your goodness that appealed to him. Quite the opposite.'

Now Judas appears at her side, whispering hard against her ear. 'For centuries, a Hunter has not broken ranks. And then you go rogue. Strange, indeed. Then, stranger still, Hunter 696B departs. But this is what intrigues us the most,

Hunter 696B is a far more fearsome predator than you and yet the High Command of the Sinestra devote all their attention to your loss. Because even the High Command suspect that Dali played a part in it.'

'He played no part.'

Judas smiles. 'Still so loyal!'

Lola thins her lips, cracking each word with the precision of a whip. 'He . . . played . . . no . . . part.'

'And yet he is deeply involved with your retrieval.' He thuds a mission file against her chest. 'My orders to kill you. Signed by Dali.'

Lola grabs the file, throws it to the floor. Judas tenses, eyes wild as he lurches forward. But Brother Jolusa raises his gloved hand, halting him.

'From the moment Dali offered to shield our holy books, there were those within the Chiro Scuro who suspected him. We believed he had a secret motive. He was looking for information. Some gobbet, deciphered from our texts, that would allow him to predict the Mosca's rise.'

Brother Jolusa rolls up his hood, turning to Judas. 'Did you not hear me? I said return her weapons.' His gloved hand jerks and Judas reaches into the shadows. He pulls out a belted cache of guns and knives. Slings it to the floor.

The old monk turns and, although the hood masks his eyes, Lola can feel them upon her. Like thumbs, pushing down.

'Who knows how long you have, child. By leaving the Sinestra, you condemned yourself to live off just your last dose of span. Unless you had the forethought to bring a supply with you?' The head within the hood cocks, awaiting an answer. Then slowly shakes when none comes. 'So then, the clock is ticking. Put whatever time you have remaining to good use. Serve the cause of righteousness and deliver us from Dali.'

Judas offers his arm for support as the old monk shuffles towards the door, one final question slipping free.

'Ask yourself this, child. What do you really know of him?'

And then, the door creaks. And they are gone.

Lola stands alone. Her weapons about her. The *Fuga* spread on the floor. And the door open.

She could just take her guns and leave. Or take her guns, shoot the old man and maybe even the Judas dude – and leave. That sounded all right.

Or she could take a moment and think things through. It has always been her weakness that she acts first, thinks later.

'Ah, cher, those trigger-wits of yours . . .'

Lola grunts, something close to a laugh. Maybe the old man is right. What the fuck does she know of Dali?

What can I remember?

She closes her eyes, summoning an image of Dali's long face. But the image is hazy. Her memories of the Sinestra had not been touched by Fan Fan. But just as when you cut out a tumour, you have to excise a lot of good tissue around it. So she had lost many memories of Dali and her time in the Hypogeum.

And what she does remember is random, snatched . . . dreamlike. Like *Alice's Adventures in Wonderland*.

'Off with his head!' That was the Queen of Hearts.

Dali always carried a pack of playing cards. With the gold insignia of the Sinestra upon the reverse: two long keys, back to back with their teeth turned out, the two loops together like eyes. A skull, is what Lola always saw. And she saw this design every day. It was painted on every door along the corridor where the Hunters had their quarters. Identical doors, stretching down Kingsway, like a pack of cards laid out in a line of Solitaire. She counted the occupied quarters once and, by coincidence, there were fifty-two Hunters currently in service.

Their rooms are simple, almost monastic. But the food is good and the Sinestra provides meticulous medical care.

And the confines of the rooms matter little. Most Hunters spend their days in the training arena, constantly sharpening their fight skills. Knowing that their Tormenta foe will be doing the same.

But as Lola walks that corridor, with the occasional Hunter lifting their head to glance at who passes, she knows what controls their loyalty. Their hatred of Tormenta makes them fight, but what keeps them obediently returning to the Sinestra for the rest of their lives is life itself.

As long as they serve, they will be served span. And their life will be infinite.

And whilst the life of a Hunter may be hard, the Sinestra offer a better proposition than many of the other Lo'World divisions where misfits such as they – neither dead nor alive – eek out eternity.

Lola continues along the corridor to a staircase that spirals down towards the training arena. The metal shudders under the heavy boots of Hunters that descend in silence.

Lola looks down at her own feet. They are bare. She wiggles her filthy toes.

Maybe train later.

That's the thing about forever. There's always later.

She swerves left past the staircase and towards a giant set of doors at the end of the corridor. The gold-scripted sign above the arch reads: 'Archivum'.

A PAIR OF SNAKESKIN BOOTS stride down the dull vinyl floors of the Hypogeum. The heels are spurred with rowels made from spinning hearts. Although as they spin and invert, they look more like spades.

The boots enter the Archivum and halt by the Senior Archivist's front desk. The hairless little man raises his head and stokes his welcome with as much fury as the rule of silence will allow.

Dali smiles and nods, aware of what provokes his

irritation. He follows the Archivist's laser gaze to a table in the centre.

It holds a pile of books, stacked high on all three sides like a barricade. The ancient gold text on each spine reads 'Collegio Romano'.

From behind the books comes the rhythmic buzz of ear-buds and the occasional involuntary half-sung phrase. Dali reaches across and withdraws a stack, revealing a pair of bare feet, perched on the table.

Lola sits behind, a book open on her lap, tapping a pencil to the bass-line. She smiles as she sees Dali and pops out her buds.

'Hey, Père D.'

Dali glances back towards the Archivist who ogles them above his spectacles.

'He doesn't like you playing music.'

Lola exhales and punches off her player.

'He doesn't like you marking the books.'

Lola lays down her pencil.

'He doesn't like . . . you.'

Lola gasps, faking horror.

Dali patiently clasps his hands behind his back. 'Yo' could make yourself more popular by adherin' to the simplest rules. For example, keeping to your appointed collection time.'

He produces a glass vial that shimmers with a blue liquid. 'Word reached me yo' forgot your dose.'

Lola takes the vial, uncorks it and downs the span in one gulp. Dali nods, satisfied. 'I'd be most grateful if yo' could remember to attend. My duties don't include Room Service.'

Lola returns the vial to him. 'You know, Père D, the fact that I forget should make you happy.'

'And yet I feel no such elation.'

Lola leans forward, pressing home her point. 'First thing most Hunters do on their return is claim their span, because that's what keeps them coming back. The fact that I forget must mean that I'm happy just to be here.'

Dali runs a hand down the pillar of books. '. . . and always right here.' His fingertip taps the top book. 'What are yo' looking for, cher?'

Lola shrugs, leans back. 'Maybe nothing . . . maybe everything.' She thuds shut a huge book in her lap. The cover's title reads *Codex Gigas*. 'Don't you think Hunters should stretch their brains?'

'They should tend their wounds.' Dali points to a recent scar at the cusp of her left breast. It has an unhealthy yellowish tinge. 'That looks odd.'

'Next mission I'll take a bullet to the other one and make them even.' Lola tugs down her vest, making her point but revealing more skin than Dali finds comfortable.

He twists his head away, masking the movement with an averted cough. Then he snatches up another topic. 'I also hear that yo' have been absent from training.'

Lola rises now. Leans deep across the table. 'With the greatest respect, so what?' Leans deeper still, their faces almost touching. 'I've never failed on a hit. I'm as fast as I need to be.'

Dali holds her gaze. They are chin to chin. 'Confidence close to arrogance.'

Lola inches closer. 'And which one are you?'

HER EYES BOLT OPEN, the memory vanishing. She looks about the old crypt. Something echoes from its walls. A sound she knows too well: the rasp of metal on bone.

Her hands whip about her body and, clad with weapons, she exits the crypt into the catacombs beyond. The low tunnel, as if blown like an instrument, delivers a dreadful sound. Heavy sobbing.

Gun drawn, Lola pursues the sound, to discover in an alcove the shuddering robes of Brother Jolusa. He is hunched over the body of Judas, his breath coming in sharp jags as if he is performing some effortful task. At the sound of her approach, his hood swivels round and he gathers Judas to him. The naked torso is wrought with wounds. Brother Jolusa inhales and sobs again.

Lola sinks to Judas's side. His skin is still warm, but he is dead. The weapon still impales his heart. With a quivering hand, Brother Jolusa pulls it clear.

It is Dali's clave.

Teeth gritted with grief, he thrusts it before Lola. 'You know this device! Is it not proof enough?'

But Lola's focus is not on the clave. It is on the hand that clenches it. The old monk's glove has been removed, revealing a contorted claw, twisted not from disease but an ancient burn. Jolusa hurriedly drops the clave and sinks his limb once more into the leather. Then he gathers Judas into his lap, stroking his hair.

'Dali's name was once Tret. And our name defines our destiny. Dali was ever the traitor!'

His eyes flash beneath his hood, finding Lola. Burning deep.

Lola nods. Slings her rifle across her back and exits into the dark night.

30

THE BACK SEAT of the Ford Tahoe smells of cinnamon and vanilla. Mo'Zart has had time enough to enjoy this sweetness. His face, slicked with sweat, has been stuck to the leather for over six hours.

Donuts. Someone sat here and ate donuts. And there's a whiff of coffee. *Damn, I'd love a hot, black . . .*

He winces and his fingers subtly rise to explore the back of his skull. It oozes blood like jam. An hour before, a similar blast of pain had brought him back to consciousness. But he's keeping his wakeful state to himself, until he can remember what happened at the Treble Belly Diner and how he ended up in this car. And whether the two cops up front intend to help him – or harm him. So for now, he's going to keep his busted head down.

A man's voice comes from the driver's seat. 'How much further?'

Bianco lolls on the passenger side, her seat reclined. 'Not far.'

'I haven't seen one sign for Swamp Gravy.'

'It's hard to find. It's a hideaway.'

The Tahoe rolls to a halt at a fork in the road. Two dirt tracks wiggle away through the heavy undergrowth.

'Which way?'

'That way.' Bianco jerks a hand to the left. Siggurson wrenches the wheel, churning mud as Bianco suddenly throws her hand to the right. 'No, other way.'

Siggurson stabs the brake, kinks an eyebrow.

Bianco shrugs. 'Didn't I just say – it's hard to find? And most times I'm driving. Kinda automatic pilot. And o' course most times I'm not distracted by a bomb-site where my biceps used to be.' She points to a wound on her arm, crudely choked by a neck-tie.

The Tahoe swings to the right and Mo'Zart lurches across the back seat. He knows who these cops are; it was his job to set up the briefing session. They are hard-core homicide detectives, both with reputations for getting results. He's read their histories. So he knows that he had better fill in the gaps of his own recent past – and fast.

He remembers arriving at the Treble Belly Diner . . . spying those blond dreads in the back booth. He sits with her, takes a gulp of the coffee that she has waiting for him. It tastes weird, kinda like cherries. He remembers talking and talking – and then a blast of pain.

He grits his jaw, bracing himself against the back of the seat as the road turns rocky and the chassis bucks and bounces.

Siggurson grips the wheel like a bronco rider. Glances at Bianco, who clamps a hand to her wound.

'Still raw?'

'Like sushi.'

He turns his eyes back to the road. It's fast sinking into mud. In the distance, across the bayou, is a lone hut on chicken-leg stilts.

'This is where we're going, Baba Yaga's shack?' He shakes his head. 'I'm trusting you on this.'

'You made the decision not to call for back-up at the factory. The right decision. But from that moment, we put ourselves off the radar and now we have to stay that way. At least until we know who ordered that strike and who the intended target was.'

'But that gives us a few days at most. Then your chief and mine are going to start asking questions about where we are.'

Bianco shakes her head and smiles. 'Ah, young Skywalker, you have so much to learn.' She reclines back in the seat. 'SCURO will have tied that off before you even got the summons. As far as your chief knows, you've been seconded for a special operation. Too high up for him to have clearance. No information on when you'll be back . . . *if* you'll be back.'

Siggurson turns in his seat now to face her. 'All right, Einstein, so you gonna tell me how you know so much about SCURO?'

Bianco rests her head against the cool of the window, feeling that familiar bayou heat rise on her neck, sink down her thighs. She shifts on the leather. 'I could tell you a whole lotta things, Bambi. But better that you ask Lola.'

'Who's Lola?'

She jerks her head towards the cabin. 'You can make that your first question.'

'And what about him?' Siggurson glances at the body of Mo'Zart on the back seat. 'He may wear a SCURO badge, but his key let the killer in. You think he knows anything?'

'He doesn't know how to keep his mouth shut, that's for sure. But I'd say she loosened him up.'

'He was drugged?'

Bianco sniffs the air hard. 'You're not getting that? Pentathium oxide. Smells like cherry pie. One dose and this little virgin woulda told her anything.'

'I don't think so.' Siggurson shakes his head. 'Pentathium oxide leaves crystal deposits at the corner of the mouth.'

Bianco hikes herself around to get a better look at Mo'Zart's inert face. 'I see crystals.'

'That's cane sugar.'

'It's Pentathium crystals. I aced you in chem class, remember that?'

'I remember what sugar looks like.'

'All right, so you want me to taste his face? Cos I will. I will taste that kid's face.'

Mo'Zart launches upwards, suddenly wide awake. 'She's right. Detective Bianco is right. There was something in my coffee. Tasted like cherries.'

Bianco blips a *told you* at Siggurson and then turns her eyes to Mo'Zart. 'Kid, you got instant likeability.'

She looks back to the window. They have reached the bayou's edge.

A large, brown hand pulls open the passenger door. Fan Fan's head, piled high with yellow hair, bobs into the car. Her eyes go straight to Siggurson. 'He's pretty.'

'He's a cop.'

'He's a pretty cop. And you're a pretty cop. Now ain't that somethin'?'

Bianco grimaces and moves to exit. The old woman still hovers at the door. 'Fan Fan, may I?'

'Cher, if you don't, I sure will.' The old woman cackles, her smile just for Siggurson. Until she sees Mo'Zart shuffle out of the back door.

Her eyes sweep up and down his scrawny frame, then she throws a question over her shoulder to Bianco. 'Your lunch got a name?'

'That's Agent Mo'Zart. We're keeping him on ice. In case we need him.' Bianco unhooks the rope of the raft, ready to make the drift across the bayou. Glances up towards Lola's cabin. 'She around?'

Fan Fan appears behind her. 'No, child. She's been gone fo' a while.' Bianco tightens her grip about the rope. 'She'll be all right. She always is.'

Bianco looks up to see Siggurson arrive beside her. She tosses him the punt pole. 'I'm guessing you'll be great at this.'

Minutes later, Fan Fan is leading the way in her own boat, rippling across the soft waters as dusk descends. In the raft behind, Bianco and Mo'Zart sit either side of Siggurson, who slowly punts.

Bianco loosens the neck-tie about her arm, probing the wound. 'So, skipper, with Lola gone, I'm gonna have to do my best to make you understand this weird new world you just walked into. And you, kid' – she jerks her head at Mo'Zart – 'you gotta back me up, because it takes some very powerful persuasion to grip a human mind and make it open . . . make it listen to truths beyond imagining.'

Siggurson lets the punt trail in the water. Looks at Bianco. 'So what made you listen?'

'Big fat gun.'

Siggurson smiles. 'Well, I've got nowhere else to go. And not much else to believe in. So let's start.'

Mo'Zart cautiously raises a hand. Bianco shrugs. 'What's that, a bathroom request?'

'I was just . . . just going to suggest that maybe we start with the incident that brought Detective Siggurson to SCURO's attention.'

'You read my report, kid. You already know why I was there.'

Bianco leans forward. 'Maybe he does. But I don't.'

Siggurson nods, and looks out at the bayou as if searching for the right place to begin.

'There was a psychiatrist, a woman, Dr Jellowitz. She was hired by the Commissioner to counsel officers who suffer trauma on duty. Maybe guilt that they failed to save a victim, or maybe they shot and killed the wrong person. The stats on uniform suicides are rising.'

Bianco leans forward, instantly hooked.

'But there was something not right about Dr Jellowitz. I couldn't put my finger on it. Nothing specific. Just that . . . the questions she asked, the way she probed . . . as if her intention was to dig the hurt deeper.'

He pauses, and then punts the pole harder, continuing. 'So I decide to do some digging on her. Find out her background. And I come up with nothing. The only information I can get is that since she started acting as the precinct psychiatrist, the suicide rate has gone up. Two officers in ten months. So I tell this to the Chief. But he blows it off. And nothing changes. She's still practising.

Then one night, by chance, I see her out in the parking lot of a bar. And I confront her. "Who are you, lady? Because my gut says you're no psychiatrist." And she answers my gut pretty directly, with this hammer blow. Next thing I know, I am fighting a woman. Which goes against everything I am, but on this occasion she's turning what I am into pulp and unless I fight back, she's going to kill me. She had such a fist on her . . . and speed. Unbelievable. Then she whacked me hard in the back of the skull and I fell.'

Siggurson pulls the raft to a halt as it comes alongside the cabin. 'I made a report. And a few months later, I get the call from SCURO.'

Mo'Zart claps his hands on his thighs, his confidence thawing. 'That's absolutely correct. SCURO had their suspicions about Jellowitz. And you confirmed them.' He uncurls his thin legs and follows Bianco, who steps up from the raft and on to the porch.

The soft wood bends as Siggurson squats to tie up the raft. 'So who is she?'

Mo'Zart tentatively swings an arm about Siggurson's shoulder as they mount the steps. 'Dude, let me tell you a lil' somethin' about girls like her.'

FIVE LONG HOURS LATER, Siggurson lies awake on the porch swing. A small, floral quilt suggests that this has been turned into his bed for the night. From one end of the frame, a lamp dangles. But Siggurson's eyes are set on the glitter of stars above as inside his skull, his brain sparks with an explosion of new information. A fresh vision of the world. He shifts a hand behind his head like a pillow, staring out into space. That one question we've all asked: are there other beings out there? Suddenly it is answered. Yes, there are other life forms. But they're not out there. They are right here. Walking amongst us. Looking like us, acting like us, silently planning. Patiently waiting.

Bianco and Mo'Zart had given him a moment to absorb

the existence of Tormenta. Sat around the fire, empty bottles of Old Artemis glowing with reflected flames, he knew they were being patient. Probably remembering how they had reacted, when they first heard.

Siggurson's reaction was to shoot off a mag of questions.

'So Tormenta live for centuries and they don't decay. But their bones must show age under the microscope. That means if a Tormenta's body were ever found and a pathologist got hold of it, the bones would show the body to be unnaturally old. They'd be exposed.'

Mo'Zart had fielded this one, leaning back. 'Sometimes Tormenta do make mistakes, they fail to feed and they die. And sometimes Hunters neglect to properly dispose of a body after a kill. But for all the times that this has occurred, it has never exposed the existence of Tormenta. Because neither the Sinestra nor SCURO wants that. Mankind is to be protected. Tell him the truth and he may try to fight back himself, which would mean inevitable defeat. So if a Tormenta body falls into human hands, that event is concealed.'

Bianco, stripped down to her vest, is dousing her wounded arm with the liquor. 'That was how I first got hooked into this. I was investigating the homicide of a club-owner called Gina Avner. She was a Tormenta – not that I knew – plying this Goth girl death-is-beautiful grift. Teenagers fall like plums if you squeeze them right. And Gina was good. Then she turns up dead in my precinct morgue and the pathologist laughs as he shows me the bone report. This kid is one hundred and ninety years old. Now back then, that result struck me as pretty funny too. And I'm thinking, damn, this case is getting weirder and weirder, because just a few months before we'd had a report of a suicide in Gina's club. A girl called Maddy Pool. But when we got there, no Maddy. No body at all – just a carbon burn ring on the floor. So I make my report and next thing I know my chief tells me SCURO are taking over the investigation and I'm to keep this' – she twitches her nose – 'clean and clear out of it. Then I get the summons to the debrief and I'm smelling the lilies.'

'So you're telling me no one has ever retained evidence of them?'

Bianco shrugged. 'Tormenta know what they're doing. They're good. They never stay long in any one place because a grift can only play for a while before it starts to draw attention, like you sniffing out Dr Jello-tits.'

'They have to keep moving, like sharks.' Mo'Zart uncorked a fresh bottle, offered it to Siggurson. 'If they hang around, not only would their grift grow old, but people would start to notice that they don't age.'

He twirled a finger through his dreads as if unwinding this information directly from his brain. 'They are born into human bodies and, just like the rest of us, that body can dictate what you do in life. Let's say you're a Tormenta and you find yourself in the body of a pretty little girl. The smart thing may be to hit fifteen and stick. Because there's a bunch of grifts that are gonna work for you: the Little Lolita, the Heartbreaker, the Jump-a-Juvie —'

'The what?'

'It's a popular one. You seduce a nice family man, then drop the bomb that you're under age. That turns a momentary lapse into statutory rape. Just add whiskey and a gun and, most times, you got span. Or let me give you another example. You're a guy, prone to fat, not so fine-looking. You might decide that a little grey at the temples and some senior swagger will generate the best grifts for you. So you let your human body age until you reach just the right amount of reassuring seniority. Then you can ply something like the Gimme-All-You-Got grift. You hide yourself in society as an investment broker and wait until a nice rich client entrusts you with their fortune. You keep them happy with some fake paper profits for a while and then, when you need your next hit of span, you pull the plug and they lose everything. Most rich folks would rather eat a bullet than starve in the gutter. So, boom – span. I could go on, but you get the picture.'

'So if they keep taking span, let's say more than they need just to live, can they get younger again?'

Mo'Zart shook his head. 'No. But they'd sure like that capability. There's much about their bodies they don't understand – just like we don't understand how cancer happens or why belly-fat sticks. And like us, Tormenta are always trying to figure out ways to evolve and become even better. But so far, they don't know how to use span to reverse the ageing process.'

'But they do know about spandex.' Bianco chucked her empty bottle on the pile.

'What?'

Mo'Zart turned to Siggurson. 'She means SpanDX. This is, I guess you could say, a form of synthetic span.'

'Which would be needed to feed the Hunters. Because they are part-Tormenta.'

'Bang on, Bambi my man. You're gettin' this fast!' Mo'Zart rolled a gappy smile. 'All right, so listen to this. The Sinestra laboured long and hard to develop an extract of span that could be used, kinda like fuel, to top up a Hunter's tank. They tried many formulas, working under the project code name of Dextra . . . kind of an opposite play on Sinestra, I guess. And, finally, the tenth formulation worked. And span Dextra Ten became spanDX.'

Bianco raised her bottle with a smile. 'Hence spandex. It stretches your life.'

Mo'Zart looked at Siggurson. 'You've known her a while, was she always this funny?'

'No, it's a new symptom.'

Bianco ignored them, pressing on. 'You know my first question? How come Tormenta don't just get together, overwhelm humanity and set us up like farm animals. Then they can just milk us for span. Forget all about their grifts and take the easy route. It's like us having to persuade a cow to die so we can get the meat, instead of just smashing its skull.'

Siggurson nodded. 'Smart question. And the answer is . . . ?'

'Kinda scary.' Mo'Zart grinned and then fell strangely silent.

His eyes lowered to the last of his liquor as he swilled it round the bottle, in no hurry to deliver this final revelation. Then he stiffened his spine, sunk his drink and continued. 'Like I told you, Tormenta are sharks. They hunt alone. And they defend their territory against other Tormenta who may try to come in and feed in their waters. This competition and distrust amongst them has prevented them from ever operating in unison. But if a Tormenta were to rise with the power to unite them, to show them how different the world would be if they worked as one force . . . then everything would change. And mankind would be finished.'

Mo'Zart looked up now, mouth tight. 'The book I was translating . . . the *Kata*. It predicts that this Tormenta will rise and lead his kind to domination. A messiah called the Mosca.'

'Hey, those flies are gonna bite ya.'

Siggurson jerks, almost falling off the swing. Bianco is standing above him, pointing to the lantern. It swarms with insects.

She reaches out and kills the flame, plunging the porch into darkness. Only the moon illuminates them now.

Siggurson hoists himself up on to his elbow. 'You can't sleep?'

'This kinda stings.' She tweaks her arm, now bound in clean cotton.

'Let me see it.' He beckons her closer.

'Big feet. Big hands. You don't look so gentle.'

Siggurson smiles. 'Trust me.'

Bianco lowers herself on to the quilt, unwraps her wound. With careful fingers, Siggurson probes the tender split. 'The tissue has a lot of previous scar damage. You been caught here before?'

Bianco winces. 'Maybe. I don't remember.' She feels him probe deeper. Grits her teeth to talk. 'So anyway, doctor, I got a question. How come you knew about that other doctor, the psychiatrist?'

'I was referred to her for therapy.'

Bianco jolts. Not from pain this time, but surprise. Her voice stays cool. 'You were seeing a shrink?'

'My chief made it mandatory. To check my emotional status, I think that's what they called it.'

Bianco silently suffers the discomfort of him rebinding the wound. Feels she can't make a sound in case a question escapes.

But as Siggurson ties the last knot, he takes her shoulders and turns her towards him. Knowing what she is burning to ask.

'When my mother was shot, I was with her. The bullet passed through her body, impacted my head and lodged inside my skull. The doctors told my father that the best option – the only option – was to leave the bullet in there. It may not move. It may stay in one place for ever. In which case, I will live.'

'And if it does move?'

'Then I'm dead.'

Bianco looks away. His calm is unsettling her. 'But then why become a cop? Why do a job that gets your head cracked every goddamn day? Why not do something quiet: work in a library, in a bookstore . . .'

'And what – die a little every day?' Siggurson shakes his head, smiles. 'I'd rather live myself to death.'

His finger traces a scar down her neck. And then slides to her shoulder where another old wound still leaves its bite. 'You're not so very different. Throwing yourself into the front line every time. You've fought every sort of psycho.'

'But you've fought a Tormenta. That's pretty impressive.' She feels the heat of his eyes upon her. 'I haven't . . . not yet.' Swallows hard, forcing a laugh. 'So I guess, once again, you've gotten there first, Siggurson.'

His hand is still on her shoulder. The touch is light but to Bianco it feels as if gravity is sucking his skin into hers. She makes her mouth speak. 'So, tell me about it. What was it like?'

'I don't remember much. It was so fast. Unreal. I'd never seen anyone move like that. Like her limbs were on fire. And when she hit me, the force of it . . . but then I landed a blow. Just here.' His hand touches Bianco's sternum. 'And I felt her skin. Just for a split second. But it was warm, soft. Then she threw me back. I hit a wall. She thought I was knocked out. She let her guard down, just for a moment. But I took it. Pulled my gun and got a bullet away. I saw it draw blood from her, just here . . .' His hand is now on on the curve of Bianco's neck.

She shivers at his touch. Breathes deep. 'Then what happened?'

'She spun me round . . .' His fingers trail down to Bianco's breast, circles its soft cusp. '. . . and she hit me.'

Bianco's voice is just a whisper. 'Where?'

'Just here.' Siggurson takes her hand and places it on his cheek.

'And then?' Bianco leans in deep, mouth open.

Siggurson descends. 'I fell.'

31

Lᴏʀᴅ Cʜᴀɴᴄᴇʟʟᴏʀ Vᴀꜱꜱᴀɢᴏ ʟᴜʀᴋꜱ ɪɴ ᴛʜᴇ ꜱʜᴀᴅᴏᴡꜱ. His back is against a set of iron doors that shudder and boom.

Although he has never passed into the room behind, he knows what lies there. Huge cylinders that drive the Helix Vivat.

The carved sign above the doors declares the room as the 'Ingenium'. Vassago has previously pondered on this rich and ancient term. The word 'engine' shares the same stem as the word 'ingenious' and appropriately so. Just as an engine pumps away, so a mind will churn ideas.

Vassago's fingers idle by the lock. The only key to the Ingenium is in Dali's charge.

Ah, Dali, what pistons of ingenuity pump and plot within your mind? Why do you spend so long in the Helix Vivat chamber?

Though this question may tantalise, it does not trouble Vassago. A mere trifle compared to the greater question he has concerning Dali.

What madness caused Dali to first betray the Legion of Gehenna?

Vassago would never forget that fateful day, one summer in 1857.

He and Dali had been bestowed the greatest honour by the Legion: the task to seek out and awaken the Mosca. For the first time in centuries, the Legion had succeeded in finding the human vessel ahead of the Sinestra. The sign had been clear. An explosion had occurred at a munitions plant called Harris Cox. The factory sign blazed bright in the flames, burned down to the last length, which now just read 'S COX'. And amongst the mayhem of staggering, blackened victims caught in the blast, there walked a small boy. He dragged a burning toy in his hand, a wooden puppet of a bird – a stork. At the sight of it, Vassago had gasped in excitement. Without doubt, the harbinger: Scox.

Dali gathers the child and with Vassago at his side, he bears him away to a quiet spot and raises his clave above the boy's chest.

He pauses, hearing the distant, distraught shrieks of the child's mother, searching for her boy.

Before Vassago can stop him, Dali ushers the child up, slapping his legs hard to propel him out of the darkness and towards his mother, who gathers him up with wrenching sobs.

Vassago stares at Dali, aghast. 'You have condemned us both!'

Their defection to the Sinestra was the only path now open to them. Despite an instinctive reluctance to absorb these one-time enemies, the High Command of the Sinestra knew that their inside knowledge of the Legion of Gehenna would prove invaluable.

Vassago shivers as if waking from a dream. His eyes flash wide, and then narrow to slits as they glimpse a shadow, moving between the pipes of the Helix Vivat.

Vassago slides into the light. Coughs discreetly, then: 'Dali?'

The familiar lean silhouette emerges, buttoning his jacket. 'Vassago.'

'During office hours, I'd prefer you to use my title.'

'O'course, Lord Chancellor.'

Vassago never tires of the strum of those words across his heart. The many painful years spent in Dali's shadow are now just a distant memory.

He would like to think that his promotion is testament to his greater qualities. But deep down Vassago knows the truth. Dali's brilliance will always outshine him. It is only the quirks and foibles exhibited since he joined the Sinestra that have made Dali unsuitable for promotion. It was struggle enough for the rank and file of the Sinestra to accept the admission of two Tormenta. But they had no alternative. They needed these defectors if they were ever to get an answer to the question that plagues them.

Who are the Legion of Gehenna and what is their true purpose?

The actions of the Legion run counter to Tormenta behaviour. As a species, they are loners and ferociously territorial. They do not welcome the arrival of other Tormenta on their patch. And yet the Legion quests tirelessly to awaken more and more of them.

Vassago's instinct was to immediately divulge everything to the Sinestra, so great was his desperation to find sanctuary. The Legion were no doubt already in pursuit. But Dali, of course, kept his heels cool. He assured full disclosure, in time. And promised that when they understood what credo drove the Legion, they would find both him and Vassago endlessly valuable . . . and eternally grateful.

And so the years had passed with Dali keeping himself to himself and Vassago slowly, surely rising up the ladder, surpassing his former master.

Oh unsurpassable joy!

He casually strolls forward, allowing his hand to trail long the giant banks of oscilloscopes that map every pulse of the Spanorama. He watches for Dali's quake of displeasure. Vassago knows how Dali hates anyone to touch his beloved machine.

'Why do I find you here, Dali?'

'Perhaps because yo' are looking.'

Vassago taps one of the flashing scopes. 'And what are you looking for?'

Dali's eyes go to the glass gauges that dance green, like living emeralds. 'I find it beautiful.'

'To the untrained eye, I do agree it is a mesmerising miasma. Each pulse and wave crashing to the next. But what might the trained eye see?' Vassago leans in deep towards one scope. The green light bathes his face, giving him a deathly pallor. 'Do you recall, in our former lives when we were so misguided and misruled . . . our doctrine was quite contrary, even in the smallest detail, to that of the Sinestra. For example, in the Legion we were told that span does in fact hold a memory of its former self. And this being so, it would theoretically be possible to track one particular skein of span and follow its arrival into human form. You recall that lesson, do you not, Dali?'

'I recall my lessons in grammar and rhetorical questions do not require an answer.' Dali moves to walk on but Vassago side-steps, blocking his path.

'But my real question is this. What do you believe, Dali? Given time, could this machine track one skein of span all the way through to the human realm?'

'With patience, all is possible. And now, Lord Chancellor, I have a question of my own. What is your intent in coming here?'

Vassago rolls his neck like a goose. 'Intent? That's too harsh. I come in hope.' He jerks a smile. 'You and I, we are the same, Dali. We should be allies, not enemies.'

'You are my enemy? I am most grateful fo' that clarification.'

Vassago stiffens. Forcing his smile wider. 'Ah, how we joust, we two!' He leans forward, pulling Dali close to him in a cold embrace. 'You can trust me.' Grasps him tighter still. 'For we two are one.'

Something in Dali's body pulses. Like an unsheathing knife, he pulls himself free from Vassago's embrace.

In insolent silence he exits.

Vassago feels spittle gathering in the corners of his mouth. Swallows it down, smoothing a calm expression across his face. Turns to a shadow that silently appears behind him.

'I think my point is made, sir. He defies *The Manifestum*, which clearly states that span has no memory of itself. He is, for want of a better word, a heretic. And a dangerous heretic. For he can be searching for only one measure of span . . . and you and I both know what that is.'

A head of white hair appears. The height and extravagance of the wig reveals that this is the Commander General of the Sinestra. He walks forward, hands clasped tight behind his back.

'Increase the surveillance. If he makes a move . . .' The Commander General hesitates, as if the evidence before him somehow jars with his gut instincts.

'. . . I am authorised to act?' Vassago keenly completes the order.

Silently, the Commander General nods.

32

A MATCH SPARKS, then drops into a glass ashtray. A sheet of paper catches alight, curling tight in the flame.

Words written in thick ink cover the paper, but the fire gnaws at every edge. The opening line is already gone. The following sentence is consumed up to:

the police case notes, discovered three years ago by Judas. These documents suggest that the root of Agnus Day's madness lay in the fact that he never grieved for his daughter. Instead he threw himself into his study of telomeres. When he could not break the link between immortality and cancer, he grew steadily mad. It was at this time that he began to believe that he was seeing the ghost of his daughter. The image of a young girl would appear at his window, sometimes leaving messages written in the condensation of the glass.

Every message says the same: that he must take his own life and join her.

All evidence in his laboratory suggested that he obeyed this ghostly command. But no corpse was found, just a carbon ring. This is because the 'ghost' at his window was an artful Tormenta called Jezebeth Hooger. She saw the opportunity to exploit the loss of his daughter and taunt this wretched man to suicide. On that fateful night she waited in the shadows for him to place the noose around his neck.

But Jezebeth was inexperienced. She knew the dangers of snatching a span too soon, but all the same she lost patience as his body twitched and spasmed. Her haste meant that he was delivered to the Sinestra and was returned to Earth as a Hunter. For years he performed his duties well. No longer the frail man he had been, he stood strong and fearsome. His only weakness was the memory of his daughter. No amount of mental training at the hands of the Sinestra could erase her memory. But the Hunter did a good job of keeping his pain hidden, leading his handlers to believe that he was done with his human past.

Then one day, in a filthy skin-joint, he sees a girl dancing in a cage. She looks so much like his daughter, his heart pounds. He drinks heavily, eyes locked upon her swaying body. He doesn't know what animal urge is driving him – grief, lust, anger – but he slides money across the bar, enough to buy her for the night. The girl is Jezebeth.

She's plying her new grift; seducing men and then exposing her tender age. She's had some good success, with quite a few family guys, God-fearing salesmen and the like, who'll gas themselves in a garage sooner than face a charge of statutory rape.

Jezebeth doesn't recognise the man who buys her that particular night.

But it is done. A Hunter and his original Tormenta are reunited.

The result was the madness of Agnus and the murder of Jezebeth. Bloody and brutal and most bizarre. For when they found her carved-up corpse, it bore a prophecy, written in blood and ink. An account of the end of mankind.

And so it is that I suspect the greatest mystery may be solved. That this forbidden union is indeed the first step towards . . .

Flames gust upwards, snatching the last words away, crackling them to ash. A silhouette relaxes back behind a desk. Reaches for a deck of cards. Shuffles slowly.

Fascinating. Perfectly fascinating . . .

A card is selected from the centre of the pack. Laid face-up on the desk. The Ace of Hearts.

What are the chances!

A long finger strokes the gold edge of the card. This chance is real. And so close. The chance to infinitely change this world and the next, for ever.

And so . . .

It is time to leave the Hypogeum.

In truth, he quite enjoyed his last perambulation. The pomegranate martini was surprisingly good. So he will walk abroad again.

Not walk of course. He will ride. And in some style.

Humans may be pitiful, but for their invention of the automobile, they deserve praise.

Particularly for the grace and might of the Mercedes Maybach.

A marvellous machine.

33

THE PEAK OF A CHAUFFEUR'S CAP TILTS DOWN.
A hand nudges it back up. The cap is too big. Maybe
because she's a woman. And maybe because the cap was
made for her father. Mercedes Toolan comes from a long
line of drivers. Her father named her after his favourite
manufacturer and probably set her destiny there and then.
But she loves her job. Even on nights like this.

She tips the cap back once again, hauling the car off
road.

This wasteland is known as the Wrips. An abandoned
dockside where whores heave up and down like whalers.
As Mercedes steers half a million dollars' worth of car
between the derelict warehouses, all the security advice
from her Toolan forebears comes to mind. She knows
the drill. Headlights off. Vehicle tracking on. Isolate just
the near-side back window as operational. The rest of the
vehicle goes on lockdown.

A knuckle raps on the glass partition. Mercedes jerks,
thrown from her thoughts. *For Chrissakes, who knocks on
the glass any more?*

This is a fully tricked-out Mercedes Maybach with a
voice-activated intercom system. Where has this dude
been for the last twenty years? She had thought there was
something odd about the way he dressed. Kinda . . . *English.*
No, weirder than English. More like —

— A second rap, harder this time. Mercedes squashes
the brake, bringing the car to a smooth halt. Her gloved
hand depresses the intercom. 'Anything you require, sir?'

She knows he can hear her. The sound of his breathing

ushers from the speakers. But nothing more.

Mercedes mutters, releasing the button. 'Suit yourself, Mr Strange Suit.'

She looks at the shuffling buffet of whores on offer. Grandpops always said you could tell more about a man from his choice of whore than his choice of suit. Mercedes cracks a smile. *Then this guy must be something south of evil.*

Her cap slips down. This time as she shunts it up, her eyes bolt wide. Someone – *something* – is hobbling from the darkness, heading towards the car. And the opening back door signals that they do so at her client's request. It looks like a woman, a long skirt flapping, a tattered goatskin bag slung across hunched shoulders. But as the figure approaches, Mercedes can see no face, just yellow eyes. But she is sure, it's a man. No, weirder than that. *It's a monk!*

She feels the door thud shut behind and waits for the rap on the glass to drive on. None comes. But a chill strikes, creeping up the back of her neck. Something don't smell right about this. And Pops always said, listen to your nose.

And look with your ears.

Mercedes presses the intercom button. The client switch has been disabled. First thing any chauffeur tweaks. The client thinks he has set it to privacy, but the driver can override.

Mercedes has done this many times before, she likes to think always with good reason. But never has she heard a conversation such as this.

It begins with a long rattle of breath. Then a voice comes, cracked with age. Must be the monk.

'Good . . . good evening, sir. We meet again.'

There is no response. Another haul of breath. 'Have you perhaps had time to digest the report I sent on Agnus Day? I wrote every word, exactly as Judas told it to me.'

Silence, just the creak of leather. The old man presses on.

'And this evening I can report more progress, sir. The

rogue Hunter, 101A . . . she has been turned to good effect. She now believes that Dali is the traitor and she is bent on his destruction. And Judas is dead.' A grunted laugh. 'The famous fearsome Hunter, slain by an old man such as I! Proof indeed that misplaced trust cuts closer than a razor.'

A rasping silence.

'Is there anything more you require, sir?'

A response comes, in the form of clicking fingers. Some kind of command.

'Ah yes, I did not forget. You were very clear that I must return it.' The whisper of metal, withdrawn from fabric. 'Might I ask how you acquired it without detection?'

Again, no response. Just the chink of glass as the drinks cabinet is opened and a bottle is removed.

'You are most generous, sir. Most generous.'

The car door clunks and then comes the sound of feet, departing.

Mercedes looks in her side mirror to see the hunched old monk shuffling fast across the Wrips.

What in God's name was all that about?

And what object had the old man returned to her client? She had heard the sound of something long and metallic, withdrawn from inside his robes.

A gun. He's given him a goddamn gun!

Mercedes sits rigid, picturing the back of her head like a pumpkin conveniently placed at arms' length for smashing.

The silence in the car never sounded so loud. Then —

Tak! Tak!

Her head flies forward, jolted by the sound of the knuckle-rap on glass. Mercedes obeys the order, eases the gas and pulls away.

In the back of the Maybach, the client sits in virtual darkness. A row of white teeth places the face in the centre of the long leather seat. The amount of exposed enamel reveals the client to be smiling.

And the laugh that erupts reveals it to be Vassago.

211

It is all coming together, just as he designed. A plan of keen complexity.

Hardly the work of an *imbecile*!

His smile snaps down to a grimace. That was the word that Dali had chosen to describe him when reporting to the Legion on Vassago's first disastrous attempt at an awakening.

He had been working as Dali's apprentice for some time and seen him perform the ritual frequently. The day came when Dali deemed him ready to perform his own. A girl-child had been found, ripe and ready. Dali had stood back as Vassago pulled his clave and sank it into the girl's chest. He waited for the awakening to begin, but instead the girl's body began to writhe and squirm. A madness came upon her and she rose up flailing wildly, screaming and pounding her head against the wall as if bent on self-destruction. It was too late when Dali yanked the clave from her chest. She fell dead. And Vassago's clave hung from Dali's fingers. Only then did Vassago see the truth. The clave was not his. He had fallen prey to an ancient trick, wrought upon him by the Chiro Scuro. These wretched monks would forge false claves, bless them with holy water and then exchange them for the real thing. The Brotherhood's name, meaning 'hidden hand', came in part from their need to remain in the shadows of the Church. But there was another, darker practice behind the name. As men of God, they could not kill by their own hands. But neither could they passively stand by when their powers of detection alerted them to the imminent awakening of another Tormenta. So the monks trained themselves, with a fanatical zeal, to be wondrous fingersmiths. The Legion member would feel no more than the brush of a shoulder in a crowd and the deed would be done: a false clave planted. Because this device would ultimately be wielded by some other hand, they would have committed no sin.

Having fallen foul of this tactic, Vassago was accused

of negligence, and in disciplining him, Dali spared him not at all.

Now Vassago will show a similar rigour. Dali will be ridiculed, routed and ripped apart. And what pleases Vassago most is that this will be ensured by the same trickery that trapped him. Over the last few months, upon each meeting, Vassago had forced an embrace upon Dali, his purpose ultimately to use this moment to switch Dali's clave. Vassago's nimble fingers had been well prepared. Hour upon hour of practice had culminated in a successful rehearsal, in which Vassago had supplanted Dali's favourite deck of cards with an identical pack. Dali neither felt the subtle switch nor, as the days went by, did he seem to notice that the cards were not his own.

And every game of Solitaire that Vassago played thereafter, twisting Dali's cards between his fingers, fed his confidence that Dali's clave would easily follow.

Vassago strokes the clave that rests on the leather. His plan is now to return to the Sinestra with this bloody instrument and news of Judas's death. What further evidence of Dali's treachery could they need?

And with all suspicion focused on Dali, Vassago can quietly set about the next stage of his plan. To subtly place himself close to the Moera – and wait. For the Mosca will come, drawn irresistibly to its counterpoise. Then Vassago will watch keenly for the sign of Scox to finally determine in which human vessel the Mosca resides.

Vassago will then awaken him and return to the ranks of the Legion – a hero!

THE CITY LIGHTS glitter through the tinted glass. The client's gloved hand presses a button on the control panel and the glass partition slides down.

Mercedes flashes her eyes up to the rear-view mirror.

'Anything I can get you, sir?' In the reflection, she sees his finger gesture to pull over. The Maybach rolls to a halt.

213

The partition remains lowered. Mercedes understands that she should, as a courtesy, face her client. And she is indeed curious to see his face. And yet —

— her spine seems to fight against her, resisting the twist. So she must force herself round. And in the darkness cast by the tinted windows, she can see no face. But her eyes go to a long, metal shaft on the seat. She tenses, then exhales, seeing now that it is not a gun. Just a large, key-like device.

She pumps a smile. 'You know sir, you still got another hour of rental'

He says nothing. And she feels that same chill seep down her neck. 'Perhaps there's somewhere you'd like to go?'

Her cap slides down. She nudges it up, forcing a laugh. 'I gotta small head.'

She doesn't even see the gun. And the silencer means that nobody hears it. Just a sharp *Tak! Tak!*

Vassago slides it back inside his jacket. Looks at what's left of Mercedes' head.

Real small now.

34

BROTHER JOLUSA FEELS A SPLASH of rain. A storm is coming. He hikes his robes to speed away across the Wrips, weaving between the whores, his hood pulled low. The girls grab at this monk, just as they would any john.

Thunder booms. His speed increases.

But still one whore follows him, proving particularly persistent. Perhaps she has noticed that he clutches something tight within his hand and assumes it to be valuable.

To her it would be worthless. But to him, it is everything. *Life itself!*

He slides a blue glass vial into his goatskin bag. Buckles it tight. How many lives has he betrayed in its pursuit?

He quickens his pace as he feels the girl closing in.

His breathing rasps. He cannot delay. He needs the span! He glances down at his hand. The flesh is now so rotted that the rising wind can shear it from his bone. He must find some dark corner, escape this girl's attentions and immediately imbibe.

He swerves into a warehouse. An old earth-moving machine is rusted with its claw outstretched, as if offering Jolusa concealment. The old man shuffles within its giant embrace. Throws back his hood and hurriedly uncorks the glass vial. Raises his fleshless fist, ready to chug it. Then —

— the vial is snatched away. Jolusa shrieks, twisting his head to see who assails him. From the darkness steps the girl. She lashes a hand about the old man's plashy neck, pinning him to the wall as his gloved hand desperately flails, trying to reach the vial that she holds a taunting distance from him.

Her face lunges forward.

It is Lola.

She sweeps her lips close to his ear. 'One word exposed you, old man. *Traitor*.' Her grip tightens. 'How could you know that Dali's name was once Tret?'

Sputum oozes from Jolusa's mouth, like a squeezed orange as Lola presses on. 'Y'see, Brother Juicy, ol' Père D didn't share much. And he certainly did not share with many. So there is no good way that you could come by that information. But he told me things. And here's one pearl from the wise man: never trust a priest who keeps his hand hidden. I think some holy man taught him that lesson the hard way. And I think that was you.'

Rain plummets through the roof, striking Jolusa's hairless head, mulching the flesh into a putrid gravy that trickles down his crown. 'Now, I am guessing that you trade secrets for span. The good news is, I'm in the market to buy. Bad news is, life just got cheap. So I'm gonna need all the secrets you got.'

Jolusa gargles his agreement. She loosens her grip just enough. He draws breath. 'I am in the service of the Legion of Gehenna. Six months ago, one of their members commissioned me . . .'

'No, no, old man. We are going way back, right to the day when you first met Dali. I want to know everything.' Lola thrusts his head hard against the wall. 'And you better hope I believe you.' She slides the vial inside her belt.

'Hunter, I can give you proof.' His eyes urgently dart to his goatskin bag. 'If you permit me.' Lola nods, but keeps a careful hold as his hand sinks inside the bag and emerges with a letter.

The paper is so old, it frays at the creases. She recognises the meticulous script as Dali's. But the words? Could the same cold hand she knew so well, the one that withdraws at the most accidental of touches, be the same that penned this passionate appeal?

Rosa, my beloved!

I have been gone from you so long, you must think me dead. And in truth, I am. My heart died the moment I left you and though I might still breathe and my body perform this physical charade, I exist not. Life without you is worse than any death.

I must tell you now what came to pass the night when you were last mine.

Our kiss sealed a promise. That I would leave and make my fortune, so that your family might accept me. All I asked of you in return was to meet me again. The day you turned twenty-one, you would go to the Church of Our Lady's Tears on the corner of Parliament Square. I promised to be there, to claim you as my bride.

But how could I know that just moments after we exchanged this vow, I would fall and my heart impale upon the Romeo spikes below your window?

My life ended, Rosa.

But a new life began. One in which I was forced to immerse myself, driven by one sole desire: to forget you, my love.

The pain of separation was unbearable and never lessened. For so many years, I hid my sorrow until I reached an inevitable catastrophe. When I would overturn my world.

You will understand better, when you have read what became of me, but here I will say just this. I was ordered to commit an act that would unleash a lasting war against mankind.

But I refused.

Not from pity – I cared little for mankind. What stayed my hand was my love for you, Rosa. All humanity would suffer from my action, so I saved the world – solely to spare you.

I wanted you to live to see your twenty-first birthday. For in my heart, an idea had taken root. If you had ever truly loved me, you would keep to our avowed reunion.

With no word from me for so many years, you would have every reason to believe that I had forsaken you. But if you loved me, as I loved you, then your heart would compel you to come to the church.

And so I came and hid myself amongst the shadows. I could not let you see me. How could I ever account for the monster I had become?

I waited all day, in such exquisite agony. Feeling dusk fall behind the church windows. And then, as the last of the day disappeared, I saw you. Your face was veiled but I did not need my eyes. My half-corrupted heart sang out to you, as you looked about the church, searching for me. I heard you whisper my name. And I felt your sorrow as you stood there, utterly alone – as you so believed.

My heart raged . Every muscle in my body yearned to reach out, touch you and say, I am alive! I am here! I kept my promise!

But then you were gone, stopping only to kiss the gloved hand of the old priest who stood by the door.

I decided in that moment to write you this letter and entrust it to that priest, so that he might pass it on to you when you next come to church.

Read on. For in the pages that follow, I have described all that I was and all that I have become. And I implore you, once you have this understanding, ask yourself one question: Can you still love me?

If the answer is yes, my dearest, then send me word by this priest. And we shall be together once more and this time, for eternity.

For eternity is what my new life offers. I will begin my account with this wondrous element, so you may see how

Lola turns the page over. There is no more. The rest of the letter is missing.

Her grip clenches, posing her question so clearly, she need say nothing. The old monk squirms, the rain making him slippery in her fist. 'I no longer have the rest of the letter. I burned it. It was just an explanation of his Tormenta awakening, his days in the Legion, his defection . . . all events of which you know, nothing more.'

'No doubt he paid you handsomely to deliver this letter. And you betrayed him.'

'I wanted no part of this lover's subterfuge. But then he produced a purse and yes, I did begin to warm to the role, a lovers' go-between. And perhaps I would have even performed my duty. But the girl killed herself. Just hours after leaving the church. A broken heart, or so I heard. So I kept the letter, useless now, and opened it. This was no sin as I was no priest. I had been defrocked, long before. Had Dali seen my hand, he would perhaps have guessed.'

Jolusa raises his scorched claw. 'The Jesuits are brutal.' His eyes fix upon it. 'But I deserved this discipline. My life was one of sin.' The old man's eyes suddenly narrow with half-remembered glee. 'Can you imagine, then, my elation when I read Dali's explanation of span? The ultimate elixir! With span, I could live life for ever and forestall my assured destiny in hell. And so, using the information supplied within the letter, I sought out the Legion of Gehenna and struck a deal. I gave them proof of the traitor Dali's whereabouts and in return, they supplied me with span.'

The happy recollection of this smart barter rouses a chuckle, cut short by Lola's fist, which finds nothing funny in it. Jolusa resumes his story with a straining inhalation.

'The Legion demanded that whilst I persist in living, I serve their cause. I was directed to infiltrate the Brotherhood of Chiro Scuro and report back on their activities. And so under the name Brother Jolusa, I began my life of espionage. With much success. Even Judas was an easy dupe.'

He crinkles a smile. 'Turns out, I lie real good.'

Another boom of thunder delivers a torrent of rain, roaring through the roof. Lola shouts to be heard above the gale that rises. 'Who were you meeting tonight?'

'I don't know.' Jolusa's eyeballs bulge, her fist closing. 'That is the truth! I have never seen his face.'

A slice of his own rotted face falls away, pounded from his

skull by the torrential rain. Jolusa shrieks. 'I am dying!' His clawed hand grasps at Lola's coat, imploring. 'My span!' He can see the blue glass vial, tucked into her belt. 'I must have it!'

Lola does not release her grip. She watches with cool fascination as the rain strips the remaining skin from his face, a long-delayed death at last devouring him.

The last of his lips wash away with the words. 'I trusted you!'

'Guess I lie better.'

35

DALI'S BOOTS APPROACH the doors of the Ingenium. The iron booms and shudders, like bone-plates that cage a raging heart. His hand withdraws a long key, cranks the lock and eases one weighty door aside. He enters a chamber that heaves and pumps with four cylinders, conjoined by a vascular mass of wires. The noise is deafening but Dali seems oblivious. A pressing purpose urges him on and he turns sideways to slip between a slew of pistons.

He reaches another door. This one is so low, at speed it could be missed. And the key to open it is so minute that one might think it winds a clock.

Dali has no time to waste and enters quickly. The tunnel that lies beyond the door is tight and dark and he has to bend and shuffle to enter it. The walls are laden with dials and gauges that extend into the darkness. These machines do not form part of the Helix Vivat. They are the fossilised remains of the old telecommunication system that once occupied Kingsway. In its day, it represented the cutting edge of human technology. When Dali first discovered it, he was full of admiration for the system's ambition. And he found himself musing upon how far human telecommunications have come since these early days. He'd heard that modern governments can listen into every mobile telephone conversation made across the entire globe. And by taking just a snippet of a conversation and feeding it into a computer, they can track down one voice from the cellular roar of billions.

Perhaps this was his inspiration. For the thought would not leave him.

Somewhere in that vast expanse of span was the measure that once belonged to his beloved Rosa. What would he give to find that span! To watch it arrive once again in human form . . . to feel that she is alive.

Not that he would make an approach. That was never his purpose. He just wants to feel that somewhere, in the temple of another body, Rosa still waits for him.

This thought – idle at first, then compelling – proved potent. And he found himself pondering on how small a fragment of voice was needed by the human computer to tune into one person. Could he not then find a fragment of Rosa, isolate its frequency and then tune the oscilloscopes of the Helix Vivat to search for her span?

But here his hatchling plan halted. For what did he have of Rosa? What fragment of her could he conjure up that might provide her frequency?

All he had of Rosa were his memories.

And then one night – a breakthrough came. He was in the Archivum making a small amendment to one of the books of the Collegio Romano. It was a biography of Brother Magen and it mentioned that he often drank an alcoholic distillation called Artemisia. The biographer called it a poisonous brew and even suggested that it might be the cause of their master's hallucinations. Dali felt compelled to add a footnote. He wanted to point out that *Artemisia* is the scientific name of the wormwood herb and, therefore, the drink referred to was probably no more than absinthe. A heady liquor but unlikely to engender the vast and violent visions that plagued Brother Magen.

As he made this footnote, a memory sparked in Dali's mind. He was transported back to his early days in Louisiana, when he was just a boy, sailing on the trader ships. As part of his initiation into the crew, he was taken to a filthy corner of New Orleans known as the Artemisian Quarter. On every corner stood an absinthe house. The plan was to find him a whore. But young Tret's curious eye was drawn to the other dark doorways of the quarter – the mambo parlours. Inside a sailor could find a cure for every pox or ill. Tret heard tell of one cure offered by these women that struck him as exceedingly strange, and yet, many a sailor requested it. It was the removal of their memories. As duty pulled them from port to port, perhaps never to return, what many a sailor wanted was to forget the faces of those they loved. To have every memory of the face they adored cut from their minds. And the old Mambos skilled in this craft would – for a bottle of Artemisia – happily oblige, sometimes carving entire decades from a man's memory. On the walls of the parlours hung hundreds of poppets, little dolls sewn up from skin. Tret heard tell that each poppet held a man's memories, keeping them safe lest he should one day want them returned. The curious boy had asked if a man had ever come back to reclaim his past, but his sailor comrades ignored the question, instead shouting down this sour talk, keen as they were to concentrate on Tret's initiation.

Dali never forgot this mambo magic and it instilled in him a firm belief that memories are made of matter. They are as much a part of our body as blood and bone.

And as he mused upon this, the idea struck him. Hard and wonderfully sharp.

If Rosa existed in his memory, then a sample of her as real as blood could be summoned forth from his own mind.

Which is why, tonight like every other night, Dali comes to this secret tunnel and places, with painful precision, a series of needles deep into his skull.

The needles are soldered in bulbous lumps to wires that have clearly been stripped from elsewhere. These connect, via heavy brass jack-plugs, to the back of an oscilloscope extracted from the Helix Vivat.

The pulsing green signal jumps as the last plug clunks into place. And Dali grimaces, feeling the first jolt of the needles. A thread of blood runs down his scalp. The ready kerchief that Dali wields suggests that he suffers this often.

And then he exhales and closes his eyes. Silently mouthing her name as he searches for her in his memory. And upon finding her, he smiles. And opens his eyes, locking them like missiles on the scope. Watching as the green light sweeps round and round. Waiting for that particular fluctuation.

One day, Rosa my love . . . one day . . .

36

'It's dead.'

'It's not dead. It's asleep.'

'Spiders don't sleep, stupid.'

A stick pokes at a tanged black mass. It is stuck at the centre of a web, strung between the iron legs of a park bench.

Lola shifts along the seat, giving the two little girls some space to conduct further experimentation. The girl who wields the stick is a snub-nosed golden cutie. Her playmate has raisin eyes, stuck in a little muffin face. She tries to take the stick from her blond friend, who prods at the web.

'Don't tease it. You'll kill it.'

Cutie-Pie twists to Mini-Muffin. Lola sees the furious look delivered.

Kid, just leave it. Better she torments the spider than you, because she is bent on hurtin' something.

Too late. The stick lashes out.

'Spiders should die because they are ugly. Just like you.' The stick misses, but the words hit their mark and Mini-Muffin struggles to her feet, her voice rising to a sob as she lumbers away.

Lola shakes her head. *Damn, I sure hope that I was one of the cute crowd.*

She has no memories of her childhood. Fan Fan removed all those. She doesn't know why, but Fan Fan musta had her reasons. As far as Lola knows, her life began when she woke up in the Lo'World with Père D's old face smiling down at her like a 'gator.

Lola swings out her long legs. Runs a hand through her

cropped, blond hair. *Cutie-camp. For sure.*

She folds her arms, scans the park. Taps her boot. *They'll be here soon.*

Children rough and tumble before her. A tornado of teasing, taunting, tears and tantrums. Lola smiles and shakes her head. It's the one thing that always gives her pause for thought. She may hunt Tormenta to save mankind, but, truth is, your average vanilla human is still a pretty vicious creature. Look at what they routinely inflict upon each other: they bully as children, persecute as adults, break hearts, wreck lives. Every damn thing that Tormenta do, except Tormenta have an excuse – they do it to survive. Humans do it . . . because they can.

So why? Why save mankind?

Père D always said it was a curse of her nature, to be constantly asking questions.

'*Cher, your chromosomes may be XX but you got a helluva big Y in there.*'

She pulls her coat about her, closing out the chill. She misses him. And she knows that if he did authorise her execution, he had his reasons. There is something more at play and she is going to find out what.

She looks at her watch. Scans the park one more time. *Where are these guys?*

She gave them very clear co-ordinates and she knows that they use state-of-the-art navigation systems. That's the kind of hardware you need if you're a reclusive brotherhood with ambitions to fight evil on a global scale. Rumour has it that the Chiro Scuro have disciples buried deep in every software giant from Seattle to Singapore.

Linked to the world by their own personal iGod.

Lola jolts as the bench bows beside her. Two men have sat down. They wear long grey coats, but their robes, a dull brown, are still visible below the hem. Their feet are sandalled and fallen leaves have gathered from their trudge across the park, wet and muddy and crammed beneath their toes.

The man closest to her reaches down to flick the offending foliage from his feet. His fingers are brown and crinkled with age but the heavy gold rings wrapped about them suggests that a great authority has accrued with the years.

His voice rumbles. 'Why here?'

Lola glances at the second figure, a younger monk who pulls his coat about him, eyes anxiously scanning the park.

'I know you guys don't like to . . . venture forth. Security risk and all that. But this kids' park – safest place I know. A mass of moms on the lookout for any kinda threat. I promise you, nothing weird gets in the playground. In fact, honestly, you guys are the weirdest thing here.'

'Still your mouth!' The younger monk gawps with fury. 'You must address Primus Pater Umberto with respect!'

The Primus Pater pauses from his delicate task of leaf removal to raise a silencing finger. Then he turns to Lola. 'Our first duty is to God. So our place is within our monastery. It is for this reason that SCURO was established. To act in our stead. To be effective in the outside world.'

'Yeah, well, that would be nice.'

Umberto thins his lips, tasting insolence, but Lola presses on. 'You have one agent dead and a spy in your ranks. Or you did, until I got effective on his ass. So I think your boys at SCREW-U just found themselves way outta their league.'

'You may be rogue, but I see you have lost none of that Sinestra charm.'

'Yep, that shit sticks like tarmac.'

Umberto gathers his hands in his lap. 'The loss of Agent Bex is unfortunate. And that miscreant Jolusa is . . .'

'. . . *was*, thanks to me.'

Umberto exhales, withdrawing his feet from an onslaught of muddy toddlers. 'Can we please get to the point of this pleasure trip?'

'I have information on the Moera. I want to act upon it.'

'Yes, that much we know. We read your report.' He unfolds a tattered serviette from a diner. It is inked with hurried notes. 'An intriguing choice of paper.'

'I was kinda short on time.'

'But what intrigued me more was how you knew where to find us, with such speed.'

'I studied the books of the Collegio Romano. There's nothing about you guys that I don't know.'

The younger monk leers forward, eyebrows arched. 'You don't strike me as a scholar.'

Lola lurches, eyes hard. 'Would you prefer that I strike you as a Hunter?'

Umberto thrusts a finger, commanding silence. Then his long yellow nail descends, poking the serviette. 'This information. You say Judas was the source. And he was certain that this' – Umberto peers down at the scrawled notes – 'this Agnus Day has passed into the third state.'

Lola nods. 'That's what he believes.'

'Then if you are to act upon it, we will need to know your plan . . . your strategy. We must understand it, as that will determine what documents we provide to you . . . the right ones, to support your chosen cover story. So please, what is to be your approach?'

'Get into Morphic Fields. Get Agnus Day out.'

'That's not a plan. That's a To-Do list.'

'All right, so how about you tell me what clearances you can get me and I'll just work with that.'

Umberto smiles, his teeth tea-brown. 'My dear, I don't think you quite understand.' He pulls up the collar of his coat, successfully shrouding all but the bulb of his old, shaven head. 'There is no quarter of the globe that lies beyond our reach. We have access that exceeds every temporal investigative agencies. Over the centuries, the wealth of our church has succeeded in ensuring that our followers reach the highest office in every field of politics, military and law enforcement.'

'Kinda like the Masons?'

Umberto smiles, muttering within his collar, 'Yes, that diversion has been most successful . . .' His fingers click. 'Brother Scarbo, the corroboration documents, please.'

The young monk pulls a large envelope from beneath his coat. Passes it to Umberto.

'These documents will get you access to the prison.'

Lola pulls out a set of papers.

'Thereafter, as you seem keen to improvise, I refer you to the appendix page. If anyone questions your activity, ask them to call one of the names on this list. Your authority to act will be corroborated.'

Lola's eyes widen as she reads the names. 'Man, when you say you have guys at the top . . .'

'You're impressed. How wonderful. You've no idea how much that means.'

Now it is Lola's turn to flash her eyes at the old man's sarcasm. He smiles and sinks his hand into his sleeve, removing a final piece of paper. A ragged remnant, containing a dense extract of text.

'This, I suggest, you digest.'

Lola takes the piece, examining its fragile state.

'We collected it from a source within the prison. It confirms that Agnus Day is plagued by visions and these prophecies have wrought a considerable hold over the inmates at Morphic Fields.'

'So you believe that Judas is right?'

'Ah, my child, what I believe . . . let us not venture there.' His old hand rises, wafts. Dismissing her.

Lola stuffs the papers inside her coat and with a scout's salute she rises from the bench and departs across the park.

Brother Scarbo leans in, his head respectively bowed.

'Primus Pater, can she be trusted with such a mission? If what she says is true, that the Moera is rising, then that must mean . . . ?'

'. . . that the Mosca rises also.' Umberto sinks deeper

229

into his hood, muffling his voice. 'Yes, my son. He comes to bring his dark dominion. But God will not forsake us.' Umberto conceals the last of his face. 'The Moera will rise . . . must rise.'

Brother Scarbo places his hands together, the prayer-like pose serving to quell a rising tremor. 'But, Primus Pater, is it not the sworn duty of the Chiro Scuro to always seek the Moera . . . to act as its guardian? How can we send a Hunter on such a quest, untested and alone?'

Umberto's eyes roll within the gloom of the hood, coming to rest like hot coals upon Brother Scarbo's pale face.

'She will not be alone, my son.'

37

'You sure it's dead?'

'Of course it's dead.'

Mo'Zart nudges a charred creature about his plate. 'So what you callin' this food?'

Bianco wipes a slice of bread about her plate. 'With Fan Fan, you never know. She just pulls something outta the bayou and fries it to death. Mystery meals. Kinda Agatha Crispy.'

Mo'Zart leans into a laptop that stands open by his plate. He vigorously stabs at the keys and his long dreads jiggle about the collar of a pink and yellow bowling shirt.

Bianco jabs her fork towards the shirt. 'So what you calling that look?'

Mo'Zart doesn't take his eyes from the screen. 'I guess when Siggurson threw me in the back of the car, he didn't see my weekend bag.' He returns for a moment to his breakfast, chasing the meat with his fork. 'Turns out I'm a bleeder. The suit was real messed up. So the old lady gave me this.'

'Real tasteful.'

Mo'Zart pauses, the fork hovering in front of his mouth. Then his nose twitches. 'And what's that smell?' He twitches his nose closer to his plate.

'That's not breakfast, that's breakdown . . . decomp.' Bianco leans back towards an open window. Peers out at the shallow waters below. 'We need some pike to come by. Those things can rip through a corpse like a wood-chipper.'

Mo'Zart baulks. 'You have a body out there?'

'Nope.' Bianco swats her hand as a blow-fly buzzes. 'Whole bunch o' bodies. Bundled up like dust bunnies.

'Mo'Zart shakes his head. 'This place is fizzucked up.' Chews on his last bite and tries to cut another.

Bianco watches him struggle. 'Kinda bony, ain't it?' She leans back, nodding. 'Yeah, I'm pretty sure it's pike.'

Mo'Zart blurts the mouthful back on to the plate, shoving it away. Wipes a sleeve across his mouth and then pulls the laptop towards him.

'How old is this thing, like what – an Atari?' He lowers his ear towards a whirring sound. 'Processor is full of bugs.'

Bianco is stalking the room with a rolled-up newspaper, following the drone of the blow-fly. 'It's all we got here. But you're a bona-fide brainiac, so you should be able to log on with a waffle-iron, right? So keep trying.'

The blow-fly lands on the window frame. Bianco raises her arm. Then lowers her eyes to the porch outside. Siggurson sits on the steps. Beside him, carefully laid out, is a row of weapons. He examines each one. She watches his fingers deftly snap and slide one magazine after another. And her body tenses, a visceral memory of his hands sliding down her belly.

Did last night mean anything to him?

Bianco mentally swats herself. *Think straight!* Siggurson has a bullet in his head. He's trained himself to live in this moment and not think about the next. One night with her isn't going to smash down that wall.

Ker-resh! She has walloped the paper against the wall, shattering a china plaque. The pieces fly high and then clatter to the floor.

The fly casually drones on.

Mo'Zart chirrups from behind the screen. 'You get it?'

Bianco bends to pick up one of the pieces, a multi-coloured fragment. She's seen this plaque a thousand times. The piece she holds is the beak of a hummingbird. The picture shows the bird's glittering wings spread wide like the rising sun. There is a Taino proverb underneath. Fan Fan has told her what it means. Bianco can't remember exactly how the old woman translated it, but she knows that it is an ancient warning of sorts, something about mortal dangers at sunrise.

And right now, it feels as if it's giving her a warning: *What happens at night might not feel so smart in the morning.*

She jolts up as Siggurson strides in. 'You got it?'

'I'm working on it.' Mo'Zart hunches lower over the machine.

'How much longer?' Siggurson slides the magazine from a Luger.

Mo'Zart raises his hands above the screen. 'Look at my fizzingers. They're cramping. You're asking me to go through every case that Gobis handled. That dude was old. He could have been a cop for thirty years.'

'I'm guessing, thanks to you, he's retired with a bullet now.' Siggurson clicks the magazine lock.

A chair scrapes back. Mo'Zart rises. Leans on the table, head low. 'Is this how it's going to be?' His face rises from the mass of dreads. 'I made a mistake. I let my dick do the thinking and that bitch outsmarted me with a cup of kookie coffee. But I am going to make that right. And you need me. Because you're looking for one homicide report with no name and no date and only a brain like mine could find that with a dead-beat laptop and a connection so weak you might as well use voodoo as Wi-Fi. Maybe you should think on that.'

A silence quivers, his declaration made.

Siggurson slides the Luger into his belt. 'To get back to your original question. Yes. This is how it's gonna be.'

A sound comes, the slap of water, snatching Siggurson's head towards the window.

Bianco waves a dismissive hand. 'That's just 'gators.' She drops down into into a chair beside Mo'Zart and lays a hand on his shoulders. She feels the muscles tense, ready to rebuff her. 'I know you wanna make things right, kid.

233

So you got no choice – you crack this. Because it was the report Gobis wrote that got him and Agent Bex killed. Not you. So keep fishing. And get yourself off the hook.'

Mo'Zart lowers his shoulders, drags a sleeve across his eyes. 'I guess if I could come up with the right key words, I could launch a spider. That could get through ten thousand files a second, the whole police database. But I'd need the right word. One that would be relevant to that particular report. But I never saw what he wrote. Never even spoke to the guy.'

Bianco slumps back in her chair, her mouth dropping open as an idea drops, big as a bowling ball. 'Sulphur.'

'What?'

'Try sulphur. "Damned sulphur." That's what Gobis said, right before Bex came in. I thought it was weird at the time but stood in that old factory, with the masks on and the stink of lilies, everything felt weird.'

Mo'Zart shrugs. 'I can try it.' Fingers fly across the keyboard and then he jerks his head towards Siggurson. 'What about him? Maybe he has more.'

Bianco turns to Siggurson, who is standing by the window, scanning the water. He pulls the Luger from his belt and thrusts out of the door.

'No, I'm pretty sure we've had all there is to be had from him.'

At the bang of the porch door, Mo'Zart looks up. 'Where's he going?'

'Takes a while to get used to the sounds of the bayou. He thinks he hears something, but it's just a sly old 'gator.'

'They dangerous?'

'They sure are. Man-eaters. Nothing more dangerous in the bayou.'

She sits back in the chair. Then —

— bolts up. *There is one thing . . .*

And she hears it. The crunch of bone. And racing through the door – she sees it.

Siggurson slamming hard against the wall, his nose already bloody and his arm jerked high, an inch away from cracking from the joint. The final thrust averted by —

'Fucking stop, goddammit!' Bianco thunders down the porch.

Siggurson expels a gasp, shot with blood. Peels his eyes from the wooden wall to see Bianco approaching. She comes to a halt. One hand now upon her hip, the other gesturing to whoever holds him.

'Siggurson, Lola.' Her hand swings back. 'Lola, Siggurson.'

The fist about his neck releases. He pulls his face from the wood. Turns to see the figure behind him. Body like a gun barrel. Blond hair cut like a bullet.

He cranks his neck, flexes his fingers.

Bianco shrugs. 'Lucky for you she wasn't hungry.'

She turns to Lola and the two women fist-bump. 'You've been gone a while.'

Lola looks from Siggurson to the door as something in a pink and yellow shirt bursts out. 'So it would seem.'

'We got a lotta catching up to do.'

Lola's eyes assess the kid as he approaches. The bowling shirt, the screw-top dreads, the voice unbuttoned to an awestruck mumble.

'You must be . . . I mean, are you an actual real-life one-time-dead super-charged —'

Bing! – The computer chimes as if the cookies are baked. Mo'Zart's body jolts, then jigs with mounting excitement.

'And you know what that means. That sound. That means, my dear frizzles, that I have a hit. I have found it. I have found the file!'

He bounds off, his dreads alive and shirt flapping.

'Who's that?'

'His name's Mo'Zart. And he's not as stupid as he looks.'

'He couldn't be.'

38

IT IS DEAD, even though the eyes seem strangely alive. It is a trick of the candlelight, the flicker caught in two shards of mirror that sit where the eyes should be. The skin is human, but hardened and yellow, stitched together with black sutures. This voodoo poppet is one of many that hang from the wall.

A black hand reaches up, perusing the poppets, touching one and then another before finally selecting the one that hangs at the very end of the line.

'Come, come, my little one. You are where it ends.'

Fan Fan's fingers close about the doll, lifting it down. She wraps a shawl about the little head as she lowers herself into a rocking chair.

Her face flashes back and forth in the candlelight. Her lips are stained black and her jaw is layered with a beard of cracking white paint. Her fingers, daubed with red, nudge back the folds of the shawl, revealing the neck of the poppet. A jagged line of red encircles it.

Fan Fan's eyes roll upwards. Hanging from the ceiling is what's left of a crow. The head has been ripped clean from its neck. The last of its blood drips onto a silver plate below. The plate holds long, black thorns, soaked and sticky.

Fan Fan's fingers tweak a thorn from the pile. Her throat produces a throbbing chant as the spike hovers. With a howling incantation, she thrusts the thorn down hard into the head.

HES DEAD! *His neck is severed, splitting apart as if it's blowing a kiss. His long, dark hair is thick with blood as* *he falls . . .*

Lola bolts awake, clutching her head, the memory searing through her brain. Staggers to her feet, lurches to the cabin window, inhales hard, head down.

Her shoulders heave as the pain passes. She lifts her eyes, bloodshot and wet.

Flips open her phone. Stabs a number. As it rings, Lola's body ripples, awakening fast.

The line connects.

'Dammit, Lola.' The voice is clotted, but clearly Bianco. 'What the hell time is this?'

'Time to go.'

THE CLOCK ON THE CAR DASH FLASHES 4.15 A.M. Lola's fingertips are cold from the kinked blood supply so she uncurls her grip from the steering wheel. Rolls her neck.

Mo'Zart and Bianco are in the back, silent. Maybe asleep. They are obscured by four large, black suit bags that hang from a hook. Beside her is Siggurson.

She's been driving for five hours down the straight and narrow road that leads to Morphic Fields. All roads lead here, it seems. The Gobis file that Mo'Zart found was that of Jezebeth Hooger. That takes them to Agnus Day, her killer. So too does Lola's mission. No coincidence. Something is massing, drawing from all quarters. And accelerating. Lola feels it.

She pushes on the gas. Relaxes her head back. Feels the *ba-boom-ba-boom* of the road studs under the tyres. The car is drifting. She pulls it back into the centre of the narrow lane.

Siggurson rolls in his seat. He too is drifting. Asleep now, but not for long. Any moment he'll speak, certain that he's been awake all this time. Lola glances at his face, loose and soft, cheeks softly billowing with each breath. Would he care that she had seen him in this gentle state? She can't remember what guys care about. Maybe she's never known that kind of thing.

Maybe no guy has ever cared for me.

Her head suddenly jerks. That same cold, sharp pain as something pierces her memory.

Black hair. Blue eyes . . . his face, bloody.

She exhales with the ache.

'Maybe I should drive.' Siggurson hauls himself up, drags a hand across his mouth, reaches for the soda can that slides across the dash. Lola grips the wheel tighter.

'I'm fine.' Accelerates, arms straight.

'You like to drive?'

'Crazy about it.'

Siggurson sets down the can, nodding. 'You don't trust anyone else.' He arches his back against the seat. 'So, after all the talk last night . . . one thing's troubling me.'

'Just one?'

'I like the details to fit.'

'I bet your house is pretty.'

Siggurson exhales, patient. 'If a Tormenta is born into a human body, do they know what they are, right from birth?'

The hanging suit bags peel apart like a stage curtain and Mo'Zart's head pops through. 'Can I field this one, boss-chick?' Lola says nothing so he grasps this silence as permission to proceed. 'I struggled on this particular question but Agent Bex had a great way of explaining it. Like a story.'

Mo'Zart sweeps the bags to one side, clearing his stage and then reaches forward to lay a hand on Siggurson's shoulder. 'Imagine you're a little boy.'

Siggurson swings his eyes to Mo'Zart, like a pair of wrecking balls. The small hand shrinks back and he quickly changes tack. 'Not you . . . just any boy in a backwater town, middle of nowhere where tolerance is thin. You have feelings, desires. Unusual desires. Because you don't like girls. You're a boy . . . who likes boys. You don't understand where these feelings come from, or why you are different. And you sure as hell don't tell anyone. As you grow up, you hope that these urges will go away. But they don't, they get stronger. And so you start to explore them . . . in absolute secrecy. You try to find books that might explain it; you find yourself looking at other kids to see if anyone looks back at you with the same secret buried in their eyes. Then one day you venture out, determined to act upon what you feel and you have your first encounter. And it is hellish. A mess. Frightening. But you know that you are going to do it again. And next time, you'll know more. Understand yourself better. You'll learn by trial and error. You will start to become what you truly are. And once you are active – still keeping your secret from friends and family, who see no change in you, other than perhaps a welcome end to your adolescent shyness – you do meet another, just like you, with all the same feelings. And together you exchange information. And through that, you grow further still. Eventually you discover that there are many like you, moving unseen through society. You all keep the secret and thus you all thrive without interference.'

Siggurson nods. 'I get the parallel.'

'But y'know, some never discover the truth at all. If a G-Man don't find them, a Tormenta might go through life driving people to despair, maybe hating themselves for it, and never even knowing why. They just live and die a plain ol' mean bastard.'

Siggurson scratches at his stubble. 'So some are awake, some are dormant.' Siggurson turns to Lola. 'And you, what are you – you're like one part human, one part Tormenta?'

'She ain't no fizzucking cocktail, man!' Mo'Zart slams his hand down on the seat. 'Don't you get it?' His hand rises behind her and hovers as if wanting to touch a live power line. 'Lola is as good as it gets.'

Lola flashes her eyes at Mo'Zart in the rear-view mirror. *Down, boy.*

Siggurson shrugs. 'So you tell me, Lola, how do you see yourself?'

'In the mirror. Just as often as I can.'

The reflection of Bianco's head rises up from the back. 'Are we there yet?'

Mo'Zart slumps back. 'We're eighty miles from the prison but a long way from him really gettin' it.'

Bianco runs her tongue across her teeth, fluffs her hair. 'Kid, we've had time. We've had proof. He's had six hours and home-brewed liquor.' She leans forward to Siggurson. 'It's fucked up. But as cops, what do we do?'

'We fuck it down a notch.'

Bianco nods, leans back. Her eyes return to the window. 'We're heading into a storm.'

Mo'Zart dips his head. 'An unholy storm.'

'No – that storm.' Bianco's finger pokes at the window. Up ahead a lightning bolts shears down to the desert floor. She puts her hand up to the window, shielding her eyes to get a better view. Then —

— her neck flies back in a violent jerk as the car slams to the left, churning across the road.

Lola's hands are off the wheel, clutching her head. A spasm rips through her body as she writhes in her seat, twisting wildly as the car spins out of control.

Siggurson lunges, grabs the wheel, pulls it down hard, tightening the spin until the axles spiral to a halt in a stink of burning brake-pads.

Silence – as one by one, they lift their heads. Look about them.

Lola is the last. A thread of blood unravels from her nostril. She drags her sleeve across her nose. Turns to Siggurson.

'You drive.'

BOOK III

39

THE MEMO ON THE ENVELOPE IS HANDWRITTEN and
says only: 'Read this, then call me.' He pulls a single sheet
from within. The print is faint, a poor photocopy. He holds
it closer to the light.

Ray D'Sola was born twenty-two years ago as
Osca Bosque. His parents were well established in
the Rio de Janeiro jet-set. His father, a plastic
surgeon, married only once but changed his
bride's face with tireless dedication. Osca grew
up believing that Egyptian mummies got their
name from being covered in bandages, as this was
his perception of his own mother.

On evenings when his parents entertained, Osca's
hair would be slicked and his shoes polished. A
maid would then usher him through to the lounge,
where his father would instruct him to play
Chopin's Étude No. 4. After the polite applause
that greeted the end of his choppy performance,
he would be removed back to his rooms.

The only occasion when any attention was paid
to young Osca was at the age of twelve when a doctor
diagnosed him as suffering from meningitis. Osca
had fallen into a coma and the news was broken
to the parents that the child was not expected to
survive. His mother wept, dabbing her eyes to stop
her mascara running. In fact, she lingered by his
bedside so long, she almost missed the party she
was due to attend.

His father prepared for the worst, tracking down a colleague from medical school who was now known for his beautiful mortuary work. He could guarantee a beautiful corpse, which in Rio meant a great deal.

His parents were adamant; no expense was to be spared. However, the costs were ultimately limited to a number of irritating cancellation charges. Osca lived.

Perhaps it was born out of a desire not to disappoint his parents, but when the child emerged from his coma, he insisted that he was in fact quite dead. He maintained that he could feel a constant swarm of flies about him, attracted by the stench of his rotting guts. He referred to a residual red blotch on the back of his hand (a disfigurement typical of meningitis) as his ´death-spot´.

Osca was swiftly diagnosed with Cotard´s Syndrome: an unshakeable belief that one is a walking corpse.

Physical illness was regrettable but for his parents, madness was one affliction too far. The Bosques took the opportunity of a move to New York to redefine their relationship with their son. At the age of thirteen, with every comfort he could wish for, the boy was locked up in the penthouse suite of his parents´ skyscraper apartment.

For hours at a time, sitting all alone, he would stare at the windows of the surrounding buildings. They looked like picture frames, enclosing vignettes of life. He requested a telescope and soon found that time passed quickly when peeping on one´s neighbours.

He began to draw on postcards, mimicking the shape of the New York windows, capturing the illicit behaviour that he witnessed within.

Sometimes he would glimpse moments of happiness, acts of kindness. But more often than not what the boy saw and recorded in obsessive detail were extracts of despair. These were his favourite. They excited him. He knew that this was not right ... not natural. But it was the reality of what he felt — and evidence of his own contention that he was indeed dead. Only a corpse could have a heart so hard that the sight of a man blowing his brains out (as the boy had recently witnessed) would raise a smile and generate an appetite. For that was the way he described the pang he felt.

His life (or death-state, as he preferred to term it) changed entirely when he was fifteen years old. One of Osca's many nursemaids had taken a particular interest in the boy. It broke her heart to see him locked up and alone, with just his endless postcard sketches. She discreetly arranged for a psychiatrist to visit, a soft-spoken woman with the fortuitous name of Dr Mother.

Dr Mother began by talking with Osca about his 'death-spot'. What if she could make it go away, would he then be alive? Osca confidently assured her that he had tried everything to remove it (the burn from an attempt with bleach had made it only bigger) but he encouraged her to try if she wished.

The following day, Dr Mother returned with a tattoo artist whom she introduced as Mr Todd Lily. He looked at the ragged-edged blotch on the boy's hand. After a little consideration, he got out his needles and began to work. An hour later, he blotted the skin and told Osca to take a look. He had transformed the blotch into a blazing sun-burst. The shape was perhaps a little uneven, but the effect could not be denied. The death-spot was gone.

This was the beginning of Osca's new life. Dr Mother had birthed him anew.

At seventeen, he changed his name to Ray D'Sola, emancipated himself from his parents (taking with him a hefty payment to keep his 'imprisonment' secret) and set about creating a new persona.

Ray D'Sola became an artist and a business whiz. At nineteen, he had turned his postcards into an installation at New York's prestigious Hunkypunk Gallery. From there, the Revelation Project had sprung.

Beginning as an underground project, people wrote anonymous revelations about themselves on postcards and left them hidden about the city, inside library books, beneath coffee cups in Starbucks. The human urge to declare their darkest thoughts and exploits found voice and the project soon transferred to the internet, spawning a global audience and (of course) merchandise. Books, events, flash-mob parties, all themed with the desire to confess our darkest deeds.

The media, jerking its knee at another internet trend, rushed to link the Revelation Project to an increase in young suicides. The broadsheets worked hard to find individuals who submitted an anonymous postcard and then went on to take their own lives.

With a wonderful aptness, Ray D'Sola immediately set up a suicide help-agency called *Rays of the Sun*. Manned entirely at his own expense, its dedication, innovation and ground-breaking outreach program rapidly put all other suicide agencies to shame. The media felt the moral high ground ripped from beneath them and the Revelation Project continued its unbridled ascension.

He turns the paper over. The reverse is blank. Clearly just this one page has been prised away from its rightful owner.

He pulls the phone close. Dials a number. It connects on the first ring.

'You've read it?'

'Yes, Marta, I've read it.'

'And?'

'It is pleasingly accurate.'

'They want to run it in the weekend edition. Centre spread.'

'Marta, I have made my fortune from the secrets of others. I was bound to become a target. We both knew this day would come.'

'It calls your mental acuity into question.'

'You mean it portrays me as a loon.'

'Yes.'

'Do you think I'm a loon, Marta?'

'I think you're a fool if you ignore this.'

'So, as my attorney, what do you propose, Marta?'

'We offer them an exclusive, an on-the-record interview. Your whole life story. They'll want some gristle, but at least we control what bones we throw them.'

'If that's what you suggest, then I agree. Make the call. Put it to bed. And then – to bed with you.' His voice softens. 'I can tell from the echo that you're in that marble tomb you call your office.'

'It's still light outside.'

'My dear, that's the moon.' He sighs. 'You really do live up to your name, don't you, Marta? You are the constant martyr to my cause.'

'If that means you work me to death, then yes.'

'Ah, Marta, you once again turn it to a joke. But I know what you have sacrificed for me, for all your clients. These last ten years, when you should have been falling in love, building a family, having a life, you have spent chained to your desk. And now . . . you have left it all too late.'

The familiar silence comes. That glorious absence of sound that is, in itself, the sound of the target being hit. She doesn't know how to respond to a compliment that cuts so deeply.

'I'll speak to you tomorrow, Ray.'

'Yes, Marta, sleep well.'

He hangs up the receiver and jots a quick memo. He'll get another bottle of her favourite bourbon sent over. As a thank you . . . and a fail-safe, to be sure that she always has sufficient alcohol at hand for when the tragedy of her pointless life finally punctures her heart.

D'Sola settles back into his chair. The black leather blends into the shades of granite and slate that clad his vast Manhattan penthouse. He plugs a set of headphones into a laptop. Clicks his inbox and retrieves his daily email from the duty therapist at Rays of the Sun.

It opens with a host of audio files attached, each labelled with a name. He transfers one after another to his desktop.

This ritual began as a piece of PR. He made an undertaking some months ago to visit the agency on a regular basis. The purpose was to display his involvement in its operation. On one visit, a worker keen for him to understand their methods played a tape of a call received that day – a heart-breaking account from a man who sits with the phone in one hand and a gun in the other. Ray had listened in rapt silence. All those present had been struck by his determination to listen to the very end. Such consideration, from the entrepreneur whom so many called a con-man.

Since that day, Ray has insisted on getting the tapes sent to him regularly, such is his active and on-going involvement.

D'Sola looks at the file names. Sees one labelled 'Dolores'.

He smiles. *That bodes well.* The name Dolores means

sorrow. He selects the file, relaxes back, stretches his legs and unbuttons his fly. As a despairing voice plays through the headphones, his hand trails down to his groin. And once again he finds that familiar sensation rising . . . that appetite he felt as a child. But now, as a grown man, the feeling has gained a hardened, more urgent edge. His blood pumps as he listens to Dolores, slurring her words as she pops pills and swills whiskey. She drones into the phone, increasingly oblivious to the male counsellor on the end of the line. And then her final death-sob comes and D'Sola groans with pleasure. His head lolls; his hand falls away.

He knows this is wrong, so very, very wrong . . . but every man has his particular lusts. Just so happens that D'Sola's fetish is . . . *what would you call this?*

What is the word for someone who gets sexed up on suicide? That perplexes him still. D'Sola has surfed for solutions. He's invested in some very expensive therapy. He's even read books. And come up with nothing. It's not necrophilia. It's not sadism. It's something . . . *other.*

There are days when he feels he might be the only one in the world who feels this.

But never a day that he cares.

He slips off the headphones and buttons-up his fly.

He can keep this secret. We all have secrets. He looks about his apartment, filled with artwork from the Revelation Project, and smiles. Then he turns at the rasp of a subtle cough. In the doorway stands a squat man in the grey of a chauffeur's uniform.

'Will you be needing the car again tonight, sir?'

'No, no, Wilson. You may leave.'

'I appreciate that sir. My wedding anniversary, so she'll like to see me home on time.'

'Of course. But I'll need an early pick-up tomorrow. Regretfully I must meet with . . . people.' His hand flicks across his diary. A name is scrawled. 'Wilson, do I know a Marty Starr?'

The old man shakes his head. 'I don't recall that name, sir.'

D'Sola flips the diary shut. 'I'm sure all will become clear. So off you go. And have an enjoyable evening.'

'Oh I will, sir. Much to celebrate. God is good and my world is a happy place.'

D'Sola clips a smile and memos himself to replace Wilson with someone a little less blessed.

40

MARTY STARR SITS UNCOMFORTABLY HUNCHED with a cell phone at his ear. A voice barks from the speaker. "Call yourself a producer? You can't produce shit, Marty. So either you get this mess sorted or you're finished. You get me?" The line goes dead.

He lets the mobile slide from his hand. It falls into a hammock of trousers that's gathered at his ankles. He is sitting in a toilet stall.

Marty sighs. He kinda misses the days when phones had a cradle and calls would end with a resounding *ker-lunk*. At least you knew they were over.

You're finished, Marty Starr. You can't produce shit.

He rises from the toilet and stares into the unsullied bowl. How true. Even his bowels have turned against him.

Squeezing from the stall and pulling tight his belt, he shuffles to the basin. Stares into the mirror. Lolls his tongue. He needs a shave. Dammit, his tongue needs a shave.

He exhales, barely fogging the glass. *You're dying, Marty. And you know who's killing you.*

It's the band. Marty Starr has managed Stork from the very start, when Fell Watson was the lead singer. Death metal was just beginning, but Fell immediately understood how to harness despair to the same three chords and make platinum sales. Self-scarring, suicidal teens swelled their fan-base, even before Fell blew his vocal cords out of the back of his neck with a revolver.

Marty was under pressure from the record label to get a replacement – and fast. He wondered where he would find a kid with the same authentic aura of death. But life is strange, and on the day that Fell's funeral was up-loaded to YouTube, a guy walks into Marty's office – Japanese, maybe . . . hard to tell behind the curtain of black hair – and declares that he's the one. Says his name is Hash-Tu.

Marty listens to his demo and it blows his mind. He can't get the contract printed fast enough.

But six months on, he is feeling the pain of this hasty decision. Hash-Tu has raised the affinity with suicide from something obscure to the central core of the band's existence – or impending non-existence, depending how seriously you take the lyrics of their songs.

Hash-Tu's deadly antics on stage are now drawing criticism from the mainstream media, as suicidal postings on Facebook constantly reference Stork lyrics.

The head of Scorpious Records laid it out to Marty in their last bitter exchange: Stork are one high-school shooting away from being dropped by the label.

The launch of the new album *Rocker Lips* is fast approaching. Hash-Tu wants to stage a performance outside a prison as an execution is taking place inside. He plans to call the event The Rocker Lips Apocalypse. The rest of the band, who revered Hash-Tu like a lethal Jesus, insist that this is a brilliant idea.

All Marty knows is that they can kiss goodbye to Walmart stocking the album. Marty has put his own money behind this release. If the album fails, he's finished. He begs the band to see commercial sense. As they slam the door behind them, Hash-Tu challenges him to come up with something better.

Two bottles of Grey Goose later and Marty has nothing. Just a liver so swollen you could mash it to pâté.

A bible lies abandoned on the floor. In his drunken desperation last night, he must have leafed through the final chapters, searching for any compromise on the theme of Apocalypse. It lays open at the Book of Revelation . . .

. . . and then inspiration strikes: the Revelation Project.

This is the answer!

He will persuade the band that the album launch should be done in association with the Revelation Project, with CDs hidden alongside postcards about the city. Hash-Tu is sure to love the tacit heritage of self-death that comes with the Project. Meanwhile, Marty can claim to the label that Stork is aligning itself with a reputable counselling agency that has done so much good work in the field of teen suicide.

It is a slam-dunk, a win win . . . if only he can persuade Ray D'Sola to agree.

Marty blinks again into the washroom mirror. On the other side of the door is the vast marble lobby of the Revelation Project's headquarters. His appointment with D'Sola is only minutes away.

He rolls his tongue about his mouth. It looks and tastes like feathers. Marty is rarely given to nerves but everything is riding on this.

And he is not the only one vying for D'Sola's attention. It took two weeks just to get this meeting and sitting in the lobby is another contender, with another pitch to hitch their wagon to the Revelation star.

Marty inhales and exits, eyes flicking to his competitor who fidgets in the lobby.

Dr Torgus is careful not to look up. She refuses to be deterred or distracted. She has her pitch memorised. She keeps her eyes fixed on her hands, casually folded in her lap.

She's recently taken to wearing gloves. Sleek, black-leather affairs. The purpose is to conceal the liver spots that leopard her hands, but the effect is to suggest a constant readiness on her part to commit murder. And right now, motive mooches dead ahead in the shape of a man shuffling from the bathroom in a cheap chino suit.

Torgus clenches her jaw. It had taken a week of studied silence to convince Duggin that she had abandoned any ambitions concerning Angus. Then, with the Governor's attention eventually averted, she approached the Revelation Project. Call by clandestine call, she clawed her way through the entourage of Ray D'Sola, at last eliciting his private office number. With an audience achieved and the day finally upon her, she is crushed to find herself in competition with others, clamouring for his commercial attention. It seems that D'Sola likes to keep the pressure up. Likes to see people sweat.

Her competitor settles into a seat on the opposite side of the table. Torgus feels perspiration prick her armpits. She lifts her elbows to allow the air to flow and skilfully disguises the move as a reach across the table, gathering one of the glossy books. She feigns interest in the title, but then – her hands twitch in an unexpected flash of genuine curiosity. The book she holds is entitled *The Poems of Archilochus*. Torgus flicks through the thick, silky pages. Archilochus' work is very obscure. D'Sola must be quite the aficionado of Greek poetry to know of him. A smile cracks her thick lipstick. Torgus is an ancient Greek name. Her roots are in this culture. Has she perhaps stumbled upon the most perfect ice-breaker?

The door to D'Sola's office swings open.

Dr Torgus and Marty Starr look up together.

41

IT IS ONE OF THOSE LOUISIANA DAYS when you just can't beat the heat. No point fighting it. Might as well just pop that top button and stretch out those legs as far as you can.

Police Chief Willy Lyon has been heeding this advice the entire day. He thuds a pair of buckskin boots upon his desk.

His officers have their own lil' wise-crack: 'You know what the Chief's name is short for? Willy Lyon-His-Ass-All-Day.' But he doesn't care. It don't bother the Chief at all. He runs the station his way and it works. All about good delegation. Which is why he likes to have a lotta female officers. Back at county hall, the Sheriff thinks that Chief Lyon is some kinda poster boy for progress, recruiting all these women. But here's the truth. They work harder. Simple fact, they just do. Quicker with their case load. Quicker with the coffee.

Chief Lyon smooths a hand across his head, taming a mass of sandy hair that circles, via sideburns and a beard, around his entire face. Pulls a file from his desk. Then he opens his mouth to shout a name, demanding attendance. A yawn bubbles up at the same time, turning the summons into a gargling Tarzan-like bellow. In the operations room beyond, where the Chief's many and varied noises are well known, Detective Blaise Dunkel rises to answer the call.

He appears at the door, swilling his coffee. 'You want me, Chief?'

'As a matter of fact, I don't. I want Detective Bianco, but she's been assigned to some tip-top this-that somewhere or other, so I'm settlin' for you. It's a suicide.'

'That sure is her speciality.'

'And she frapps a fine iced latte.'

'Yeah, they are good.'

'But you're the best I got right now. So this one's yours.' Chief Lyon skims a finger across the file. 'It's a suicide, no doubt about that. Forensics show GSR on the victim's hands and he's a drinker. Got a hospital record that says he's tried this stunt before. Just about sober enough this time to get the gun in his mouth, I guess.'

Dunkel slurps the foam from his coffee. 'So what's to do? Sounds like we can wrap it and stack it.'

'Wrap it and stack it?'

'That's what my old Chief —'

Lyon's boots thud to the floor. 'This ain't Walmart, son.' He hauls his huge chest up to his desk. 'You're new and maybe my candy-sweet karma has confused you. But I have earned a little kickback. Thirty years of service. Took four bullets, thank God, none in the ass. So I do things right. You best learn that. And what we got here' – he wafts the file – 'is a little clean-up in aisle four.'

He flicks to the last page. 'There was another person present . . . a kid called . . . I dunno, there's no name, just a number. Says here he's some kinda rockstar.'

Dunkel grimaces, as if another shot of shit has just been added to his coffee. 'That so, sir.'

'Yeah, says the band's called Stork. Some kinda new fusion . . .' He peers closer, frowning. '. . . death-metal grind-core. You ever heard o'that?'

'I'm a little bit country, sir.'

Dunkel catches the file as it frisbees towards him.

'Dig some. Usual questions.'

'Sure, boss. And . . . what are the usual questions? I mean, if we know it's a suicide?'

'Reckless endangerment, son. Gotta be sure the kid didn't push him to it.'

'Oh, sure, that, yeah . . . I got it, sir. I'm on it.'

Lyon tilts back his chair, shaking his shaggy head as the detective disappears down the hallway.

For a guy called Blaise, he sure don't burn too bright.

ON THE WALL OF THE INTERVIEW ROOM an old-fashioned digital clock flips numbers, marking the seconds and generating a relentless *shik-shik-shik*.

Sat on one side of the table is a male uniformed officer. Opposite is Hash-Tu. His long black hair hangs like a curtain across his face.

In his hand is the pen he was given to sign his statement. He tap-taps it on the table, finding the off beat with the *shik-shik-shik*, creating a nerve-jangling non-rhythm.

The officer grips the edge of his chair, veins pulsing with tension. Wanting to reach across the table and skull-fuck the kid with the pen. But he can't. The freak isn't even under arrest.

He's helping with their enquiries.

As the door swings open the officer bounces to his feet. 'All yours, Dunkel.'

His exit has sufficient speed to generate a waft of air that peels apart Hash-Tu's hair. Just long enough for him to glimpse the sweating detective that now settles into the seat opposite.

'Sure is a hot one today.' Dunkel runs a finger round his collar and then opens the file, papers clinging to his palm. 'We'll try not to keep you long. A few questions, is all.'

Hash-Tu stares at the shiny face before him. Breathes deep. Smelling the detective's discomfort.

'If you could just explain to me what happened.'

Hash-Tu says nothing out loud. But his mind unfolds the question with great care.

The beginning part, he can explain. He was in his dressing room. It was the last night of the official tour. Marty was there. He was drunk, of course. Raging and weeping, begging Hash-Tu to reconsider his decision to stage a concert outside Morphic Fields. It was bad enough that Stork would choose to perform as an execution takes place, but to select the death of Agnus Day – a perverted child-killer – that will kill the album.

'It's fucking goddamn professional suicide! I'm begging you . . .'

Marty had fallen sobbing to his knees and once again, Hash-Tu felt it rise within him . . . that very particular thrill that comes when he witnesses a person in the throes of despair. It's been this way his whole life. The misery of others feels like silk upon his skin.

Guess that's just the way I'm wired . . .

He tells Marty that he has brought this upon himself. He had promised the band a collaboration with the Revelation Project and in truth, Hash-Tu had liked this idea. The project's creator, Ray D'Sola, was someone he wanted to meet because the guy's an artist in death. His personal contribution to America's suicide culture deserved recognition. But Marty had clearly failed to impress, as D'Sola selected another project with which to partner. When Marty delivered this news, Hash-Tu experienced an emotion that he later identified, with a little research, as disappointment.

So the sight of Marty prostrate before him, pleading and pawing, provided him with some small pleasure. One that would be improved if Marty would just kill himself. That's what Hash-Tu wanted. That's what he always wanted. This was his sickness. This was his drug.

And this is what he cannot explain. Not to himself. Certainly not to this decaff detective.

So he opens his mouth a fraction and provides just this: 'He was sad. He pulled a gun. He shot himself.'

Detective Dunkel writes rapidly. The gathering momentum suggests he's expecting more. So the pen hovers mid-air as Hash-Tu concludes not so much a statement, more a Haiku stanza.

'That's all you know?'

'Yes.'

Hash-Tu isn't lying. It may not be all that occurred. But it is all that he knows. The rest of what ensued is beyond his understanding.

As Marty lay dead, gun in hand, brains in bits, Hash-Tu felt the most tremendous urge to kneel and press his lips upon the man's cold mouth. He sucked hard, aware at first of the dead tongue drawing up into his mouth, then – fighting a gag reflex – he sucked some more and he felt it . . . something rising out of Marty, pulsing, alive, released from this dead shell. Entering him as he inhaled again, sucking harder, swallowing it down and feeling . . .

What?

. . . an incandescent euphoria. A deep need, spectacularly satisfied. But as the giddy high passes, Hash-Tu wrenches his mouth from Marty's corpse. Rises to his feet.

No way of knowing what had just occurred. What he now felt.

This may take a little more research . . .

He sits back in the interview chair as Detective Dunkel passes him a card with the station number on.

'If you gain any further insight . . . understanding . . . into what happened, please let me know.'

The card sits, unclaimed, despite the fact that Hash-Tu is quite certain he will be seeking further insight and understanding. But not into Marty's death.

Into why he has never felt so alive.

42

GOVERNOR DUGGIN IS A SHORT MAN. Very short for his weight. And always short for his age, right back to his childhood days. At five years old, even on tippy-toe, he had not been able to see inside the long wooden box that lay in the front room of his house. But he knew that his mother was inside it. She had been there for a few days, surrounded by white lilies. Kept close until her burial, as was traditional. But with the fifties boom, his parents were the first generation to get central heating and no one in the family had stopped to think of the ripening effect this might have upon a corpse. And so, although young Duggin was unable to see his mother's body, he sure could smell it. And judging by the way the brown and withered lilies stank, his mother he imagined looked the same.

Then came the day that four men in identical sharp black suits appeared at the door. They had come to take her away. At the time, young Duggin was unaware that the removal of his mother roused any horror in him. But then, two years later, his father took him as a treat to a music show. The first act on was a doo-wop quartet, The Fly Boys. They walked on to the stage in their identical sharp black suits and young Duggin felt hot, clotted bile rise up in his throat, erupting from his mouth and splattering across his lap. He recalls hearing a voice scream out that he wants the men to go away, but it didn't feel as if the voice were his. The most intimate memory, the only thing that he recalls as feeling real, was that his vomit smelled sweet as lilies. Amid his screams and violent squirming, his father held him down, trapping his wrist against the seat, embarrassed, insistent.

'The men won't hurt you, boy. Just stay for the first song.'

Duggin suddenly bolts from the memory, roused by a sharp, female voice.

'Let's begin by getting something clear.'

He looks up. Four sharp black suits stand before him. Two women. Two men. It's the brunette who speaks. 'This prison is ours, Governor. For as long as we want it.'

Duggin smears his palms along his thigh. These agents had walked in unannounced and spread themselves in a line across his office, hands clasped up front, the pose identical . . . disturbing. It has taken Duggin until now to master his childhood chill. He looks to the window. The rain beats, relentless, but the rhythm calms him. He breathes deeper, slower.

Until the brunette breaks out from the line and begins to pace the office. 'We are here because word has reached the Federal Bureau of Prisons that, under your command, a disruptive force has been allowed to spread unchecked within Morphic Fields.' She curves around a bucket that collects rain from a crack in the ceiling. 'You've permitted one prisoner, Agnus Day, to gain a psychological hold over the inmates, and that's one sure way to make the Bureau snippy. So we have been despatched with full authority to nip this niggle.'

Duggin blinks as if Bianco's words are individual jabs in the eye.

'Now, I don't know what your personal record is on the control of narcotics and firearms, but let me tell you this, there is nothing more dangerous in a prison than the spread of an idea. And you have allowed, without intervention, the entire inmate community to develop an addiction to the prophecies of one man.'

She straightens her lapels, rolls her hands, knuckles down, upon the desk. 'Our brief is to clean this mess up and, with your cooperation, we'll pass through like a dose of chlamydia. You won't feel us. But if you stand in our way, start swinging that dick – you'll be pissing blood. Do I make myself clear?'

She reaches inside her jacket and produces a thick sheaf of official-looking papers.

They slap against the desk. With a hesitant hand, Duggin slides on his spectacles. Scans the contents. Then, in disbelief, draws the papers closer still. These clearances are mighty high. Sky high. A man might get a nose bleed just from reading the signatures.

And then, the papers are gone, swept up in Bianco's hand as she rolls them tight, replacing them within her jacket.

'I will be heading up this operation so I'll need an office and a dedicated phone line.' She clasps her hands behind her back. Walks down the line of her fellow operatives, passing Siggurson. 'We will need a barber for a head-shave and a set of prison blues. The library must be cordoned off' – she slaps a hand on Mo'Zarts's shoulder – 'and get him every gigabyte you got.' She walks on past Lola with just a razor's edge of a glance and . . . says nothing.

Then she turns her back on Duggin. 'Our first objective is to debunk Agnus Day in the eyes of the prisoners. Make them see that his voodoo-pallooza prophecies are bogus. Once he's robbed of their respect, his hold is gone – and we can haul his ass from Morphic Fields without fear of reprisal.'

Duggin appears to be listening but his eyes are on Lola. He stiffens as she breaks from the line, moves towards him.

Bianco shoots her cuffs. 'And let's be honest, Governor, you don't want Agnus here. He's been nothing but trouble. So I'm pretty sure a lot of what I've said sounds good to you.'

Duggin puffs his cheeks and puckers his lips into a balloon-knot of contemplation. Lola's close on his right side, but still he risks popping one last question.

'So I assume that the Federal Bureau has cleared all this

with the Ministry of Justice and Washington?'

Lola leans in. 'I want to kiss your mouth to stop you saying such ridiculous things.'

HER UNDERWEAR IS SOMEWHERE. She wore black, of course. Her best Victoria's Secret, because this was to be her big seduction. The vinyl floor in Duggin's private chamber is dark grey, turned black by dirt, and Dr Torgus had removed the thong with such alacrity, the elastic launched across the room. Now the only secret of this underwear is where the fuck it landed.

She had been hiding on the other side of the door, waiting for her weekly meeting with Duggin, and today she was keen to get to the meat of it. Then those four agents had walked in.

On the other side of the wood, pantyless and gasping, she had listened in horror to their mission brief. They were going to take Agnus from her.

Not possible! Not now! Not so close to the arrival of Ray D'Sola . . .

With her old face and broken credentials, still she had succeeded in persuading him to come. Just to witness, with his own eyes, the sheer mountain of material generated by Agnus Day. More than a book . . . an installation. A phenomenon. Nostradamus for a new generation. Secrets of the past. Revelations for the future. Dr Torgus remembers telling herself to *shut up!* as she pitched the idea in D'Sola's office, hurling reason after reason at the coconut of his head. And then – joy of joys – the word *yes* had been handed to her. The smallest word, which felt huge in her arms as she walked from the office, giddy and giggling.

Now she has nothing. No hope. No plan. No panties. And their chilly lack is forcing her to tweak her stride, when every muscle in her body urges speed.

Her hands contain the swirl of her skirt as, flanked by two guards, she minces in tight-hipped, tight-lipped silence down the central prison corridor, arriving at the final corner cell. The one with the window.

A SLENDER FINGER WAFTS BACK AND FORTH. Grotteschi lies on his bunk, white iPod buds plunged deep into his ears. Inside his head, Mozart's Requiem unfurls. The slim device is a treasured perk from a guard who was particularly troubled by a note from Agnus. The actual wording of the revelation now escapes Grotteschi, but he had found a mild interpretation that gave the guard relief.

Grotteschi inhales as the key descends to a mournful B flat, then yelps as he is sharply yanked upright. His eyes bolt open to find Dr Torgus bursting into his cell, guards behind, jangling keys.

'What is the meaning of this!'

He is silenced by a hand that thuds his hump against the wall, holding him fast. The face of Dr Torgus thrusts forward, an inch from his. He can taste her breath: coffee and stomach acid. She raises her thumb and forefinger, the merest pinch apart. 'I am this close . . .'

Grotteschi shrinks back. 'Less than, I'd say." Her spit hits his lips. '. . . this close to getting everything back.' She stares, eyes wide, fogged by her fury. 'My reputation. My life. And then this happens.'

'Must *this* happen?' The guards are ripping up his room. Yanking blankets. Grotteschi squirms.

Torgus curls her upper lip like the rising safety gate on a band-saw. 'They show up with their papers, as if my plans count for nothing. Giving me no chance to change his mind, to put my case, to put my ass on his face until he says yes! That's all I wanted!'

'So reasonable, thus phrased.'

The guards tip out his drawers as Torgus grinds on.

'So now: a change of plan. I am forced to go beyond those means.'

'Beyond the ass?'

A guard reaches under the bed. Pulls out a pair of shoes and a small wash-bag.

'You understand, I must have total control.'

'That may require medication.'

The shoes are searched with probing fingers and the wash-bag is unzipped, soap spilling. Torgus swings her eyes to the bed as the guards comb through the contents.

'. . . everything must be in my possession. All that you have is now mine.'

His pockets are turned out like dog-ears. Gum-sticks fall. Grotteschi gestures down. 'Can I minimise the mess by confessing now that I keep two balls in my scrotum?'

His insolence receives a sharp punch to the sternum. He falls heavily to the bed, his sudden weight forcing something to dislodge from the springs below.

A box hits the concrete floor with a thud.

A guard falls to his knees, retrieving the Nike shoebox. He peels off the lid and presents the contents to Dr Torgus. A mass of paper shreds, covered in text.

She takes the box, cradling it in her arms, looking at the many prophecies within. 'This holds the future that Agnus saw. And now, it is my future.' She strokes the box, a smile rising. 'What *is* the meaning of this . . .' She lays her hand upon the lid, exhales and, with a spin of her heel, she is gone.

The cell door slams and clunks. Grotteschi lowers himself to the bed and sweeps aside his precious soaps from the pillow. He pokes his pockets back within his pants. And then he lifts an arm upwards, snaking it beneath his shirt to where his twisted spine lurks. Out of his collar, Grotteschi pulls a handful of paper, the bundle reducing the size of his hump. He then carefully slides them into the pocket next to his heart. He had sensed that such a raid might occur and had prudently secreted the most precious of the papers beside the most untouchable part of his person. He smiles and, with a soft grunt, settles back down on to the bed below.

He listens to the rain battering against his window. How unnatural that this storm should be so unrelenting.

The skies know it. Heaven itself is horribly aware. *Something comes . . .*

From the moment of his encounter with Ring-Pull, Grotteschi knew that momentous events were now unfolding. He could not know what form it might take, nor when the catastrophe might come. But he knew that fate had dealt him a card to play in this game.

He slides in his ear-buds and sighs as the glorious requiem floods his ears. *If this duty brings death, then I am ready.*

And the scattered soap fills his nose with the scent of lilies, the traditional flower of the funeral.

Lola's boots step out on to the prison roof. The flat surface swims with rainwater. She pulls her long coat about her and strides to the edge, forcing ripples hard to the gutter. She hears the boots of a guard follow, two paces behind. Clad in black waterproofs, he looks like a slippery tadpole, slung with a gun. Young Officer Trill has been assigned to accompany this agent, but halfway across the roof she holds up a hand, commanding him to stop.

She sweeps her eyes across the roof and spies the four-metre tower of a ventilation shaft. Rusted rungs creak beneath her weight as she mounts it, rising up, high enough now to survey Morphic Fields in all its sodden shame.

The surrounding desert has drunk its fill of water but the storm tortures it with more, forcing it to swallow rain that bubbles back up, rising around the prison perimeter like a burgeoning sea.

Flanked on all sides by five-metre fences, Morphic Fields seems to float like a frigate, torn from the world by the black water. The watchtowers at each corner groan in the wind like masts.

Lola closes her eyes. She did not come here to look. She came here to feel. To release, for a moment, that Tormenta streak within her . . . that shard in her soul. If another like her walks within these walls, shark-like, she will feel it.

Lola breathes deeply, opening the mental cage in which she imprisons her darker self, and instantly, the power she has disciplined herself to access only for combat bursts free, roaring through her mind and body. Lola tenses every muscle, riding this beast, feeling it rage, following where it leads. Opens her eyes, her every sense heightened now. Ready to search.

Is he here? Is the Mosca already amongst us?

And then she feels it. Like the death throes of a dark star, a wave of energy rises from the entire prison and breaks across her body.

She staggers back. Struggles, stumbling, to find her footing, her body quaking.

Officer Trill splashes up to the base of the tower. 'Ma'am, you all right?'

Lola says nothing, hauling heavy breaths. Trill tips up his hood, his young face twitches, a mess of emotions. 'Thought you were gonna jump for a moment there.'

Lola thrusts out a hand, commanding him to stay back from the tower as she fights with herself, forcing her Tormenta streak back into its cage. It resists, screaming inside her head, trying to wrest control of Lola's mouth to force her to flash a smile at the guard below and say, '*You've thought about jumping, haven't you, kid? Because you feel the evil that approaches. You sense it coming. So maybe you should jump, before it pushes you.*'

Lola grasps her head between her fists, forcing it down, expelling a jagged grunt as she slams her mental cage shut and condemns that sliver of her soul to darkness once more.

Slowly rises. Eyes wet with strain. She stands above Trill, a pulse jumping wildly in her neck.

He flips a faint smile. 'It'll pass, ma'am. We've all had it . . . kinda feelin' outta sorts. I blame the rain.' He tugs his dripping hood. 'No good for the brain.'

With a tidal splash, Lola jumps down.

It's gonna take 127 steps to get back down from the roof. Trill had counted them on the way up.

He has taken to counting and collating his surroundings: light bulbs in the corridors, floor tiles in the washroom. He likes to keep his mind occupied. To stop it wandering.

Because Officer Trill's brain has recently been prone to restless roving.

And now he's finding it harder and harder to deny the knocking dread inside his head.

He accelerates to keep up with the agent. She now strides towards a set of steps that lead underground to the Medical Isolation Cell.

And as they descend, he finds himself counting a fresh set of steps. Mouth shut, but shouting the numbers loud in his mind.

Sixty-four, sixty-five, sixty-six . . . the emergency ward of Morphic Fields lies deep beneath the prison, hewn from the bedrock. The steep stairwell and the many doors lend the ward its security. It also spares it from the rain and this tunnel is one of the few places in the prison that remains unflooded.

Sixty-seven, sixty-eight, sixty-nine . . . They reach another door. A guard shuffles to his feet, tips back his cap, exposing a face that's pale and wrinkled, as if his years of subterranean duty have rendered him unable to survive in sunlight. He cranks his key in the lock and swings his door to reveal another stretch of steps. Then he turns, his eyes fixing upon the blond figure who accompanies Trill. As she moves to pass, a book is thrust hard against her.

'So must ye descend before ye can rise.' The guard's voice rattles with unreachable phlegm.

Lola stares at the old guard as Trill swiftly dips between them, snaring the book and waving it harmlessly. The cover is emblazoned with a mass of golden crosses. 'It's just an ol' bible. He's taken to passing it to anyone who . . . descends.' With a thin grin, Trill turns. 'Now, Bob, I don't think this agent needs your protection. She looks pretty handy to me.' Trill strains a laugh as he eases past the old guard and pushes the door wide for Lola.

She thuds down into the darkness and Trill follows. They silently sink deeper and Trill feels the beat of his mind against his skull. He breathes hard and looks down. In his hand is the bible. He knows for sure that there are forty gold crosses on the front, but he will count them again . . . and again.

ON THOSE OCCASIONS when Officer Molloy found himself on Isolation Duty, he would always volunteer to take the final stretch of corridor, guarding the last door before the cell itself. His reasoning was that if he is to be forced deep into the bedrock, he might as well take the spot with the sweetest acoustics. Because Officer Molloy loves to sing and on this last stretch, the granite walls provide a wonderful echo.

But the stone no longer resonates to his tenor. He hasn't sung for a while. Not since his beloved Trudy left him. Ripped from his arms by the revelation that his mistress is pregnant. Just as Agnus had predicted. On the paper he gave Molloy was written one word: 'Scox'. Grotteschi translated that as a stork, foreboding evil. News of this baby would wreak destruction – and, as ever, Agnus had been right.

I shoulda listened to him!

'You hear me, Molloy?'

Molloy spins round to see Trill standing before him.

'I said, open up.'

His finger gestures to the door behind Molloy. The sign reads 'Medical Isolation Cell' but the heavy rack of locks confirm that the purpose of this room is less about care and more about concealment.

Trill's thumb now jerks over his shoulder. 'The agent here wants to talk to Agnus.'

Molloy jolts as a blond figure steps from the darkness. She looks like a woman but scares him like a man.

He gathers himself, rubbing his narrow chin. 'Is that so? The agent wants to speak with Agnus.' Molloy pulls up his keys and cranks the lock, baring his teeth in what could be a grit of strain . . . or perhaps an amused grin. 'Well, let's see what we can do, shall we?'

The door swings wide. Inside a figure sits, withered and wild with hair. On the wall behind, lit by tiny, flickering lights, is a metal frame.

Lola enters. Takes up a position in front of Agnus. He doesn't move.

She lowers to her knee to find his face. And then she sees that the metal frame is a surgical device. Tubes coil from his chest and wires connect his head to a monitor, the flickering lights of which create the strange illumination.

His eyes are wide, unblinking.

And his mouth sags open, dragging air, but locked into a silent, catatonic gape.

Lola rises to her feet, pulling out her phone. She flips it open. It connects in one ring. 'Can you talk?'

BIANCO SNAPS HER PHONE SHUT. Increases her pace. She thinks better when she walks. Just as well: she's got a lot to think about and a long way to walk. The rain means that she and her escort of guards can't cut across the yard to reach the library, so they are making their way through the long circumference of corridors. The two guards each push a trolley stacked with prison files. The wheels squeak, and to Bianco's ear they seem to repeat an insistent question. 'So . . . ? So . . . ? So . . . ?'

So what are we going to do now?

She looks to see the guards are pointing left. That hallway twists away into the distance.

'Why not down here?' She points to the broad, grey corridor before her.

'Ma'am, that way takes us through the gym. The prisoners are taking their exercise in there, on account of the rain.'

'So?'

Bianco flicks her fingers, a gesture to open the gym. The lock turns and an electronic motor heaves the doors apart.

High up on the observation platform, armed guards prime their weapons, put on point by this entry.

The command is yelled for all movement to cease and the gym falls suddenly silent. Each prisoner compensates for this enforced immobility by charging their eyes with a body's worth of muscle, punching their weight at Bianco, following her every step across the vast room. Their faces are tattooed with a gang mark that Bianco knows very well. She has seen these horizontal stripes cross-hatched by the bars of a holding cell many times. These prisoners belong to the Petra Loa. And in the centre is a giant of a man, who lumbers forward. The distant rifles prime and point, but Kon'Verse is allowed to approach. Bianco feels as if her limbs are made of metal and this giant man is a coil of magnet. His eyes draw her to a halt.

'You will fail, if you fail to see him.'

Bianco's eyes flick up to the gantry. The guns are trained upon them but something tells her the weapons are poised more to ensure her attention than to contain this convict.

'See who?'

Kon'Verse lets the basketball in his hand drop, like a god releasing a planet to its fate. And the sound of it striking the floor seems to act as a signal. The guns withdraw and the exit door slowly grinds open.

Bianco strides out, breathing hard, furious at herself. Throws back one glance, finding all eyes upon her.

Stiffens her spine, shaking the feeling that she is trapped inside her body.

And yet, somehow, these prisoners seem free. Unconfined by these walls.

She pounds down the last few yards and thrusts open the doors to the library. Mo'Zart is already inside with a fleet of guards who unload boxes of inmates' records.

Bianco fires two words, like warning shots. 'Plan B.'

She signals for the guards to leave them. As the doors swing shut, she turns to Mo'zart. 'Agnus is alive, but a dead-end. Lola's seen him. He can't talk. There's nothing he can give us.' She paces round a tower of boxes. Drops to a desk. Pulls a clean pad of paper towards her. 'I need to write while I think.' Frisks her pocket. 'You got a pen?'

'Just this one. But it's red.' Mo'Zart pulls it from his shirt.

She snaps her fingers for him to throw it. Snatches it from the air and scribbles with the nib until the red ink flows. 'I don't like to write in red. Reminds me of school. Like Teacher has corrected me. That I've got it wrong.'

Mo'Zart drops into the chair beside her. 'But we've got it right, right?'

On the pad she draws two pin-men. 'We know what we've got to do. Find the Mosca. And find the G-Man who has been sent to awaken him. That ain't changed. Just how we do it.'

'And how fast we do it. I looked up the medical notes. Agnus has gone into some sort of vegetative coma three weeks ago. Now, if this is some kinda chrysalis stage, then the Mosca has had time enough to close in. Both he and the G-Man could already be here.'

'But we'd know if the Mosca had been awakened, because hell would be hopping, right?'

Mo'Zart nods. 'I'd say we are in time . . . but by how much?'

Bianco taps the pen like a metronome, quickening the tempo of her thinking. 'If Agnus can't speak, then we get hold of everything he wrote and we talk to every prisoner that spoke with him. Whatever information we get, we have to piece together ourselves until it shows us who the Mosca is. And as for the G-Man . . .' She jerks the pen at the files on the trolleys. 'Those are the employee files. We look at everyone who's arrived in Morphic Fields since Agnus began to have his visions.'

'I've already made a start on the prisoner records.' Mo'Zart jerks a thumb at a two-foot stack.

'You read all those while I was gone? I was thirty minutes, tops.'

Mo'Zart taps his skull. 'That's kinda my thing. And I found this.' He unrolls the file in his hand and spreads it on the table. 'It gives me an idea about what we should do first.'

A finger sharply taps the table, halting him. 'You know why it's called Plan B? It's short for Plan Bianco. I'm running the show. I say what we do first.'

'So you got me boiling these exceptional brains, and you don't want to taste the gravy?'

Bianco says nothing. Mo'Zart looks at her. The silence strains, broken only by Bianco's tapping pen. Then: 'So what you waiting for, kid, an eight-bar intro?'

Mo'Zart smiles, peels apart the pages. 'It's a classic bait and wait.' He taps the name on the file: '*Charles Grotteschi*. This one prisoner was closely associated with Agnus. Very close. He acted like a kinda interpreter, decoding every revelation. So all we gotta do is get Grotteschi to open up to Siggurson.'

'And how do we do that?'

Mo'Zart pulls out a page from Grotteschi's file. 'I know every book this dude ever checked out of the library and one in particular . . . gives us an opportunity.'

Bianco takes the prison file, flicks through it. 'Grotteschi's done time. An old con like him will smell a cop through kryptonite. The minute Siggurson makes an approach, starts asking questions . . .'

'He won't. Grotteschi will come to him.'

'Why?'

'Because he'll find Siggurson irrestistibizzle.'

45

GROTTESCHI'S FINGERS CRAWL OVER THE MUFFIN in his hand. He is pulling it apart but not eating it.

He finally prods a lump between his lips, but it lodges in his mouth, parched dry by excitement. His eyes are locked on the prisoner sitting opposite him in the canteen.

The morsel squats in his throat until his brain finally engages and pumps words from his mouth, forcing the muffin to expel in an explosion of crumbs. 'That's some big ol' bullet hole you got there.'

The freshly shaved head of the man opposite bears a cratered scar above the ear. The eyes rise, stare at the hunch-back, then sink back to the meal. Grotteschi knows that it's hard to get a new con to talk. The smart ones stay silent until their position in the hierarchy is first confirmed by their fists.

But Grotteschi cannot wait. He'll risk retribution.

This is just too extraordinary to ignore!

The strange events leading to this moment began earlier that morning. Grotteschi turned up for his trustee duties to find his book-trolley parked outside the library doors. The duty guard informed him that the library was – for the moment – out of bounds. This being so, the books ordered by the inmates had been loaded on to the trolley, ready to go. At the time, Grotteschi barely cared about this wrinkle in the system. In fact it spared him the task of trawling the shelves to collect the same old sticky paperback porn.

Quite happily he took the trolley from the guard, along with the delivery list. With his good eye already monocled, he wandered off, pushing with one hand and holding the list with the other, scanning the titles and cell numbers. Then, with a muted squeal, the monocle pops from his eye. He comes to a halt. Pulls the list closer.

There it is. In black and white. His name, and beside it, a book to be delivered. But he has not ordered it. Not this time. In truth he hoped never to see it again.

It is the *Bardo Thodol: The Book of the Dead*.

Who would have sent it to him? Who knew of his encounter with Ring-Pull? Not the guard who escorted him; he never set eyes upon the book. Only Ring-Pull . . . and so now, only Ring-Pull could be sending it back to him.

But why? As a threat, a taunt? No, no, this made no sense!

Grotteschi was certain that, in that one fateful encounter, he had seen the true spirit that now occupies Ring-Pull's mortal shell. It is the spirit of Tenzin Nara, a gentle, seeking mind who sought to help him in his search for the truth to Agnus' visions.

He would not tease.

. . . but might he share? Yes, yes! This is the answer!

Tenzin Nara wants to send Grotteschi a message, a clue. And so, with a trembling hand, he pulls the book from the trolley, rattles the pages back and forth – and then he finds it: a fly, squashed between the covers. Its sticky body has been used as a crude glue to affix a scrap of paper.

Just as he said . . . The Beast of Flies . . . the bringer of death. Most certainly this message is for him.

Grotteschi peels the note free. It is short and elegantly written in red ink.

A BULLET IN THE HEAD. HE SHOULD BE DEAD.
BUT HE DID NOT DIE.
AND THIS ONE MAN
CAN TELL YOU MORE THAN I.

Now, a few short hours later, Grotteschi finds himself

277

before this man.

It must be he! That bullet wound to the head, so deep, and yet he lives. This is the man that Tenzin Nara foresaw.

And now Grotteschi must engage with him, find out what he knows. Share with him his own meagre findings.

But where to begin? He may be quite unaware of his destiny, oblivious to the answers that lie within his bullet-ridden brain. The wrong approach may break no silence, only bones.

Think, Grotteschi! Think! But all that comes is the most common of con greetings.

'So, how long you got?'

The shaved head rises again. This time he speaks. 'Life.'

Grotteschi scours the face before him, searching for a clue that this man knows of their shared destiny . . . some awareness of the realms beyond.

And then it comes. The man leans closer. 'But not necessarily this life.'

46

'*Will you quit scratching.*'

Mo'Zart's voice crackles from a tiny device lodged inside an ear. Above the ear is the scar of a bullet wound. Siggurson's finger scratches at it again.

'*C'mon, sounds like we've wired up a canine.*'

Siggurson grimaces. Drops his finger.

He stands in his cell, tin bucket in hand. It is slop-out time. He waits for a bell that finally shrills. His cell door slides open and he steps out on to the iron gantry. Below and above him, the cell doors clunk and shunt and a hundred slop-out buckets clang down on the walkway. Siggurson grits his jaw. Undercover in a jail always stinks. The buckets are emptied and he eases back against the wall. From the gantry above, droplets shower down. *I am outta here before shower-time comes round.*

He turns his eyes straight ahead. Sees Grotteschi outside his cell, talking to one of the guards. The merest flick of his old finger gestures towards Siggurson.

IN THE LIBRARY, Mo'Zart is surrounded by open files and laptop keyboards. A speaker crackles as Siggurson's mic picks up another voice. The tone is gruff, with the edge of a whisper.

'*The old hunch-back tells me you got a talent, a talent for . . . metalwork. He wants to show you round the shop before the shift begins. I've given that my blessing. And if I ever need a blessing in return . . . I may call upon your talents. Do you understand?*'

Mo'Zart's dreads dance as he swivels in his chair from

one terminal to the other. Fingers punch up information.

'This is good, Siggurson. I got the workshop log here. Grotteschi's in there every day. That says to me that he thinks it's a place of safety. He's taking you to his sanctuary. Looks like he's buying it.'

Bianco leans forward, her pen tapping like a conductor, slowing the beat. 'Don't underestimate the old guy. He's smart.' The pen taps on, counting down to her conclusion. 'We're gonna need another beat. Some kind of detail that'll convince him Siggurson's got the gift.'

IN HIS EAR-PIECE, Siggurson can hear Mo'Zart's fingers hammering at the keyboard. And in his cell, summoned by a sharp hiss, he looks up to see the finger of the guard reach in and beckon him out. The finger then wordlessly directs him towards Grotteschi, who is already on the level below. The hunch-back urgently jigs back and forth, signalling to Siggurson to come down and join him. As he descends the metal steps, Mo'Zart's voice buzzes in his ear.

'This guy Grotteschi has got some kinda good gizzle going. All sorts of favours. A CD collection, art books, cigars . . . but most of all, soap.'

IN THE LIBRARY, the speaker now transmits the echo of footsteps. A change of surface. Concrete. Siggurson must be entering the workshop.

Mo'Zart rattles at the keyboard. '. . . and when it comes to his soap, Grotteschi will accept only one fragrance, lily of the valley.'

A heavy clang of metal pops the speaker. Mo'Zart cranks the volume as another voice comes, muffled by fabric and movement. But it is clearly Grotteschi.

'We have these pieces. Different shapes, different fixings. Our job is to put them together. We rarely know what the end item is destined to be . . . a plumbing fixture, a valve perhaps. And never do we have instructions. Perhaps they

existed once, a mystery all of its own. So the trick is to examine each piece, until the piece speaks to us and tells us where it goes.'

Mo'Zart dinks a frown 'Why is he telling Siggurson this?'

Bianco recognises the careful tone. 'The guard is too close. Grotteschi can't speak freely.'

'I was just saying to Office Bilfinger here, I saw those dextrous hands of yours and I knew that your talents should be applied to the metal shop.'

Mo'Zart nods to Bianco, her instincts right.

'So he's allowed me the chance to show you the ropes before the shift begins. Officer Bilfinger knows what a puzzle this work can be . . . and he has had some personal experience of my own ability to solve puzzles, isn't that right, officer?'

'Let's begin. And the first task is to wash our hands of all trace of grease. So, officer, I'll just show the new boy where the basins are.'

A rush of water drowns the sound of the mic. Mo'Zart fiddles with the pitch, thinning the bass to bring out the thread of conversation. *'Please, my boy, don't use that faecal treacle they call liquid soap.'* The disdain in Grotteschi's voice crackles the signal. *'I have something of my own.'* The rustle of a pocket, the crinkle of wrapping paper. *'Lily of the valley.'*

Mo'Zart taps furiously, then he pulls the mic close. 'Mary's tears. That's another name for the flower. Tell him that, then wait for my cue.'

Siggurson twists off the tap. Turns his head to Grotteschi and delivers in an empty monotone, 'Mary's tears.'

Grotteschi slowly pulls his hands from beneath the faucet. Water drips from his fingers. And in his eyes, something bubbles.

'You know about Mary's tears? That is such a rare extract of knowledge.' Grotteschi watches as his new apprentice closes his eyes.

'Your mother's name was Mary . . . and you lost her when you were still a child.'

'Did this come to you in a vision, my boy? Tell me! Do you . . . do you then know about my mother?' Grotteschi staggers back, grasping the edge of the sink, gasping for air. Forcing his mouth to form words. 'Yes . . . yes . . . you see everything.' He hauls in a deep breath, forcing himself to be calm. Then he peels his one good eye upwards. 'When my mother bathed me as a child, she would cry. She always assured me it was nothing . . . just the soap. That the fragrance was Mary's tears and with her name being Mary, it was bound to make her eyes water. A kind story, to keep me from knowing that what truly made her weep was the sight of my crippled spine.' Grotteschi heaves a deep sigh. 'She took her own life and many cruel tongues wagged that no mother who loved their child could do such a thing. But I know my mother loved me . . . why else would she spare my hurt and blame her tears on the fragrance of lilies?'

A hand launches out and grasps Siggurson's sleeve, quivering with an ecstatic energy. 'Your gift is strong, my boy.' He stares deep into Siggurson's eyes. 'And in you . . . I sense that your mother . . . your mother somehow has made you what you are. Gave you life, but also death . . .'

Another commanding bell rings.

Mo'Zart DIALS THE VOLUME DOWN as the bell's blast threatens to blow the speaker. Then he turns to Bianco and sucks in a low whistle. 'That's some game-play from Siggurson. He's got Grotteschi believing they share some mommy-bizzle. How'd he do that?' Mo'Zart returns to his keyboard, shaking his head in admiration.

Bianco says nothing. But her mind twists a smile. *Ah, Grotteschi, you've got the gift and you don't even know it.*

The roar of a machine rises. The bell marked the start of the metal-shop shift. Mo'Zart tries to adjust the pitch again but nothing comes.

'I can't get anything over this. Sig's on his own.'

'So we wait.'

THE JIG-CUTTER IS A TWO-MAN MACHINE and, at the sound of the bell, Grotteschi is quick to claim it. It will keep Siggurson at his side and their conversation can continue. And it suits Siggurson's purpose, also. The blade descends every ten seconds and its piercing squeal means that Siggurson's answers to Grotteschi's questions must be cut short.

'My boy, what do you know of Agnus Day?'

'I am here because it was destined.'

The blade screams, churning sparks. Grotteschi waits for it to rise, impatience riddling his feet. At last, it lifts. 'You have seen him in your visions?'

'I hold a book. And in the book, I see the meaning . . .'

Grotteschi squirms away from a spray of sparks. 'Agnus brings us a warning but I cannot decipher it. Which is why I prayed for one such as you to be sent.'

MO'ZART TRIES THE VOLUME AGAIN and winces as the jigsaw grinds from the speaker. 'Still nothing.'

Bianco looks up from a stack of files. 'We wait. And while we wait, we read.' She slams a file shut. Quickly pulls another. 'So far I've counted a hundred and seventy new intakes to Morphic Fields since Agnus got here. Anyone of them could be the Mosca or the G-Man. Without something from Grotteschi, I'm gonna die of paper-cuts.'

Suddenly – the flush of a toilet. Siggurson has made it to the confines of a cubicle. His voice hisses from the speaker.

'Listen up! This is what I've got so far. Agnus wrote hundreds of prophecies, thousands maybe. All of them cryptic, most of them crazy. But according to Grotteschi,

some do hold a deeper meaning. Two in particular. Grotteschi calls them the Poet and the Painter. Don't ask me why. Thing is we gotta get these pieces and . . . piece them together. To see the bigger picture. So the one he calls the Poet, that prophecy was given to a heavyweight called Kon'Verse. Grotteschi has arranged for me to have an audience. Kinda loose arrangements tho' . . . basically, he's just given me a code word that should stop Kon'Verse from pushing my teeth so far down my throat I gotta clean them with a toilet scrub. If I can get close, get him to talk, maybe he'll give up the prophecy and we can get to work.'

SIZE THIRTEEN BOOTS THUD across the concrete floor. Siggurson's eyes are set on a hulking kiln. The Petra Loa gang move amid the hot pipes. They are not working, but the guards make no attempt to coerce them.

As Siggurson nears, he feels the heat of their eyes upon him. He takes a final pace. Looks up – a long way up – to find Kon'Verse's eyes.

He's surprised by the crack in his own voice. Coughs to claim control of it. 'So, you interested in Greek?'

Kon'Verse stares at him in silence.

Sigurson feels as if he's cut the red wire and the bomb's still ticking. One of Kon'Verse's crew takes a step forward, head cocked like a rooster.

'You wanna say that one more time?'

Unsure that he does, Sigurson inhales. 'Greek . . . poetry.

Sound worse. The gang moves a step closer, but a low exhalation from Kon'Verse moves them aside like a hot thermal. And the merest twitch of his giant hand signals that Siggurson may approach.

'Grotteschi sent me.'

Kon'Verse inhales and slowly lowers himself to sit on the base of the kiln, like an iron throne.

'Then we will talk of one thing.' He spreads a hand on each thigh. 'The meaning of my revelation.' His fingers are thickly tattooed with roses. They clench, rippling thorns. 'Time was, Little Bit rapped and his words were cheap. And he soon found himself a foe. Got into a dissing-war. Things got outta hand. His foe's daughter ends up dead. Little Bit didn't pull the trigger. Maybe one of his crew. But he ends up here.'

From his pocket, he pulls a folded piece of card, passes it to Siggurson. It bears the words in a savage scrawl:

Came he once as Archilochus with words that killed. He will come again by that same name.

'At first, I could find no meaning in it. The hunch-back told me Archilochus was a Greek poet. What was I supposed to understand from that? And yet I knew Agnus intended this for me. So I meditated upon it. And I found my meaning.'

A tattoo of thorns climb up his neck, as if they bear his head like a wind-blown bloom. 'I cursed my imprisonment as unjust. But then this revelation showed me the truth. What killed little LouAnne Titley may have finished with a bullet, but it started with my words. I was guilty. And suddenly, with that realisation, the anger that raged inside me subsided. And there came great peace. And I knew that I must make amends. That Little Bit must die to pay for her death. And so I killed off that identity. And Kon'Verse came to be.'

He gently smooths the crumpled card across his palm. 'This is the meaning that I took from Agnus' words. A meaning that spoke to me and made sense of my fate. But I know that this holds another meaning. One that relates to all mankind.'

Siggurson stares back at the black eyes upon him, feeling their gaze enter deeper through his skin as Kon'Verse leans in close.

'The hunch-back may be fooled by your games. But I

know the truth, lawman. And I know this too – that you were sent here for a purpose. So take this . . .'

He slides the scrap of card towards Siggurson. '. . . and set its meaning free.'

47

THE MOUTH OF AGNUS DAY sags uselessly. He can't talk. So Lola has gone to Plan B. She's ordered up every cassette of his police interviews and psych assessments.

Lola stands beside his bed, the tapes spread out on the blanket. She picks up the first. In the underground gloom of the ward, she can barely read the label. She twists it to catch a glimmer from the flashing lights of the medical machinery. It says 'Property of Sulphur City Police Dept. Interview: Agnus Day'. She slots it into the player. Plugs in her ear-buds and sits back, eyes closed as the old tape hisses and pops into action.

A long burst of tone. Then a gruff voice announces:

DIX: The time is twenty-two hundred, June sixth. This is the interview of Dr Agnus Day in connection with the homicide of Jezebeth Hooger. Attending officers are Sergeant Don Dix and Detective Judah Gobis. Dr Day has been offered an attorney and declined. Please confirm this for the tape.

AGNUS: I decline an attorney.

[The sound of a chair scraping back.]

GOBIS: So, Agnus, can I call you Agnus? Y'see, I feel I know you. I've worked a case on you before, [A cigarette lighter snaps, a deep inhalation.] As fate would have it, I was the investigating officer on your suicide. Or what we thought was your suicide. Guess I can wrap a ribbon around that one now. But I remember it well. It was all about your daughter. That's what we thought. Her death. That's why you took your life. But

here you are, very much alive. But Jezebeth Hooger is
dead. So you need to tell us about that, Agnus. Tell us
everything that happened tonight.

AGNUS: My duty was to protect her. To save her.

DIX: To protect who, Jezebeth?

AGNUS: To save her.

GOBIS: Hey, where's our manners, Agnus? You smoke, don't
you? Here's a fresh pack. Crack it open.
[Cellophane crackles. Chairs creak.]

GOBIS: [whispering]: I think he means his daughter. She
died of cancer and he was supposed to be a cancer
specialist. That was the guilt that pushed him over
the edge.

DIX: So he's confusing Jezebeth with his daughter.

GOBIS: He's got seven pints of someone else's blood down his
shirt, Dix. I think he's confused about a lotta things.
[A throat-clearing cough.]

GOBIS: So, Agnus, can you tell us about your daughter?

AGNUS: I will tell you about Maddy.

DIX: Your daughter's name was Lily.
[A fist thuds on to a table.]

AGNUS: Are you listening? You must listen. It is important that
you remember this.
[The voice of Agnus becomes strangely clear, not
thick and stilted as before. Sharp as a pin.]

AGNUS: The first thing you need to understand is that Maddy
Pool was an ugly child. Blubber skinned. Thin hair, like
an insect nest wrapped around that large cranium.
Her teenage years brought no improvement. All
those vile hormones just swelled her body, bigger
and bigger.

So she took a job that kept her in the shadows. A
coat-check girl in the kiosk of the Sewercide Club. This
underground music den ran in the old pipes beneath
the city. It was the creation of Gina Avner. Now,
Gina was a cream-skinned delight, with a lithe body

pierced and tattooed into a temple of pain. The girls who frequented the club were equally spectacular creatures, wrapped in black and obsessed with death. Nothing made them so happy as despair. Particularly the despair of others. Maddy was taunted by Gina without mercy. The naughty girl once slid a razor blade beneath the kiosk window and told Maddy to cut that ugly face right off her skull. And every night, as the thin, gorgeous girls danced into oblivion, Maddy would wonder if death, so celebrated in this club, might be just the thing to set her free. And so, one night, she walks to the river and lets her huge body roll in. She tries to breathe the stinking water in; she wants to welcome death. But something in her fights back. Refusing to die. Rejecting death. And her legs beat and her arms crawl and her fingers find mud and, heaving hard, she drags herself from the water. Lies on the edge of an old abandoned reservoir, into which the river empties. Glad that she is alone to wallow in this shame. Not shame that she attempted suicide. Shame that she lacked the courage to see it through. Regretting already that she permitted her primal instincts to overwhelm her desire to die.

And then she sees him. A boy . . . a man. A little older than herself. Black hair. Blue eyes. Walking through the reeds. He says he's an entomologist – a fly-hunter. He didn't mean to disturb her. But seeing her distress, he stays. He reaches out a hand and gives his name: Kave. An unexpected friendship sparks. For Maddy, it quickly grows to love. And so, just days after that first bizarre meeting, she cannot contain her joy when he says he wants to take her on a date. And he insists that they go to the Sewercide Club, so all the girls who taunt her can see her in the arms of an adoring man.

When the night comes, oh, Maddy's excitement

is quite marvellous! She can barely slick her lipstick straight. She has squeezed herself into a red dress that so constricts her blood supply, her face is soon a matching crimson. But she will endure it - just for tonight. Because this is her night. And when Kave takes her hand and sweeps her into the throbbing club, she is delirious. They dance and swirl until she is giddy. So giddy in fact that she can't be sure of the exact moment when Kave's hand slips from hers. And without her glasses she can't be certain that what she's seeing is real. So she waddles closer. And there it is. Gina Avner, her long cream arms wrapped around Kave, kissing him deeply.

The last thing Maddy remembers is crashing into her kiosk, ripping off her dress, pulling out the razor blade from the back of her diary and slashing it across her wrists.

And as she falls to the floor and her head rolls, she sees a shadow in the doorway. And she knows it is Kave. He rushes to her side, gathers her in his arms and brings his lips down to hers. She feels his kiss . . . but it's not a kiss. Something other. He is sucking hard, an unnatural force dragging something from within her.

But she will not give in to death. And just as she did beneath the water, she fights back. Rising up, swallowing back down what Kave had tried to siphon from her and then —

— nothing. Blackness. Until Maddy's eyes bolt open and

Lola's head jerks. Eyes blink hard in the half-light.
Have I been asleep?
She looks down. The audio-machine lies on the floor, cracked and crazed as if it has fallen from her grip. She picks it up, frowning. The cassette inside is knotted into the

mechanism. Which makes no sense.

It was playing. She heard it. All that stuff about . . .

She snatches up a folder and tugs out the printed interview transcripts. Flicks through. And finds – nothing. No mention of Maddy Pool. No record of that part of the interview. Lola chucks down the papers and hitches herself on to the bed to sit crossed-legged before Agnus.

If it wasn't coming from the tape, then it was coming from him. Somehow.

This is some kinda weirdo voodoo.

Lola stares at him. With his skin all stinky and yellow and his head spiked with monitor needles, Agnus looks like one of Fan Fan's thorn-headed poppets.

She always said they spoke to her.

So speak to me, Agnus. Tell me who Maddy is.

Silence. Nothing moves and then —

— a hand rises.

Not his . . . but hers.

Lola watches, wide-eyed and mystified, as her arm extends, fingers pulling a wire from the monitor board of the machine. Its sharp tip draws blood from her finger as she yanks it free. Then, inhaling hard, she forces the thorn-like tip deep into her scalp. A trickle of blood runs down her forehead as her fingers pull another wire, thrusting it into the other side of her skull. Her obedient hand returns to the machine, stripping the wires and thrusting them into her head until her cranium is linked to Agnus' by a silver web.

Blood streaks her face. She stares up.

This is what you wanted.

His mouth still sags, but she clearly hears his voice.

It is necessary.

What do you want me to do?

To remember.

His voice suddenly explodes like a bullet within her skull.

Know thyself.

Lola's body arches in the grip of a violent spasm. She

291

reaches up, one hand clawing at her head to rip the wires free, but her other hand wrestles with her wrist, fighting against herself as memories flood her mind.

She sees the heavy-set face of a girl, eyes swollen and red. And she knows – this is Maddy Pool.

And she knows – *this is me.*

She feels herself entering a lumbering body. And she hears the shrieking taunts, feels the sharp jab of fingers. And the hot burn of shame. She tries to run, but as if in a dream, her legs are leaden, refusing to escape.

Then blackness and —

— another torrent of memories, faces, voices, tears and screams, crashing down upon her, drowning her. She gasps for breath as if the past is bursting her lungs and then —

— blue eyes. Black hair.

Kave! My saviour!

Her breathless mouth. A kiss. Her hand in his.

And love. Such love. Like sunlight. Warming her body and then —

— it burns. It scalds her heart. It boils her blood, so she must cut her skin to cool it down, to let it chill against the ground.

And then he bends to take the last of her.

Kave! My traitor!

Her lifeless mouth. A kiss. Her span in him.

LOLA LEAPS FROM THE FLOOR, roaring, fighting back. Ripping free. Spinning to her feet as the guards burst through the cell door, weapons primed.

Molloy's eyes bulge.

The agent's blond hair is clotted with blood. It runs in thick streaks down her face. She ranges back and forth, breathing deeply.

Taking neither his eyes nor his rifle from her, Molloy chucks a command over his shoulder to Trill.

'Go tell the Governor.'

Trill's voice trickles from the darkness behind. 'Tell him what?'

'That Agnus is awake.'

Lola turns to Agnus. And watches as his sagging mouth now tightens into a smile.

48

BIANCO GLANCES AT THE SIGN ON THE LIBRARY WALL that reads 'Quiet Please', then inhales and bellows at the top of her voice. 'Two-Nine-Three-Six-Four.'

'OK, I'm getting closer.'

Mo'Zart is deep in the library and high on a ladder, running his finger along the reference numbers on the uppermost shelf. 'Scroll down and see if he took out any others on Archilochus.'

Bianco taps the computer. The page lists all the books checked out from the library by Grotteschi. She shouts over her shoulder, 'No, just that one.'

'I got it!' Mo'Zart pulls a book out, jams it between his teeth and scoots down the ladder like a fire-fighter, landing with a thud. He bounds across the library.

Bianco snaps her finger, encouraging speed.

Mo'Zart wipes the cover on his thigh, drops into a chair, flips the book open. Bianco hovers behind, leaning deep.

'So what have we got?'

'Apparently, no sense of personal space.' Mo'Zart tucks his shoulders tight. 'It don't help with you bent on my shoulder like a crow.'

She leans in deeper still, black hair swishing. 'In Taino, Bianco means crow. So it is my natural state to perch.'

She jabs her finger down hard on the book and Mo'Zart grunts, pressing on. Flicks the pages, each one bearing a poem. The paper is yellow and stiff, crackling in his fingers.

Bianco's nose is almost in the crook of his neck. 'What are we looking for?'

'I don't think the answer is in the actual poetry. Agnus

talked about Archilochus himself, the man. And when he says he came once before, that has to be a reference to the Mosca. We know the Mosca has come many times before and the Sinestra have always successfully struck before the G-Men could arrive to awaken it. So maybe there is something that links each incarnation of the Mosca. We find that, then we know what to look for in this new coming.'

Bianco glances again at the tattered card Siggurson was given by Kon'Verse. 'This says that he'll come again by the same name.'

'We can't take that literally. The Greeks love to play with their names.' He raises a finger, skewering an example. 'Plato's name was actually Aristocles, but he got the name Plato from being fat – *platon* means broad. So first we find out what we can on our guy.'

Mo'Zart spreads wide a page entitled: 'Archilochus: Extracts of his Life' and Bianco snaps her fingers. 'Read it.'

Mo'Zart dips his head, eyes scanning like a printer.

Bianco snaps again. 'Out loud.'

Mo'Zart sits up, book in hand. Clears his throat.

'The poet Archilochus was born in 680 BC on the Greek island of Paros. He was famed for the savagery of his verse, which would often take prominent dignitaries as their theme and subject them to vicious ridicule. In Greek society, one's reputation was valued above all else and to be reduced to a laughing stock, for many, meant ruin. Numerous accounts of performances given by Archilochus would make particular mention of the strange pleasure that he appeared to derive from seeing men and women crushed by his poetic scorn.

'However, despair struck Archilochus himself when he fell in love with a beauty called Neobule. Archilochus courted her earnestly, but her father, Lycambes, grew ever more opposed to the union as Archilochus' reputation for cruelty grew. When he ultimately withdrew his daughter from the engagement, Archilochus set his mind on vengeance.

'At the feast of Demeter, where all of noble society was gathered together, Archilochus rose and delivered the most scathing attack of his career. The poem's subject was Lycambes and his daughter. They were mercilessly parodied until both ran weeping from the feast.

'Soon after, their bodies were found hanging in the temple gardens. Father and daughter had committed suicide, crushed by Archilochus' words.

'The poet was inconsolable. He cried out that he did not know what so possessed him to drive others to their destruction. One account records him tearing the robes from his body and crying to the sky, "What beast lives within me, that I must be a stranger to myself?"

'He wandered into the desert, imploring none to follow him. But intrigue followed him to the end. According to an account rendered by a scribe in Lycambes' household, an unknown man attempted to pursue Archilochus as he fled. His name is not recorded and the scribe notes that he was unfamiliar with the strange Legion the man attested to serve. When he questioned him as to his intent, he replied, "To kill Archilochus, if you so call it death."

'However, in a final twist, before the legionary could reach him, Archilochus was slain in a duel by a man known only as Corvus.'

Bianco is pacing, thinking aloud. 'I see a connection. Archilochus killed through his words. And Kon'Verse, his lyrics . . . his rhymes . . . they got a young girl killed. Just like Neobule.' She flexes her fingers as if the idea is growing in her grasp. 'I looked into his eyes and I saw something there . . . something beyond the natural.'

Mo'Zart shakes his head. 'If Kon'Verse were the Mosca, his every instinct would be to kill the Moera. And I've read the records. Kon'Verse has been close to Agnus all along and the old man ain't dead yet.'

'I say we play safe. Get him locked in isolation.'

'I say we need him.'

Mo'Zart sees the steel grit in Bianco's eyes. He holds up a hand. 'Will you hear me out?' He flaps the hand, beckoning her over. With his other, he punches up an image on the screen. 'You know how I got recruited, right?'

Bianco walks around the desk towards the screen. 'The Voynich Manuscript at Yale. That's what SCURO uses. Like a brain magnet.'

Mo'Zart scrolls through online images of the book's strange pages. 'This chapter is right where I'd got to in my translation when Agent Bex found me.' His finger jabs to one page, singling out a symbol in one corner. 'This is the sign for Scox. And Scox, the flaming stork, is a herald, so it always appears close to the symbol of the fly . . . the Mosca.' His finger sweeps to a winged rune.

'Like the Lord of the Flies?'

'That's the devil himself . . . let's say that the Mosca is one of his fierce lieutenants. But this is what I want to show you.' He points to a thin, triangular rune. 'This symbol is known as *thurisaz* or, in Anglo-Saxon, *thurs*. It appears frequently alongside the symbol of the Moera.' He points to a sign that resembles three threads, intertwining as one.

'So what are you saying?'

'*Thurs* is the rune for protection and defence. It means thorn. Now look at this.' He leans across to another computer that displays the prison records. Taps in a reference number. Kon'Verse's file picture comes up. Tattooed rose thorns climb up his neck and reach across his jaw.

'He chose those tattoos because his name – his birth-name – was Ursus Blackthorn.' Mo'Zart swivels to Bianco. 'And that shows us his destiny. Like Judas with his black rose. And Brother Spino . . . in Latin, that means thorn. Kon'Verse is just one in a long line of guardians.'

'So he's not our guy . . .' Bianco exhales, fists clenching against the edge of the desk. 'Where does that leave us?'

Mo'Zart spreads his hand over the poems of Archilochus, then he folds the wings of the book shut. His eyes flicker as if a thought is passing through his head like a butterfly.

Bianco sees his expression. 'What is it?'

Mo'Zart grimaces, failing to capture the idea before it disappears. 'Your name means . . . crow?'

Bianco exhales. 'Yeah, so?'

Mo'Zarts twists his pencil in his dreads as if trying to unscrew an idea that is buried too deep. 'Could it be that there's . . .' He snaps back into focus. 'It's nothing. Maybe nothing. We need more to go on.'

'But tell me we've got something here. Does Archilochus hold some clue to the identity of the Mosca?'

Mo'Zart nods, chin in hand. 'It's one piece of the puzzle. We just don't know where it fits.'

49

'You crazy whack-snatch! What the fuck have you done?'

'If you'll just let me speak —'

'I'm sick of that mouth of yours! It sucks like mud and spits up trouble.'

The raised voices are muffled by the door, but Officer Trill knows how to skulk. His parents' refusal to get a divorce and readiness to get drunk meant that Trill perfected early the art of lying low and listening up. He moves his ear close to the hinges.

The Governor and Dr Torgus are really going at it.

'Woman, you're destroying me!'

'I would never hurt you . . .'

'You'd pull my colon out through my cock if you thought it would drag you outta this shit.'

'Ray D'Sola is a celebrated philanthropist. I've persuaded him to come here . . . to meet you. To memorialise a prisoner . . . your prisoner . . . in your prison.'

'You're an idiot.'

At a bellowed command Trill is quick to appear, flapping through the door in his waterproofs. He sees Governor Duggin behind his desk, kneading the back of his chair, killing the leather.

'Get over here. I'm kinda sick o' shouting.'

The officer moves closer, finds himself beneath a crack in the ceiling. The rain splatters down the back of his hat.

'Trill, I'm finding it tough to talk to Dr Torgus without getting testy, so I'd like you to tell her just what you told me.'

Trill turns to Torgus. Her hair is wet and stuck against

her scalp, grey roots showing. She looks like a raccoon spooked from a trash can.

Leaning back against the desk she muzzles a grimace. 'Tell me what, exactly?'

'Ma'am, Agnus Day has woken up.'

Duggin strides towards the window, snatching up a pack of cigarettes. 'I had a chance, one sweet-chilli chance to get Agnus swept outta my chimney, nice and quiet: an unconscious con. But now all my bunting goes right back in the fucking box. One whisper that he's awake and the Petra Loa will be baying to get him back.'

Torgus drums her nails upon the desk. 'So – I have a proposition.'

A dart of her eyes suggests that Duggin should dismiss the guard. As the door closes behind Trill, Torgus eases herself forward.

'What about this. You do not return Agnus to the cell-block. Instead, you declare an on-going concern for his health. He would, in your opinion, fare better in the care of the infirmary. That means he rides the prison train across the desert. To ease his journey, I will administer one of the many anti-anxiety drugs that I am licensed to dispense. The dose will be necessarily high, such is Agnus' state of distress. Sadly, he will respond adversely to the sedation and never regain consciousness. As the federal agents will no doubt insist on traveling with him to the infirmary, they will be aboard the train to witness his death, in full knowledge that you, Governor, are miles away in Morphic Fields. You clearly had no hand in his unfortunate passing. I doubt they will demand much investigation as his death puts a very final end to their concerns about Agnus' undue influence.'

Duggin chews the filter of his cigarette. 'And what do you want in return?'

'Next to nothing. I simply want the chance to sell Ray D'Sola the publishing rights to the prophecies. To do that, I first need Agnus to assign the rights to me.' Torgus reaches inside her jacket and produces a document. 'Once I have his signature, I will . . . sedate him.'

'And Ray D'Sola?'

'His interest is in Agnus so he'll bypass the prison and accompany me on the train.' She moves in closer still. 'You won't feel a thing.'

Duggin's face relaxes a twitch. Torgus seizes the moment. 'Trust me, honey . . . it'll work.' She slides her fingers down, finding his groin.

As she urgently pulls and caresses, Duggin hisses through tight teeth, 'Trust me, Torgus. You won't feel a thing.'

50

'THIS MAY HURT.' Lola yanks out the last needle from Agnus' scalp. He doesn't flinch, even though the fast removal pulls some flesh. Blood dribbles down his face. Lola has no time to wipe it clean.

By coming back to life like this, Agnus has condemned himself. Any tolerance the Governor may have had for their interference will surely cease now that he can officially put Agnus back on death row.

She runs her fingers through her hair feeling her own scalp clotted with blood. Breathes deep.

I just need . . . to think. But there's no time.

She turns to Agnus. His eyes follow her about the room as she paces, planning her next step.

Those memories . . . that's who I was. But what matters now is what I am. What I must now do.

Above her she hears the clang of the doors. The echo of boots. Guards are approaching.

She bends down to the frame that suspends Agnus, her fingers flying as she unties the tethers that bind him. 'I am here to protect you. But I don't know how long we have. So tell me what you know. Who is the Mosca?'

Agnus stares at her with milky eyes. His mouth slithers. 'I am here to protect you.' The dull tone suggests he is simply repeating the sounds from Lola's mouth.

She pauses in her task. Finding his eyes: 'Do you understand me? Do you know who you are?'

'Do you know who you are?' The same droning echo, then his eyes spark. His voice sharpens. 'You are Maddy Pool.'

Now Lola grasps his jaw, turning the emaciated face to meet hers. 'Who I am does not matter. Who is the Mosca?'

The heavy footsteps pound closer. Lola accelerates her efforts to release his limbs.

'I'm taking you from here. You come with us. And we find who the Mosca is.'

'Cease now!' The roar from Agnus rips across her face like hot steam and his freed hand snares her wrist, hauling her close. 'You will let this happen. Events must take their course. Until the time comes.'

'What time?'

'You will know.'

The guards burst through the door. Lola's eye blaze, burning down the fuse of the last few seconds. 'How will I know?'

Agnus' eyes close and his neck wilts. His words now slide and slur. 'Not how . . . what . . . *what* you will know. That will change everything.'

51

DUST RISES FROM THE BACK OF A PEW, flurried by a sigh. Grotteschi is on his knees. Beside him is Siggurson. They are in the dark arches of the prison chapel.

Grotteschi whispers, but the slate walls amplify each syllable. 'So you have the Poet. Now to the Painter. But where to begin this next revelation?' His old hands, clasped in prayer, hold a shred of paper. 'Let us start with Father McDees.' He rises with a groan and slides on to the pew. 'He was the chaplain at Morphic Fields when Agnus first arrived. I always liked McDees – or McSqueeze as he was commonly known amongst the inmates. He was an ex-con . . . did five years for corporate blackmail, went to jail and found God.' Grotteschi grunts a laugh. 'The prison system does not attract the highest calibre of churchman. And consequently we at Morphic Fields were allotted this old lag. And very few attended his confessional. Would you want to open your darkest secrets to a one-time extortionist?'

A creak of wood sparks Siggurson's head to rise upwards, his training kicking in. He disguises the response by clasping his hand in prayer, mimicking the old man.

'Worms, my boy. This place is riddled.' Grotteschi shifts, easing the pressure on his shins, finding a temporary respite. 'McDees was a clever man; I find that most blackmailers are. And, at the outset, he and I enjoyed many a conversation on the topic of Agnus, when I was sure that this new inmate was pulling a con all of his own. McDees and I both admired his creative commitment. Until McDees got a revelation all of his own, thrust into his hand by a gibbering Agnus.'

Grotteschi slides the paper from his fingers and conceals it in his palm. 'I will share the note itself with you momentarily, but first let me get to the kneebone of this story. The revelation spoke of a painting . . . this painting.'

Grotteschi points upwards. Hanging on the church wall beside them is a heavy-framed picture. It shows three women, draped in white robes, spinning thread.

Grotteschi exhales, struggling up to his feet. Puckers and puffs dust from the brass name-plate.

'This is *The Three Fates,* or, to give them their original Greek name, *The Moera,* painted in 1692 by the Dutch artist Emanuel de Witte. According to myth, by the spinning, pulling and cutting of their thread, the Moera determine our lifespan. Strange how that echoes Agnus' work on the human lifespan and telomeres.'

His hand unrolls to show Siggurson the shred of paper, upon which a single sentence is scrawled.

The master Chiro Scuro Emanuel de Witte atrophied the fly of the fatal three.

Grotteschi waggles the paper, urging Siggurson to take it.

'When McDees received this revelation, I knew that the "fatal three" must refer to the "three fates". It was the only one of de Witte's work that made sense. So I persuaded McDees to order a copy of the painting so that we might study it. This is a cheap facsimile, but adequate for our purpose." He pokes in his monocle, peering at the brushstrokes. "Now I have to assume that Agnus made an error. In his haste, he misspelled chiaroscuro, omitting the "a". Chiaroscuro means "light and shadow" and it is an Italian style of painting. But here is the first twist of the mystery. Emanuel de Witte did not paint in the Italian style, so why would Agnus call him a master of this art? And then there is this to consider . . . The Three Fates are women. In de Witte's work, the face of the Fate who cuts the thread, and so determines death, is decidedly masculine. Do you see that . . . ?' Grotteschi's eye, made huge by the monocle, bubbles up at him. 'Perhaps because de Witte knew the work was flawed in this way, he did not sign it with his real name, but instead he used the pseudonym Kolibrie.'

Grotteschi's finger strokes the large, hard jaw of the deathly Fate. 'McDees and I pondered over this endlessly. And, oddly, I found this priest more given to fearful superstition than I. He lacked faith.' Grotteschi fumbles with a chain that hangs about his distended neck. From it hangs a crucifix. 'My mother raised me in the true faith, but when she committed the sin of suicide, I fell from the path. But now my heart has been reawakened. Whatever dark realms exist beyond this, I know that God's hand lies above them all, and that He would not forsake us. But McDees, the superstitious charlatan, did not care a fig for what the message to mankind might be. He surrendered himself to dark imaginings and saw only his own future in this revelation, believing that it foretold his own death. He became obsessed with the rope in the hand of the final Fate, as if the length of it could tell him of the date of his own demise.'

A shaft of light spears the gloom. The chapel door swings open. Siggurson turns to see a priest silhouetted in the arch. The long robes sweep forward.

Grotteschi nods his head. 'Good evening, Father.'

Siggurson studies the figure as he moves through the darkness. His eyes are on a sliver of grey metal that flashes in the priest's hands.

Grotteschi sees this keen attention and waggles his head. 'You think that is McDees? No, no. He's dead. Hanged himself with his own vestment belt. No easy task, the cord was only four feet long.'

The priest sweeps by, hidden in a hooded robe, his hands clasped about an iron cross. He disappears into the vestry. 'That is the latest in a long line of feckless fathers who have been despatched since the suicide of McDees. Not one has yet lasted a month before appealing to the Cardinal for a transfer. It seems that Morphic Fields gives these sorry celibates the chills. But I digress. Your mind must be applied to this alone.' His old hand strokes the painting and then lowers to Siggurson's shoulder, pressing down with surprising strength. 'I shall leave you now, to contemplate. Let the meaning come to you.'

Grotteschi crosses himself and kisses his crucifix. 'Agnus is trying to show us the truth. And I know that somewhere in this painting, there is a sign . . . to show what comes.'

52

HER PAINTED NAILS stab at the keypad of her phone. D'Sola picks up before she even hears it ring.

'You are extremely tense, Dr Torgus.'

She flinches, shaken. 'Why do you say that?'

'I have an app that tells me how tightly you are holding your phone.'

Dr Torgus swallows, confused, exhaling only at the sound of D'Sola's laughter.

'A joke, Dr Torgus.'

She tries to return the laughter but emits only a tight cough. 'Mr D'Sola, there's been a change of plan. No, not a change . . . a modification.'

She looks in the mirror. Her fingers try to revive the drowned hairpiece that sprawls across her skull. 'You should ask your driver to take you to the railway terminus behind the prison. We will be travelling with Agnus to the prison hospital. I have all the materials with me. We will have every opportunity to . . . take care of business.'

At the other end, D'Sola is silent. Dr Torgus becomes agitated. Then —

'Is this the only . . . modification to your original proposal, doctor?'

'Yes, absolutely. Everything else remains exactly as we discussed.'

She can almost hear the chill of D'Sola's smile.

'There is a great little app that I recommend. It gives you instant word definitions, Dr Torgus. I suggest you look up the meaning of "exclusivity".'

The line goes dead.

RAY D'SOLA HANGS UP HIS PHONE and slides it into his pocket. He leans back against the white leather of the seat.

The windscreen wipers of his Rolls-Royce Silver Ghost sweep away the solid desert rain with the kind of smooth silence that sets you back two million dollars. The driver's voice is delivered by a walnut speaker. 'I still can't quite be sure what it is, sir.' Wilson takes a hand off the wheel and tips back his chauffeur's cap. Stares hard through the downpour. Rising between the road and the distant bulk of Morphic Fields is some sort of metal structure. 'I'd say it's a music stage, sir. Because that bus' – he gestures to a vehicle ahead, swarming with kids who goon against the glass, '– looks to me like it's full o' fans o' some sort. But I can't read the name painted on the side, on account of all this blessed rain. So . . . Well, my sweet Lord!' Wilson leans forward and points up to the heavens. 'Will you look at that!' The solid black sky above Morphic Fields is splitting apart and sunlight shears through like a band-saw.

Wilson shrugs, killing the wipers. 'These desert storms are mighty strange.'

'A detour, Wilson. Follow that bus.'

The vehicle is bumping down a slip road, heading across the desert towards the structure.

Wilson yanks the wheel, churning dust. 'As you please, sir.'

D'Sola estimates that it will please him not at all. As the car passes the bus and nears the structure, he can see that it is indeed a vast performance platform. Scaffold poles catch in the fresh sunlight, reflecting gold. Roadies roll drums of cable and haul generators. And above the stage, a banner rises. It bears one word: 'STORK'.

A collection of black-clad boys sit on the ground beneath a sunshade, surrounded by a swarm of assistants. This must be the band. Heads down, they appear uninterested in any attempt to usher them from the canopy. The only movement comes from a blade that flashes as it is passed from one band member to another, each taking a moment to score a fresh cut in their exposed forearms.

The assistants pump their walkie-talkies, summoning security as shrieking fans are disgorged from the bus.

The Rolls slides between a row of metal barriers that are hurriedly hauled into place about the canopy. A pale-faced assistant, waving a clipboard, flags down the strange car.

'Here is just fine, Wilson.' D'Sola ignores any attempt by the assistant to gain his attention. His eyes are locked upon a figure who rises from the band and walks towards the car. A long, lean boy whose face is hidden by a curtain of black hair.

The back door breathes open. D'Sola's voice rises from within, smooth as smoke. 'I think we should talk.'

Hash-Tu spins the blade in his fingers as he sizes up the sleek machine, but no sound slides out from behind the hair.

D'Sola smiles. 'Oh, that's right. You shoe-gazing gonzos aren't much given to conversation.' He leans an inch from the vehicle. His face catches in the sunlight. 'Beautiful, isn't it.' He gestures to the sky, bright and clear. 'I hope it holds for your performance.'

A flash behind the hair shows that Hash-Tu's eyes are moving. His torso twitches a fraction closer. D'Sola smiles.

'Good. You know who I am. So can we put an end to this performance?'

'Are you here to see me?'

'Quite the opposite. I was not expecting to see anyone at all.' D'Sola's hand gestures towards the massive form of Morphic Fields. 'It is Agnus Day who brings you here?'

Hash-Tu nods.

'Ah well then, please come.' D'Sola beckons the boy to join him in the vehicle. 'Wilson here can entertain us with another acre of desert.'

From behind the barriers, fans whoop and holler as they catch sight of Hash-Tu. Two girls in the crowd stretch their necks, straining to catch a glimpse of him as he slides into the car. In a breath of dust, it bears him away across the desert.

One girl turns to her friend. Her green eyes are acid wide. 'Hey, Livi, he's comin' back, right?'

'Of course, Ghost. He'll come back. He always comes back.'

THE INTERCOM BUTTON IS FLICKED TO SILENT. Then D'Sola's finger rises, taps his lips. He is in no rush to speak himself. A moment of silence will allow him to gather his thoughts. Examine this emotion rising within him.

Shall I call it anger? Dr Torgus had promised him exclusive access to the phenomenon of Agnus Day. That was one element of this venture that had attracted him, the fact that he could deny the privilege to anyone else. He had also been drawn by Dr Torgus's knowledge of Archilochus, a poet for whom D'Sola has an unbridled passion. And of course her obvious emotional fragility was . . . appetising.

But the proposal itself, to publish the convict's prophecies, seemed tenuous at best.

However, curiosity had prevailed. The slaughter of that child-whore in Sulphur City was intriguing and D'Sola felt a strong compulsion to be in the orbit of the one who wielded the knife.

But now that he is here, he finds some death-metal interloper has come to worship at the killer's shrine and share him with the world.

So the urge – the cold, hard longing that unfolds within him, like a many-bladed device – perhaps it is anger?

D'Sola relaxes back and moves to the more delicious dilemma: *what to do with this anger?*

He glances at Hash-Tu, who stares out of the window. D'Sola wonders if he rehearses in the mirror that tilt of his chin, high enough to elegantly stretch his neck like a wading

311

bird, but not so high that his hair falls free from his face.

And then the black hair swings as Hash-Tu turns towards him, his eyes narrowed to a glittering strip. 'Does the silence make you uneasy?'

D'Sola smiles. 'I think I'll stop you right there, glum-drop. You seem to be confused. Perhaps because your experience is more commonly that you are the weird one. The scary guy. The one who makes those around you . . . uneasy.'

As he speaks, D'Sola feels his own breathing strangely accelerate. He clenches his jaw, forcing control over his lungs, determined to finish his discourse. 'You don't make me feel . . . anything. *Nothing* makes me feel anything. But I think . . . in fact I know, with an awful certainty, that I can make you feel something.'

Hash-Tu slides hard into the door, producing the blade from his fist. 'Don't touch me, you fucking sicko.' His hand lashes and blood flies. Hash-Tu thrusts again, but slower now, unsure how it is that he draws so much blood from D'Sola when his blade does not appear to be connecting with him. And then, as he tries to raise his arm a third time, he sees it: his own hand, thrusting the blade into his own chest. Blood bubbling beneath his T-shirt as a hole opens wider.

Hash-Tu writhes, screaming, rupturing red across the white leather. Unable to stop his own hand as it hacks and hews.

D'Sola looks on, breathing hard, enraptured. The broader he smiles, the further the hole rips.

Until Hash-Tu shivers and spasms into the footwell.

D'Sola continues to watch for some minutes. The boy is exceptionally dead but D'Sola feels the need for a moment's calm to examine what emotion it is that he now feels.

He is an educated man but he's not sure that there's a word for this. His finger quivers with such ferocity he can barely secure it upon the intercom switch.

'Wilson, would you kindly stop the car.'

The Rolls relaxes to a halt. The door is swept open and D'Sola exits. It is only as he stretches his arms wide and walks from the car, grinning at the vastness of the desert, that Wilson sees the bloody carcass on the car floor. The chauffeur's hand lunges inside his jacket and pulls a gun. He looks at his boss, who smiles, utterly calm.

Swallowing hard, Wilson jerks the gun towards the corpse. 'Now, boss, you wanna tell me what's happening here?'

D'Sola inhales and then turns his eyes on Wilson. 'Wilson, I really don't know. But it is rather wonderful, don't you think?'

D'Sola seems to ripple with a strange energy. His gaze fixes on the old man. 'What do you want to do with that gun, Wilson?'

Wilson goes to speak, but something emanating from D'Sola seems to leaden his tongue, stultify his brain. 'Sir . . . I . . . I . . .'

'You don't want to kill me, do you, Wilson? On a lovely day like today, with the sun so strong on the back of your neck? You want to put that ice-cold barrel against your hot head and pull the trigger, don't you, Wilson?'

'Sir . . . I . . . don't.'

But then Wilson feels it, the chill of the gun touching his temple. And his eyes slide to one side to see that his own hand steers the weapon.

'That's right, Wilson. Your world is a happy place.'

Impossibly . . . irresistibly, Wilson's thumb peels back the priming pin and in a jolting blast empties his brains out through his left ear.

D'Sola looks at this fresh corpse, thumping into the dust. Feels a power rip through him like an execution volt.

Something is happening. He doesn't knows what. But he knows this: it feels good. It feels right.

D'Sola bends to collect the car keys from Wilson's

clenched hand. And then, before the conscious thought can find a voice inside his head, he submits to the urge to plant a hard kiss on the old man's mouth.

D'Sola then twists away, drags a sleeve across his lips.

In an afternoon of first-time feelings, that last one, decides D'Sola, is definitively the most fucked-up.

53

'Again. Slower.'

Bianco looks at the books spread open in front of Mo'Zart. He nods and brings his finger back towards an old art book that's open on an image of *The Three Fates*.

'This face here' – he taps the strong, masculine features of the last Fate, then sweeps his finger to a book of portraits open beside him – 'is this man right here.'

Bianco looks from one image to the other. 'And that is who . . . and that means what?'

Mo'Zart draws his fingertips into pincers as if conducting the most delicate part of the symphony. 'Each revelation is a clue to the identity of the Mosca, but Agnus was careful that each message could also be connected to the person to whom it was delivered – because that knowledge will help us to decipher it.'

Mo'Zart pauses, letting each fact chime before moving on. 'What links Kon'Verse and Archilochus is that they both killed through the power of their words. McDees was a blackmailer and so was this guy.' He taps the portrait of the man before them. 'Jornis de Wijs.'

Mo'Zart's finger rises now, moving faster as if the music of his logic is gaining tempo. 'Look at where the artist placed the face of de Wijs in *The Three Fates*: on the body of the Fate called Atropos, the one who cuts the thread . . . the Fate of Death. That is where the word "atrophy" comes from. And here in the revelation, it says he "atrophied the Fly". Do you see? Isn't it perfect?'

Mo'zart is on his feet, as if ready to receive applause, but his audience of one stands with her arms folded.

'Everything. From the beginning.'

Mo'Zart nods, tips up his palms. 'As you want. But it begins in the seventeenth century.'

He quickly flicks through a huge art book, selecting a painting. It shows a serving maid pouring a pitcher of beer for a sleeping huntsman, who has a dead goose hanging in his arms.

'Back in seventeenth-century Holland, there was what I guess you could call a craze in high society. It was all about these: proverb paintings. Here's one example, a tavern maid pouring a hunter a pitcher of beer. Charming and harmless, you'd think. But you'd be wrong. Every painting was intended to carry a hidden meaning, concealed in the symbols of the picture. And the message could only be cracked if you knew your proverbs well. So solving the riddle was like a seventeenth-century equivalent of doing a crossword puzzle. People would spend hours staring at them, searching for clues. And they were motivated to solve the meaning. How else could they be sure what message the giver of the painting was sending to them? Was it a message of love, or an insult, or even a threat?'

Mo'Zart gestures to the picture of the tavern maid. 'Look at this one. Do you see that the pitcher she holds has a crack? That refers to an old proverb about a cracked pitcher not holding its beer and it means that whoever sent this painting is saying, "Man, you can't handle your drink." And the goose with the limp neck . . . there's a Dutch proverb that likens a man's inability to get it up to a goose that can't raise its head. I could go on, but you get the point. Whoever sent this painting was giving the message: "You can't hold your beer and it's making you impotent." Perhaps it was sent by a disgruntled wife – who knows? This particular painting is clearly meant to be just a bit of fun. But the messages contained in some paintings were far more sinister. And none more sinister than those sent by Jornis de Wijs.'

Mo'Zart turns the book round so that the portrait of a man's sallow visage faces Bianco. 'De Wijs was a blackmailer and he hit upon the idea of sending paintings that concealed references to secrets that could defame and destroy high-society figures. All he needed for his plan was an artist willing to create the paintings according to his instructions.'

With a flick of his finger, Mo'Zart draws Bianco's eye to a book of paintings. 'This is the work of Emanuel de Witte. He was perfect for Jornis's plan – a bankrupt, willing to do anything to save himself. He created the paintings as Jornis prescribed. The blackmail victims were quick to read the messages hidden in the unwelcome art delivered to their door. Some paid the price to the blackmailer, whom they knew only by the pseudonym signature in the corner of the painting, *Kolibrie*. But many – those who could not pay the extortionate demands – took their own lives rather than risk exposure. In short, Jornis drove them to suicide. And de Witte, who loathed himself for the part he played, eventually took his own life. He hanged himself – but not before completing a painting of his own design.' Mo'Zart now returns his hand to *The Three Fates*. 'This was his final work and in it, he left a hidden message to be found after his death. One that would expose to all society the identity of the deadly blackmailer who had been plaguing them. On the body of the Fate of Death, de Witte painted for all to see the face of Jornis de Wijs. So everyone would know that he was the mysterious Kolibrie. De Witte left the painting to be discovered on the day of his suicide. Two days later, Jornis was found stabbed through the mouth. Most assumed that the killer was one of his blackmail victims, but an eye-witness gave testimony that the knife was wielded by a man called Corbin Kraal. In normal circumstances, the Master of the Burgher Guard would have pursued this villain Kraal, but none mourned the death of Jornis De Wijs and the stranger was allowed to slip away unhindered.'

Bianco says nothing, waiting for the silence to signal the end of this account.

She shakes her head. 'The shit you know.'

'Now we gotta put it all together.' The book on Archilochus bears his picture on the front. Mo'Zart adds it to his stack. 'This is what I think. Agnus is showing us that Archilochus and Jornis were both incarnations of the Mosca. Neither reached their awakening. So if we can find what links Archilochus and Jornis, then we'll know what links them to the next incarnation . . . the one that comes now. We look for that link – we find him.'

'And kill him.'

'Right.'

Mo'Zart gathers the mounting pile of books to him. 'We can do it. Just gonna take time.'

The shriek of an alarm cuts the air, echoing from the walls, filling the prison. The door to the library suddenly thuds open. Officer Trill appears.

'Ma'am, the Governor says we got trouble. Big trouble. Right now.'

A TUMBLER OF RUM SWILLS. Governor Duggin slugs the shot back and pours himself another, crimping the phone between his neck and jowl.

'With all due respect, Agent Bianco, I must ask that you pay heed to my greater experience. I had no option but to order a lockdown. If we fail to take immediate action, we are sitting on a whole barrel o' trouble.' He swigs a second time, emptying the glass. 'The reality is that Agnus Day has regained consciousness, which benefits neither your plan nor mine. Once he is back amongst the inmates, his control will return. So we have but a short window to remove him from the prison. Now, our means of discreetly so doing are limited. With a hundred miles of desert in every direction, getting anything out of Morphic Fields is a challenge.'

He pauses. 'Agent Bianco, would you excuse me a

moment, my officers have arrived and are awaiting orders.'
Duggin claps a hand over the mouthpiece. 'Very good,
gentlemen. Very smooth. My compliments to H Block.
Those Haitians are real masters of rum. Now load it up.
All of it.' Five officers nod, approaching a stack of barrels
in the office, each taking one and rolling it out. Duggin
smacks his lips, returns to his call.

'So this is my proposal. Each Friday night a train arrives,
dedicated to Morphic Fields. It transports inmates due for
trial, or those in need of advanced medical treatment . . .
in short, a line to the outside world. It is well armed and
built for this purpose so I want you to have no qualms as to
security. There will be guards and munitions aboard. Now,
today is Friday and the train is due. I say we put Agnus on
it and defuse this situation.'

He pauses, allowing Bianco to respond. His face relaxes.
He is hearing what he wants. Leans back.

'I'm glad that you agree, Agent. This is the only way to
remove the rag from the barrel.'

54

GROTTESCHI'S MONOCLE GLITTERS as he stands tip-toe on his bunk-frame and peers out of his cell window to the flood-lit desert below. A solitary rail track stretches from the dark horizon to Morphic Fields, where it thrusts between giant concrete cubes assembled as a platform.

The surface is checkered with the pools of light, and guards, in their pale buff uniforms, move in and out of the shadows. Grotteschi squints, counting numbers. This is a bigger turnout than the usual bon voyage brigade. Grotteschi watches them shunt across the cubed platform like chess pieces.

And then black makes its move.

Four dark suits appear. Federal agents, he's sure of it, fanning out to take up position at each corner of the platform. Grotteschi does not know what their purpose is. But he does know that Siggurson is one of them.

He watches as Siggurson turns his face up to the prison, as if sensing that one good eye is upon him. Grotteschi crinkles a smile.

He is not aggrieved by the deception. How can a fraudster such as he cast judgement? And further, he forgives them for a reason they could never understand. Their deception bears a strange truth. Siggurson is not a visionary, but without doubt he is outside the norm. Life and death is no simple thing with him: somehow, those forces coexist within his head. And what awaits him is the strangest fate – neither life nor death, but something other.

Grotteschi feels this with all his heart. A heart now awoken to God, who speaks clearly to him. He clasps his hands together in prayer.

'Holy Mary, Mother of God, you have sent them to keep Agnus safe. So I ask that you bestow your protection, Holy Mother.' He sinks lower, burying his nose between his freshly washed hands. Breathes deep.

'Mother . . .'

ON THE PLATFORM, A RADIO CRACKLES.

'This is bad.'

'*This is good.*'

'Good how?'

'*You think I would have agreed to this without an advantage?*'

'Which is?' Lola releases the receive button on her radio, looks across to the far corner where Bianco stands, radio to her lips.

'*We know the Mosca is drawn to pursue the Moera. So if Agnus gets on the train, the Mosca will feel compelled to follow. And that means our search area gets smaller. In the prison, we'd be looking amongst two thousand people. On the train we're gonna have maybe fifty.*'

Lola nods. 'This is good.' She turns at the rattle of gurney wheels. 'They're bringing Agnus now.'

Two guards steer the gurney. Agnus is bound to the frame by leather straps. Bianco looks on from across the platform.

'*He can't talk?*'

'Won't talk.'

'*Does he know who we are?*'

'He knows who I am.'

'*What do you mean?*'

'It means I don't trust him.'

Mo'Zart's voice cuts across the transmission. '*We must trust him. He's all we have.*'

From his corner, Siggurson watches. '*But he's barely alive. How can we be sure that the Moera will emerge from*

321

that? Maybe he's malfunctioning. You can wire a bomb, but it doesn't always detonate.'

'*So with or without his help – we find the Mosca.*' Bianco raises her hand and jerks it forward, a signal for them all to board the train. '*Lola, you stay close to Agnus. Siggurson, there's an observation wagon; the monitors cover the train. I've told Duggin that's ours.*'

'*Copy that. Where will you be?*'

Bianco strides towards the train. '*Everywhere.*'

A **WATCH TICKS**. Dr Torgus feels the whir of the second hand as if it were drilling into her wrist.

He should be here!

Her eyes scan the platform and then sweep again to the half-lit dirt road that leads to the terminus. The train won't go until those agents are aboard, so for these few brief moments, she is glad of their presence. She watches as they walk from the far corners of the platform.

Slowly! Slowly! Just a few moments more . . .

Then she sees a figure mount the steps to the platform. Her eyes widen in welcome, then instantly thin. It is only the prison chaplain. What confused her was the speed of his approach. She has never known any chaplain to show an ounce of alacrity to travel with the sick. She strikes a match for her cigarette and allows herself a smile. They will actually be in need of a priest, once she has put Agnus into his endless slumber. The chaplain will no doubt be delighted to prove himself so useful.

She sucks her smoke into life and flicks the match into a trash can. Her eyes return to their sweep of the platform and the road. As the two agents board the train, she pulls out her phone, reluctant to disturb him, but desperate now. It does not ring before he answers.

'Yes?'

'Mr D'Sola, the train is about to depart.'

'I can see that.'

Dr Torgus swivels her head the length of the terminus. 'You're here? I don't see you. Do you see me?'

'My dear doctor, you are thoroughly conspicuous.' And then she hears it. A crackle and whoosh as the trash can beside her ignites, a blazing beacon. She leaps to one side, hair swinging. Looks up to see Ray D'Sola is on board the train, his shoulder casually propped against the window of the Governor's private carriage.

55

THE SOUND OF A MUFFLED SCREAM HAS A SPECIAL QUALITY. The stoppered mouth means the cry is forced back down the throat, resonating in the belly. This particular body, however, is as thin as a piccolo and makes a pitiful sound.

Stripped to the waist, bound and gagged, a man is crammed beneath a wooden frame. An altar of sorts. It rocks back and forth to the trundle of the train and is one of many crude fixtures that dress the carriage as a chapel of rest. It is here that the corpses of those inmates who fail to survive the journey are placed. Such is the fate of many who receive a shank to the guts and do nothing but bleed for two hundred miles.

But now the chapel is splattered with blood from the many deep cuts that cover the man's body. And on his forehead, the knife arrives to bite again – once, twice – making a raw V.

A voice whispers.

'Now my dear chaplain, let me be clear. I intend to carve my entire name upon your face. By the time I reach the "O" I suspect that I shall be upon your eye. But you could end this agony. Simply take the blade and draw it across your neck. It is suitably sharp, I think we can both agree on that.' The bound man howls beneath his gag, writhes away from the blade. But the knife pursues him. 'Your death is certain. All I ask is that you take your own life. You will, assuredly, do a kinder job than me.' A scream drenches the cloth. But still the captive does not take the knife.

'Ah well. I shall leave you to your wounds. But I will return.'

A THICK COTTON WAD IS SHOVED INTO AN EAR. Molloy grimaces and pokes the wad deeper. Turns to Officer Trill. 'That done it?'

Trill looks at a streak of blood that runs down Molloy's neck and sticks to his collar. The source is the plugged ear. He nods. 'Looks good.'

'Damn thing, been weeping like a wound o' Christ. I don't know what's happenin' to me.'

'Maybe you can get a doc to take a look when we get to the hospital.'

'I'm not hanging about for that. By the time today's batch has been processed, we'll be heading back.' He jerks a thumb to the wagon behind. 'There's gotta be more than fifteen today.'

'Eighteen in total. Seven wrist-slits, two belly-shanks, four bone-snaps, five unknowns.'

'You counted them?'

Trill nods.

'There's something wrong with you, boy.'

'I'd say there's something wrong with all of us.'

They turn at the sound of the wagon door sliding. The black robe of the chaplain sweeps through, his hat pulled low.

'Afternoon, Father. Can we help you?'

The chaplain pushes past the guards, brings his face against the observation slot to the inmates' wagon. 'I've come to see Agnus Day. I hear he is somewhat . . . sick.'

Molloy forces himself between the window and the chaplain, irked at this intrusion. 'He's not in there. Governor said he was to be in solitary.' A twitch of Molloy's head indicates the next carriage down. 'Governor also said no one was to enter.'

'Might I just look in?' The chaplain wafts a hand at this simple request. But Molloy's eyes go to the fingertips. They glisten with sweat.

He adjusts the wad in his ear as he thinks. 'I guess there's no harm in just looking.' He leads the chaplain to the window of the second wagon. Taps the glass with his knuckle. 'That's Agnus. As he lives and breathes.'

The nose of the chaplain is all that protrudes from beneath the hat and now its pointed tip presses against the glass. 'Who is that in there with him?'

'An agent, I don't know what federal flavour. Not my business.'

Sweat runs down the glass and Molloy sees its source is the chaplain's chin. The collar below is drenched and sticky.

'Are you all right there, Father?'

Yellow eyes swivel beneath the brim and Molloy instantly understands that this enquiry also falls beyond the bounds of his business. In a flash of black, the chaplain is gone, striding down the carriage.

Molloy ambles back alongside Trill. 'Another new chaplain, I guess.' Shakes his head, ear-wad waggling. 'How many chaplains we had since Agnus came, eh?'

Trill shrugs. 'Ain't been counting.'

HE FEELS THE WAGON DOOR SLIDE SHUT behind him. Removes his hat and sweeps away a thick slick of sweat. Vassago needs span.

He hasn't fed since his last official ration from the Sinestra and that dose is proving lamentably weak. And that accursed chaplain is refusing to comply. Vassago had believed he would submit readily. The way he begged and pleaded at the outset of the attack, clawing at Vassago's stolen robes, hanging about his thighs and weeping. But once bound and gagged, he became resilient, refusing to sully his soul by suicide. But Vassago will break him. He must, so that he can feed and gain strength and then pursue his greater quest. His fingers fumble with a fold beneath his robe, then close about the cool shaft of his clave. He has his precious tool. Now all he needs is for Scox to do its duty and blaze beside the body that bears the Mosca.

Then he will act! He will plunge his clave and awaken the Messiah.

Ah, glory so long since denied me! He can almost hear the voices ring in adulation from his brothers in the Legion of Gehenna.

Vassago smiles. With a hand wet with sweat, he slides open the door to the chapel carriage. And a muffled cry rises.

56

BIANCO SPINS THE CHAMBER OF HER MAGNUM SHUT. 'I'm checking out who's on this train.' She glances at the bank of monitors in the observation wagon. They flick between cameras.

She looks over to Mo'Zart as her muzzle points to Siggurson. 'Fill him in.' She holsters her weapon. 'And if something boils inside that soup you call your brain, you let me know.'

Siggurson gestures to her weapon. 'How'd you keep hold of your gun? They did a weapons strip when we boarded.'

'Maybe I got more places to hide one.' Bianco slides it down the belt of her pants. 'Or maybe I got two.'

As she exits, a monitor captures her image. Siggurson watches her disappear into the next wagon.

'She thinks she can handle this alone.' Turns to Mo'Zart. 'She can't. So make this story fast.'

Mo'Zart nods. 'You got it.' He lifts up a book. 'Once upon at double time there was a poet. His name was Archilochus.' Taps the front cover of the book which bears his picture. 'Archilochus had some wicked rhymes. No doubt he was an incarnation of the Mosca, but he was silenced by the knife of a man called Corvus.'

Siggurson nods and rolls his hand for Mo'Zart to move on. 'Two thousand years later, the next incarnation of the Mosca is this guy.' Mo'Zart produces a copy of *The Three Fates* and points to the face on Atropos. 'His name is Jornis de Wijs but he too was halted before his awakening. Because the signature on this painting exposed him as the blackmailer Kolibrie and he was killed by Corbin Kraal, an assassin.'

Mo'Zart pauses. 'That's all we have. But I believe it's enough. We find what links these two . . . and that will lead us to the next incarnation.'

Siggurson takes the picture of *The Three Fates*, studies it. 'You said the signature exposed Kolibrie. There's no signature here.'

Mo'Zart scoots closer. 'That's the thing with these proverb paintings – no words. You gotta guess the symbizzle.' He jabs a finger at the corner where a signature should be. A tiny humming-bird flutters in the shadows. 'Kolibrie is Dutch for hummingbird and, in their proverbs, it signifies blackmail. The hummingbird sucks sweetness from a flower, like an extortionist, draining his victim. And Mr Kolibrie, gotta say, he was good. After his murder, his fortune was turned over to the Church. Town records show it as ninety thousand guilders. Today, we're talking about twenty million dollars.'

He taps the portrait of De Wijs, a finger circling the narrow eyes. 'Can you imagine if he had been awakened? The Mosca, with all that money and power behind him? And you know what, I think that de Wijs knew that he had a destiny waiting . . . he was aware. More than the previous incarnation. Archilochus caused others hurt, but he was just a poet, and the urge to torment drove him insane. De Wijs was rich with a deep reach into European society. And he relished the pain he caused. He made a business out of it. Big business.'

Mo'Zart leans back. 'If the Mosca were a serial killer, you know what the cops would say: he's escalating. Each incarnation is richer, more powerful. And with a greater love for what they do. So this one that's coming . . . he's gonna be a natural born world-shaker.'

'So we kill him in the shell.' Siggurson snaps the book shut.

Mo'Zart's radio crackles. It's Bianco.

'*You still talking?*'

Mo'Zart clicks the button. 'Getting there.'

'*Get quicker.*'

Mo'Zart puts the hand-set down. Looks at Siggurson. 'Who made her leader?'

'Darwin.'

Mo'Zart smiles. 'Yeah she's gotta lotta tooth and claw, right.'

'You wanna get your opposable thumb off the button. I can still hear ya.'

Mo'Zart stuffs the radio into his belt and Siggurson pushes the books back towards him. 'You better crack this, kid, or she's gonna make you eat crow.'

Mo'Zart nods. 'True to her name.' He rams a finger into his dreads, twists deep. And then —

— his eyes rise. A smile ignites. 'And ain't that a thing. Crow . . . they're both called Crow.'

'Who?'

Mo'Zart leaps to his feet, hands alive. 'Corvus is Latin for crow. And Kraal is Dutch for crow.'

'So what? We have a link between the assassins. That doesn't get us any closer to the Mosca.'

Mo'Zart raises a finger. 'Unless of course . . .'

BLACK HEELS SLIDE ACROSS THE METAL FLOOR as the train lurches round a bend. Bianco's hand slams against a window, steadying herself. She resumes her approach towards two uniformed guards who stand outside the prisoners' carriage.

Molloy stiffens, flashing the pips on his shoulder as Bianco flashes only a smile.

'Gentlemen, how are ya?'

'Popular, this afternoon.'

'I'm looking for the passenger manifest.'

'You mean a list of everyone on board?'

'We can call it that.'

Molloy prods the wad in his ear. 'We don't have one.'

'So you don't know who's on the train?'

'If it's got a gun, it's a guard. Cuffs, it's a con.'

'What about civilians?'

Molloy shakes his head. 'Ain't no civilians on this train.'

Trill dips in. 'Apart from the guy with Dr Torgus.'

Molloy stretches his neck. 'Well, obviously apart from *that* guy.'

'What guy?'

'Let me check with the list that we don't have and get right back to you.'

Trill dips again. 'He's in the Pullman, ma'am, centre carriage.'

Bianco nods, spins on her heel and strides away down the corridor. Molloy throws Trill a hot eyeball but the young guard shakes his head. 'She's a federal agent, Wally. It ain't smart to lose it with an agent.'

'I was not losin' it.'

Trill waggles a finger at the ear-wad. It now oozes with fresh blood. 'I think you lost a little too much brain.'

As Bianco walks down the corridor her radio bleeps.

She pulls it from its pouch. Mo'Zart's voice blasts. '*How good is your Greek?*'

'I can fry cheese. That's it.'

'*No, no . . . the translation. The meaning.*'

'The point?'

'*They both mean the same thing. Kolibrie is Dutch for hummingbird. And Archilochus . . . that's hummingbird in Greek. The name. The name is the destiny.*'

'So we're looking for a guy called hummingbird?'

'*Or something that means hummingbird.*'

'Fuck, I never want you on my team in Pictionary.'

Siggurson's voice cuts in. 'Get serious, Bianco. Because this is all we got.'

'Hey, I'm serious mysterious.' She slides the radio back, quickens her pace and whispers to herself, 'I'm checkin' names and shooting' brains.'

57

A FINGER TRACES THE SCARS OF A TATTOO. It wraps around Lola's biceps and ripples as she flexes her fist. The original ink design has been corrupted by a knife. It once displayed her Hunter number: 101A. But when she went rogue, she had taken a blade and cut the digits deep, turning them into letters to create a new name to go with her new life: LOLA.

But the scars had never healed and often, they still open and weep.

The blood trickles down her arm. She turns away, knowing there is no tending that will work. Her eyes go to the many surgical drips that feed into the arms of Agnus, which lay inert above the blankets.

And in the gloom of the windowless wagon, she contemplates again the same silent question.

How can this be the saviour of mankind?

Everything that she knows of the Mosca tells of a fearsome force, so commanding that all Tormenta will fall into his thrall.

And this pale shank of flesh is all that will stand in his path?

Then Lola inhales, stiffening. She must have faith.

Because after all, what was I? Maddy Pool, a girl too scared to live her life. And look at me know. I changed. He will change.

There must be another stage in his evolution. Perhaps it takes the Mosca to first appear and this rising causes the Moera to emerge.

'I wish to rise.'

The sound of his voice jolts Lola from her thoughts. Agnus is twitching a finger towards a metal plate on the bed.

'There is a mechanism.'

Lola snaps into action, leaning forward, finding a panel of buttons. Stabs one. The bed slowly grinds until Agnus sits upright.

'Is that good?'

'No, it is agony, but I will endure it to set my eyes upon you.' A shifting sparkle from his sockets suggests that his eyes are travelling the length of her body. 'I find you most . . . becoming.' His blackened lips crack into a smile. 'And tell me – what am I?'

Lola says nothing, her eyes hard upon him as, suddenly, his face sags. Then it bulges and twists, as if a fist churns within his skull, stretching his features into a reptilian grin.

'I asked you a question. What am I?' The hissing voice does not pause to draw breath. 'I will tell you what I am. I am the last and the most wretched of the three. The half-made thing!'

His hand thrashes outwards, grasping at Lola's torso. 'But, vile miscreant that I am, I deserve to live.'

The goal of his clawing now becomes clear. He scrambles for the vial of span. Taken from Jolusa, it now hangs from Lola's belt.

'I can smell it! Give it to me!'

His body lurches upwards, then snaps and spasms, arching back as if a bolt shoots through his spine, seizing his muscles. Shrieking, he falls against the bed. His face drops. And, still gasping for breath with his mouth pressed to the pillow, his voice mumbles.

'Do you know who I am?'

Lola finds her voice. 'You are the Moera. You were three – now one.'

His cracked lips ease into a smile. His head nods. 'Agnus was the first, the Father. Weakened by his loss. And then came the Hunter, strengthened by his training. And then came the Maniac . . . driven by his lusts.' He raises his hand and stares at the limb as if it were still freshly drenched in blood.

His voice comes, a sorrowful whisper. 'She was just a child.'

Lola watches, as if mesmerised by the small, pale hand. Which suddenly lashes like a viper, grasping at her belt.

'Give me life! You don't deserve it! What were you, eh? What were you!' He struggles for breath, overwhelmed by his fury. 'You were such an ugly and despicable girl. No one liked you. No one cared for Maddy Pool. And then he came along and you were so stupid – oh! So monumentally stupid that you let yourself believe a boy as beautiful as he could want a creature like you. Suicide – you lacked the spine for even that! And now you dare to hold life in your hand and deny it me? Unworthy bitch!'

Agnus hauls himself back, roiling and writhing on the bed, his body a battleground. But his eyes are still cold and in control. 'You will obey!'

Lola jolts as the muscles in her shoulder tighten. Then a searing pain comes, as if a cold steel rod is being forced into her arm, pulling her like a puppet, thrusting her hand down towards the vial. With a grunt, Lola pulls back, the heft of her resistance smashing her hand into the wall.

A voice shrills from within Agnus, 'Stop! She is just a child!'

Then the same mouth contorts into a grimace, hissing, 'She is just another whore for slitting.'

Lola's hand quivers as it is ripped from the wall and forced down towards the vial, fingers brushing the glass. She clasps her other hand about her own wrist, trembling with the effort of self-restraint. Until —

'Cease this!'

Her hand drops free. Lola looks up. The face before her reflects neither sorrow nor maniacal fury. What Lola recognises is the cold resolve of a Hunter. The voice is clenched tight.

'The Father will speak and you will listen. We have little time before the other rises again.'

And in that moment, the mouth drops, pale and loose. And Agnus hauls a rattling breath, then another, deeper, as if trying to blow out a fire inside him.

At last, words come.

'I am three and I am one . . . but I am not the Moera.'

Lola leans close, measuring her words. 'But the *Kata* confirmed it. You have passed through the three states. And Judas —'

'— believed what he wanted so desperately to believe.'

'Your visions . . .'

'They were real. And with purpose. For I am the lamb, the sacrifice. My death will pave the way for the true Moera.'

Agnus grimaces, as if quelling pain. Struggles for breath, and in the silence, Lola drops her head into her hands.

'But if you are not the Moera, then the Mosca . . . we will not find him here?'

'Oh yes, the Mosca is very close. He must be, for he is drawn to the Moera.'

'But then who?'

'You! You . . .' Agnus lurches forward, stiffening his lips, seeking control. But fury overwhelms him, and the bitter wretch within him completes the sentence to its own design.

'. . . you are a stinking whore! Filthy as the Jezebeth who stole from me! My life! My life!' His hands flail wildly, clawing at the air. 'But I got it back, unwittingly perhaps. For I just stumbled on the secret . . . one that you already knew! But brainless worm that you are, you wiped it from your memory!'

His eyes bulge, straining with fury. 'You want to remember, don't you? You have to remember, or you will never get your span back, never pass into the third state . .

. so think! Think! What did I do to that little bitch before I ripped her belly open? I fucked her, Lola. I fucked her until she came.'

And with a gasp, his throat kinks and he slumps back against the bed. His face is still twisted and sunk deep into the sheets, almost suffocating his mouth. Lola cannot tell who it is that speaks.

'You know what the French call an orgasm? A *petite mort* – a little death. They say some part of you dies when you reach ecstasy. That a little of life itself slips from you and that's what makes the thrill. And they will never know how right they are. Because that is how a Hunter must redeem their span. Bring the Tormenta to ecstasy and when they reach release, the span comes with it. In that moment' – his fist suddenly launches upwards – 'it can be snatched back.'

The hand hangs in mid-air and then falls limp and tumbles back down. Angus rolls on to his back, freed from the sheets, eyes wide and cold.

'To Jezebeth, I was just another trick. Neither she nor I knew the fates to which we condemned ourselves as we raged across that bed.' He hauls in a deep breath. 'I roused Jezebeth and in her moment of release, my span was delivered back to me.' He exhales, blood dribbling between his teeth from the exertion. 'Three become one . . . but not in me. I am no trinity. Just a travesty. A wretched and accidental chimera.'

His hand reaches out towards her. 'The true Moera is aware. It has a fixed purpose. Seeking out its span, it seduces knowingly . . . to come . . . to become.'

His eyes burn into hers. 'What do you seek, Lola? What drove you to leave your duty?'

'My span . . . to reclaim my span.'

Agnus smiles, as if his mind, like a frail raft, has weathered the storm and pulled into its harbour.

'Yes, child.'

And as his eyes stay fixed upon her, demanding more,

Lola feels words rise in her throat as if pulled out by wire.

'I . . . I am the Moera.'

Agnus nods and withdraws his hands back upon his chest, almost in prayer. 'And if the Mosca rises, you too must be ready to rise. So you must reclaim your span. If you do so knowingly – wilfully – you will not suffer as I did. You will instead pass into the third state. This is your destiny. And so, as the lamb who came to lead you, I have only one last thing to impart.'

Agnus holds out his hand, a frail finger beckoning her closer. Lola leans in. And with a roar, Agnus lashes out, snaring her wrist, pulling her closer, grinning maniacally at his subterfuge. 'I will live!'

She feels his grip weaken as a voice bellows, not from his mouth but from the chamber of his neck, which now bulges like a bullfrog. 'Release her or die!'

His eyes still blazing, Agnus shakes his head. 'No, Hunter. I shall not!' Lola is forced down on to the bed. His fingers claw.

But as he strains to pull Lola the last inch, the voice that comes next is that of a roused father.

'You shall not hurt her!' Then his mouth twists again, a sliver of scorn. 'You are the weakest! You have not the courage to stop me!'

His fingertips clench against the vial, so tight a crack appears in the glass and then —

— something whips past Lola's face. It's a surgical tube, exploding from Agnus' neck. He howls, his grip weakening. Lola breaks free. Bolts upright to see Agnus writhing as the remaining surgical drips burst out of his body like fireworks, ignited from within, spraying blood and plasma. Soaking the ceiling until finally the tube into his trachea explodes outwards, blasting a gaping chasm in his neck through which the last of him escapes in a whistling rush.

In the silence that follows, Lola stares at the flesh vessel that was once so many and is now none at all.

58

'My skirt's too short.'

Dr Torgus twitches on a velvet stool and her hand flies to her mouth, clamping her lips. She makes sure a smile is fixed before she unmasks it.

'I don't know why I said that. I apologise, how foolish.' As her hand sinks lower, it brushes her skirt, tweaking a tug.

A man's hand reaches past her, pulling a bowl of cashews closer. 'My presence disturbs you.'

'Mr D'Sola, no. Please don't think that.'

'I think I will.'

A silence hangs.

'Martini?' The syllables tinkle down like broken glass. Torgus slides from the stool and moves behind the bar. It stretches the length of the Pullman carriage. She turns, flashing her hooded eyes wide. 'Let me guess how you like it – real dirty and with olives?'

'And without the eyeballs.'

Torgus blinks, feeling her smile stick to her teeth. She turns towards the bottles. Trails a finger across the labels. 'It seems . . . we have no vermouth.'

'Then a whiskey.'

A moustache of sweat clings to the hairs of her upper lip. She licks it away. All of the bottles are empty.

'No whiskey either . . . how foolish.'

'Then what?'

She turns back to face D'Sola and her eyes catch on a stack of barrels concealed beneath the mahogany counter. It is Duggin's prison-brewed liquor.

'We have rum.'

'Then you have redemption.'

Torgus pulls open the cooler, tips an ice-tray and hails down cubes. 'I hope this may redeem me further.' She nods towards a folder on the bar. It spills with papers. 'Please take a look. I think you will find the prophecies arresting.'

She turns to the cooler, replacing the ice-tray. And with a subtle hand, she pulls from the shelf a small pharmaceutical vial.

With her back to D'Sola she inserts a syringe and fills the barrel of the hypodermic. She hears D'Sola flick through the papers.

The needle slips into her pocket. And D'Sola closes the file. 'Intriguing, certainly.'

Torgus swoops, emboldened. 'I have a campaign all planned. We tap into the online community that the Revelation Project has already grown and we launch Agnus to a new generation, looking for a prophet.' Her eyes are wide, begging for a response.

'An unusual name . . . Torgus. Annie Torgus.'

She flinches, confused by D'Sola's sudden change of subject. Gathers herself, leans back against the bar. 'Annie is short for Anstice. It is Greek.'

D'Sola smiles. 'Now I understand your appreciation of Archilochus.' He leans in close. 'For most, his vicious words hold no appeal. People find him . . . crushing.'

Torgus forces herself to speak, to mask the weight of her breathing. 'Anstice means resurrection. That's me, you see, I cannot be crushed. I will always rise again.'

D'Sola's fingers are now sliding under the cuff of her blouse, easing the silk upwards. Torgus inhales, unable to move at his touch. Unable to distinguish between the pulsing sensations of fear and arousal that travel higher with each thrust of his fingers. Until the fabric rips and exposes on her forearm a tattoo. A long-beaked bird.

'And what is this?'

Through dry lips, she whispers. 'A stork. That's what Torgus means . . . in Greek.'

D'Sola is close now, his lips almost upon her. 'So here you are, a Greek bearing gifts.' His hand slams down on the file. Suddenly withdrawing from her. 'So you will understand that I cannot trust you.'

Torgus blinks, thrown from his thrall.

D'Sola is all business once more. 'I need to see some evidence that you have ownership of these papers.'

Torgus smooths her jacket, using the move to check that the syringe is securely in her pocket. 'Agnus Day will assign the rights before the train arrives, Mr D'Sola. Now I suggest you sit back and relax, peruse the writings. I shall shortly return.'

Wrapping a smile across her jaw, she moves towards the carriage door, thrusting her hips as if she imagines D'Sola's eyes are upon her.

Then she halts with a sudden untidy stagger. The door bursts open.

Stood in the frame is Bianco. She rips a smile. 'Bon'swa, as we say in the swamps.'

Torgus opens her mouth, releasing a hiss of surprise. But she is too slow to summon words as Bianco's arms thrusts past, beckoning D'Sola to exit the wagon.

Torgus inhales, swelling her resistance. 'This gentleman is my guest and you cannot just . . .'

Bianco address D'Sola over the invisible shoulder of Torgus. 'I need you sir.'

D'Sola sweeps forward. 'That request from one as lovely as you, I can't resist.'

He exits into the corridor and Bianco slides the door shut, erasing Torgus's face behind. She turns to the dark, sleek figure who stands so very close to her. 'I need your name.'

'Marry me and it is yours.'

Bianco says nothing. D'Sola smiles, nodding compliance. Passes her a thick, white business card. Watches as her eyes scan the glossy print. 'And might I ask your name, Agent?'

'My name doesn't matter.'

'Oh, I think you know that names matter a great deal.'

He snares the card, draws it back. Bianco flinches, surprised by the move. Disturbed that she allowed it to happen. She flexes her fingers. They feel slow, reluctant.

'I suspect that my name is not what you hoped for. I have disappointed you.' He pockets the card. 'Men are always such a disappointment. And you, Agent Nameless . . . ' He leans in close, dragging his nose up the curve of her neck. 'You smell like a woman who has been recently . . . disappointed.'

Bianco moves sharply away. Except that she doesn't. Her mind gives the clear command but her body is deaf to everything but the sound of his voice, strumming the tiny hairs of her ear.

'What was it . . . one night and then nothing? Not even an acknowledgement that it happened? I think he is blameless. The fault is yours. You just don't have it. That thing that men want. The va-voom, the moves. You are a fuck to forget, Agent Gameless.'

Bianco feels herself fall back against the wall. Her eyes closing. His breath caressing her lips.

'I don't think we should see each other any more.'

Silence, then —

— she opens her eyes.

The corridor is empty. He is gone.

59

THE TIP OF A BLADE circles an eye-socket, sinking deep and creating a perfect 'O'. Vassago leans back, admiring his work. The letter completes his name, now carved across the sweating face of the chaplain.

'So I ask you again, would your merciful God want you to suffer? Is suicide a sin when it ends such anguish?'

The chaplain's eyes, sticky with blood, stare upwards. Vassago flinches away. 'You look at me with all your fancy faith as if I am not worthy. A lesser thing than you! Well, I have a creed. I have belief! It is my faith that forces me to wreak these wounds upon you . . . and my faith is strong.' The knife hovers, ready to strike again.

And then the chaplain opens his mouth and murmurs, 'Tell me of your faith.' Vassago bends lower as the priest whispers again, 'What do you believe?'

Vassago thins his lips, which crack and crumble with decay. 'What I believe . . . you could never comprehend.'

Blood oozes from the chaplain's mouth as he struggles to form words. 'Perhaps if I understood your creed, I could find a rationale that would allow me to comply . . . allow me to exit by the means you wish.'

Vassago is now bent double, his shrivelled ear close to the chaplain to glean every word. He feels hope rise within him. 'So you are saying that if I explain my faith, you will do as I bid?'

He feels the priest's head rock in his grasp – a nod!

'Then I tell you this. I believe that the Mosca will come and unite all Tormenta. He will show us the strength that comes from acting as one and, once joined in combat, we will usurp humankind and bend them to our needs. This will be done when the Messiah comes. And I, Vassago, shall be the one to bring forth his glory.'

'His glory . . . or yours?'

Vassago stiffens. 'A glory I deserve! Where so many have failed, I will succeed! And my place within the Legion will be restored.' His fingers tighten about the chaplain's skull. 'My name will be forever honoured.'

The priest's voice is now no more than a gasp. 'True worship is what the soul does unseen. Faith is to forget the self.'

Vassago's skinless fingers feel once more for the knife. 'I do not think, churchman, that we are walking towards common ground.'

He folds the chaplain's fingers about the hilt and places the edge to his throat. 'So now, do as I bid and take your life.'

The priest twists a thin smile. 'I have done as I was bid.'

The knife falls, unused, as death at last gathers up the chaplain, rescuing him.

Vassago throws back his head and howls in frustration. Rises up, paces about the wagon. His eyes catch in a mirror. His flesh is now withered down to the bone. He lifts his hand, sniffing it, recoiling from the stench. More than decay, he reeks of defeat.

He has no span. He has no sign of the Mosca. And now – he has no time.

A loud knock batters at the door.

OUTSIDE THE CHAPEL WAGON, Officer Trill raps his knuckles again.

'Father? Are you in there?' His fingers try the door. It is locked. He knocks a third time. 'Officer Molloy sent me. He says that you should come. It's Agnus . . . he . . .'

Trill stops. Molloy had given him strict instructions not to say too much. All he had to do was ask the chaplain to come to Agnus' wagon. If, for any reason, he would not attend the body, then Trill was to insist he stay inside the chapel. Molloy wanted the train on lockdown. So two options only. No arguments.

Trill wrinkles his lips, irked by the lack of response. The priest must be in there if the door is locked from the inside. He glances up at the fire axe, braced above the door. One swing and he could gain entry. But that might be beyond the bounds of Molloy's directive.

So Trill knocks a final time. 'Father, either you come with me or you stay in there until we arrive. Choice is yours.'

From inside the wagon comes a loud metallic creak. And then the thud of boots on the roof.

Sounds like the chaplain has exited through the skylight.

Trill frowns. That option, Molloy had not covered.

60

THE NIGHT WIND RIPS THROUGH LOLA'S CROPPED HAIR. She sits on the roof of the train as it hurtles through the desert. Her eyes are wide but fixed on nothing . . . on everything.

Beside her is the open skylight through which she climbed to find this rushing sanctuary. The bolted cover, which gave so easily to the force of her fist, bangs in the buffeting air. Then Lola's boot strikes out, smashing it back against its hinges, again and again until, with the last furious strike, the cover shears away.

Lola watches it tumble free, spinning high.

And a thought flies upwards, filling her head. How wonderful would it feel to hurl herself from this roof and fall into the roaring air. To be free, for a moment. And dead for ever.

An easy for ever. A tiny loss. After all, what is she?

No memory of who I was. No knowledge of what I am. And no will for what I must become.

Her fists clench and a fury rises. A fierce refusal, finding form.

Who forces her to be the Moera? Who tries to bend her to this destiny? She leaps to her feet. Her head falls back and a roar rips free, ricochetting against the sky.

'Who are you?'

Her body drops and racks.

And, as if her furious sobs are rising high and chilling against the sky, a rain falls, cold and hard. Returning her words in stinging blows. Battering down, soaking her face and mocking her rage as nothing.

HIS BOOTS, THOUGH HEAVY, MOVE WITHOUT A SOUND.
And he is able, oh so easily, to observe her. She stands
with her back to him, battered by the wind but feet firmly
planted, muscles tight. So unaware, so rapt in some strange
fury that Vassago knows he could – in one step, one push –
joyfully remove her from the roof.

But he has another purpose. And that must take
precedence over pleasure.

He slides another yard.

She is a Hunter, certainly. He knows the stance. He
would even say he knows the smell. Each time his duties
as Lord Chancellor forced him to visit the training arena,
to feign an interest in their fitness, his nostrils burned with
their stench. That residual humanity in them that ages and
stinks like milk. And their new Tormenta trait that, to
Vassago's nose, refreshes the air like liquid nitrogen.

He smells this now. But over and above those fumes,
another fragrance comes. One that he inhales so deeply he
can taste it on the back of his tongue.

The smell of span!

He knows not how, nor why, but he is certain that this
Hunter carries a vial. So he will take her by the neck, and
take it from her.

He readies his arm and then —

— she turns.

She is young and lacks the scars to prove experience.
Vassago tilts his chin so she can see whom she opposes.

She doesn't flinch. Her fists rise up.

Vassago nods. Almost smiles.

This Hunter has some nerve.

Above the roar of the wind, he thrusts his voice. 'You
bait me, Hunter? Then you cannot know me.'

SHE KNOWS HIM TOO WELL. She's heard Père D speak
of him many times, and at the shaping of his name, her

mentor's lips would thin like razor blades. With such hatred between them, she never understood why they defected together. But they did and now Vassago has the same illustrious pedigree as Dali: the best of the Tormenta breed, a G-Man no less, strengthened further by the skills and secrets bestowed by the Sinestra.

If she were just a Hunter, she would know she cannot beat him.

But she is more. Much more. And she will prove it.

Lola grins.

You don't know what I am.

Thuds a step forward, fists bristling, inviting attack. Then —

— her head cracks back. Her jaw jerks high. Her lips burst blood. Punch after punch, Vassago assails her – faster, harder, keener. Stumbling and dazed, her fists flail and fall. She cannot pierce his complex attack, which sends her this way and that but always into the cut of his knuckles. Her eyes rock in their sockets as his punches pound down the front of her face.

Then his hand stiffens to a blade and scythes into her sternum. As the blows explode through her body, blood erupts, spewing from her mouth like a blow-hole. And amid the crimson spray something glitters blue. Arcing through the air. And Vassago's hand lunges forward, clawing at Lola's body, roaring as he pulls forth a smashed vial.

His jaw drops, wailing wildly. 'My life! My life!'

His fingers close about the glass, jagged like a blade. Leering down, hot spittle flying. 'Then your death.'

His hand jerks and the glass is thrust deep into Lola's belly, churning in the wound as his furious fist flings Lola from the roof.

61

THE TATTOO ON THE BACK OF D'SOLA'S HAND
expands as he clenches his fist. The image is a sun with rays reaching out. The jagged design is shaped by the dark blemish of dead skin beneath that it attempts to conceal.

In his fist he holds a thin silver case, containing business cards that bear the same logo. He snaps the case shut.

'Will there be anyone else on this train to demand that I identify myself?'

'I apologise, Mr D'Sola. We need tolerate these agents for just a few hours more. They are a necessary evil.'

'I find unnecessary evil much more entertaining.'

Dr Torgus lets his words fly past her like arrows. She doesn't know where they come from, nor even if she is their target. She smooths her jacket, checking the pocket once more, and strides into the corridor, coming to a sudden halt as Officer Molloy appears, gun raised, approaching fast.

'Gonna have to ask you to return to your carriage, doctor.'

She retreats, feeling the Pullman door swing back open behind her. Then she gathers herself. 'I need to check on Agnus. His physical condition is my responsibility until we arrive at the hospital.'

Molloy gestures with his rifle for her to step back. 'Then your duties just got a whole lot lighter.' His eyes shoot up at the sound of boots on the roof of the train. 'Whereas mine now . . .'

'What is going on?' Torgus attempts to make her tone stern.

Molloy's eyes are still locked on the roof. 'Agnus Day is

348

dead, doc. And that agent . . . well, she's all gone.'

Torgus reels back, caught at the elbow by D'Sola's firm grip.

'Dead, you say?' D'Sola's voice almost cracks with laughter. 'This is something of a setback, is is not, doctor?'

'I'd say. I'd say that for sure,' Molloy responds as if these recent events crush only his plans for a quiet turn of duty.

He thrusts the doctor back into the carriage with the tip of his gun. Pulls the door shut. Then moves on, prodding the cotton wad deeper into his ear.

62

THE PAIN IS UNBEARABLE. But so is the beauty.

Sunlight is ravaging Siggurson's retina and he wants to close his eyes. But he can't. He has to look at what glitters before him.

No muscle is under his control. The pressure in his skull is mounting, forcing his body ever further beyond his reach. But his mind echoes, unleashed and loud.

This will pass. It always passes.

He has known these attacks since boyhood. The tingle that starts in his fingertips. Travels upwards, twanging tendons, pulling his body into an agonising rigor. And then the vibration begins at the back of his brain, as if the bullet has sprung wings and is beating against the grey, curling current of his cerebellum. Then his senses dip and distort. First sound fades away. Then his mouth moves, shaping thoughts he can't control. Siggurson knows that by the time the attack has reached this stage, he will have sought solitude.

As a child, he used to make believe that he was a superhero who must hide away as his transformation comes and goes. And, in truth, he does get a power of sorts. With his senses distorting, he can see the simplest things in extraordinary detail. As if every atomic particle were revealing itself.

And now, braced hard against the wall of the wagon, it is not Mo'Zart's face, ripped with confusion, that holds his eye. Instead Siggurson stares at a blow-fly. It hovers in mid-air, an inch before him, caught in a slender ray of light that refracts from its wings in iridescent rods of red, gold, green and blue.

Siggurson's mouth is moving. He knows this by the soft billow of air across his tongue. But he doesn't know what he is saying. And he hears no sound.

But he sees the fly, a ball of sunlight. A thief of colour.

IT IS A BEAUTIFUL GUN, COLD AND SMOOTH. Bianco watches her fingers drift down the length of the barrel.

The rifle is fixed to the wall. One of many that flank the wall like iron ribs.

She knows that she is in the munitions wagon. What she can't remember is how she got here.

In the corridor . . . that man, his lips so close . . . his voice . . . and then, he's gone.

As if clutching at the fog of a dream, Bianco forces her mind to retrace her steps. Steps that staggered and stumbled. She saw the door to the munitions wagon. She wanted to enter. Was forced to enter.

And then . . . she remembers opening her eyes to this glory of guns.

Bianco's hand drifts towards a rack of high-velocity hand-guns. She wants to bring her fingers back but the tips seem drawn to the Magnums, as if magnetised.

The voice in her head that questions her actions is small – a whisper. But something in Bianco tells her to breathe in, to swell that voice. Heed it!

Move your hand away from the gun. The beautiful gun. That would feel so good against her skin. Her fingers curl about the handle, popping it from its mount. Drawing it down towards her temple.

Drop the gun.

It is cool. And hard. And it would push that bullet in fast, so far.

Drop the goddam fucking gun!

With a roar, Bianco slams her hand against the steel floor of the wagon.

This is him! This is what he wants! Ridiculous! You

351

barely spoke. Barely touched. He just gave you his card.

And his name was . . . was . . .

A blast of static rips against her ear. And only now does she realise that she is lying on the floor of the wagon, her legs spread as if she dropped like a cut puppet. Her radio, sprung from her belt, lies by her ear.

From somewhere deep inside her brain, she is certain she knows this voice.

'*Bianco, you read me?*'

Mo'Zart. His name is Mo'Zart. Bianco tries to move her hand towards the radio. Her fingers resist.

'*Bianco, pick up. We have a situation here.*'

She grits her teeth, grunts and shoves her arm as if poking it with the stick of her mind. Fingers grasp the hand-set, press the button.

'I hear you.'

'*Siggurson's down. Not down . . . but out. Not out. Not here.*'

Bianco rises up, feeling her mind shiver and shimmy, finally slipping free. She exhales through tight teeth. 'Again. Slower.'

'*You weren't responding, so Siggurson said he was coming to find you. He got up and then – it happened.*'

Bianco rolls her neck, the rest of her body returning to her. 'What happened.'

'*Nothing. That's the thing. Nothing happened. He just froze. Like someone flicked a switch in his head. I don't think he can hear me and he's making no sense. Just keeps saying the same thing, again and again.*'

'What?'

'*That the fly has stolen the colours of the sun.*'

'I'm on my way.'

Bianco rises to her feet. *The bullet. Must be the bullet.*

Deep in Siggurson's brain. Not deep enough to kill him . . . not yet. But clearly deep enough to inflict these seizures. These hallucinations.

The fly . . . stealing the colours of the sun.

And now Bianco feels an idea impact the back of her head, hard as a shovel.

. . . the Fly so loved the Lily, to woo her he stole the colours of the sun.

Bianco keeps walking, thudding her fist against her temple, forcing the rest of the memory to drop into her mouth.

. . . and so it was that the Fly became the hummingbird. And his name was . . .

Bianco closes her eyes. *Think! Think back!* And then she sees it.

The china plaque on Fan Fan's wall. The one that the old woman told her about a thousand times. Always the same story. The Lily . . . The Fly . . .

And his name was . . .

She clenches her fist. Pounds it against her thigh. And then she remembers . . . smashing the plaque. And placing the pieces back together, making the words of warning from that old Taino proverb.

Beware of . . .

MO'ZART SCREWS HIS FACE, listening hard '. . . of what?'

'*Guacariga!*'

'Now you're talking crazy.'

Bianco's voice is breathless, rasping from the radio. She's walking fast.

'*Just do what I say. You got eyes on the Pullman?*'

Mo'Zart punches up a screen that shows Dr. Torgus with a male guest at the carriage bar. 'I see a man.' He peers closer, eyes suddenly widening. He recognises that face.

Bianco's voice pounds from the radio. She is increasing her speed. '*Guacariga is the Taino god of death. He's always shown in the form of the hummingbird, because he was cursed for stealing his colours from the sun. And in*'

English, Guacariga translates as "rays of the sun".'

Mo'Zart's eyes now bulge, swelling with realisation. He open his mouth, but a deeper voice comes from behind.

'Ray D'Sola.'

Mo'Zart spins round as Siggurson's head lolls back.

Mo'Zart grins and bellows into the hand-set. 'And Elvis is back in the bizzle.'

'Then we got ourselves a hunting party.' Bianco's radio clicks off.

Mo'Zart drops his hand-set and claps his palms on Siggurson's shoulders. 'Man, what just happened?'

Blood threads heavily from Siggurson's nose. Mo'Zart averts his eyes, forces his smile wider. 'Thought you were dying just then.'

Siggurson staggers to his feet, breathing deeply. 'Not then.' He raggedly drags a sleeve across his nose. 'But maybe now.'

He turns and lurches towards the Pullman.

63

TORGUS TAPS HER WATCH. The second hand has stopped. She taps again harder, but time refuses to revive. She can feel the first rays of sunrise through the metal slats of the Pullman window. There can be only another fifty miles to go.

'It is all too late, isn't it, doctor?' D'Sola slowly unsheathes his commentary, every word a fresh inch of bared steel. 'Too late for your body, so old and ugly now. Don't you feel the flesh falling away from your bones like ham?'

Torgus quivers, feeling the cut of each syllable. The pain is sharp . . . but thrilling.

'Too late for your reputation to be redeemed. Too late for your life to have any meaning at all.'

She finds her eyes drawn to her own hand. Seeing it in awful detail. The hairs that curl from the back of her fingers. The fatless veins that bulge, blue as ink. And as if her arm is a snake, charmed upwards by the sound of D'Sola's voice, it rises . . . floats.

Fascinated by her own actions, she says nothing as her fist suddenly drops and clumsily swipes the file of prophecies to the floor, the papers gathering at her feet.

'There is nothing to live for now, is there, doctor? All that awaits you at the end of this journey is the indignity of decay. Can you smell that sickening sweetness? Does it repulse you, doctor? I believe it should.'

Torgus begins to unbutton her own blouse, thrusting her fingers across the loose, wrinkled flesh of her breasts. Unzips her skirt. It ripples to the floor, piling upon the papers.

She feels her head rolled by her own neck muscles, which twist like a tourniquet. She is made to look at the tall glass of rum that stands on the counter. D'Sola is filling it to the brim. Passing it to her.

'Shall we have one last drink, doctor, to your one last glory?'

Torgus's eyes slowly lift to meet D'Sola. Entirely held within his thrall, she brings the drink to her lips. But her mouth remains shut. And with a determined jerk, she splashes the spirit down her chin. Dribbling it between her breasts and down her exposed belly.

'Cigarette, doctor?'

D'Sola strikes a match and hands it to Torgus who – silently, obediently – grasps it. Then opens her fingers, letting the match fall on to the papers at her feet.

The flame ignites, instantly finding the fuse of alcohol down her body. Licking upwards, her loins hot at last.

64

Something crawls across the roof of the chapel wagon. It is Vassago, his chin so low it almost grazes the metal. Grunting and sniffing, he pursues a splattered trail of span.

That I should be reduced to this! Truffling like a pig!

Borne on the billowing air, the span has spread the length of the train. Vassago inches on, licking and grubbing, sucking up what dregs remain, knowing that this will give him only hours more.

Then his nose twitches, snagged by another smell.

Smoke!

His head cranks up. An acrid carpet ripples down the train, forced by the wind. He can't see where it originates until, with a raging blast, flames burst up from the farthest carriage.

And Vassago slowly rises to his feet. His eyes lock upon the fire that draws him down the train; his boots gather speed, breaking out into a thudding bound as he leaps from wagon to wagon, arriving at the shattered skylight filled with fire.

Drops to his knees, forcing his face against the searing heat, staring down into the carriage.

And then he sees it. Flames rising up a woman's naked body. She writhes and wails, thrashing across the floor.

And there on her arm – a tattoo. Vassago's eyes seize upon it. Inked black and tall. A stork!

Scox! The sacred stork! The blazing beacon sent to guide the Legion's search. And so . . .

His eyes sweep the wagon. And there he sees him: the

man who watches unmoved this immolation.

It is he!

Vassago grasps his clave, thrusting his boots, crashing down through the skylight.

D'Sola turns. Breathing hard, aroused and so enraptured by the death of Torgus that at first he cannot determine what it is that interrupts his pleasure.

Then his eyes narrow, locked on the grey, gracile creature that lands, uncoiling, before him. It wields a metal shaft. D'Sola wants to step back. But his body, beyond his control, thrusts upwards as —

— Vassago plunges the clave down. Releasing it to stand proud in D'Sola's chest.

Vassago grins exuberantly. *It begins!*

Falling to his knees, he bows his head, bellowing an exultant welcome to the long-awaited Messiah. Throwing his arms high.

Feeling blood splatter down.

He lifts his eyes, to find that his Messiah is – gone.

65

'It has to be somewhere!' Bianco's voice blasts from the radio.

Mo'Zart responds as he runs down the corridor, his eyes flashing left and right, looking at the walls, the roof. 'I don't see one.'

'Look harder.'

'I'm heading for the guards' wagon.'

Mo'Zart's mind is racing. If he had built this prison train, where would he put the emergency stop?

He bursts through the connecting door to the guards' wagon, gaining speed and then slamming hard against the wall.

The corridor is suddenly flooded by guards. Guns drawn, they are responding to the fire alarm triggered in the Pullman. Mo'Zart can't move, flattened by the surge. Can't even lift the radio to his mouth as he hears Bianco's desperate cry.

'Find that button and push it or what's gonna stop the train is my fucking body on the tracks!'

HER FEET HANG ABOVE THE RACING GROUND. Bianco has one hand clamped about D'Sola's neck. His unconscious body is in her grasp. Her other hand holds them both against the train door, which swings open, sucked out by the wind. Mo'Zart's got ten seconds to stop this train.

Less than ten. Vassago has burst from the Pullman and is striding down the corridor, reaching out for D'Sola, roaring wildly. Blasting blood, as something strikes him hard from behind. Vassago buckles to his knees, revealing Siggurson poised with a fire axe in his fist, pulled back and ready to deliver another blow.

Siggurson's eyes go to Bianco. She wrestles D'Sola hard against her chest. He is regaining consciousness.

One word bursts from Siggurson's mouth: 'Go!'

Bianco doesn't look down. Holds Siggurson's eyes to the last. Lets go of the door and clutching D'Sola —

— she jumps.

Vassago rises up. Flexes his fingers in a rippling beckon before folding them into a fist. Turns to face his assailant, eyes ablaze. 'Let's go.'

Siggurson nods, grunts. Swings the axe, but Vassago is too quick, snatching it from his hand and thrusting it back, clubbing the blade against the side of Siggurson's skull. He reels back into the Pullman, stumbling and dazed, but rises up ready as Vassago appears through the smoke in the doorway. Siggurson leaps through the spreading flames, dives over the charred remains of Dr Torgus and lands behind the bar, a space shielded from corpses with room to fight. With a thud, Vassago is on the counter, pacing its length, swinging the axe and looking down at Siggurson like a bear in its pit. Flames gust about him, rippling across the floor. Vassago sees Siggurson's eyes glance below the bar.

'No hiding place, I fear.'

Siggurson's leg kicks forward and as Vassago hears it connect with something below, he senses danger. Too late, as the barrel of rum propelled by Siggurson rolls into the flames and ignites, spewing up a wall of fire, blasting the axe from his hand and forcing Vassago from the bar. He lands and turns, the heat haze blurring his vision. Does not see the flash of steel as a bar stool swings and smashes down.

But not into the back of his skull. Vassago is too nimble. The edge of the stool scythes air and strikes the bar, bouncing up as Vassago snares it, twisting the momentum of the blow back on itself, using this to thrust it forward.

And, like a sledge-hammer, it crashes into the back of Siggurson's skull.

Knocking him down.

Nailed, for the killing.

Vassago lunges, then stops at sound of guns priming. Turns to see a slew of guards surge in.

66

'What do you see?'

'I see you, Agnus.'

His face is above her.

Lola doesn't feel her mouth move but still, she hears her own voice. 'Which one are you?'

'Of the three, I am the greatest. I am love. And I will not forsake you.'

A hand moves across her eyes, plunging her into blackness. And now Agnus' voice comes not from above her, but from within her.

'What do you see?'

A light flickers as if her eyes are opening, but she can feel her lashes still intertwined. The beam shines from the back of her skull and the images are projected on the reverse of her retina, inverted, swirling, confused. Snatches of sound, crashes of colour.

'I don't know what I see.'

'What do you feel?'

And that answer comes instantly. 'Afraid.'

And suddenly the images blaze forth. She sees a torrent of red.

Blood —

— from Siggurson's head. He is face down, eyes locked, mouth open. Above him stands a howling figure, raising a grey, skinless fist.

Vassago. Lola hears her own whisper but feels no breath pass over her lips.

'You see clearly now. You feel it.' Agnus' encouragement no longer comes in words. Lola feels him urging her on as if he has a hand about her heart, squeezing the beat to quicken.

Lola's voice rises, panting. 'Vassago needs span. He hears them coming.' Her muscles twitch and tense. 'They have guns. They feel strong.'

She sees the first wave of guards burst into the wagon, weapons thrusting as Vassago spins to face them.

'They don't understand.'

Vassago's jaws drop wide and in a storm of glistening limbs that sweep back and forth, up and down, he wildly conducts a chorus of carnage, ripping the guards belly to chin, mouth to ear, nostril to eyelid.

The steel walls of the wagon run thick with blood and flesh like an abattoir and screams rebound from the metal.

Lola feels the hand rise from her eyes.

'I must stop him.'

'Yes. That is what you must do. But you are dying, Lola.'

'If I am to become the Moera, how can I die?'

'Vassago tore a hole in your belly. Threw you from the roof. You fell between the wagons. Now you are lying, twisted and broken on the couplings, silent and unseen.'

'I should have defeated him. Where is my strength? What must I do?'

"Give up, Lola.'

She tries to move her body, but it is as if her flesh is made of water and the command to her muscles is like a breeze upon the surface.

'Give yourself up. Set yourself free. Because to receive the strength to win, you must first surrender.'

Lola grits her teeth and grinds her muscles again. 'It is my destiny! I must have the strength!'

'The power of the Moera is not from you, it is *through* you.'

The heat of his hand hovers above her heart. 'The plan is not yours and the path is never of your making.'

His voice dwindles, like a wick with a final drop of wax. And the light dims.

'If you are ready to surrender, declare it. Cry out, "Take me! Use me!" Do this and the world will turn to give you victory.'

Lola opens her mouth, this time feeling the muscles respond, shaping the words. At first just a whisper.

Take me.

And then her voice bursts forth. A roar.

'Take me!'

'I've got you.' A hand heaves her up, dragging her beneath the arms. 'I'm gonna get you somewhere safe.'

It is Mo'Zart. With strained grunts, he shunts Lola backwards through a wagon door, into the smoke-filled corridor, finally heaving her into the cover of the munitions wagon. Sets her down, gasping for breath. His face is thick with smoke soot.

'The G-Man impaled the clave and D'Sola's gone. So if Bianco survived the jump, she's out in a thousand acres of desert with the Mosca.'

Lola grabs at a rung of the gun-rack on the wall, hauling herself upwards. The slit across her abdomen yawns wide, exposing red gums of muscle.

Mo'Zart lowers his eyes, 'Have we lost this, Lola?'

Lola grips the bar harder, pulling straighter. 'I'm just beginning. And first is Vassago.'

Mo'Zart leaps to his feet. 'The G-Man? Forget it, Lola. You're all busted up!'

Lola wraps her fingers about a Winchester rifle that is braced to the wall.

Mo'Zart tries to grab her. 'He's gonna have you on your knees!'

With one tug, the restraining bolts shear away and the gun pulls free. Lola turns her eyes to Mo'Zart.

'Have faith.' She slides the gun across her back. 'The world will turn and make him kneel first.'

67

SHE FLIES THROUGH THE AIR. Her back arching, her arms spread wide, soaring. Then swooping, falling now, gathering speed and smashing hard to the ground, an arm cracking backwards at the shoulder.

Bianco gasps, sucking up dust. Peels open an eye. Above her, a figure shimmers, hazed by the fluid in her eyes that still swills from the impact.

It is D'Sola.

He reaches down and grips her body a second time, lifting her up with impossible ease. Hurling her up in the air again, further this time, with a playful spin as if this act is born from exuberance, not fury.

Then, tiring of this too-easy game, he looks about the desert for a bigger distraction. And sees the sun, rising red above the horizon. And with the clave still impaled in his chest, he begins to bound towards the streaking rays.

Bianco struggles to her feet, her right arm hanging like a snapped wing. She pulls her Magnum. Grits through the pain.

The muzzle quivers in the unfamiliar grip of her left hand.

68

A KNIFE POKES OUT OF MOLLOY'S EAR; it doesn't plug like a cotton wad, but the blood has ceased to flow. Now that he's dead.

Vassago pulls a gun from Molloy's mouth and rises up, stretching his torso. It is now healing with fresh flesh as the siphoned span begins to take effect.

He looks down at his skin with the expression of an unhappy bride. This isn't what he wanted at all. The tissue is thin and slow to grow. He ripples his lips in disappointment.

He had persuaded Molloy to end the agony of the knife's slow entry into his skull by blowing his own brains out. Vassago then fell to his knees and siphoned the span.

But something had caused Molloy, for many days before, to bleed from the ear. Vassago would say a tumour by the taste of it. The man had only days left to live and so what Vassago siphoned is useless.

He needs more. Enough to buy him time to get the Mosca back. The awakening is under way, but he needs the Mosca in his care, so he can relish the moment of his triumphant return to the Legion.

So Vassago inhales, scouts about the smoke-filled carriage to find another fix.

The flames are high now, licking at the ceiling, seeping out into the corridor. And the heat is horrible. But Vassago sets about his task with a flurry of hoisting kicks, bouncing bodies from the floor, looking for one that still lives. And then he hears it: the music made by the instrument of misery.

A pained exhalation.

And then he sees it: a body by the bar. Still moving.

Vassago strides across the wagon. Time is short and so he begins his opening argument as he approaches.

'You have a choice. You can burn to death, an excruciating exit. Or you take the chance to end your own life with a single clean and painless shot.'

The hand of the crawling victim reaches up through the smoke, grasping wildly as if searching for the gun.

'An excellent choice!' Vassago smiles and mocks a bow, like a Maître d'. Pulls a weapon from one of the nearby dead guards and empties the chamber of all but one bullet. Folds the smouldering fingers of his victim about the butt of the gun.

Then he drops to his knees, ready to feed.

The thumb of his victim peels back the priming pin.

Vassago swipes his tongue, wetting his lip. 'If it makes you feel any better, your suicide will not be in vain.'

The victim's finger closes about the trigger and pulls. The bullet rips through his skull. His final breaths come in short, hard jags.

Vassago twitches, listening to the dwindling gasps. And his ears are alert also to the crackle of the flames that race ever closer.

He bends down to the gaping mouth. Perhaps a breath comes, he cannot be sure. But the smoke of the fire is belching hard down the back of his neck.

He cannot wait. Vassago slams his jaw down and begins to inhale. And rising up comes a pulsing coil of span. Disappearing gulp by gulp into Vassago's gullet.

Then, bent double as he swallows, Vassago halts. Amid the heat of the fire comes something cold upon his neck. He rises to find the massive barrel of a Winchester rifle thrust against his skull.

Releasing the half-sucked span, Vassago twists round. And there she is, that strange Hunter. One hand clamped to her bleeding belly, the other toting the gun to his head.

Vassago smiles. 'Will you grant the last request of a

dining man?' He dabs his lips. 'I should like to know your name.'

'It's spelled just how it sounds.'

A deafening *ba-boom* blows Vassago's head from his shoulders.

The force of the recoil thrusts Lola back, staggering into Mo'Zart who catches her behind.

'Now can we get outta here? If those flames reach the munitions wagon, the whole train is gonna blow.' He pulls her arm about his neck, supporting her. He gives a backwards glance and then —

— wrenches to a halt. His eyes lock on the body beneath Vassago.

'Siggurson! That's Siggurson!' The blue eyes are wide and staring and a length of half-sucked span still trails from his mouth.

Mo'Zart lurches towards the body as if to gather him. But Lola's fist flies, snaring Mo'Zart by the throat, pulling him close.

'He's gone. And we have to go.'

With one thrust, Lola hurls him from the wagon as the flames explode in a fresh wave of fire.

She alone looks round to see that amid the many corpses, Siggurson's body has now gone. Leaving just a carbon ring.

And as the flames lick into the munitions wagon Lola leaps from the train, blown high by the blast.

69

LOLA ROLLS LIKE A BOULDER, churning dust. She crashes to a stop in a stubble of bushes. Shakes her head, shunting her eyes back into focus. Rises up.

About her are bodies. Arms outstretched. Legs bent back.

Lola drags a sleeve across her nose, stanching the smell of clothing fused to smoking skin. Moves amongst the bodies in slow strides, rolling ribs with her boot, looking at the blackened faces revealed as the corpses twist round.

The bodies stretch far into the desert. She inhales, tips back her head and yells his name. 'Mo'Zart!'

Listens for a response. None comes. She continues onwards, boot swinging, rolling one by one.

And then, as a cadaver tumbles over, Lola sees a face she recognises.

Not Mo'Zart.

It is Brother Scarbo, with the shaven head and those eyes that once looked upon her with such misgivings. One of them is now circled with the final letter of a name scored deep across his face.

Lola kneels and strokes the wild eyes shut. She thinks back to her meeting with Primus Pater Umberto. He must have decided in that moment to assist her with more than just papers. He pledged his faithful aide to thwart the Legion, keep her safe and speed her cause.

Lola reaches down, her hands moving urgently across his body, cracking his contorted legs straight, looking for what she knows must be there. Because a brother of the Chiro Scuro would come with only one purpose in mind.

To perform the deed for which they are famed. The art of the hidden hand.

And as Lola wrenches back the monk's rigored arm from his belly, she sees it.

A clave.

And she smiles. *Is there a chance that he succeeded?*

The monk's plan would have been to use all his cunning to get close to Vassago. The Brotherhood often use a technique called the 'wise whisper'. They offer a great wisdom, an insight, a prophecy – but deliver it in a voice so hushed that their quarry is forced to lean ever closer, allowing the monk's gifted fingers to accomplish their goal. To steal their clave and replace it with a perfect replica, blessed by holy water.

If this replica is then used in a Tormenta awakening, madness will result.

Lola holds the clave in her hand. Twisting it, looking at every detail, even though she knows that her eyes are not skilled enough to distinguish between a true clave and its replica.

So she can only wonder, did Brother Scarbo do as he was bid? Did he succeed?

If this is the replica, then Scarbo was killed before he could make the switch.

But if she holds Vassago's true clave, then . . .

A shadow suddenly falls across her. Lola turns, gun drawn, to find Mo'Zart standing above her. Covered in ash, he looks pale as a ghost. But the choking cough that racks him hard shows he's alive.

Lola rises, grasping Mo'Zart about the shoulders as he breathes deeply, straightening up.

'I thought you were dead.'

Mo'Zart shrugs, head up. 'Dead ain't what it used to be.' He looks about at the corpses, then his eyes suddenly widen.

'Bianco?' He looks up to a swarm of crows, circling to

the west. 'She's out there with him. You think she's gonna make it?'

Lola's fingers close about the clave.

'She's gotta chance.'

A maggot! I was but a maggot of a man! And now I am emerging from my skin. I am becoming what I was always destined to become!

D'Sola pounds across the sand, his body rippling with an insuppressible energy. He can feel a force unleashed, pulling his skin apart as his new self writhes free.

His eyes blaze, set on the sun that creeps above the horizon.

'I shall rise! I am the dawn! I shall steal the light and bring forth a new age of darkness.'

Another surge racks his body. And he feels fresh words forced into his mouth. But only one sound comes out. A shrieking caw.

'Fly! Fly! Fly!'

D'Sola clamps his jaw shut. But now his arms bolt from his control, thrusting out, flapping crazily.

With a gargling howl, D'Sola heaves his limbs back towards his chest. He wraps his fists about the clave, sinking it deeper, digging the metal down to find the power he first felt. But all he feels now are his fists betraying him as they wrench the metal like a tin opener, ripping a lengthening split down his body.

BIANCO STEADIES HER LEFT ARM, keeping the muzzle locked tight on D'Sola as he runs wildly through the desert. His fingers are clawing at the clave. But with every twist of the clave, the volume of his madness increases. The metal burns hot, blistering his palms, but still D'Sola feels compelled to wrench and twist it, forcing blood and tissue to spill like chum in a sea of sand.

He is screaming. In agony, Bianco must assume. But amid the cries there seems to be half-formed words, crazed jabberings.

She primes the Magnum as D'Sola begins to crank his arms again, as if trying to fly.

Bianco narrows her eyes against the glare of the rising sun, then —

— D'Sola takes to the air, arms flapping, rising high. Higher.

But it is the power of a high-velocity bullet that propels him. Thrusting him upwards for just a beat of his arms before his back explodes. And as he falls, he swoops and swirls. Because there is no ground below him. The bullet has blown him over the edge of a ravine.

And from the sky descends the murder of crows, cawing crazily, following his body down.

SHE HAS NO TEETH SO SHE SUCKS THE MEAT OFF
THE BONE, then chucks the chicken wing to the floor of the
flat-bed truck.

Mo'Zart can't take his eyes off her. She's a hooker, for
sure. And old for her trade, maybe the neck-end of fifty.
Looks like the Momma-Ho of the bunch. There are five
girls in total and Mo'Zart skims a glance across them all:
stick-thin and thickly rouged, with hair whipped up by the
wind into a cotton candy chaos.

They sit one side of the flat-bed truck, facing Mo'Zart,
Bianco and Lola.

Momma-Ho reaches into a grocery bag on her lap and
pulls out another piece of chicken. Starts sucking, squeezing
grease down her chin. Then jerks a finger at the bag on
Lola's lap. 'What you got in there?'

'Human head.'

Momma-Ho looks at Lola's blood-stained torso,
Bianco's broken arm slung in a belt and Mo'Zart's face,
a shade deeper with smoke. 'I know a place you can get
chicken.'

The truck bounces high as it hits a deep rut in the desert
road.

'Not much further now, my dears.' The voice comes
from the driver's cabin. At the wheel is Sister Vermilion
Rose. Her huge face turns, wimple flapping. 'Five miles, no
more.'

A cigarillo droops between her lips and her hands that
wrench at the wheel are covered in tattoos. 'It's a little bitty
town but there's a sheriff's office. Got a phone that works

and a deputy that don't. But I hope that is sufficient for your needs.'

She flashes a tobacco-toothed smile to her new companions.

Mo'Zart musters a smile back. He is sure that her church does wonderful work providing succour to street-walkers, but he had felt a ripple of reservation when the truck first pulled up and offered them a lift. The mission banner painted on the side read: 'The White Lily of the Trinity'.

Mo'Zart had whispered to Lola, jerking a finger at the name, 'It's a sign.'

'It's a truck.' And with that, Mo'Zart found himself bundled aboard by Lola's boot.

And in truth they had been walking for an hour across the desert before they hit a road and then another hour had passed before they even heard the chug of an engine.

The heat was unbearable and so was the silence. No cars. And less conversation. Neither Bianco nor Lola wanted to talk. But Mo'Zart did.

Maybe they're used to this kind of crazy, but I still got questions.

'Why would Siggurson do that?'

Lola said nothing, just paced the roadside, eyes on the horizon.

Mo'Zart persisted. 'Why shoot himself?'

Lola still paced, but now she elected to speak. Slowly, as if she was piecing events together in her own mind, step by step. 'He faced death, every moment of every day. The frag in his brain was like a ticking bomb. This way, he could control the moment of his death – and make it count for something.'

Lola fell silent for a moment, as if deciding whether to say more. Finally: 'He saw me in the doorway. He saw my blood. He knew that I would need Vassago to be vulnerable if I were to stand a chance. He'd already watched him siphon the other guard. So Siggurson knew how to bring Vassago to his knees.'

Mo'Zart hung his head, eyes down. 'Then he sacrificed himself for us.'

Bianco snapped her head round. 'He's dead. We're alive. It's over.'

Sitting in the back of the truck, Mo'Zart glances over at Bianco. She hasn't spoken since. Which he finds strange. Such a cold comment to make about Siggurson. Maybe she really never liked him. Or maybe she liked him too much.

Or maybe she hasn't spoken because there's nothing more to say.

Mo'Zart looks out at the desert. A distant column of black smoke rises above the horizon. He exhales, resting his chin in his hands.

We're alive.

And it is over. *

*ADDENDUM

LONG CUFFS GRAZE ACROSS A CARD TABLE. Dali is dealing out a game of Boo-Ray, the first time in a long time that his deck has been used for anything other than Solitaire.

Seated across from him is the Commander General. He sucks on a cigar and gathers the cards dealt to him.

The rules of Boo-Ray demand that you show to your opponent two of the three cards in your hand.

And as Dali contemplates his hand and takes a sip of the Commander General's finest Vesuvio Port, he ponders on the rectitude of his decision to show the Commander General only two of the three pieces of evidence that he received against Vassago.

The items had arrived neatly boxed. So tight and tidy in fact that the thought never occurred to Dali that the sender might be Lola. She was not one for doing things right. But clearly, her time as a renegade has sharpened her skills with bubble-wrap.

Dali had first lifted out the note. Written in her hand, he knew that instantly. He recognised the style from the dense notes she'd made in the margins of all those library books that so perversely held her attention.

And no one but Lola would begin a missive to him 'Cher Père D'.

He scanned the contents quickly. The letter made no mention of her leaving. No reason as to why she quit his loving care. But Dali no longer held out hope that this particular hurt would be healed by explanation.

The letter told him only that the enclosed clave

belonged to Vassago. And the severed head - oh yes, there was, in all its stinking glory, a severed head – that delight belonged to Brother Scarbo. The name carved across his forehead was clear despite the shrinkage of his skin. A signature declaring guilt.

The letter was not signed. It finished with the words 'I miss you, Père D'.

Ah cher, tu es perdue . . .

Dali deliberately lost the letter for ever in a flame and handed over to the Commander General only the clave and severed head. Vassago's absence had already aroused suspicion so these items easily elicited a verdict.

Dali returns his attention to the game as the Commander General sets down his cards - two Jacks. Dali sets his own face to an expression of engaged interest.

'We owe you an apology, Dali. But in our defence, once we learned what had befallen Judas . . . and the considerable evidence presented by Vassago. The case for your treachery seemed strong.'

'Ah, is that how it *seemed*, sir . . . ?"

The Commander General pauses, exhales. Point taken. 'We gave Vassago's testimony too much credence.'

'If my reputation is restor'd, sir, I ask for no more.'

'Apart from our gracious tolerance of your . . . personal project. Something that you should have disclosed to your superiors much sooner.'

Dali taps his nose, the length of his cuff concealing his mouth. 'Perhaps I feared ridicule.'

'I suggest instead you fear failure. She is lost to you.'

'Sir, there is much that we don't understand and I, for one, relish our ignorance. Because in the darkness, there may hide hope.' Dali twitches a smile. 'I will find my Rosa.'

The Supreme Head bites down on his cigar to free up a throaty cough. 'Your turn, I believe.' He gestures to the table and Dali obliges, making his play – two Threes.

'No word on Vassago's betrayal must escape. We may

have successfully thwarted the Legion of Gehenna once again, but they will draw encouragement from this breach.'

'Understood, sir.'

'This is the closest they have got. Chilling indeed that Vassago succeeded in applying the clave.' The Commander General stifles a shudder. 'We must increase our vigilance.'

'Sir, I recommend that we begin the trainin' of a new Hunter with immediate effect. We focus him from th' outset to do nothing other than track down the Mosca, when he next rises.'

The Commander General digests this thought. 'This is somewhat unorthodox . . .'

'Sir, yo' said it yourself. The Legion is gettin' faster and better informed. We must respond . . . adapt. I just ask that yo' consider my proposal.' Dali slides a file across the table.

The Commander General fills the silence by sweeping up Dali's losing pair and sucking hard on his cigar. 'First time I've played and I've won.' His hand descends upon the file, resting gently.

Dali nods and smiles, ever the grand master.

(11)

HER BELLY IS STRETCHED into the bright bulge of late pregnancy.

Bianco leans back into the swing on Fan Fan's porch. She is barefoot and shelling peas, a world away from the hardened cop. But at the first ripple of a raft, she has a gun in her hand, primed and pointed at the foot of the steps.

Lowering it with a smile as she sees the familiar blaze of blond hair.

Lola mounts the steps, eyes on Bianco's belly. 'So when were you gonna to tell me?'

'When I started showing. Or when you showed up. Whichever came first.'

'So here I am.'

'And here we are.' Bianco pats the bump.

'It is Siggurson's, right?'

Bianco tosses the gun on to the porch. 'You see me with one goddam guy and so you assume it must be his. Like I don't get guys. I actually get a lot of guys. I've dated two detectives at the station. I have a life outside of you, you know.'

'But it's Siggurson's, right?'

Bianco shrugs and smiles. 'Either that or this baby is the second coming. I ain't been swung since this swing.' She pats the old cotton cushions.

Lola drops into the seat. Glances at Bianco's bump. 'You gonna be all right doing this alone?'

'I'm not alone. I got Fan Fan. I got you.' Now Bianco raises one hand to Lola, a finger tracing some small, fresh scars across her forehead. 'You look pretty much in one

382

piece. Guess I was worrying for nothing.'

Lola smiles but she feels that Bianco's eyes are still hard upon her. 'So tell me, Lola, what's been keeping you away, if it ain't been the fighting?'

'I've been thinking.'

'Shit, now I am worried.'

Lola rolls her shoulders. Chin down. 'I had to figure some things out. Make some decisions.' She lifts her eyes, turns to Bianco. 'I gotta tell you. Something that Agnus said about the Moera . . .'

Bianco suddenly jolts and gasps, her hand on her stomach. 'Got his daddy's big feet.' She shifts, easing her spine. Looks back at Lola 'So . . . what did Agnus say?'

Lola shrugs. Smiles back at Bianco. 'Ya know what, it can wait. Let's just celebrate what's inside of you.' She smiles and rests a hand on the dome of Bianco's belly. 'Never seen you so big.'

Bianco shrugs. 'I'll lose it again. You musta been over two hundred pounds when you were Maddy and look at you now.'

'So you're pretty sure about all this?'

'I know it's gonna change everything, but this baby is part of me, my future.' She resumes her pea-shelling. 'I like to fight and I can fight most anything . . . but destiny, that's always gonna get ya.'

She jerks her head to the cabin behind. 'Now go find Fan Fan. She's been keeping a barrel of Old Artemis for your return. Thinks it's her best brew yet.'

A ROSE BENDS AS A KNIFE STRIPS IT OF THORNS. They fall into Fan Fan's lap.

Her yellow hair, piled high, flops back and forth as she rocks in her chair. And her voice floats. 'Ah, child, yo' been a long time comin'.'

'I'm here now.' Lola exhales silently, as if ridding herself of the last chance to change her mind. 'Because there's

383

something I need to do . . . a man I have to find.'

The only sound is the creak of Fan Fan's chair.

Head down, Lola continues. 'He has something that belongs to me.' She swings off her long coat. 'And so do you, Fan Fan.' She lowers herself to the floor. 'You have my memories.' Lola crosses her legs, back straight. 'And I want them back.'

The rocking chair halts. Sharply, mid-creak. 'You sure you ready?'

'I don't have a choice.'

Fan Fan heaves herself up from the chair, on to her feet, turning round in lumbering half-steps. And then Lola sees her.

Her face is painted white with eyes blackened into empty sockets. A rictus grin is painted red across her lips. And from her hand hangs a little skin poppet. A jagged red line circles its neck and its head is spiked with thorns.

'Then let's begin.'

Fan Fan lifts the doll, cradling it in her arms. She pulls a thorn from her pocket, drags it through her lips, loading it with spittle. Holds it above the doll's head. 'Close your eyes, child.'

The thorn thrusts down.

And Lola convulses, a bolt of yellow light blinding her. The light refracts from golden letters, embossed on the cover of a leather book. They spell *Codex Gigas*. It lies open in her lap. She is in the Archivum, slowly turning the pages. Her bare feet are propped up on the table.

The voice of Fan Fan drifts over the memory.

'This is where you spent so many hours. Pouring through the books of the Collegio Romano. You felt drawn to them. Perhaps the first sign of your destiny . . . the way the books called to you. And within the pages of Brother Magen's book, what did you find?'

Lola's eyes are dilated wide. And she can see the page before her, as if it is held again in her hand.

Lola recites the passage, word for word.

And this is how it may come to pass. The Hunter must find the Tormenta that took their original span. And when they find that host, this is how the span must be redeemed. They must rouse that Tormenta to ecstasy and in that moment of release, as something of life is lost, the span escapes and can be snatched.

'And so you came to your dark discovery. That the Sinestra had lied to you. They said that you were neither dead nor alive and so you had no other fate but to be a Hunter. But in truth, there was another path . . . one that would return to you your original span. In one crude act of union, you could get your life back. From the moment you made that discovery, you could no longer serve the Sinestra's cause. Because you had one of your own. You were going to find Kave.'

Fan Fan thrusts down another thorn.

Lola jolts as her head fills with an explosion of green. A dirty green. Perhaps once a peppermint but now a putrid shade, stained by nicotine.

It is the wall of a smoky salsa club. Tables dot the edge of the room, lit by velvet lamps, worn thin.

Young men, slicked with hair oil and sweat, heave large-boned ladies about the room to a salsa beat.

Beneath a corner table, long legs swing. Not to the music, this twitch follows a quicker tempo. A tell-tale sign of impatient tension. But the body feigns a relaxed pose. One hand holds a drink, bombed with cherries, and the scarlet dress clings like paint. Cut low and strapless, a swathe of flesh flows free. The tattoo around the biceps reads LOLA. Another tattoo that reaches down the back of her neck is a twisting metal spike.

And at her heart, rising across the swell of her breast, is a black lily.

Lola's eyes are on the dance floor. Amid the forest of

tall, waggling wigs, she finds the face she's looking for.

A man. Dark hair. Blue eyes. He wears his shirt open to the navel and lets his long hair sweep free. And feeling the diamond drill of Lola's stare, he turns.

It is Kave.

Fan Fan's voice comes like a whisper, as if she is sitting alongside Lola at the table.

'From the day you left the Sinestra, you devoted every waking moment to tracking Kave down. And seeing that face, those eyes . . . that night came back to you. At the Sewercide Club. When he took poor Maddy on to the dance floor, turned her once, twice and then released her. Taking the hand of the beautiful Gina. Kissing her hard, as all those faces turned to Maddy, jeering, pointing, pushing, punching as she tried to escape the dance floor. To escape her skin by slashing it with razor blades.'

Lola uncrosses her legs beneath the table, the twitching becoming a furious tremor. She breathes deeply as she watches Kave finish the dance and kiss the heavily jewelled hand of his lady partner. He then turns and walks towards Lola, eyes set on her like lasers.

Fan Fan's voice breathes on. 'Here was your chance for sweet revenge. Kave would never know the true identity of this assassin, so transformed, so beautiful. A real Cinderella Killerfella. And he came to you, so willingly . . . so unaware.'

Kave sinks into the seat beside the blonde in the red dress. His voice rings in her mind.

'This is very beautiful.' A finger points to the tattoo of her name. 'But it robs me of the chance to ask your name.' His eyes glitter, locked on Lola's face. 'So I will have to engage you in conversation by other means.' Lola feels his eyes sweep down across her body, lingering on the tattoo at her heart.

'The black lily. Highly poisonous.' His fingers approach as if to connect with the soft rise of her breast.

Lola cuts him a smile. 'One touch and you're dead.'

Kave sweeps his fingertips closer still to her flesh. 'We've all got to go sometime.'

Lola's hand flashes and snares his fingers and as she twists his wrist to snapping point, she swivels from the chair and slides away, disappearing through sequins and smoke.

Knowing that Kave will follow.

A heavy rain is falling outside. The rush of tyres and splattering gutters drown the sound of footsteps. But Lola senses he is close behind.

She takes a deliberate turn into an alleyway.

She hears the echo of his boots.

She turns. And Kave faces her. He reaches out, as if inviting her to dance. Lola tilts her head in assent, spinning round as if to enter his arms, but instead delivering a crashing blow to his neck with the side of her hand.

Kave rolls with the blow, exiting the spin with his fists ready, swiping her jaw, twisting her round and then snaring her waist, hooking her spine to save her from the ground. For a beat, she dangles across his arm like a tango queen until Kave jerks hard, cracking her back, forcing a cry from her throat. Then she drops as her leg swings high, kicking Kave in the side of his skull. He rocks backwards, stumbling hard. Snaking round so fast that Lola is still rising from the ground as he grabs her from behind, clamping her body, his mouth to her ear.

'I did not know who you were.'

Lola tenses, but her voice remains calm. 'And who am I?'

'You are one of us.' Kave inhales deeply, sweeping his nose up the length of her neck. 'I can usually smell one of our kind. But not with you.'

'Must be the soap I use.'

'Or perhaps you're a Hunter.'

Lola doesn't move. Letting the silence hang until Kave continues, his tone still hushed.

'A Hunter, I always think, has a gentler fragrance. I

guess it's their residual humanity. But if you were a Hunter, you would have killed me in the dance club. And you didn't . . . well, perhaps you killed me just a little bit.' She feels his lips smile against her ear. 'Broken heart.'

He slowly releases her.

'So let's discuss what brings you to my beat. This is a small town. No room for two, so I'm not about to toss you for the territory.'

Lola flexes her fingers, arches her back. 'Why would I want this dump?' She kinks her hip. 'And why would you?' Shakes her head. 'Something doesn't fit. The old gigolo grift in a dead-beat town, plied by the mighty Kave?'

He runs his tongue along his teeth. 'Then you've heard of me?'

'I wouldn't get too psyched. What I heard is that you've lost it.'

'Things change. By choice.' He pauses, turns his head away. Then smiles. 'I have been alive a very long time and I have done amazing things. I don't think there's a grift I haven't perfected. So I started setting myself new challenges. I once even found myself wondering if I could get someone to kill themselves because they were too happy. I was making up new rules just to stay interested in a game that was becoming too easy. What we do . . . it used to take real skill. People were tough, tenacious, unbreakable. Now I sometimes wonder if we actually drive them to death at all. I think we could just sit right back and let the world do it for us. It's like everyone is lining up along the edge of the ravine and all we have to do is give the final shove – and what's to love in that?'

'You're saying you ducked out because you were bored?'

'Maybe I just wanted to live a little. You ever thought about that, Lola?' He raises his arms, warming to his theme. "We spend all our time conspiring and conniving, duping and demeaning . . . just to get more life to carry on doing the same thing. We live for ever . . . but I don't think I ever lived at all. Until that day.'

'What day?'

Kave smiles, his fingers brushing her arm. 'I know your name. But I don't know who you are.' He leans in, whispering, 'I'd like to know. So – let's spend some time. We've plenty to spare.' He releases her fully, walking away. 'I'm at the Salsa Shack on Mondays and Wednesdays.'

Lola calls after him, 'I don't dance.'

'Yeah, for sure. No rhythm.' He flips his collar up against the rain. 'We could just talk. Which doesn't take timing.'

'Unless it's comedy.'

'Very funny.'

And he slowly slides into the darkness. That bursts into red. A pain blazes through Lola's head as Fan Fan digs in another thorn.

'You went back to the Salsa Shack. You had no choice. The seduction of Kave was going to take time. You kept up the pretence that you were a Tormenta. So you could draw him closer, win his trust.'

The red haze melts into her red dress as she spins and fast-steps across the floor. Kave has her by the hand. The music blares and Lola finds herself throwing back her head and singing as the band breaks out into Cuban beats.

And drifting above the music is Fan Fan's voice.

'You told yourself that seeing Kave at the club was a good thing. Dancing with him, feeling your hand in his, it would keep your fury fresh. Never let you forget what he did to Maddy.'

As Lola and Kave move to the heaving rhythms, their bodies collide, wrap close, uncurl and then spin back tight.

If they fight like dancers, then they dance like lovers.

'And you told yourself that this tantalising closeness would rouse him faster, so you could throw him to your bed and get your span back.'

The music changes to a rumbling grind and Kave pulls Lola close, locking their hips, his mouth wet against her hair.

'But this was a lie. It was all a lie. The truth was a terrible thing. You were falling in love with him. Just like before.'

'No'! Lola's voice rings out from the walls of Fan Fan's cabin. She is up on her feet, eyes wide, grasping at the doll in Fan Fan's arms, wanting this to stop. Her words come in angry bursts. 'That's not true! It was all an act. To make him want me. I hated him!'

Fan Fan says nothing, allowing Lola's ragged breathing to relax. In the calm she asks, 'Do you want to stop? We can stop. The choice is yours. Always has been.'

Lola sinks back down to the floor, her head lolling forward. Fingers balling into fists of tight control. 'No. We go on.'

Fan Fan takes another thorn and nestles the doll deep into the crook of her arm. 'Very well.' She thrusts hard.

A blast of blue. Sunlight on water. Lola and Kave sit by a vast lake. It captures the sky like a mirror.

They are not talking but the silence between them seems easy.

Lola speaks first. 'So this is it?'

'Yes. This is living.'

'But we're not doing anything.'

'Yes we are. We're doing nothing.'

Lola shrugs, not getting it.

Kave smiles and reclines back on to the bank, kicking off his shoes. 'Don't underestimate it. Doing nothing is hard. You never know when you're finished.'

Lola falls back to join him, staring at the sky. 'But this isn't what Tormenta do.'

'It's what people do.'

'But we're not people.'

For a moment Kave says nothing. Then he rolls on to his elbow. 'I don't expect you to understand.' His mouth momentarily tightens. 'Nor any Tormenta. That's why I've never spoken of it before. But now, with you . . . I want to talk.' He nudges Lola's face towards him, demanding her attention. 'A while back, I took a measure of span. From a girl. Not all of it. I fucked up. The mighty Kave fucked up. Only the second time in quite a few thousand years, but still . . . it happened. I don't know what became of the girl, maybe the Sinestra swept her up, who knows. But I know what happened to me.'

He pauses, as if passing the last exit from this confession. 'When a span is half taken, you know the human gets Tormenta traits. But if the Tormenta gets tainted by any human traits, those traits are easily crushed, squeezed out like pulp. So I didn't expect to feel anything, apart from fury that fresh span had slipped my grip. But this girl . . . it felt different.'

He glances away, his eyes on the lake. 'I met her by a lake, just like this. She was nothing much to look at. Lonely, vulnerable . . . an easy siphon. And yet . . .' He shakes his head, eyes down. 'There was something about that girl's span . . . it was strong. I couldn't shake the taste of it. And the high it gave me . . . messed me up. Made me feel things I had never felt before. Made me look at my life as a Tormenta and see that it was just an existence.'

He sits up now. 'I mean, we laugh at mankind for being so dumb and weak and persuadable. Because they love and hurt and trust. Emotions that we just don't understand. But I'm no longer sure that makes them weak.'

He turns to Lola. 'One human will lay down his life for another. Without even knowing their name. Humans care. They cleave together. Tormenta can't even share one acre of ground without ripping each other to pieces. And I guess what I'm saying is . . . I like the way that her span made me feel. I like the fact that it lets me love.'

And she knows that he is going to kiss her. The kiss that Maddy had longed for, eyes closed on the dance floor.

So now Lola closes her eyes and she waits.

And she feels it. His lips. His kiss. Where everything

391

began. And where everything must end.

Lola opens her eyes and the sunlight burns white, blinding her.

She blinks and slowly the sun haze swirls into prisms. Balls of colour, that stream through a stained-glass window.

Lola is in a church confessional. Through the grille she can see the outline of a monk.

Fan Fan's voice is a whisper, as if respecting the peace of the church.

'Now you found yourself troubled . . . conflicted. Could you trust to your heart when Kave had deceived you before? And what of your span? You had given up everything, turned the Sinestra against you for this one quest and now you're thinking that you cannot go through with it. Because you love him.'

Lola's head is bowed in the shadows of the confessional.

'You sought solace . . . wisdom. You went to the church by the old soap factory, the White Lily of the Trinity. You knew from your training that it was a safe-house for the Chiro Scuro. There you found a monk who would listen to your story, advise you perhaps. Brother Fidel was kind and patient. So you told him the truth. The Brotherhood has no great love for the Sinestra, so they would keep the secret of your desertion safe. And Brother Fidel was much intrigued when you told him of how you studied the books of the Collegio Romano – a collection of works that the Sinestra had still failed to return to the Brotherhood, almost two centuries on.'

Brother Fidel's voice seeps softly through the grille. 'You said that you have questions and seek answers.'

Lola's voice comes clear. 'I am aware that since the theft of Brother Magen's writing, much of your knowledge has been lost. So I am not asking what you know, Father, just what you believe to be so.'

'Very well, my child.'

The inhalation from the adjacent box is deep, held long.

And then: 'If I take back my span from the Tormenta that stole it, will they die?'

'Yes, we believe they will. But no Hunter is taught how a span is reclaimed, so it has never been proven.'

'But I know, Father. I have discovered the means for myself.'

'How . . . how did you discover it?'

'It was in the *Codex Gigas* of Brother Magen. The very last book I read. And I read them all. Every one.'

'All of them? But that's . . . impossible. It is a library in itself!'

'I know . . . and reading came hard. I never had the patience before. But these books, they spoke to me. They drew me.'

'. . . as if their call lay beyond your control?'

'Yeah, I guess.'

Brother Fidel's voice is barely more than a whisper. 'Just as the legend says. The books are like a magnet to the chosen mind . . .'

A silence ensues from the monk's side of the confessional. Lola continues. 'So I want to know if I can redeem my span without causing the death of the Tormenta.'

Now the monk speaks, giving a short, abrasive cough.

'No . . . I believe not. Death must follow. A Tormenta can release span into the body of another Tormenta, but not back to its original host.'

Now it is Lola's turn to fall silent. 'Then I have no choice. I must leave. Harden my heart to him and return only when I can bear his loss.'

'That is your only hope, my child.'

'Will you help me?'

'Of course . . . but how?'

Another silence. And this one persists. Until Brother Fidel is forced to quit his box and open the door to Lola's side.

To find her gone. All that remains is a piece of paper. A note addressed to Kave and a request to Brother Fidel written on the reverse: 'Please see that Kave gets this.'

The note is not sealed, written in haste on a page torn from the bible that rests in the confessional.

Kave,
I have to go away. If you love me, wait for me. I will return.
Lola

'DID HE GIVE HIM THE NOTE?' Lola looks up at Fan Fan, like a child still hoping that this story might turn out well.

Fan Fan reaches out, smooths Lola's hair with a gentle hand. 'It is nearly over, child. But close your eyes.'

She takes the final thorn. 'This one will hurt.'

As she thrusts it between the eyes of the doll, Lola spasms back, a blackness engulfing her.

And Fan Fan's voice comes distant and distorted as if carried by the solar wind across the universe.

'You went to cool your heart. And nothing sets it faster than the chill of death.'

Lola's eyes stare out from a face set like stone. A splatter of blood arcs across her cheek as a blade flies in her hand.

From her grip, the slit neck of a woman slides free.

'You went on a killing spree. You slaughtered every Tormenta you could find.'

As dark as her eyes, the twin barrels of her shotgun rise. Blasting smoke – and a man explodes across the dashboard of his car.

'You wanted each kill to refresh your hatred of Tormenta. Remind you of what brought you here. Teach yourself a lesson in vengeance.'

A bullet shears through a young girl's neck. Lola cranks and reloads her automatic.

'You were merciless.'

A smart-suited guy backs away, hands up in surrender as the bullet carves out his heart.

'You had everyone looking for you. Tormenta were running scared.'

Lola stands high atop a warehouse. The wind-torn factory sign behind her reads 'The Soft Soap Factory'. Like an eagle, Lola stares down at a church far below. White paint curls from its walls, like the petals of lilies.

'The day came for you to return. You felt ready, capable of the ruthless subterfuge, to look at him with eyes of love and then drag the life – your life – from his body.'

Her eyes sweep to the distant neon rooftop sign that flashes 'SALSA SHACK'.

'Like all good Hunters, you would observe him before he knew of your return.'

She pulls a set of high-powered binoculars and scouts the streets around the dance club.

'You have been long gone. Your absence may have caused his heart to cool.'

A flash of black hair. Lola zooms in. *It is him*. She zooms closer.

'For all his talk about believing in love, you may have fallen from his affection the moment you left. Because Kave is a liar, a deceiver, a Tormenta . . .

'. . . a believer.'

An image fills the binocular lenses. A black lily, tattooed across his heart, wrapped with a ribbon that bears the name 'LOLA'.

Her mouth opens. Then she immediately rips the threatened smile from her lips.

She will not be diverted! She will complete her plan. Seduce him. Steal back her span.

Lola descends the rusted fire-escape of the factory, arriving on the sidewalk. Scarlet heels stride towards the dance club.

'You would be just how he remembered you. That knowing smile, those diamond eyes. And now your lips will tell him that by leaving him, you proved to yourself how much you want him.'

The red dress swings with every step as Lola approaches the club.

'The lily tells you that Kave's feelings for you are real. So you will assure him that you feel the same. Your heart is his. You love him.'

The little red shoes hasten, suddenly breaking out into a run.

'And these things that you tell yourself, you suddenly realise are not lies intended to seduce him. They are true. You do love him.'

Lola is laughing, tears running down her face.

'All thoughts of vengeance are forgotten. You do not want your span back, for you know now it would be no life without him.'

Lola bursts into the club. It is in darkness and empty. Her eyes search the shadows. Wanting to call out his name, but something halts her. A sound.

Breathing, hard and strained. Like someone dying.

Lola paces towards the back hall, eyes wide, fearful. And then she sees him.

Not him at first. At first she sees the woman. Naked, strong and beautiful, writhing on top of Kave, who grasps her hips, grinding her down, groaning in ecstasy.

The woman has black features but pale skin. A strip is painted across her eyes, like a honey-bee. And long, albino dreadlocks ripple as she rocks and rides Kave's body. And with a roar, Kave explodes into her body and she shrieks wildly as she arches high.

Lola stands rooted, open-mouthed. Plain little Maddy Pool, watching Kave kiss Gina Avner on the dance floor.

Just the same.

Except Maddy had run to cut her own throat.

Lola sinks back into the shadows and pulls her blade. From the covering darkness, she watches as the albino woman gathers her clothes, throwing them about her as she exits the club.

Kave heaves for breath on the wooden floor, his body dripping with sweat. He rises and turns at the sound of footsteps. And as he sees Lola's face he smiles, barely feeling the chill of her blade. Only the warmth of his blood lets him know that she has cut his throat. He falls, the blood pooling fast from his neck, running behind Lola as she walks away, as if her red dress is melting like a popsicle.

'You don't look back. Looking back is what hurt you in the first place. Those memories of Maddy . . . those are what made you fall in love with him again. Now the past is done with. Kave has deceived you for the last time.'

Lola's face is set hard, denying the tears that fall. They are lost in the rain that now pours as she walks through the streets.

Ripping off her scarlet shoes, she feels the sidewalk swill beneath her feet. Hurls the shoes to the flooding gutter. Wipes the knife blade clean against her dress as she walks. Feels the wet satin cling to her thighs. She looks up to see the church of the White Lily of the Trinity. Bursts through the doors, her skin cold, her fury burning. Spins round with her blade up, thrusting it against a throat.

Forcing to the wall a man who yelps in fear.

It is a young monk.

He burbles, finally finding his voice. 'I know who you are.'

Lola lowers the knife, her hot eyes unblinking. The brother blusters on. 'Brother Fidel said that you would return one day . . . he told me to watch, to wait faithfully. He had not long to live, so he knew he may not be here when you returned . . . to give you this.'

He pulls a letter from within his robes, holds it before his face like a thin shield. 'This letter tells of something wonderful. That's what Brother Fidel said. I haven't read it . . . that would be a sin of transgression. He said that only you must see . . .'

'I saw enough.'

The young brother shrieks as the knife flashes, slicing past his face. The letter is snatched, speared on its tip. The young monk wipes away the blood from his eyes. Gone too, is Lola.

'YOU NEVER READ THE LETTER.' Fan Fan sets down the doll and strokes Lola's eyes, forcing them to open.

'You came back here to me and I had never seen you so crazed with grief . . . with anger. The pain was jus' too much for you to bear. You had fallen in love, to find it as sharp as a Romeo spike. You told me everything and then begged me, right here in this very room, to burn the letter and to remove every memory, every thought of Kave. You told me to leave you with just enough of your past for you to know who you are now . . . and what you must do. Enough for you to function in your duty as a Hunter . . . but child, not enough to *live*.'

Lola looks up at the old Mambo. 'Did you burn the letter?'

'No, child. Because I knew this day would come.'

Fan Fan's eyes go to the row of poppets, hung on the wall. 'Each one o' them holds a little of what I took from you. But this one . . .' She looks down to the doll in her arms. 'This one holds the truth.'

She takes a knife and slits the throat of the doll, along the jagged red line that circles its neck, now revealed as stitching. Its thorny head falls away and rolled within its body, like a spine, is a letter. Fan Fan pulls it out, smooths it flat against her lap, offers it to Lola.

'Might you read it aloud, child?'

She pushes a candle closer as Lola unfolds the papers.

Inhales . . . finding her voice.

Lola,

My time is short. So I leave you this letter, so you may know the truth.

Let us begin by returning to the night of our first meeting. You believed that your only goal was to redeem your span. You knew nothing of the Moera. But I did.

Years before, the 'Fuga di Spino' came into my hands. This book had been brought to the Brotherhood by Judas. He was engaged in his own lonely search for the Hunter who would pass into the third state.

When you confessed to me that you felt drawn to the works of Brother Magen, my suspicions were aroused. Could it be that you were destined to be the Moera? Then, when you further confessed that you felt compelled to reclaim your span, I was utterly convinced. But you slipped through my fingers, disappearing into the night, leaving only the note addressed to Kave. But I could not stand idle, I had to do all within my power to ensure that, upon your return, you would see your calling through to its completion.

The sole obstacle to this event was Kave. That is to say . . . your love for him. So I prayed for guidance. I asked God, 'What should I do?' And the answer came: Do as she bids you. Deliver the letter. And so I went to Kave. I must confess that I was fearful to be in the presence of something so ungodly. But as I observed him read the words that told of your leaving, I witnessed what I believe to be a miracle. In his eyes - the eyes of a Tormenta - I saw real hurt. And, emboldened by this, I risked my life. I asked him if he wanted salvation.

And he met my eyes and he said yes.

What followed was a strange exchange. I told him all that I knew of you, of what you are. Of what you must become. Of the Moera.

And despite my fear of his hurt becoming fury, I told him that what stood in the way of your destiny was him. Because for you to enter the third state, he must give up his life. And you loved him too much for that.

But there was hope . . . If he were to release your span into another Tormenta – one for whom you had no affection – then you would reclaim your span from them without hesitation. And your transformation into the Moera would be complete.

He told me that he would comply. His only wish was to see you fulfilled.

Then I told him of the sacrifice that he must make. He must renounce all his Tormenta ways. This would be the price of his soul's salvation. He must live as a human . . . die as a human.

He agreed to this covenant. We told no one and in secret we strove to find the perfect vessel into which he would decant your span. We needed a Tormenta who would succumb to both his seduction and yours.

We found the one. Her name is Bee-Bee. All the information you need is on the reverse of this letter. A Hunter of your calibre will have no trouble tracking her down.

Kave will complete his task before your return. Then he must leave. And you and he must never meet again. As succour to your hurt, I offer you this from the gospel of 1 John 4:18: 'Perfect love casts out fear, because fear is torment.'

Kave loves you. So know that what he does, he does for love.

And so my heart goes with you, Lola, heart of the world.

Forever,
Fidel

The letter falls and Fan Fan reaches down, pulling Lola upwards, forcing her to stand.

Black eyes meet blue. "So what you gonna do, child? Choice is yours. Always has been.'

Lola says nothing. But her heart answers.

Find Bee-Bee . . . take back my span. Become three . . . and so become one.

A NEEDLE PIERCES TENSE FLESH. Black ink spurts. The needle sinks again, faster now, the metal flashing as it gains speed.

The machine is forging a tattoo. As the design takes shape, it becomes clear that it is a number. It arches across the curve of a huge muscle.

Dali peers closely as the ink and blood bubbles and sets. Then inhales to project his voice above the jabber of the machine.

'I have been accused of favouritism in the past and to that I plead guilty. But the way you came to me, how could I not adore you?' He pulls a handkerchief, dabbing at the blood that dribbles down the arm. 'The most fundamental error . . . and yet still Vassago commits it. He could not wait until the life had left your body.'

Dali tuts as he tucks the handkerchief away. 'Your training has been longer than usual, because your duty as a Hunter is unique. Unlike your associates, you will not be hunting Tormenta. You will seek out only the Mosca.'

His last word rings loud as the machine stops, the number complete.

Dali gently dabs the arm, blowing on the flesh to cool the sting. 'You step into some big shoes. The last Hunter to bear this number was amongst the greatest ever to serve the Sinestra.'

He takes a stride back to admire his new protégé. The quiver of his cuffs suggests a huge satisfaction.

'I have been permitted to train you for this one task because the Legion's last attempt demanded that we raise our game. And in addition to a dedicated Hunter, we have installed a new security measure into the Helix Vivat.'

Dali taps a shiny, giant oscilloscope that is plugged into the dash of the machine. 'In exchange for the High Command's gracious toleration of a particular pastime of mine, I have applied my private research to the design of this device.'

He leans low, huffs upon the glass and buffs it with his cuff. 'This scope is tuned to the frequency of the Mosca's span. It is still somewhat rudimentary as my memories of meeting him are fleeting. Yo' have to consider, it was more than a century ago and I barely glimpsed the boy. There was a fire, yo' see. And he was shrouded in smoke with just that little wooden bird in his hand. And in all honesty, my mind was much in flux, so filled with my beloved that. . .' Dali halts mid-sentence, a careful hand rising to his lips. 'I digress. Suffice to say I saw the boy.' He now clasps his hands together in moderated joy. 'The essence of the Mosca is so potent that, even with this scant information, our new scope has succeeded at last in issuing us a reading.'

Dali slides over a sheaf of papers. 'If we have deciphered it correctly, it indicates that the Mosca arrived five years ago into the body of a male child.'

His fingers tap the file. 'This contains the full report. It will enable you to locate the target.'

Dali looks up. 'Any questions, 666B?'

The Hunter steps forward, a taut body wrapped in black, moving like a shaft of midnight. The face is harder, the eyes colder – but it is unmistakably Siggurson.

He says nothing.

Dali grins. 'Then let the hunt commence.'

(IV)

THE LITTLE BOY HAS EYES ONLY FOR THE FLY. He sits in the corner of a noisy nursery. He has been excluded from the games, but he seems not to care. His dark eyes follow the fly as it creeps up the wall. With a flash of his small hand, he snares it, wrapping his fingers tight. He pulls his fist towards him and then opens it, finger by finger. The fly remains on his palm, washing its bulbous head, twitching its wings, which catch in the sunlight, twinkling with a rainbow of colours.

Even when a teacher smooths her skirt and kneels down beside him, the boy doesn't turn.

She inhales, gathering patience. 'You know that what you did was wrong, don't you?'

The boy says nothing, his eyes still set on the fly. The teacher perseveres. 'You may not have pushed Beatrice from the monkey bars, but those nasty words you said about her weight, you really upset her. And then she fell.'

The little boy turns, his eyes unblinking. 'She jumped.'

The teacher thins her mouth, attempting to hold her smile. 'Your Mummy told me that your daddy used to be bullied at school. They called him an unkind name because he didn't have a mother. So you don't want to hurt other children like your daddy was hurt, do you?'

'I don't have a daddy.'

The teacher inhales, realising that this was perhaps a bad tactic. She turns at the sound of footsteps behind her. 'Ah . . . I'm glad you're here.'

Appearing at her side is Bianco.

'He's been doing it again, I'm afraid.' The teacher pauses,

but then feels compelled to continue. 'What concerns me is that upsetting the other children clearly gives your son so much . . . pleasure.'

Bianco stiffens, instinctively rising to her son's defence. She grasps his hand. 'It is very hard for him.'

The teacher nods, trying to sympathise. 'I appreciate that. Every boy needs a father to look up to. But his behaviour is entirely inappropriate. So perhaps it would be best if you found another nursery. Somewhere better able to assist such a . . . challenged little boy.'

Bianco spins on her heel, exiting with her son in tow.

As she walks out into the sunshine, she forces a smile. Hoists her son up on to her hip. 'You don't listen to her. You do have a father and he is someone you can look up to.' She tips her head towards the sky. 'Because he is up there. And he is looking down on you.'

She squeezes his little body tight. 'No matter what you do my darling, he will be right there, watching over you. And no matter where you go, he will find you.'

Acknowledgements

To all those who recognized that my anti-social and obsessive habits would be best suited to the solitary life of a writer — thank you for your encouragement. Among them I must single out for special mention Howard Reay and Peter Lukas.

To Edward Fitzpatrick, the man who saved me the cost of a stamp by passing the manuscript to the publisher, my on-going gratitude.

To Simon Petherick, Richenda Todd and all at Beautiful Books, I appreciate your tireless work and unwavering passion.

And to Andrew Goth, my ever-lasting thanks for your insight and vision. I could not have done this without you.